Amanda Brookfield

Amanda Brookfield worked in advertising before becoming
a freelance journalist. She has lived in China, Germany,
Sweden, Argentina and America and currently lives in
Dulwich with her husband and children.

SCEPTRE

-12

Walls of Glass

AMANDA BROOKFIELD

SCEPTRE

Copyright © 1995 Amanda Brookfield

First published in 1995 by Hodder and Stoughton
First published in paperback in 1995 by Hodder and Stoughton
A division of Hodder Headline PLC
A Sceptre Paperback

10 9 8 7 6 5 4 3

British Library Cataloguing in Publication Data

Brookfield, Amanda
Walls of Glass
I. Title
823.914 [F]

ISBN 0 340 62340 3

Typeset by Hewer Text Composition Services, Edinburgh
Printed and bound in Great Britain by
Cox and Wyman Ltd, Reading, Berkshire

Hodder and Stoughton
A division of Hodder Headline PLC
338 Euston Road
London NW1 3BH

In Memory of Lucy

As Pippa pushed open the rusting black gate its lopsided hinge emitted a strangled screech that sent tiny vibrations shooting down into the roots of her teeth. After a few moments of standing at the front door she remembered that Jane and Michael's bell no longer worked and rapped briskly on the splintery wood. Pippa's own home, an airy four-bedroomed Edwardian house in Dulwich, was lovingly repainted and cleaned in a methodical way throughout each year, so she could not resist a silent tut-tut or two at the sight of the Lyttons' obvious neglect of their own property. But at the same time, she loved – and almost admired – them for it. It took courage to neglect things, she sometimes thought, a courage which she lacked completely.

'Coming,' shouted Jane from somewhere deep inside the house.

Pippa got out her handbag mirror to check her bun; her hair was so fine that it slipped out of the pins and clasps no matter how many she applied. She smiled quite warmly at her reflection, not out of vanity (she was not beautiful – her nose was too pointy and her mouth too thin), but because she was happy. She always enjoyed taking time out of her carefully constructed bustle of domesticity to visit Jane and the children in all their glorious chaos. And on this occasion she had some rather exciting news to impart, when the moment was right.

The door burst open, giving Pippa a snapshot impression of the familial warmth and brightness within.

'Heavens,' exclaimed Jane, pushing her thick, dark fringe from her eyes and hoicking baby Harriet higher on to her hip, 'is it eleven already? Lovely to see you Pip – come in. Mind the trains – Tom has spent all morning building the longest train in the world, haven't you, love?' She stooped to stroke his messy brush of hair, before leading the way through to the kitchen. 'You look well, Pippa – you make me feel a total wreck – which I am – roll on the spring term – coffee or tea?'

'I'd love some tea.' But more than that, she wanted to hold Harriet, who was pudgy and square and smiley.

'Could you take the baby, do you think?' Jane, who knew of the Crofts' fruitless – but now abandoned – quest to have a child of their own, was never sure whether to push her offspring on to Pippa or keep them at bay. 'I almost burnt Harriet with the kettle once, trying to juggle cups and things – it was when the health visitor was here – which was lucky, if you see what I mean.'

Jane moved deftly round her cramped but cosy kitchen, the soles of her black plimsoles squeaking on the cracked linoleum floor. Being so petite, she had a tendency to make Pippa, who was by no means tall, feel clumsy and large. She wore a green hairband that morning, a thin strip of dark velvet that did little to control the glossy jumble of her hair, but which drew attention to the brilliant emerald of her eyes, so deeply set into the pale, elfin face. Pippa had always thought Jane very striking to look at, not in a way that made her envious, but so that she couldn't help wanting to stare. To manage to look scruffy but attractive was an achievement far beyond Pippa's own aspirations, as was Jane Lytton's way of appearing higgledy-piggledy but happy. Pippa knew herself to be incapable of reconciling such opposites. For her happiness was impossible without orderliness, just as attractiveness was out of the question without a good deal of thought and attention to detail.

The little L-shaped kitchen always reminded Pippa of a fully-equipped caravan – everything was reachable and functioning so long as it stayed in its correct place; one thing left out or put away badly threw the whole system into chaos. Tom's paintings, together with innumerable creations out of tinfoil, cardboard and string, filled every inch of space between the bulging cupboards and shelves, giving the effect of some crazy wallpaper of modern art. Along the window-sill which overlooked the back garden, several trailing plants fought for space amongst pots of herbs, cookery books and a large bowl overflowing with safety-pins, paper-clips and rubber-bands.

'Any news of the extension?' she enquired brightly. Ever since the Lyttons had moved to Cobham, when Tom was not yet two, they had been talking of building on at the back.

Jane sighed. 'Oh, I don't know, Pip. It's so much money. Michael says we'd be better off moving again, but it's a bad time to sell – we just go round in circles when we talk about it. I've rather given up thinking about it, to be honest.' She sat down at the small pine table opposite Pippa and stirred milk into their mugs of tea. Thinking about the extension only made her cross. The move out of London had been her idea to begin with, but Michael had got very enthusiastic in the end. They both fell in love – as she remembered it – with the cottagey feel of number 23 Meadowbrook Road and had enjoyed making plans to improve and enlarge it. But when their requests for planning permission ran into trouble, Michael started to go sour on the whole project. His recollection of their house-moving episode was now based on the belief that Jane had pressurised him into making a decision before he was ready. Perhaps she had, perhaps he was right. Jane wasn't sure any more. She wasn't sure about a lot of things.

'Well, Tim said that Michael is dead set on going ahead, even though you've still only got permission to add on one room.'

'Really?' Jane wondered if other wives found out quite so much of their husbands' thoughts from other people. She laughed quickly, before issuing an automatic excuse for her ignorance. 'Michael's been working very hard recently – it makes him absent-minded – I keep telling him he'll leave his head at the office one day and not just his briefcase.'

'At least that bank of his has eased up on the travelling side of things. When Tim's gone it's for weeks at a time. His trips are longer than the holidays he's selling.' She sighed. 'I do get lonely, you know,' she added in a bleating baby-voice to Harriet, who looked puzzled and put Pippa's amber necklace in her mouth by way of a response.

'She's teething, as you can see,' said Jane, offering her daughter a rusk. She hoped Pippa was not going to start on about the wearing demands of Travelmania – the tourist business that Tim had started after leaving the city, which boasted exotic trips at affordable prices. Pippa was unremittingly sweet, but prattled on a bit sometimes, in the way that some people did if they had no burning commitments in the hours ahead. During the early years of their acquaintance, when Jane had not progressed much beyond pasting Tippex for Moretons publishers, Pippa had an enviably pressurised job as PA to the managing director of a prestigious London advertising agency. But after a couple of years of failing to conceive a child, Pippa's doctor had warned that stress at work might be taking its toll on her hormones and recommended that she take a break. Though her resignation from the agency was billed very much as a temporary measure, complied with for prudence's sake alone, it somehow became permanent and – like the desire for babies that had prompted it – impossible to discuss. With the instant success of Tim's business went the last traces of a possibility that Pippa might return to work. She even started hinting, with wry little smiles, that Tim would disallow such a thing – as if it had become one of those male-pride issues that wise wives learn to humour.

While Pippa talked about Tim's long absences Jane tried but failed to keep her mind from drifting upstairs to the five or so loads of washing that lay strewn across the landing and bedroom floors, together with the thought of Tom's wet mattress, which needed scrubbing and drying before the smell of urine was completely absorbed into its soft foam interior. As her musings moved on to an alarmingly broad shopping list of food, clothes and shoes, she began to wonder vaguely why Pippa had been so insistent on inviting herself over and how long she was planning on staying. Since their relationship had arisen from the longstanding friendship between their husbands rather than any instinctive liking for each other, what intimacy they managed never felt entirely natural.

Having quietly wished Pippa was gone Jane immediately felt guilty and invited her to stay for lunch.

'Oh I'd love it, if I won't be in your way.'

Harriet was wiggling impatiently, clearly bored with her allotted lap and looking for new distractions. Soggy rusk stuck in blobs to her face and bib. A few gooey fingerprints were visible on Pippa's fluffy jumper. She tried to wipe them with a tissue when Jane wasn't looking, but Jane had already seen and was ready with a damp cloth and apologies on behalf of her daughter.

'Silly of me to wear it, I know.'

'It was certainly a little optimistic, to visit this house in such a lovely thing.' She touched the soft grey wool with the back of her hand, suddenly conscious of the grubbiness of her own sweat shirt and faded jeans.

'Tim gave it to me. It's got llama in it or something. He brought it back from Peru – for my birthday,' she added shyly.

Jane clapped her hand over her mouth. 'Oh Pippa, I forgot, you should have told me. Oh no, I feel awful.'

Pippa was blushing, regretting a little that she had dared to mention it.

'It's only a wretched birthday. Thirty-eight is not exactly a reason to celebrate – especially not in my case.'

'But of course it matters. I mind terribly about my birthdays. I love presents and being taken out to dinner and all that sort of thing—' She stopped quickly, remembering that her birthday that year had been quite horrible. It was a Saturday. Tom, wanting to mark the occasion, had promised to deliver breakfast in bed to both his parents. Michael had to be forced not to go down and intervene while the smell of burnt toast curled its way up the stairs. The toast was quite black, heaving with butter, but otherwise okay. The boiled eggs had been put into water in a saucepan but never boiled. Jane, who was relieved that Tom had heeded five years of warnings about never touching the knobs on the stove, even given the desire to cook an egg, bravely cut the top off her runny offering and dipped a wedge of the charcoaled bread into the grey-yellow slime. Tom stood in solemn silence, watching from the end of the bed.

'Tom,' said Michael, 'you haven't cooked the egg. It's not cooked, see?' He picked up the egg and held it out. 'It's still cold. When you cook something it goes hot. It's all liquid inside. Look at Mummy's.'

But Mummy, charged with a fierce reflex of protective love, was spooning large dollops of the phlegmy offering into her mouth and rolling her eyes with pleasure.

'Jesus, Jane – how could you?' said Michael with a laugh. 'You'll be sick.' He turned back to his son, still smiling. 'Well tried, Tom – just ask for help next time, okay?'

But it was not okay, as Jane had known it would not be. Tom's day was ruined. Her day was ruined. Just one mouthful would have been enough, just one mouthful for love's sake. But he wasn't like that, her husband. Michael liked things one way or another, black or white, like his tables of figures at work. If something wasn't cooked that was meant to be cooked, you didn't eat it – whatever the circumstances. Such an attitude no doubt worked wonders in meeting rooms, when heady negotiations for debt-rescheduling and long-term loans hung in the balance, but it did not do so well at home. Michael, who felt it was wrong to be chastised for honesty, and that Jane, as usual, was being over-protective of their first-born, refused to melt and admit he had been wrong. Jane, out of some kind of inverted revenge, refused to go out to dinner. Michael ate bread and cheese watching *The Bill*, while she pretended to read upstairs.

'There's nothing more depressing than a bad birthday,' she said firmly, shaking off the memory. 'I bet Tim's got something lovely lined up for tonight.'

'He usually gets tickets for a show or something, but he never lets on till the last minute. One of those funny rituals we married couples go through,' she added fondly. 'Actually,' she got up to look out of the window, her fingers fiddling absently with the yellow beads of her necklace, 'Tim has been moodier than usual recently. I know he's a bit of a one for sulks – not like Michael at all – but this time I really feel something is up.' She eyed Jane, who was stacking the dish-washer very busily behind her. 'He hasn't said anything to Michael, I suppose?'

'Not that I know of.' Jane pulled a bottle of white wine out of the fridge door. 'Let's celebrate just a little. It's only supermarket stuff, but quite nice. I've got lots of tail-ends of smelly cheeses to go with it. A birthday lunch of sorts.'

'You're very kind, Jane. I don't know where I'd be without you.'

Such comments always threw Jane off balance, since she never felt able to respond in kind. Pippa was a dear friend, but not one that she relied on totally. Not like Julia, say, whom Jane had known since school and whose presence in her life – usually down the end of a phone line – was intermittent but vital. Like Pippa, Julia had no children, but didn't mind at all. She was not married either, or even close to it. Having recently set up her own antiques shop in North London, she was totally involved with that.

With Pippa, there had always been a subtle imbalance in the relationship, brought on by Pippa's at times embarrassing admiration for Jane's marriage to her husband's best friend. The fact that the Lyttons had managed to have children quite effortlessly only contributed to Pippa's perception of their marital bliss, at the same time fostering a tic of awkwardness between the two women which no amount of goodwill could entirely smooth away.

They sat down to French bread and cheese, while Harriet slept and Tom watched *Thomas the Tank Engine* on the telly.

'I made a big decision last week,' blurted Pippa, now frantic to broach the subject beating in her head like a pulse.

Jane sipped the wine, which was a little tart, but pleasantly cold.

'Something exciting?'

'Very.' Pippa cut off a wedge of Brie and put her knife down. 'I'm going to go for IVF. I know I always said I wouldn't – that if nature wouldn't take its course it was wrong for us to interfere – but I've changed my mind.'

'Pippa – that's – that's amazing.' Jane's mind floundered in search of appropriate words; she very much wanted to say the right thing. 'How terribly brave. What are the chances? Isn't it very expensive? Will it hurt? What does Tim think?' A couple of years previously the Crofts had formally resigned from the ranks of would-be parents, confessing to close friends that the strain was too much and they wanted to concentrate on enjoying themselves instead. Though Jane had nurtured suspicions as to Pippa's true commitment to such a way of thinking (compared to Tim who had shown unqualified relief at their decision) she never imagined her turning round with such a bold reversal of opinion. But on seeing the warm glow of hope in Pippa's round and usually quite solemn face, she was immediately thrilled for her. She wanted to be encouraging, to help make it happen. She reached out instinctively and touched her hand. 'Oh, I do hope it works, Pip. You deserve it, of all people.'

Pippa's smile was brilliant. She pushed some wisps of her fine hair, glinting now with slivers of silver, out of her eyes. 'If points for trying count, we do deserve one, I suppose. I know this sounds terrible,' she went on carefully, 'but I think I would have liked to have had a miscarriage, I really would. Just one. At least it's closer to being pregnant. Whereas I'm just barren, like those women in the Bible – unblessed and infertile.'

'Oh Pippa, don't say that. Anyway, some of those Bible women had babies when they were old and supposedly past it.'

'Well, I'm nearly past it, which is why I've decided to take drastic action. It's now or never, Jane.'

Jane rummaged in the fridge for a bunch of grapes to add to their spread. 'And Tim is all right about it, is he?'

Pippa took a deep breath. 'Tim doesn't know. Not yet.'

Jane stopped, bunch of grapes in hand. 'That's a little fundamental isn't it? Are you sure he'll—'

'Yes. Absolutely. He's got to.'

Jane knew they were on dangerous ground. The desire to have a child was totally primeval – unarguable, once it took hold. She knew because Tom hadn't been planned, not for one second, and yet when she found out that she was pregnant, one drizzly morning three years into her marriage, she sensed at once that she was in the grip of a force far stronger than anything she had ever experienced. It was inconvenient to say the least, and certainly unwise. She was by then working as an editorial assistant. Michael had just started a phase of extensive travelling and she felt very distant from him. He would come back exhausted but hungry for sex, pushing into her in a way he never had before, ungenerously, without tenderness. It was confusing. To be wanted in such a basic way was new to her – she was scared by the lovelessness of it all. Out of bed they ticked along as before, as if nothing had changed. It had made Jane start to wonder if love mattered after all, lying buried as it did behind the daily negotiating and arguing of married life. But when Tom was conceived as the result of one such unemotional sexual encounter on a humid August night after Michael had been in Cairo for ten days, Jane decided at once that she should have the child. It felt like fate – out of her control entirely. And then, after the birth, it felt like love, the real thing, the thing she had always hoped to get from marriage.

'Are you going to have any more?' asked Pippa, as Tom appeared, looking screen-dazed and pale.

'No, I'm full thanks – but you go ahead.'

'I mean children, silly, not cheese.' They both laughed, which made Tom suspicious and needing an explanation; by the time they'd finished trying to tell him what they had found so funny, the moment for answering Pippa's original question had passed, to Jane's relief. It seemed mean to admit to Pippa – of all people – that she did not want any more children. Harriet, loved and treasured as she was, had been produced more for Tom's sake than anything else. Jane was very careful about contraception now, even when Michael was all rough and lustful.

2

Michael sipped his mineral water, enjoying the silent expectancy, the power he wielded in the meeting-room.

'It's not a question of *if*, Antonia, but *when*.' He looked round the table of faces, knowing he now commanded their full attention. Antonia, a bristly and ambitious newcomer to the department, began making a few notes, to cover the moment of put-down. She wondered if Michael Lytton disliked her, whether his frequent challenges were personal or professional.

'It's a market we can no longer ignore,' went on Michael, deliberately looking at his watch to show that he felt the meeting should draw to a close. 'I'd like to see detailed data on investment opportunities relevant to our special interests by the end of the week. Antonia, perhaps you would like to head up the investigation.'

She nodded, not sure whether to be pleased or offended. It would be a lot of work, but then there was the enticing prospect of earning credit points by doing it. Everyone began packing away their papers and shuffling out of the room.

'You are happy to take on this job, are you?'

She looked round in surprise, having thought the room empty. 'Absolutely. No problem, Michael.'

'Good. If you need any help getting started, don't hesitate to knock on my door.'

'Thank you.'

With a quick smile he left the room, leaving Antonia with a blurred impression of businesslike kindness riding on whiffs of expensive aftershave.

Michael sauntered back to his office with his hands in the

trouser pockets of his double-breasted suit, whistling quietly through the tiny gap between his two front teeth. It was a noise he made when he was happy, when life played into his hands and he felt in control of its multifarious demands. Adrenalin still pumped through his veins from the meeting, from handling it – and the prickly but promising Antonia Fielding – so well. Although it was Friday night he felt in no hurry to go home, wanting instead to climb down more gradually from the high generated by a hard but successful week's work. A quick drink in the bar perhaps, a half of bitter with Terry or George before hacking back to Cobham. The idea was tempting.

As Michael made his way along the maze of plush, neon-lit corridors that linked the offices of his firm of city bankers like sections of a honeycomb, he tried not to think about the journey home. He dreaded the swarms of rushing commuters, the seedy filth of the south-eastern trains, the fifteen-minute walk the other end. It had been mad to move out of London, quite mad. The next move, when the market picked up, was going to be right back in again, he would see to that. Never mind Jane's rural idyll. It was totally impractical, unless one could afford a flat in London as well. But Michael did not relish that idea either. He had never liked being on his own and had no desire to revert back to a part-time bachelor existence of cheese on toast and baked beans out of a tin while watching junk on the telly. Home life might be noisy and grating at times, but there were many comforts that made up for it.

In the end he persuaded John Procter to have one for the road. But then Terry joined them and they decided to make it two. As Michael was on the point of leaving the MD came in and asked him how far his department had got in looking at Polish markets. Feeling on the ball and superbly able, Michael updated him at length, before rushing back upstairs to see if Antonia had gone home and to ask her to have her presentation ready three days earlier than planned.

'Tom waited up for you.'
'You shouldn't let him, I've told you before—'
'You said you'd be early.'
'Did I?' Michael frowned, having genuinely forgotten the

promise that was lightly made but hungrily received by his son. 'I got held up. Things began to happen just as I was leaving.'

Jane, who had heard all the excuses many times before, mechanically set about laying the table and serving out food. She wasn't in the least bit hungry. The meat had held up well, but the baked potatoes were hollow and tough, their skins like cracked leather. It was nearly ten o'clock.

'It was Tom's concert,' she said, 'he did his solo on the recorder.'

'Oh shit.' Michael, who was ravenous, spoke with his mouth full. He chewed vigorously and swallowed before continuing. 'Jane, love, I'm sorry.' He reached out and put his hand on her arm. She continued eating very slowly, puting only the smallest amounts in her mouth – a flake of potato skin, half a mushroom, a soggy carrot. She did not want to forgive him. The pattern was all too familiar. The repetitiveness of it all depressed her immensely. Last time it had been a parents' meeting. Next time it would probably be the carol concert.

'It doesn't matter.' She pulled her hands on to her lap and fiddled with her wedding rings. One of the tiny gold claws holding the diamond in place was sticking upwards, leaving the stone dangerously loose. The claw itself was as sharp as a needle and caught, irritatingly on everything she handled. She pressed it now, hard, into the top of one of her fingers, feeling at a great distance from the pinpoint of pain.

'I'll apologise to Tom in the morning. Was he very upset?' He put in another mouthful.

She was honest enough to hesitate before answering. Tom wasn't a child who got very obviously upset. At the tender age of nearly six he had already developed a daunting capacity for suppressing his emotions. Jane knew about his feelings from the way he walked, the set of his face, the funny voices he used.

'He didn't say much about it, but he wouldn't eat his supper.'

An urge to scream pressed at the back of her throat; she wanted to yell at him, to blast the words out, that of course Tom minded – because a promise had been made and broken, again, because he barely saw his father and when he did he was often critical and cross. But such outbursts, she knew from experience, got them nowhere. Michael would rant for a while about how much he slaved for his family and how little understanding he got in return and then follow this up with a hurt silence that could last for days. She always ended up having to make the peace.

'Jane, I've said I'm sorry.' His big brown eyes took on the soulful look he used to tell her it was time to step down and relent. 'Work is crazy at the moment.' He mopped up the last of his gravy with a piece of bread and wiped his hands and mouth on the oven glove that lay on the table beside them.

'Work is always crazy,' she said quietly, leaving the room to lock up the house and go to bed.

Michael, feeling guilty, but cross with his wife for being the instrument of that guilt, stayed in the kitchen for much longer than he really wanted, looking at a catalogue of home furnishings that had been put through their letter-box the week before. Jane didn't throw newspapers and magazines away until the house threatened to be overrun by the damn things. Michael hit the glossy pages with the back of his hand in a sudden rush of frustration, causing the magazine to fall to the ground with a slap. He stared down at a chic sitting-room of navy blue and sandy yellow, complete with a designer mother and child playing happily on a colour-coordinated hearth rug. Engulfed in the bright squash of his own home Michael felt inordinately sad; when – if ever – did the gulf between how one wanted life to be and how it really was begin to narrow, he wondered.

Upstairs, Jane had left his bedside light on, laid out his pyjamas on the pillow and turned on her side to sleep. But in spite of her closed eyes and the quietness there was an atmosphere of unease in the room, generated by their conversation over dinner and all the things that the two of them had thought, but failed to say.

'Are you awake?'

'Hm.' She curled herself up more tightly into a ball, wanting very much to be left alone.

But Michael wanted reassurance; he needed to feel that he was master of his own life, master in his own home even, though he would never have put it like that himself.

He turned on his side so that he was facing her curved back. After tracing one finger down the nobbly ridges of her spine, he reached across her, his hand seeking her breasts. Jane kept her arms folded into her, protectively. She felt the hand arrive, knew what it sought and curled up more tightly still. Not now, she thought, please not now.

But the hand persisted, firmly pulling her arms out of the way, finding its way up under her nightdress, stroking, caressing, determined.

Jane did not want to make love. She was tired and angry. But she was also resigned. An honest woman – a woman who loved her lover – would say no, she thought. But Jane, as she realised with a terrible self-loathing, had got beyond the point where such honesty felt possible. Michael pushed his knee between her legs and settled his weight upon her with a grunt of satisfaction. She turned her head away and closed her eyes as he started to move in the old familiar rhythm, while his hands stroked and kneaded in a show of giving pleasure which lacked commitment and reflected his own needs rather than hers.

'Did you enjoy that?' he asked sleepily, to put the seal on his warm sense of reassurance.

'Yes,' she lied, because she was tired and wanting to sleep, and because dishonesty was so much easier than truth.

3

Mattie could not remember when she last felt less like doing anything, let alone Sunday lunch in Cobham with big sister Jane and her inscrutable husband. Even to contemplate living in a place like Cobham seemed to Mattie, who had a terrible hangover and who had never lived further than two tube stops from the West End, to reflect something close to insanity. But then, while being enormously fond of her sister, she had never really understood her motives for doing anything. She often thought that if their parents hadn't died, skidding on a sheet of black ice and through the wall of an old Roman bridge when Mattie was still in her teens, the two of them would have remained indifferent and distant. But the accident changed things for good; ever since then Jane had tried to look after her – or at least been there for her, even when she wasn't wanted. And Mattie, while resisting the sisterly mothering, was also grateful for it, knowing that she would almost certainly have fallen apart without it.

Her headache was particularly intense that morning. It was entirely usual for her to feel so bad, indeed a weekend without a throbbing head smacked of failure. Mattie, although almost thirty, liked to dance, preferably in large nightclubs with strobe-lights and the first drink free with your ticket. The anonymity of it appealed to her most of all; there were none of the hideous social rituals associated with the ill-fitting mould of her teenage years – of partners and pauses between songs. To be safely alone, yet part of a symbiotic crowd, soothed Mattie's endless ruffles of insecurity. It was also very good for the figure, she found, to dance all night long, for several hours out of every week. Taking the little tablets (which was what gave her the headaches) was the silly and expensive part, but then it was the tablets that gave such an edge to the atmosphere and energy of the thing.

After taking three Panadol and drinking a Coca-Cola Mattie began to feel fractionally better. She ran a bath and dozed off for a few minutes, her head of crazy corkscrew curls lolling heavily to one side and trailing in the water like dank seaweed. The painful notion of train timetables and organised movement was just beginning to peck at the edges of her consciousness when the sound of someone tapping on one of the windows by her front door brought her fully awake. Mattie lived in a basement flat in Kensington, the steps of which led past the two oval windows that gave her poky kitchen-diner the dubious distinction of looking like a ship's galley. She padded through, dripping wet and full of yawns, to see Julia peering in through the smeary glass.

'You were expecting me, weren't you?' she called, tossing her astonishing curtain of shining fair hair over one shoulder and laughing at the sight of Mattie, all wet and puffy-faced. 'I'm giving you a lift to Jane and Michael's. Sunday lunch. Remember?'

'Oh, thank God. Come in, come in. I'm nearly awake. Can you make coffee? I must do something about my face and hair – I can't face the world without a face,' she groaned.

'Run along, I'll see to coffee,' soothed Julia, who was used to Mattie and rather fond of her.

'I just don't see why you had to invite them, this weekend of all weekends.'

'But I told you about it ages ago. Tom, you're spilling your drink. And what do you mean "this weekend of all week-ends"?'

Michael shook the paper hard. 'I could just do with some time—I don't know, you book so much up, we could have gone away for the weekend.'

Jane almost laughed. They never went away for the weekend. Even their summer holidays were usually spent in Kent with Michael's father. Fond as she was of the old man and his big farmhouse, it irked her that they always ended up there, falling back on the easy option, the only option that required neither money nor organisation. The year before she had invested a considerable amount of energy in trying to sell Michael the idea of a family camping holiday. But he would not be persuaded; he wasn't a rubbing-sticks-together kind of chap, he protested, and never would be. Jane sometimes looked at other families she knew and wondered enviously at their regular escapes to cottages and hotels in England and the rest of Europe. She knew that it wasn't really money or time that prevented her and Michael from doing similar things, but a fundamental lack of inclination, a sinister shadow within their marriage, like a dark smudge on an X-ray.

'It's only my sister and Julia,' she said more gently, not wanting the day to face ruin so early on. 'We haven't seen either of them for ages—'

'Nonsense. You and Julia jump around doing those ridiculous exercises together at least twice a week.'

'Once every two weeks. It's yoga and I haven't been for ages.'

Michael folded the newspaper neatly back together and crossed his arms. 'It's just the thought of enduring all you women that I find a little daunting.'

'I tried to invite Tim and Pippa, but they were busy.'

Michael humphed and disappeared in the direction of the lavatory.

As she cleared up the kitchen and set about peeling apples for the crumble Jane seriously tried to think who else she could have invited that would have made Michael feel his own needs were being catered for. She knew none of his work colleagues, since he had never invited any of them back to be entertained, even when they had lived in London. While Jane would have hated pouring over recipe books in the interests of pleasing the expensive palates of Michael's various bosses and their wives, she could not help wondering about it. The fact was that apart from Tim Croft no name sprang to mind – unless she counted Michael's younger brother, Christopher, who lived in Oxford and to whom he'd never been particularly close.

Jane, on the other hand, knew loads of mums in the area, mainly through school and sitting in playgrounds, and had occasionally tried to stretch some of these friendships to include husbands. But Michael was very resistant about such things. He worked too hard to be bothered with any superficial socialising, he said; he preferred to spend what little spare time he had relaxing with his family. But as Jane heard Tom bang on the loo door and Michael's muffled roar of response from within, the notion of a relaxed family life seemed little more than a shimmering mirage, vanishing as quickly as it was glimpsed.

The moment their two guests arrived Michael came alive. Having spent the previous two hours pointedly burrowing through sheaves of work papers – much to the consternation of the children, who wanted him to play – he leapt to his feet for Julia and Mattie, issuing drinks and witty small-talk as if it was the most natural thing in the world. And Jane marvelled, not for the first time, at how much more fluently he communicated with people he knew less well, people who offered no threat of intimacy. It was incredible, seeing him now with her sister and her best friend, his bad mood apparently forgotten, his face broken into smiles that showed his handsome teeth and made them feel welcome. It was like watching a different person. Yet who was she to criticise the clicking of such switches? She did it all the time. And as she studied his display of warmth, she even felt a twitch of something like envy. It was a long time since her husband had put on such an act for her.

The weather was just warm enough for them to take their coffee outside, where they were able to appreciate perhaps the best aspect of the house. The garden was a simple rectangle in shape, not exceptionally large, but beautifully designed for a family. A tree-house, a sand-pit and a long swing gracing the outstretched limb of a huge oak were visible at the far end, on the lumpy, unkempt bit of the lawn, next to a tangle that had once been a vegetable garden.

Mattie sat cross-legged on the grass, blowing tremulous smoke-rings through her rubied lips and rocking steadily to some silent tune playing inside her head. Jane, watching the faint grey circles rise and fall apart on the chilly spring breeze, shivered and sank lower into her deck-chair. Beside her, Michael and Julia talked in an animated way about french polishing.

'How are you, Mattie?' she asked, the tone of her voice communicating the sincerity behind the question.

'Oh, you know me, up and down.' She fiddled with a dangling bit of skin near the cuticle of her left thumb. All of Mattie's fingertips were stubby and raw where she had gnawed at the soft flesh. Once upon a time their mother had painted her nails with a thick, repellent varnish called 'stop 'n grow', guaranteed to cure the habit. But Mattie, being Mattie, had pronounced the stuff to be delicious, and feasted on her chipped fingernails with more cannibalistic fervour than ever. Jane smiled to herself as she remembered the episode and then immediately felt sad. Where had it gone, all that easy anger of childhood, when the things to fight against were so obvious, so deeply felt? Grown-up enemies and sorrows were so much more of a blur; there were no goodies and baddies any more, just a confusion of feelings.

'Have you been painting?'

Mattie squirmed and looked away. 'Not really. Too bloody knackered half the time. I'll do a bit in the summer, when the light is better. It's still quite dark in the evenings – by the time I get in from work anyway.' She shook her dark curls and shot Jane a mischievous grin, out of nowhere, causing her sister a familiar, but painful, stab of motherly emotion. 'I've become a video freak. I curl up on the sofa with my duvet and a few bars of chocolate – it's great.'

Jane, knowing that Mattie was seeking a reassuring reprimand or two, deliberately held back, simply shaking her head with a smile. Mattie was a good painter; it was sad that she felt so little compunction these days to do it. Being a secretary didn't suit her – she was almost certainly lousy at it – but it paid for her rent and cigarettes. And chocolate. Judging from the blotchy pallor of her face, she had been consuming little else.

'Just you take care,' she said softly, leaning forward to give the lightest touch to Mattie's marbled cheek.

'And how about you, big sis, how are you?' Mattie stood up and put her sunglasses on as she asked the question.

'Me? Oh, I'm fine,' replied Jane automatically, staring up at the giant reflector lenses, seeing a warped image of herself, like a hunched old woman in a chair. Then quite suddenly she started to cry, terrible tears that simply spilled down her face of their own accord.

'Jane? What the—' Mattie quickly knelt beside her and took her hands. Then Julia noticed that something was wrong and came sweeping over waving a handkerchief. Jane felt spectacularly embarrassed and acutely aware of Michael sitting helpless in the deck-chair next to her, watching the scene of his weeping wife and clucking women with horror. She knew it was a truly dreadful thing to do – to burst into tears at a Sunday lunch for no reason at all. But it had crept up on her out of nowhere, stealthy and appalling, like a sudden sickness. And once she had started it took several minutes to stop. She blew her nose hard on Julia's immaculately ironed hanky.

'I am sorry, all of you – what an awful thing to have done.'

'Don't tell me, it was my new sunglasses – I can take it. I'll burn them the minute I get home.'

'Dear Mat, I love your glasses.'

'Would a drink help?' It was the first thing Michael had said.

'Thank you, Michael, but I'm fine now.' There was an expectant pause, as if all three of them were waiting for an explanation. But she had none to give.

Julia and Mattie left soon afterwards. At the door she laughed reassuringly with them and blamed it all on hormones.

'I'll call you,' said Julia with a firm look.

'What was all that about?' said Michael, his voice not exactly resounding with sympathy.

'I – I don't know.' She concentrated hard on clearing the table, instinct telling her that she had something to hide, though quite what she wasn't sure.

'Nobody just bursts in tears without there being some kind of reason for it.' He stood in the doorway of the kitchen, arms folded across his broad chest, his strong, square face set in an expression of vigorous determination.

'I suppose – I suddenly felt sad.'

'Crying and sadness are commonly associated, this is true.' His impatience made her rattle the plates. Upstairs Harriet began to cry in her cot. 'Perhaps you could be a little more explicit? After all, I don't think your behaviour could exactly be described as normal.'

'Normal?' She looked at him for an instant, before returning her attention to stacking plates. 'I don't know, Michael, I don't know,' she burst out, feeling close to tears again. 'I'm sorry, but that's the truth of it.'

'Steady on, we don't want to scare the children with all this hysteria, do we?'

Tom was standing beside his father, holding a complicated Lego construction up for approval. For a split second Jane felt that the child understood more than the man, that he was tuned into her in a way so deep that it made Michael a mere stranger by comparison.

'I say, you're not pregnant are you?' he went on, holding Tom's creation but not looking at it.

'No, Michael, I am not pregnant. There are other reasons that women cry.' She wiped the table mats and stacked them back into the box, the sides of which were badly battered, and held together with stiff, ageing Sellotape. They had been a wedding present from some distant relative of Michael's who now lived in New Zealand – brilliantly coloured birds of the world, laminated so securely that their plumage shone with as much brightness as they had on the day they were unpacked.

'Good. A baby is about the last thing we need.'

'It's a space rocket,' said Tom for at least the fourth time, but very loudly now, so that Michael had to respond and Jane could escape. At least it felt like escape, as she sidled past the two of them and got on with the immediate demands of her daughter and a messy kitchen.

But all through the domestic chores of that day and the rest of the week, the unprompted outburst of crying sat in Jane's mind like an unanswered question. She was greatly alarmed by it. To have embarrassed herself was bad enough, but far worse was the sense that she had lost control. Some fundamental ground in her life was shifting; she was losing her balance.

4

'You need a break,' remarked Julia a couple of weeks later in a tone of voice that was both scolding and kind. 'Too much bloody domesticity – baby-dribble and Hoover bags – it drives most women to drink in the end. Lay down the rubber gloves and demand a holiday for yourself.'

'Oh Julia, I can't.' Jane was trimming the fatty edges off some pork chops; the telephone was wedged between her ear and shoulder, causing considerable neck-ache, since the conversation had gone on for some time. 'You know I can't.'

'I know you won't, which is quite a different thing.'

'Michael would have a fit and who would look after the children and where would I go?'

'Rent a nanny from one of those agencies and go to a health farm. Tell Michael it's that or a divorce.' She laughed. 'Be bold, woman, demand your rights.'

Jane sighed, not in the mood for her friend's flippant confidence. 'Rights are complicated things when you're married. And anyway, all your suggestions are outrageously expensive. It's impossible.'

'Nothing is impossible, Jane,' she retorted, 'you're going woolly-headed, that's all. You're not seeing anything beyond the wallpaper.'

Even for Julia this was curt. 'Well, thanks for the advice,'

'Don't go all defensive. Tell me to shut up or bugger off, but don't curl up in that bullet-proof shell of yours – it's very distressing for those of us left outside in the cold.'

Jane put the phone back on its wall-slot next to her shelf of kitchen jars, feeling dazed and alone. Once upon a time it had been easy to love Michael. She looked at the pile of raw pork in front of her, pink and moist, streaked with white fat, and wondered if human flesh looked like that, beneath the skin. Now love did not come to her fresh and inspirational as it once had; now it was a stale remembered feeling that she had to dig from her mind with force. She started to cut the meat for the stew, but her knife was blunt and the pork resisted, its fatty streaks so interwoven with the pink flesh that she could not separate them. The fat with the meat, she thought, the rough with the smooth, for better for worse, and she gave up on her task, tearing the meat into big pieces and throwing them into the pan regardless.

Michael must have missed his train. Outside, a failing sun was casting its last beams across the garden, illuminating the spring-green of the grass and making the young faces of the leaves stand out against the dusky sky like jewels on metal. The blurred screen of a television flickered on in the upstairs room of the house next door; from the other side of the fence the hollering of an angry child broke the stillness of the evening. Jane, whose own children had been asleep for half an hour at least, took a glass of wine and sat down in one of the deck-chairs still left out on the lawn from the not entirely successful Sunday lunch a couple of weeks before. Its once shiny metal frame was now thick with rust; orange speckled with black and brown. She rubbed and picked at the worst patches with her fingers, knowing it was futile, but wanting the shine to return.

After a while she gave up and checked her watch before following the overgrown stone footpath that ran up the side of the lawn to the garden shed where she kept her cigarettes, behind an old paint tin at the far end of the shelf on the left. Having lit one, she inhaled slowly, closing her eyes, enjoying the dry burning at the back of her throat and the faint sensation of giddiness. Her hands smelt of garlic and onions; tiny shreds of pork lay trapped beneath her fingernails. Her fingertips, still greasy, slid on the cold metal latch as she closed the shed door. She made her way back down the path with quick, light steps, balancing on the balls of her feet so as to avoid the cracks in the stones.

'I see you,' a voice said.

'My God, Michael. You startled me.' She dropped the cigarette at once and ground it into the stone with her plimsole. 'I thought you'd be on the later train.'

'So I can still surprise you, after all these years.' He was in a good mood, still smiling, saying nothing about the cigarette. Though he only kissed her on the nose. 'They've changed the train times – British Rail strikes again, so to speak.' He sniffed the air, which smelt of mint mixed with smoke. 'The garden isn't looking bad.' He tugged a small twist of bindweed from the nearest shrub and put it in his pocket. 'What's for supper?'

'Pork. A sort of stew.'

He blew vigorously on his hands and rubbed them together. 'It's bloody cold though. What are you doing out here any way?'

'It's not cold, it's lovely. I thought we might eat outside.'

'You must be bloody joking,' he retorted, before disappearing back into the house through the open kitchen door.

Jane returned to her wine, casting a regretful eye at the squashed, unsmoked cigarette on the path. Perhaps Julia was right, perhaps time alone was what she needed. Time and uninterrupted sleep.

Michael came back in a thick jumper and an anorak, making loud shivering noises, but bringing the wine bottle and a glass with him. He placed them carefully on the grass before sitting down in the deck-chair nearest hers.

'Good day?'

'More or less.'

'Children all right?'

'Tom wailed at the school gates and Harriet lunged at the shelves of the supermarket like a sumo wrestler. So pretty normal all round. What about you?'

'Monstrously busy.'

'You always say that.'

'That's because it's always true. Dinner ready yet?' He patted his stomach which was flattish but soft.

'Shall we talk about our marriage instead of dinner?'

'Whatever for?'

'It might be interesting.'

'I highly doubt it,' he laughed, pouring himself some wine.

There was a terrible complacency in his aspect which struck Jane with such force that for a moment she could not speak. Had it always been there, she wondered, or had it edged into him, another component of teasing middle-age?

'Why are you in such a good mood anyway? Have you been given a pay-rise or found a mistress or something?' A rather wicked urge to shock him was in danger of taking hold.

But Michael wasn't shocked at all. He was enjoying her banter. 'No such luck on either account, I'm afraid.' He grinned and stretched, thinking of the crisp perfection of Antonia's presentation and the neat pleated slit at the back of her pin-stripe skirt. 'Perhaps I feel good because I'm almost thirty-five and not yet bald or fat or poor or lonely.'

'Those are all negatives. It's not the same as saying I'm slim and rich and surrounded by people I adore.' She eyed the thick curls of his hair, the distinguished, glinting-grey above the ears. 'You're certainly not bald.'

'And I do adore you.' He reached out and patted her hand.

She sat unmoving, unable to respond, suddenly rigid with cold. It wasn't enough and it wasn't true. He adored her according to his moods; if he felt good he said he adored her. It had nothing to do with love. She withdrew her hand and cupped her wine glass to her chest, staring into the yellowy liquid, watching a bobbing fragment of cork dance on its surface.

'I'm starving. Christ, it's cold.' He jumped up from his deck-chair and walked briskly across the grass to the section of the path where she had dropped her cigarette. Gingerly he picked it up, holding it as he might a dead worm, before hurling it into the mass of variegated ivy that grew along, through and round their garden fence in a collage of greens.

Jane went inside to boil some water for peas. Why was trying to talk about the real things so hard, she wondered, when, in many ways they knew each other so well. Once it had been simple enough. When her parents were killed and Mattie went off the rails Michael had empowered her. Just the sound of his voice had been soothing; she had loved his unflurried rationality, the way he weighed up what had to be done, assessed things, sorted them out, tackled them head on without fear.

Though she put on a sweatshirt and sat in the chair nearest

the boiler, the cold would not leave her. The pork had turned brown and tender at the mercy of the oven, but all Jane saw was pink flesh and squidgy ridges of fat. It was like seeing into the heart of the things, and it made her feel sick and sad.

5

Julia banged the side of the steering wheel with the flat of her gloved hand and then resignedly pushed the gear-stick into neutral. She should have gone another way – along the embankment and across one of the city bridges perhaps. After scowling at her reflection in the rearview mirror she looked again to check her make-up. Her lips were very red. Too red. She pressed them together several times and then dabbed at the edges with a tissue. The car behind beeped rudely. The Hammersmith traffic had shifted forward by five feet at least and she hadn't even noticed.

Her fingers reached for the radio switches, but stopped short. Her car had been broken into the week before and all its contents swiped, even the floppy box of tissues she kept on top of the dashboard and a shapeless mohair sweater that her mother had knitted years before, which she hated but couldn't throw away.

Without the distraction of music or news Julia found herself mulling over the prospect of the evening before her. She was almost as baffled about being on the guest-list as she was about why Pippa Croft should have taken it upon herself to organise such a party in the first place. Celebrating promotions was surely a wife's job. She had said as much to Jane, who was irritatingly pragmatic about it. Pippa was on an 'up', she explained, looking for reasons to be jolly, and if that included throwing surprise parties for Michael, then that was fine by her. Julia had wondered then – as she did now – whether her friend spoke the truth. She couldn't work Jane out at the moment; she couldn't get her to talk any more, either to complain or to have a laugh. Everything was fine, she kept saying, her lips closing on the word like a portcullis.

It had been hard enough maintaining a friendship like theirs over the years, given all the hoops of marriage and motherhood that Jane had chosen to fling over herself. They had had to work at it, the two of them, like some off-beat married couple who only met when other commitments allowed. The intense intimacy of their student years had been stretched and moulded into something far more dilute, something far less threatening and involved. Sometimes Julia felt that the friendship only survived by virtue of what had gone before. There was so little now to fuel it in the everyday sense of having things in common.

By the time Julia accelerated across the relative freedom of Wandsworth Bridge she was already late for the party. She whistled quietly at her own audacity as she shot through a red light and turned on to the south circular. The evening might be fun after all. Mattie was going to be there, as was Michael's brother, Christopher, whom she hadn't seen for years, and a man called Jes, who was a friend of Michael and Tim's from way back and whom she vaguely recollected as being quite amusing. Since it was a long time since she had experienced anything approximating to a 'relationship' with a man, Julia could not help allowing herself a heartbeat of speculation at renewing such acquaintances.

As Julia Durnford's looks had emerged from the knobbly cocoon of late adolescence, she had discovered the fundamental and most disturbing fact that to be stunningly attractive was frequently the most terrible burden. There was little she could do about it; no visual aids or clever dressing were required to draw attention to her glassy blue eyes and lustrous blonde hair. And her figure was the racehorse kind – that breed apart – with naturally toned long legs, strong hips, a slim waist and broad shoulders. Men, it seemed, read from an entirely different score when presented with such looks. The most obviously desirable qualities in a partner, or at any rate the ones Julia found herself scanning for, such as sincerity, understanding and an equal capacity for intellectual as well as sexual pastimes, were invariably buried under far less enticing features – possessiveness, vanity and insecurity being the most striking traits of the men she had attracted so far. In short, practically all her affairs had been a disaster, apart from one with a married man, which she tried not to remember and from which she had eventually extricated herself with more regret than she had ever before experienced.

The Crofts' sitting-room, with all its sweeps, folds and tucks of flowery cottons, reminded Jane of a Laura Ashley furnishings shop. Although several years had passed since Pippa designed it, the effect was still crisp and new; a creamy garden of silky, pastel shades, unsullied by grubby finger-marks and juice-dribbles. To complete the picture, Pippa floated amongst the floral scene like some pre-Raphaelite flower-girl, one of those wan, gowned women on the arty calendars that Jane and Mattie had bought each other as birthday presents in their early teens. Pippa's long, limp tresses had been loosely – but very carefully – pinned to the top of her head so that large wisps fell down about her ears and neck, trailing decorously amongst the large hoops of her earrings. Her dress, like her curtains, was covered with flowers and swept almost to the ground. Jane, who wore a plain silk shirt and baggy black trousers, felt, with a familiar jolt, the chasm that separated her from the wife of her husband's oldest friend.

'This is wonderful, Pippa, you've gone to so much trouble—'

'I never guessed – I thought we were going to the bloody cinema,' said Michael, not for the first time, slapping his knee and looking happily round the room at the small group of people Pippa had invited to celebrate the latest success in his career.

'He was hell to get out of the house,' put in Jane, touched, in spite of herself, by Michael's obvious delight at Pippa's surprise party and willing herself to join in the spirit of the occasion.

'I could never have organised it without your help, Jane – you've been a marvel,' said Pippa unnecessarily, getting up to offer a plate of miniature, perfectly sculpted vol-au-vents round the room.

'I have done nothing,' said Jane, which was the simple truth. She wondered if Pippa had hesitated at all before suggesting the party. More disturbingly, she wondered at herself for not minding. Life was so much easier if you just let it sweep you along. It was amazing how many things seemed to happen of their own accord.

'How are everyone's drinks?' asked Pippa, clapping her hands to conceal her panic about the evening in general and the meal in particular. She had written down exactly when each dish had to go in and out of the oven but still kept forgetting. The real intention behind the dinner, so simple in conception, had been as a pretext for cheering Tim up, jolting him out of his unremitting glumness. But her plan, perhaps wavering under the weight of the secret hopes heaped upon it, was refusing to cooperate. Michael appeared cheerful enough, but Tim's contribution to the festivities had so far amounted to little more than a menacing silence, one of those that made Pippa sure she had done something wrong, something as yet unidentified, but wholly unforgivable. Jes had added greatly to these anxieties by bringing a girlfriend. The grilled prawns were going to have to be spread very thinly indeed, as was the home-made garlic mayonnaise, which had curdled twice and which she wished she'd never started. The book said the salmon only needed forty minutes, but it had looked so huge – so disturbingly chunky and raw – that Pippa was allowing twice that amount of time. She tried not to think about the salmon as Christopher asked her how she was and said they hadn't met since Harriet's christening.

'We're just lovely, thank you Christopher,' she chimed, smelling fish and resisting the urge to run to the kitchen. 'Do you know Jes Frewin and his er—'

'Cassie,' said the woman quickly and confidently, stepping forward to shake Christopher's hand with a great half-moon of a smile that might have been more reassuring if it had not been for the purple lipstick that outlined it. 'I'm in television. Documentaries mainly. Jes and I met working on a programme on inner city violence. I think he's the best producer on the circuit.' The large smile never left her face as she spoke, nor did she seem to breathe between sentences.

'I'm sure you're right,' said Christopher, with a slight bow to them both.

Jes shook the ice cubes in his glass, looking embarrassed but pleased. 'Steady on, darling, from what I recall our friend here isn't exactly a fan of the media.'

A dim memory of a drunken argument about the intrusive power of the press stirred at the back of Christopher's mind. It might even have been at Michael's thirtieth. He was drinking a lot around then.

'Middle-age has softened my views considerably,' he said, laughing easily and rocking his tall frame back on his heels, 'though I have to confess to the unforgivable crime of not owning a television.'

'Are you serious?' Cassie turned incredulously to Jes, giving Christopher the opportunity to cast his eyes round the room and raise his glass of orange juice in silent toast to Michael.

'Don't take it personally, please,' he went on, deftly flicking his attention back, 'if I had a television I'd never read a book or listen to music. I'm totally undisciplined. If there's a box anywhere near I switch it on. It's a very alluring machine.'

A gentle nudge on his elbow from behind saved him from having to continue.

'Excuse me a moment,' he said, with generous politeness, before turning away. He was already wishing he hadn't come. He should have known better after all this time.

It was Jane who had touched him. Pippa was hovering at her side.

'We're needed in the kitchen, apparently.' She pretended to look solemn. 'The salmon is misbehaving.'

Pippa wrung her hands. 'I need to get it on to a plate and it's sort of falling apart.'

'Don't panic, Pippa. Jane will take the legs and I'll manage the head. You can direct operations.' He kissed his sister-in-law lightly on the cheek. The room was like a greenhouse, but her skin felt cool and smooth. 'How are you?'

'Fine. How's Oxford and academia?'

They followed Pippa through into the kitchen.

'I'd hardly call teaching little boys an academic challenge—'

'Well, you're writing a book as well, aren't you?'

Pippa, who had two large pink blotches on each cheek, blew a wisp of hair from her eyes and handed out cloths and cooking slices. 'Can you save your chatting for later, you two? If this bloody fish falls apart I shall scream.'

'That might be rather fun – to have a screaming hostess.'

'Christopher, behave,' whispered Jane, who could see that Pippa was indeed close to some sort of minor breakdown.

The fish wobbled dangerously on its journey from pan to dish, but held together apart from part of the tail, which was easily wedged back into place. The two helpers watched as Pippa lovingly planted sprigs of parsley along its sides and spread lemon slices across its belly and the loose bit of tail.

'It looks lovely,' said Jane, avoiding Christopher's eyes which were twinkling irreverently.

'Thank you so much for your help,' murmured Pippa, absorbed in her task. 'Would you mind asking the others to go and sit down? If we don't start on the prawns soon this monster will go completely cold.'

It took a while for the party to get going, for the single, stilted conversation between all of them to scatter into happy fragments of a more natural dialogue. Jane, listening with strained intensity to Jes's views on the role of the welfare state, felt her face aching from being fixed in appropriate expressions. She felt deeply uninteresting and uninvolved. When Jes gave up on her and turned to Mattie she experienced a surge of relief, followed quickly by a jerk of panic that her life somehow amounted to nothing more than this room full of people, whom – as it suddenly seemed – she barely knew and who certainly did not know her. Only when her eye caught Julia's did the panic subside. She was wearing a short, black velvet cocktail dress that pencil-lined the smooth curves of her body and made her long, fair hair shine like silk. She was smiling and nodding at Cassie, who had been talking very energetically at her for several minutes. Julia was on her best behaviour, nodding intently and shooting intermittent looks of encouragement at Christopher, who appeared either preoccupied or left out.

But it should have been Michael, thought Jane suddenly, the panic returning, it should have been Michael who made her feel she belonged. He was sitting opposite her, his legs so close under the Crofts' long, narrow dining-table that she could feel the brush of his knees against hers when he shifted position. He was smiling deeply, running his fingers through the dark, silvered curls of his thick hair, sipping champagne, nodding with Tim about something, enjoying himself.

She stared so hard at him that he turned to look at her, raising his eyebrows questioningly. Caught off guard, she could think of nothing to say except to ask if he was having a good time, which sounded like a probe for congratulation. At least that was how Michael read it.

'This is marvellous, sweetie. I didn't guess. Truly, I didn't guess for a second.' He raised his glass and offered a toast to his wife and to the chef.

Pippa blushed and waved her napkin.

The prawns were well received. Especially by Cassie, who listed the vitamins to be found in shellfish and announced that she had recently become a vegetarian. Though Pippa, in the light of this new information, had been most fortunate in her choice of menu, she felt duty-bound to confess that the hollandaise sauce was positively loaded with egg yolks (they had helped considerably in the long battle against curdling), and that the rice had been cooked in chicken stock. Cassie, having forgiven her hostess these oversights, proceeded to flutter her ringed fingers and talk at length about her visit to an abattoir, the stench of the blood, the screams of the dying animals and the depravity of mankind in general.

'Just as well shellfish don't have feelings, isn't it?' remarked Christopher, glancing up with a sharp smile from a project that involved lining prawn heads round the rim of his plate, so that their depleted antennae drooped decoratively over the edge.

Cassie opened her mouth, but Michael, too padded by good wine and good humour to pick up on any undercurrents of tension, got there first.

'Thought you were looking a little thinner, mate,' he said to Jes, 'now I know it's too much bloody rabbit food.'

'Oh, I'm still a raw steak man through and through,' Jes assured him quickly, sensing that he was defending far more than his eating habits.

'What about you, Mattie,' put in Jane quickly, brought to attention by a sense that the conversation was in danger of collapsing into something a little less cordial, 'weren't you off meat for a while?'

'Yeah, until I nearly hacked my thumb off chopping through one of those endless concoctions of onions, peppers, swedes and parsnips. I converted to chocolate on the spot and I've never looked back. No chopping, no mess, no washing up.'

'Chocolate?' said Cassie, as if it were a word of quite unmentionable crudity.

'Except for breakfast when I have cereal or toast. You have to wash the bowl or the plate then, of course, but nothing's perfect, is it?'

Jane sat back through all this, enjoying the way her little sister could grab the limelight in the simplest of ways. She was never afraid of saying the first thing that came into her head and simply following it through to see where it led.

There followed a sequence of uncomfortable silences and stuttering starts, finally broken by Cassie's announcement that she was about to start work on a documentary about marriage. 'My personal view – not that it will affect my presentation of the facts – is that marriage is almost always lethal.' Her eyes skewered Jes's, lovingly, for the split second it took for everyone else to notice. 'So don't go getting any ideas, darling.' She threw back her head, slowly widening her large mouth into its designer smile and unconsciously flinging the largest of her permed tresses across Christopher's cheek. He wiped the spot where her hair had touched him, absently, continuing with the other hand to twirl the stem of his wine glass.

'What a load of bullshit,' remarked Mattie, dabbing at a drop of sauce with her finger and sucking it noisily. 'Not that I want to get married,' she added, when in fact she sometimes did and sometimes didn't, depending on fluctuating levels of self-confidence. 'I can't help thinking monogamy must get to be a little dull.' There was a faint shuffling amongst those members of her audience torn between wanting to defend their capacity for sexual adventure and anxiety not to provoke any twangs of discord with their partners. Mattie appeared happily oblivious of such stirrings. 'It must be like the same person painting the same thing over and over again – in the end there is a limit to its creative potential.' Unwelcome thoughts of her own unfinished canvases, their faces turned in disgrace to the wall, and the forty hours a week she spent staring at a screen in an over-heated office, interrupted her flow. 'I suppose that's why we all find fantasy so useful – I bet loads of marriages would fall apart without it, anyway,' she concluded, with the distinct feeling that she had somehow lost the thread.

'Perhaps you shouldn't make judgements on things you haven't tried,' suggested Michael, a little stiffly, wishing the conversation hadn't been allowed to grow so dull.

'Hear, hear,' echoed Tim, giving his friend a look of unqualified allegiance.

'You forgot to mention love, Mattie,' put in Julia cheerfully, 'not that I could claim to be an expert on the subject.'

At which point Jane slipped away into the kitchen to see if she could help Pippa with the pudding. When she returned, bearing a jug of cream, Michael was pulling his brother into the conversation, with a distinct vibration of challenge in his voice.

'Your turn, Christopher,' he said, folding his arms and smiling not altogether pleasantly, 'what's the bachelor view of love and marriage then?'

Christopher's response was slow, almost languid. He looked across the table at his brother, their dark eyes meeting fully for the first time that evening, His hair was much blacker than Michael's, cut very short, giving even more prominence to the high Lytton forehead and the peculiar paleness of the skin. It was incredibly fine, Jane noticed, like a thin porcelain mask that might shatter from the slightest tap.

'Oh, I'm a die-hard romantic, I'm afraid – all in favour of life-long commitments and happy marriages.' He paused gravely. 'Though of course I keep it as well hidden as I can.' He was the first to laugh and everyone else followed suit, some element of relief ringing through the air.

The rest of the evening passed very slowly for Jane, who, as the designated driver could not help feeling sober and tired. Christopher left shortly after dinner, politely declining Pippa's offer of decaffeinated coffee or camomile tea and murmuring about the long drive back to Oxford. He was soon followed by the others, Julia kindly offering to give Mattie a lift. Jane and

Pippa spent the best part of the next hour in the kitchen, tidying up and talking in hushed tones about the chances of getting pregnant through clinical intervention, while their husbands discussed asset trading over large glasses of brandy.

'I've sort of broached the subject and then flunked out. I'm terrified Tim's not going to agree. It's so wretchedly expensive – but still we'll have to go private. There's a three-year waiting list on the NHS – by which time it could be too late for me – and even then you only get one shot at the thing.' Pippa paused, an empty wine bottle in each hand, and brushed away a strand of hair with the back of her arm. 'The thing is, Tim is just not himself at the moment. So I keep putting off asking him.' She laid the wine bottles carefully on top of many others in a box in the corner, before continuing. 'Did you notice anything tonight? Don't you think he seemed a little – preoccupied?' Pippa gave a nervous peek round the door to check that they were in no danger of being overheard. 'I'm really rather worried about him.'

'I suppose he was quite quiet,' conceded Jane, struggling to think how she could be reassuring. The truth was, she had never found Tim easy to talk to. He had always struck her as being very much a man's man, one who made a point of steering well clear of what he regarded as the tittle-tattle of women. 'But Michael didn't exactly say very much, did he? Come to think of it, none of the men did. I'm afraid Mattie did rather a lot of talking.'

'And Cassie.'

They both laughed.

'But I like Christopher.'

Jane hesitated, as always uncertain about her brother-in law. 'Yes, I like him too. But he's sort of moody – I never quite know what to make of him. Like tonight. He was really quite jolly at the beginning, but by the end he had gone all broody and silent, as if he'd had enough of us all. I never know what he's thinking, but always suspect it's something rather critical.'

'Well, he helped me a lot in the kitchen, which I thought was lovely,' pronounced Pippa, folding the last drying-up cloth into a tidy rectangle and leading the way through into the sitting-room.

On the way home Michael put his hand on Jane's knee and, inspired by a sleepy gratitude, squeezed it on and off all the way down the A3.

'It was good to see Jes after so much time – good-looking woman he's found for himself too. Not my type though.' He yawned deeply. 'Christopher's a pompous ass; I'm always pleased to see him and then wonder the hell why.'

'I'm not sure he's arrogant exactly—'

'Yes he bloody well is. Ivory tower nonsense,' he muttered, adding more strongly, 'and he couldn't even hack that, could he?'

Jane had no desire to listen to Michael's familiar tirade against his younger brother, how he had thrown away all chances of adult success by swapping university life for a small prep school, how he was almost certainly a suppressed gay.

'You know I hate to say it—' he went on. She braced herself, containing her irritation with a short intake of breath, 'but I'm sure he's a pansy.'

The choice of word fell upon her ears like the scrape of a nail on a black-board. 'I think you're wrong. I don't think he's gay – I never have.' She took the slip-road off the motorway and changed down into fourth gear.

'So you thought he was interested in Julia and Mattie, did you?'

'No, I did not. Though he may be, for all I know. I'm just going on my instincts.'

'Ah, instincts. Good, solid things, instincts.'

She realised then that he was very drunk and that it was pointless trying to talk sensibly about anything.

'And that sister of yours talks a load of twaddle. Fantasy and all that rot.' He yawned again, more deeply this time. 'No one in their right mind would take her on for life. Be more like a bloody life sentence than a marriage.' He chuckled and removed his hand from Jane's knee.

By the time they reached the outskirts of Cobham Michael was sound asleep, his cheek pressed against the window, his face squashed, mouth open, like a dead man.

A heavy rain was falling. As Jane strained her eyes to see past the frenzied, squeaky swipes of the windscreen wipers, she thought about things like fantasy, imagination and sexual pleasure with the nostalgic longing of remembering lost friends. In the last few years her capacity for such luxuries had faltered and run cold. Sitting there in the stuffy, car-heated darkness, her husband breathing softly, rhythmically beside her, she could have wept for what was lost. Not just for the sweet explosions of erotic pleasure, but for the faith and intimacy that had inspired them. It had begun as the occasional cheating – reserved for those odd times when she felt so tired and unresponsive that sex was just something to get over and done with. But gradually the habit had taken hold. Their love-making took less and less time, as Michael grew surer of his ability to arouse her and she withdrew ever more expertly into herself, hiding her disappointment behind charades of satisfaction and pleasure. Which would upset Michael more, she wondered, as she switched off the engine and turned to look at him, the duplicity of a full-blown affair, or this silent deceit already coiled deep within their bed, like a worm within a rose.

She turned to him and stroked his forehead with the barest surface of her fingertips, exploring his face, tracing the faint frown lines, the baby softness of his eyelids, the sand-paper feel of his cheeks and chin, the dry lines of his lips. He closed his mouth and smiled in his sleep.

'Excuse me.' There was a tap at the window. Jane peered out to see the wide, friendly face of the baby-sitter, Mrs Browne, standing by the car clutching umbrellas.

'Oh, thank you so much, Mrs B,' she said gaily, prodding Michael in the ribs and clambering out of the car into the black wetness. 'We're terribly late, I'm sorry.' She had to shout against the pelting rain. 'Do you want a hand, Michael, darling?'

'You mean, am I so incapacitated that I require assistance for the simple business of walking?' He spoke loudly and quite fast, as if in pursuit of the words as they slithered out of reach.

'Did he have a good time?' said Mrs Browne with a wink,

nodding her head at Michael as he walked very slowly towards the front door, head bowed against the vile weather.

'We all had a lovely time thank you, Mrs Browne,' replied Jane firmly, hating the tone of female conspiracy ringing in the question.

this one, we could both be looking for jobs – although my neck is on the line more than hers, which is only natural since it's worth a bit more at the end of each month—'

Jane, who had once grown nervous on Michael's behalf when he mentioned such meetings, drifted into a sort of trance as he talked; he had his back to her and was rooting unsuccessfully in the fridge for the bottle of champagne. It had been a habit of her parents to keep champagne in the house. Her father claimed that it made him look for excuses to celebrate rather than grumble. Thinking of her parents gave her a jolt, as it sometimes did, an electric shock of pain that passed through her without warning, a memento of the loss and shock.

Once the bottle had been angrily extracted from the drawer marked 'salad', Michael made a visible attempt to slip into a more appropriately celebratory frame of mind, though the strain showed in the rapidity with which he emptied his glass and his keenness to escape to the other room.

They ate pâté and humus with toast on their laps in the sitting-room. After the news there was a repeat of a Benny Hill show. Jane reached for the console and pressed the volume switch down a few notches.

'Hey, what did you do that for?'

'I want to talk.'

He rolled his eyes. 'Not now, please, Jane – this is funny.' He turned the volume back up. 'Anyway, what about?' He kept his gaze firmly on the screen.

'You're not listening.'

'I am, I am.' He gave her a reassuring look and then laughed loudly at something on the programme. Very deliberately, light-headed with apprehension, Jane got up from the sofa and placed herself in front of the television.

'What the hell are you playing at?' he scowled, reminding her of how Tom looked when one of his favourite videos ended.

It wasn't a great moment to have picked, she knew that, but fear at her own courage had blurred her judgement and the careful sense of timing that she usually employed in dealings with her husband. It struck her suddenly that she had shoe-horned both of them through so much that was bad – so much that should have been allowed to be bad –

by simply pretending that everything was all right. It was a hard habit to break.

'We're not getting on very well, Michael,' she announced firmly, feeling small and melodramatic.

He shook the look of irritation from his face and extended his hand towards her.

'Come and sit down, for goodness sake. We're fine.'

'No, we are not.' She ignored the hand and took a step backwards; the hem of her dress prickled with static electricity at the touch of the screen behind. Benny Hill was on a horse, singing loudly.

Michael sighed and put his hands to each side of his face, before running his fingers back through his thick hair.

'Why are you doing this, Jane, tonight of all nights?' he asked, expressing irritation rather than the desire for a genuine answer.

She started to reply, but he quickly turned the volume down and pulled her hard by the arm until she sat down beside him.

'Everything needs working at – marriage and everything else. We both know that.' He smiled and shrugged as he said this, as if making such an enlightened statement absolved him from the onerous task of putting it into practice. 'Come here and stop looking so bloody miserable.' His arm tightened around her and pressed her to him. His shirt felt faintly damp against her face. It smelt of fabric conditioner mingled with sweat. Jane went limp, focusing her attention on one of his buttons. It was a perfect, pearly white, apart from the faintest grey streak between two of the holes.

'That's better,' he murmured, stroking her head.

When Benny Hill had finished Michael murmured, 'I almost forgot – I've got something for you,' and produced a crumpled white envelope from his trouser pocket. Expecting it to be an anniversary card, Jane was surprised when a small business card saying *Georgio Beauty Therapists* fell on to her lap. In the top left hand corner was scrawled a time and a date. 'It's a present. A facial something or other. Apparently Mrs Glassbrook – the MD's wife – spends half her life there. It's supposed to be very exclusive,' he added, because Jane was so silent.

'Thank you,' she breathed at last, 'how very . . . original.
I . . . did you think of it yourself?'

'I found the card in the street – what do you bloody well
think?' In fact it had been Antonia's suggestion, when he had
let slip that he had to get back early for an anniversary meal;
his secretary had popped round in her lunch break to make
the booking.

'I'm afraid I haven't got you anything.'

'I'll forgive you,' he said softly, placing his hand on the round
of her bottom and moving it slowly over the slippery silk. 'There
are ways you could make up for it, you know.'

She forced a smile, while inside a lone voice roared with
derision and despair. Nothing had changed. She was powerless.
The failure felt all her own. Michael pretended not to see –
Michael would never see – that their marriage had plummeted
terrible depths, that they were in a silent, secret, dark place
where there was no love, no understanding, no hope.

'I'll quickly clear up and have a bath first,' she muttered,
sloping off, hoping that if she took long enough Michael would
have fallen asleep before she got into bed.

'You Lyttons make me sick, honestly, such romance – champagne and beauty treatments – after so many years, it makes those of us who do nothing but watch telly together feel quite inadequate.' Pippa's tongue curled neatly round her lips in search of stray blobs of cream. 'Tim would never think of giving me a present like that – not in a million years, not even if I spelt it out as a written request. He thinks all this beauty stuff is a big con. If he has to pay more than a fiver for a haircut he feels he's been robbed. And he hates it if I wear more than a dab of make-up.' Pippa touched the natural flush in her cheeks self-consciously before taking another careful nibble of her éclair which, in spite of her cautionary assault still splurged cream out on all sides. 'This is truly delicious,' she sighed happily, 'I can't tell you how pleased I am that you called.'

Jane had given up on her own pastry which was filled with a sickly yellow cream and heavily laced with cinnamon. After the gruesome attentions of the morning she felt badly in need of a cigarette, but didn't want to shock Pippa.

'Actually, Pip, we're about the most unromantic couple you could ever hope to meet. Michael got the idea of a facial from his boss's wife who apparently has her spots squeezed and her face pummelled every week. I'm beginning to suspect,' she went on cheerfully, 'that he wants to turn me into one of those plastic executive wives who nibble expensive spinach leaves for lunch and wear designer jackets to the supermarket.'

Pippa giggled in happy disbelief. 'I bet it was lovely, though.' She closed her eyes. 'A facial massage, hmm.'

'If you really want the truth, Pip,' Jane leant forward over the table, smiling wickedly, 'it was quite vile. A teenager, with powder caked into her acne scars, had the audacity to make very dispiriting remarks about my bumps and blemishes while studying them through a magnifying glass. She said I had a "combination" problem and asked me if I exfoliated. When I said not that I knew of she left the room for a few moments, clearly in a state of shock.'

'Oh Jane, she didn't,' said Pippa, laughing so much she had to put her tea down.

'When she put cucumbers on my eyes and sprayed me with boiling steam I thought I was going to suffocate.' Jane, enjoying herself now, slurped the dregs of her coffee and looked over her shoulder in a charade of fear at being overheard. 'I will pass delicately over the next ten minutes, the pain and shame of which have to be experienced to be believed. Suffice it to say that I felt far worse than a monkey having its fleas picked.'

'Jane, stop, please, I'm getting a stomach ache. Eclairs and laughing don't go. Anyway, monkeys like having their fleas picked.'

'The only half-way decent bit was a few minutes of massage at the end, but that was when she chose to embark on a detailed description of her grandmother's boils, which sort of ruined the effect.'

'I sincerely hope you won't tell it to Michael like this – it probably cost a fortune.'

'Twenty-seven pounds, to be exact. I'm thinking of taking a course.'

After they had ordered another tea and coffee Pippa asked timidly if she might finish Jane's sticky bun for her. 'I'm trying to relax a bit more – be easier on myself,' she said, by way of an excuse. 'Doctor's orders.' She grinned, dying to get on to the only subject that she ever really wanted to talk about, dream about, worry about.

It was impossible to explain to anyone quite how obsessive the matter had become for her, now that she had let it. Everywhere she looked there were babies, pregnant mothers, prams and push-chairs. Every advert, every press story, every TV programme seemed to be about children or parents or pregnancy. Coming to meet Jane that morning, she had glided past countless black and white images of a teenage pregnant girl, standing under the bold telephone number of a clinic that promised counselling before abortion. The very idea – knowing from the pictures in one of her endless books what a foetus looked like after only a few weeks of development – filled Pippa with a nauseous despair. Jane was one of the very few people she felt she could talk to about this blight of involuntary childlessness. To her, it was beginning to feel like bereavement without a corpse. And like bereavement it was a subject which people found hard to tackle head on. Jane was so good at simply listening, without showing judgement or pity. For it was the pity of other women that Pippa dreaded most of all.

But when she revealed quite how far she had delved into the logistics of a private IVF programme, still without a murmur to Tim, even Jane felt she had to intervene with some advice.

'Pippa,' she spoke gently, aware of the raw sensitivity of the subject, 'if you don't get Tim on board soon you're running the risk of making him feel so left out – and perhaps resentful – that he might set himself against the whole thing.'

'I just want to find out all the details of what's involved, whether I'm suitable, stuff like that. We've had Tim's sperm-count done loads of times in the past – we know the problem lies within me.' She tweaked the string of her tea-bag and studied the label for a second. 'There are all these hormone injections you have to have to produce masses of eggs; then they are collected by ultrasound and put in a freezer. It's quite amazing. I've read about loads of couples who've succeeded – sometimes first time round. Though of course the overall statistics are relatively low – a thirty-five per cent success rate – and each cycle of treatment costs £2,400—'

Jane had to put her hand on Pippa's to interrupt the flow and get her proper attention. 'Tell Tim.'

Pippa sighed and pulled out her purse to pay the bill. 'I know, I know. I just keep waiting for him to snap out of this dark mood of his. It's incredible how he sustains them.' She waved at the waitress and wouldn't hear of Jane contributing. 'It'll all come tumbling out in the end, no doubt – some problem at work, I expect – it usually is,' she added with a forced smile.

Jane deliberately took her time getting home, not minding the bad traffic or the endless series of red lights. Every so often she touched her face, hating its sheeny smoothness and the strong smell of cosmetics. Her skin had never needed much attention – a flannel and some moisturiser was the extent of her own beauty programme – much to the dismay of the beautician. She had exaggerated the discomfort of the experience to Pippa, partly to make her laugh, but above all to protect herself. What really rankled was the feeling that she had lain on that couch for an hour, her feet freezing and her mind resistant, because of some whim of Michael's. It had not been a thoughtful gift, of that she was quite certain. It was like the tea-making machine he had given her for Christmas and which he used every morning. Jane only ever drank tea at tea-time. Her hair still felt sticky from the various oils and creams that had been rubbed round the edges of her forehead and temples. On looking in the mirror in the bathroom at home she saw that it was sticking up at odd angles all round the frame of her face, as if it had been glued out of place.

Turning the taps on full, she briskly filled the basin and splashed her face with water, before rubbing it hard with a flannel. Then she fixed the hose attachment to the taps on the bath and washed her hair, using two lots of shampoo and conditioner, massaging her scalp till it felt bruised, running her fingers mercilessly through the black, wet tresses until they squeaked from rinsing.

'Let's have a look then,' said Michael, when he got in late that night, tweaking her chin to make her face him. 'Didn't they do make-up and stuff?' There was disappointment in his voice.

'Nope.' She turned her attention back to the stove. 'Sorry, no make-up. Just lots of cleansing and rubbing. It was most invigorating.'

'I thought they'd do make-up.' He poured himself a glass of wine and stood looking at her from the doorway for a few moments. 'You should wear make-up, you know, Jane, it suits you. I like it when you smarten yourself up a bit. I think it's important for a woman not to let herself go, after having children and so on. Antonia does aerobics three times a week – before work.' And with these encouraging words, he disappeared into the sitting-room.

* * *

'Michael thinks I should swap yoga for aerobics,' remarked Jane the following week, when she met Julia for one of their evening sessions with Shiro Yatzuma.

'Michael is wrong. Aerobics is the closest thing to legal torture known to woman.'

Julia cut a striking figure in the changing-room, with her mass of hair coiled into an elegant bun on top of her head, showing off the graceful slimness of her neck. She sat on the bench, a little self-consciously, pulling her long legs into her so that her chin rested on her knees.

'Is Harriet teething or has Michael been keeping you awake with long sessions of torrid sex? You look mildly shattered.'

'Both. And thanks for the compliment. I'm supposed to look great – I had a facial last week. An anniversary present from Michael.'

Julia raised her eyebrows. 'I am impressed.'

'I hated it actually.'

Jane pulled on a baggy T-shirt emblazoned with a cartoon of a frowning elephant under the words 'No Pain, No Gain' and made a silly face at herself in the mirror. All around them the other women were getting ready, trying not to look at their reflections too critically, but doing so none the less, casting hopeful glances at their profiles, patting their stomachs and yanking their costumes down to cover the bulges of their bottoms.

'I ate cream buns with Pippa afterwards, which was much more fun.' She put two clips in her hair in a vain attempt to stop it flopping into her eyes and followed Julia through into the carpeted studio.

Mr Yatzuma took his art extremely seriously and was quickly irritated by students who did not do likewise. Since this solemnity, combined with the silky brush of his cropped hair and the wide dish of his pallid face, had been know to induce schoolgirl giggles from the two friends, they took their usual precaution of positioning themselves in opposite corners of the room.

'Silence, please, ladies,' murmured Shiro, his eyes closed, his palms upturned to the ceiling. The women dutifully fell quiet and crossed their legs to begin.

Although quite broad and muscular, their instructor could twist his body into the most surprising contortions. Beside his mat a small tape-recorder emitted a form of tuneless humming, which, after the first few minutes of grating annoyance, grew strangely soothing. 'We must centre our bodies. Balance, relaxation, breathing, these are the key. These three things will make us feel well tonight.' Shiro moved round the room as he spoke, helping his charges stretch into something approaching the correct positions.

'You are trying too hard,' he said when he got to Jane. 'You have no breathing. Please breathe, Miss Lytton. Do not strain your body. No discomfort for you, please. Your face and neck are too tight.'

He knelt down beside her and began to rub her shoulders as she lay, face-downwards, pulling uselessly at her legs, trying in vain to coax the soles of her feet to touch the backs of her knees. 'Release,' commanded Shiro. 'This is bad. No good. Everything is too tight.' Ignoring the rest of the class – much to Jane's consternation – he proceeded to massage her neck, her shoulder blades and her spine, moving his fingers gently but firmly down over each vertebra and into the small of her back.

'I think I'm cracking up,' she told Julia afterwards, as they sat with large glasses of red wine and a frayed basket of stale French bread.

'Aren't we all, dear, aren't we all.'

'I'm being serious.'

'Oh, let's not be serious, please. I've had a filthy week. The weather's too good. People are much keener to browse in antique shops when it rains. Unless things pick up I'm going to have to sleep with my bank manager.'

'What if I told you that when our oriental Mel Gibson laid his hands upon me I was melted to the core?'

Julia let out a small scream and reached for a cigarette from Jane's crushed packet of ten. 'And I thought you had fallen asleep.'

'Sleep was the last thing on my mind, I can assure you. If Mr Yatzuma knew the effect of his rub-down he'd probably expel me on the spot.'

'That good, was it?' Julia raised one beautiful crescent of an eyebrow and tipped her head back to blow a perfect smoke-ring at the dingy-brown ceiling of the wine bar. 'I thought such things weren't supposed to happen to happily married mothers of two.'

'They're not.' At which point two steaming bowls of fettuccine and mushroom sauce arrived, mercifully interrupting Julia's line of questioning.

After a few mouthfuls Julia gave up on her food. 'I don't know why we carry on coming here – this stuff is too stodgy for words.' She prodded her heap of pasta and grey lumpy sauce with her fork. 'It's all out of a tin, you know.'

'It's not and I don't care, I'm starving.' Jane, used to her friend's picky eating habits, was not going to be deterred.

'I'll tell you something funny though.' Julia threw a heavy tassel of hair back over one shoulder and sat back. 'That brother-in-law of yours rang me up the other day.'

'You mean Christopher?' Jane stopped eating. 'You never told me.'

'I'm telling you now. It was a couple of weeks after that frightful evening at Pippa's, when Michael and Tim got so drunk and that vegan woman with lacquered hair and a pillar-box mouth kept delivering lectures on how we should all behave.'

'I knew it –' Jane clapped her hands, 'he likes you – I knew he wasn't gay—'

'Gay?' Julia considered the idea for a moment. 'I wouldn't say so, no. But I'm not sure that he likes me either.'

Jane pushed her plate away and reached for her wine. 'Don't play Miss Modesty with me. Of course he likes you, why else would he ring?'

'I haven't the faintest idea. He said he was coming to London and could we meet and then a few days later he said he was awfully sorry but the whole thing was off and he wasn't coming after all.' She eyed her friend for a moment. 'How well do you know him?'

Jane shrugged. 'Not very well at all. He's either frightfully shy or terribly aloof – I can never decide which. When Michael and I first met he used to be around quite a bit,' she paused, spearing a limp mushroom with her fork, 'but then I guess he went his own way and we went ours. It's Michael who's always had this thing about him being gay. They've never really got on at all. Christopher has always done the rebellious things – gone round the world, chucked in a promising career, got pissed at funerals – he was a monster at their mother's – though he's definitely sorted himself out a bit since those days.'

'A bit like you and Mattie then,' teased Julia, 'one on the tracks and one in the habit of going haywire.'

'Not a bit like me and Mattie, no,' rejoined Jane stiffly, hating, as she always had, the age-old assumption that she would go straight where Mattie would flounder. 'Mattie and I are very fond of one another, in spite of our differences, whereas Michael seems to get a positive pleasure out of knocking Christopher down, picking holes in him – maybe it's sibling rivalry – hell, I don't know.' She crossed her arms and threw Julia a mischievious look. 'But he must have contacted you for a reason.'

'Don't start match-making, please – you've always been lousy at it.' She shuffled in her chair. 'I'm beginning to wish I'd never mentioned the man. Anyway he's not my type.'

'And what exactly is your type, may I ask?' Jane was trying to be jolly, but Julia chose to take the question seriously.

'Oh Christ, I don't know. For years I thought it was so important to have a man in my life, but now only a small part of me feels that way. It's so much easier only having myself to worry about. I feel so uncrowded, so uncomplicated. Do you know, it's almost two years since I had any sex.' She lowered her voice. 'And I can honestly say that I hardly miss it at all.'

Having noticed the sidelong glances of appreciation cast at Julia by a couple of the waiters and some of their fellow-diners, Jane could not help but think how amazed they would have been to hear such things. Beautiful women were always assumed to have the best sex lives. A twist of jealousy tightened deep inside. For a moment she longed for the simplicity of living alone that Julia had described. But yet, it felt impossible to regret her life – its fallibility was integral, unavoidable. Given the time again she would have made the same decisions, good and bad, she was sure. Then she thought of the children and her stomach turned again at the wonderfulness and awfulness of it all.

So wrapped up was she in her own train of thought, that it was several seconds before she realised that Julia was waiting for her to say something.

'I said I have applied to join a dating agency and all you do is blink. I expected mild shock at the very least.'

'I – I am shocked. How – how – liberated, how brave of you.' Jane shook off her own preoccupations with difficulty, as Julia's announcement sunk in. 'A dating agency? Are you serious?'

Julia was back in her stride, enjoying the self-mockery that her own situation allowed. 'I am to be fed into a computer – bust size, brain-power, the circumference of my corns – and in a few days it will spew out the name – or if I'm lucky, the names – of my perfect partners. Modern magic. It's got to be worth a try, don't you think? I don't have time for night classes in basket weaving or Chinese painting; all my friends are married – apart from Robbie, who's terribly gay and who's great for going to the cinema and unthreatening cuddles, but who is inclined to get depressed and drag me down with him; the thought of singles' bars fills me with a deadly disgust and, in spite of what I said just now, I do sometimes miss a bit of healthy coital cavorting on Saturday nights when the rest of you are celebrating anniversaries and I've got nothing more than a book on restoring chamber-pots to keep me company. More wine?'

Jane shook her head. Then she said, 'I think I might have to leave Michael,' which made Julia tip all the dreggiest bits into her glass and put the bottle down with a thump.

'That's appalling. What on earth has brought this on? Have you had a stunning row?'

'It's not like that . . . I only wish it were, it would be so much easier. Perhaps if we'd rowed a bit more things wouldn't have got so bad.'

'You are not making sense, girl. Drink some wine and try again.' She pushed her glass across the table and leaned forward over folded arms.

'Mum and Dad argued – loudly – loads of times, but I'm sure they loved each other.'

'Mine argued too – very loudly – and loathed the sight of one another,' retorted Julia, whose parents had divorced when she was in her teens. 'Of course, you don't have to explain anything if you don't want to – not to me – though I think Michael is going to need to understand,' she added, more gently. 'Is there someone—'

'Else? No. I've told you, it's not simple like that. It's just not working . . . as it should . . . as I always hoped a good marriage should work.' She struggled to find the words, hating her hopelessness, her inability to spell it out. 'We don't really fit – I'm not sure we ever have – but it's so hard to own up to these things, even to yourself. For ages I've pretended that everything was all right – helping Michael pretend too. And when things feel really wrong, I look at the rest of the world, at all the other trillions of married couples with children and mortgages, living in suburbia, making love on Friday nights after a drink or two, yelling at the children and at each other about money and fairness, and I think perhaps misery is normal. All these other people accept it, so who am I to complain?'

'You could do a lot worse.'

'That's what I've been telling myself for ages, but it doesn't help. Whatever we had has long since dissolved – though Michael wouldn't admit it for the world.' She squeezed her fists and pressed them hard into her forehead. 'The awful thing is, I can still remember how it used to be, how I used to need him – but now I think it was all tied up with Mum and Dad, what I went through having to cope with Mattie flipping so badly after they died.'

'You're stronger now, that's all,' said Julia. 'You're a little more independent, you—'

Jane shook her head slowly. 'No, it's much more than that. Apart from Harriet and Tom, there is this great nothingness between us. I cook for him, clean for him, sleep with him – but there is no affection. We no longer touch each other in the real sense – not inside where it matters.' She laid both hands flat on the table and studied them hard. They looked dry and shrivelled. 'We have been going through the motions of marriage – and not even managing that very well.'

'You've got to laugh,' said Julia dryly, 'here are you trying to get rid of your man just as I'm starting an earnest search for one. There's got to be a lesson in there some-where.'

Having made her confession, Jane immediately felt a combination of relief and regret. An illogical urge to reassure Julia overtook her. 'I'll probably never do anything about it. It's probably just a phase. Christ, is that the time – I'll have to fly.' And in a flurry of dividing up the bill and grabbing coats she bustled herself out into the blissful cool of the streets, feeling more burdened and confused than ever.

Julia tried poetry instead of chamber-pots in bed that night, but her mind would not focus. She thought instead of the steely shutters of marriage and the secrets nurtured within, out of loyalty, fear, habit and, perhaps, love. Though shocking, Jane's admission made sense. All her uncharacteristic swings of mood, the brooding silences, the tense cheerfulness, had a context now.

In the midst of her compassion, she felt an irrepressible and complex blend of guilt and betrayal. Jane should have told her earlier. Their friendship should have allowed her to speak up long ago. The fact that it had not – that their own relationship too had failed in this way – led Julia's mind along the labyrinthine paths she hated most, towards the painful conclusion that no amount of lovers or friends or children can prevent each person from being alone. Which led her on to the thought of the dating agency and the ridiculous gamble and possible humiliation to which she had so recklessly committed herself.

But you've got to try, she told herself, as she replaced Wendy Cope's slim volume on the side-table and turned out the light – you've got to try to connect with people, to understand them, even if it drives you mad in the end.

8

Michael fiddled with his executive toy. The heavy metal balls clacked rhythmically together, the momentum of each swing starting the next. He felt jaded and fragile from a bad night's sleep. He was never any good without sleep. When Jane was breast-feeding the children he had been driven to using ear-plugs. But last night Tom had crept into their bed during the dawn hours, crawling up under the duvet to lie between them, his arms round his mother, his small cold toes seeking warmth along his father's legs. Too tired to do anything about it, not wanting to make the child cry, hoping Jane would do something about it, Michael had tossed on the uncomfortable borders of sleep until the buzz of the alarm on the tea-machine sounded in his right ear.

He picked up the picture of Jane and the children that lived on his desk and began fiddling with that instead. The frame was loose. The three of them smiled at him. Or rather, they smiled at the man behind the camera, just as they had brushed their hair for him and given him their full attention when he asked for it. Sometimes Michael envied that photographer, whom he had never met, who had been doing a 'special' on family sittings in a corner of BHS when Jane strolled through one afternoon with Harriet in a pram and Tom toddling beside. How much easier it would be to enjoy his family, he mused, if, every so often, they sat still like that for him, contented and unquestioning. As it was, family life was rushed and snatched, full of noise and things that made him cross.

Holding the photo at a distance, he tried to look objectively at his wife, to see if he could perceive something beyond the familiarity of her face. Her smile was fixed and sure, but those cat-green eyes looked away, out of the picture somewhere, to some distant horizon behind his left shoulder. Hetty was propped on her knees, floppy, pink and plump – too plump, he had said to Jane at the time, though since then her stocky limbs had begun to elongate with quite alarming rapidity. Tom sat beside them, a little apart, hands self-consciously folded in his lap. A bubble of sentimental pride burst in Michael's throat, quickly followed by a spasm of frustration. It was a devilish business being a father. The children were so demanding; they seemed to reserve all their extremes of behaviour for him – either deliriously happy or deliriously vile. They never hurled themselves like that at Jane, hollering and tugging for attention.

Tracing a finger through the thin film of dust on the glass, Michael indulged in a recollection of his wife as he had first known her, when she was a history student at Durham. Since he had been studying economics and business studies, their paths had barely crossed at first. Later on, when they grew intimate, he marvelled that he had not noticed her earlier, with her lustrous tangle of dark hair, such a dramatic frame for the small round face and startlingly sensual eyes, heavy-lidded, bewitching. He thought suddenly of the first time they made love; how she had stared and stared, holding his gaze, not letting go, even when she came, with three short gasps, her mouth slightly open, lips wet from kissing. Such intensity was new to Michael. It sharpened the focus of his life, brightened the colours of his world, made him want to get out of bed in the mornings and go jogging round dark, empty streets, for the sheer hell of being alive. The fact that such intensity had gone was not something he liked to think about, beyond the fact that he was sure it was normal. They still had sex about once a week, which he reckoned was pretty good going, even if they took considerably less time about it and Jane's eyes were invariably closed.

They had their first proper conversation one sticky June night in a queue outside a cinema. Each was waiting for their partner of the time to show up. He was going out with a Scottish girl, Fiona Yarrow, a mathematician with brilliant-red hair, film-star lips and pale, freckled skin. Jane was with a medical student called Dougie Craven, a strong scrum-half and something of a college hero. She had seemed so small and serene that, when Fiona finally appeared, running round the corner, all legs and arms, she had struck him as being somehow gangly and inelegant, a giraffe beside a deer. When the couples separated to find their seats, both Jane and Michael turned for a quick look back, exchanging a glance of mutual interest. It was a line cast between them, the ensnaring moment, the moment that ensured they would take the trouble to meet again.

'Am I interrupting?'

Michael hastily put down the photograph. 'No, Antonia, no. I was miles away. Come in. Help yourself to coffee.' He gestured at his percolating machine on a shelf by the window and stretched himself out in his chair. 'You couldn't pour me one while you're at it, could you?' He nudged the photo back into place and flipped open his briefcase.

'Not having trained as a waitress, I don't like pandering to such requests, but seeing as you look half asleep I'll treat you just this once.' Her voice was teasing and sure. She had come a long way in the last few months.

Michael wondered, as he had many times before, whether she found him attractive. It was irrelevant of course, a mere indulgence, that would have no effect on his assessment of her research into Polish money markets. But it did add an edge to office life, to have even the possibility of such a notion dangling over him. He especially liked her hair, which was long and black and straight, as crisply cut as her suits. She was tall – almost as tall as him in her high heels – and flat-chested, like one of those waif-like models who posed in shrunken vests and baggy socks.

'Terry's asked me to do some work on South America.'

'Don't worry – I'll have a word with him later on today.' Michael began sorting through the papers in his briefcase. Tom had drawn a bright red line across the front of his main notepad, together with a large, tremulous rendition of the letter T. Irritated, Michael turned to the page where he had jotted down a list of issues to go through that day. On what had once been the blank page opposite, a green and orange pirate ship now confronted him, decked liberally with cannons and pirates, who poised daintly on the tiptoes of their pin legs at odd angles amongst the rigging.

'What an original plan for the day,' laughed Antonia, who had quietly approached his desk and was leaning over with interest.

'Bloody children.' Michael ripped Tom's picture out of the book and screwed it up into a ball which he hurled, with perfect accuracy, into the bin in the corner. 'Sorry about that.'

'Don't apologise, I thought it looked rather good. How old is your boy?'

'Five . . . or maybe six. Nothing but trouble at any rate. I assume you're not in any danger of cluttering up your life with infants?'

'Christ, no.' She straightened up and briskly yanked the jacket of her suit down, pulling out imaginary creases, before seating herself in the wide luxury of one of Michael's brown-leather chairs. 'About Terry – I think you've misunderstood.'

'I've told you, I'll sort him out,' he muttered, engrossed in a column of figures from his in-tray.

'But I want to do the work, Michael. It's on Argentina and Chile. The whole place is really opening up – the opportunities are fantastic. It should be a great project. Don't worry about the work-load, I'll manage easily.' She clapped her hands together and stood up to go. 'If I didn't have to come in on Saturdays I'd feel I wasn't doing my job properly.' She laughed easily, causing her colleague a quite unexpected sting of envy, before other considerations crowded his mind.

'But you were assigned to work for me, Antonia – it's not as simple as you seem to think. It would be ridiculous to work on Eastern Europe and the southern hemisphere at the same time – that's not how we operate here, it—'

She coughed a small, unnecessary cough of politeness, before interrupting. 'I have already taken the liberty of speaking to Mr Glassbrook about it – I knew you would think that the most sensible approach, given that straddling departments is not usual policy.' She tucked a glossy wedge of hair behind one ear, 'and he seemed to think it would be fine, so long as neither you nor Terry start to feel that I am falling down on my commitments.'

There was nothing more to say. She was well ahead with all her work – one step ahead of him half the time.

'You weren't beginning to think you owned me, were you, Michael?' She grinned in a last pause at the door, before swishing lightly out of the room, a millimetre of petticoat-lace flashing at him from under her short skirt, a parting shot of teasing contempt.

When Tim Croft rang an hour or so later to ask if he was free for lunch, Michael leapt at the chance. The exchange with Antonia had unsettled him. While coping deftly with the straightforward aspects of office politics and competition, Michael was not so adroit when it came to the management of other people. He hated not knowing where he stood; wheeling and dealing in international markets was one thing, but when the matters at stake were blurry issues of feeling and opinion he invariably struggled. Most riling of all was the loss of face in being forced to share the increasingly acclaimed services of Antonia with one of the other partners. The whole business left him feeling subtly, but profoundly, threatened.

His bad mood lingered on as the taxi edged its way through the stodgy West End traffic. Halfway down the King's Road frustration so overcame him that he got out, resolving to walk the last mile to the pub that Tim had suggested, a favourite drinking haunt of theirs on the riverside near Wandsworth Bridge. Since he had left so promptly, he had loads of time to spare.

But walking was hard work too. Though summer had by no means arrived, an uncharacteristically warm day had brought shoppers and tourists out in droves. The pavements were densely layered with ugly snapshots of modern man in full summer regalia; quivering white flesh and straining seams assailed him on every side. Feeling like a visitor from another world, Michael walked briskly, his grey suit jacket carefully folded over one arm and the sleeves of his pink and blue striped shirt neatly rolled up to the elbow. After a while he found himself keeping step behind a spindly, leather-clad creature, with a cartwheel of red and yellow spikes where most people settled for hair. There was a tattoo on the back of the creature's neck, a large pair of lips that moved as the neck crinkled, pouting and puckering at passers-by. As if aware of Michael's riveted eyes, the cartwheeled head suddenly spun round; it belonged to a girl with flaring nostrils and staring black eyes that made Michael afraid.

He ducked into a bookshop and, with Jane vaguely in mind, wandered into the cookery section. Michael didn't read much himself, apart from two or three of the better known thriller writers, which he always bought in hardback a few weeks after they came out. Having flipped idly through the pages of a weighty manual entitled *Your Wok and You*, he moved further along the shelf, to find himself in the biography section. And there was his brother Christopher, his dark eyes watching him from out of a black and white photograph on a book which had been put back face downwards. He looked unconvincingly spruce and serious, like a parody of a devout intellectual. *Clough's Life and Works*, by C.J. Lytton. Although it was over a year since the book had come out – he and Jane had their own signed copy at home – Michael picked it up and opened it: '*Perhaps the first truly "modern" poet—*' With the faintest shimmer of an expectation that he might learn something new, Michael quickly turned the page to read the summary of his brother's life, which he had only ever glanced at before:

> *Christopher John Lytton was born in 1955 in Newcastle, second son of the Reverend Earnest Lytton. After attending St Peter's College for boys, he was awarded a scholarship to King's College Cambridge, where he gained a first class honours degree in Classics. As a postgraduate he presented a thesis on Greek myth and the twentieth-century novel, which was greeted with considerable acclaim and a three-year research fellowship at Trinity College. In 1980 Christopher Lytton moved to Christchurch College Oxford to continue with research, but left soon afterwards in order to travel and, ultimately, to live in France. He returned to Oxford in 1985, where he now lives and works as a teacher of English and Classics at St Stephen's Preparatory School. Clough's Life and Works is Christopher Lytton's second published work. His thesis was adapted for publication in 1980.*

Michael closed the book and studied the photograph. All his

earliest memories of his brother were tied up with feeling sorry for him. Poor little Christopher, clinging to his mother's sturdy legs; too small to climb a tree, or kick a ball, or stay up late, or fight back. And by the time he was old enough for such things Michael had given up waiting for him, busying himself instead with schoolfriends and intricate airfix models that couldn't possibly be done with little brothers hanging around, fingers up their noses, asking silly questions.

Even though Michael had long since been forced to realise that Christopher was a steely-willed, deeply independent character who would doggedly pursue his own mystifying course through life, a shadowy image of the poor, shunned little brother remained. Perhaps it was partly this that had prevented them from ever crossing the tricky threshold of true sibling friendship. But there were other, more serious chasms too, based on yawning differences of character. For Michael university had been a necessity more than a pleasure, even after he met Jane. During all of his time as a student he had itched to be done with it. To get a job, to make money – he burned to get on with the real business of life.

The fact that Christopher had been content to languish for so long as an academic, only to chuck it all in, seriously affected his elder brother's opinion of him, confirming deep-rooted suspicions of foppish laziness and a weak character. None of his extensive travels seemed to improve him in the least. Trading his scholar's gown and scuffed suede brogues for a rucksack and leather sandals that showed off slim, white feet, surprisingly small for his height, he would simply vanish for months at a time, only to reappear quite unchanged without any warning at all. Even after his long spell in France, he was the same Christopher, fluent in French maybe, but still single, still unnervingly quiet. If he regretted hopping off the academic treadmill just as he seemed to be getting the better of it, he never said a word.

Michael slotted the book back into the shelf, beside something far more exciting with a silver cover and blood-red letters for its title. He turned and bent his head to make out the words, but caught sight of the time. After all that he was going to be late. He hurried out of the shop, cursing his brother under his breath.

9

Not so very far from where Michael and Tim were ordering ploughman's lunches and pints of real ale, Pippa Croft was trying on a pair of pink Bermuda shorts and frowning. Her stomach had expanded in recent weeks, risen and smooth like a perfect cake, as if in anticipation of being pregnant. Perhaps because of this association, Pippa found that she did not mind the extra weight at all. She even toyed with the notion of phantom pregnancy, fascinated by the idea of such a thing, fascinated most of all by the force of human longing to which such a condition bore testimony.

After fighting with the waistband of the pink shorts for a few minutes, she gave up with a resigned but not unhappy sigh. Of course hormones had nothing to do with it in her case. For Pippa, food was all about relaxing; she had been treating herself a lot recently – mostly without any guilt at all – and it felt marvellous.

A far greater problem lay with her knees. Being a fine-boned, wispy sort of person, Pippa had often thought that she deserved something better than the dimpled puddings that covered her knee-caps. Many attractive fashions had been wistfully jettisoned on account of them, including hot-pants in her early teens, when her best friend, Matilda Johnson, had acquired a pair of purple velvet hip-huggers that had set Pippa's heart afire with envy.

Such renewed endeavours to expose her legs in a favourable light stemmed from Tim's astonishing announcement, very late the night before, that he wished her to accompany him on his trip to Africa, in a few weeks' time. The invitation had been issued from behind a vast bunch of flowers, an embarrassment of gladioli, irises, chrysanthemums and carnations, that provided the secondary service of shielding him from the intensely questioning silence maintained by his wife. When his morose, cherubic face did emerge – when he finally thrust the lavish bouquet into her arms – she saw that the usually irrepressible curls of his hair lay flat and damp with sweat. He looked full of guilt – sodden with it, in fact. A few weeks before Pippa had watched a compelling, awful soap-drama in which the long-suffering wife confided to a friend that she knew when her husband was starting a new affair because he always brought her flowers. Pippa thought of that wife now, as she smiled wretchedly and began clipping generous wedges off the stems with her secateurs.

'I don't think Africa would suit me, to be honest, Tim.' She reached into the cupboard beside the sink for her biggest vase. Ask him, ask him, ask him, sang a voice in her head. But she knew she wouldn't. For all the wrong reasons, of course; despicable reasons to do with being nearly forty and wanting a child. Because Tim was her best – her only – hope of that. Because that mattered more to her than putting up with infidelity and the grim fact of still loving him.

'I want you to come on this one, Pip – I really do.' His face was the picture of anguish and concern, so much so that she found an absurd compassion welling in her heart for how rotten he must feel. An astonishing clarity invaded her mind like light; never had life seemed more simple; never had she felt more clear-thinking and brave.

She cupped his face in her hands, touching the deep dimple in his chin with her thumbs. 'Oh Timmy, you fool,' she murmured, brushing his lips with a kiss. 'You don't have to take me – I'm too grown up to mind about your travels these days. I'll spoil myself while you're gone – how about that? I'll watch slushy videos and eat chocolates in bed, I promise.'

She returned to the flowers, arranging them with quick, skilful movements, tweaking off a leaf here and a stem there.

'Pippa – I love you so much—' He came up behind her and put his arms over her shoulders, burying his head in her neck, breathing hard, smelling of beer. 'Please come with me – just this once – please.'

She thought again of the wronged wife on the telly and gripped the edge of the sink. She had to suppress a wavering of resolve then; it hit her from nowhere, triggered by this appalling tipsy pleading, this clear begging for forgiveness for the unmentioned sin.

Taking a deep breath, she closed her hands over his. 'Okay. If it means so much to you. I'll come.'

Having wrung the decision out of her, he retreated, as if exhausted by the effort it had taken. He took a bottle of beer from the fridge and swigged at it, gasping between long, throaty gulps as if his thirst might never be quenched.

'You'll need some new clothes,' he declared at breakfast, his hair springy from the shower, but his eyes puffy and pink.

Pippa, whose knowledge of Africa was confined to Hollywood depictions of men in khaki shirts, darkened with circles of sweat, and sultry women who languished under ceiling fans while the natives ran riot, feared what she might have to suffer from the heat. Her skin was naturally pale and fine; excessive heat brought her out in red blotches and patchy rashes, it made her thin baby-hair cling to her scalp with all the panache of a used dish-cloth.

'I'll need a hat too,' was all she had replied to Tim, offering up her cheek for the ritualistic kiss of farewell.

'Have you anything a little longer?' she asked the sales assistant now, peering out from behind the curtain of her box-cubicle, despising her own timidity.

'Longer than Bermudas, madam?' replied the girl, in a tone that suggested she had been asked whether black could be made white.

'I mean – sort of just below the knee.'

'Culottes?'

Pippa nodded, but without hope.

The girl strolled off for a few minutes, only to return with a pair of red corduroy shin-length culottes that were clearly useless. Pippa took them, to be polite, but left them on the hanger. She pulled her own clothes back on, all the while doing a quick mental check-list of her summer wardrobe. There were a couple of things that would do – her cotton cream trouser-suit and her silk skirt with the stretchy waistband. No need to panic after all.

Standing on the escalator, she could not help glancing at herself in the mirrored wall. Her cheeks were flushed and her hair a mess. One earring dangled askew. She twisted it back into place and tried to raise her spirits by thinking about lunch.

Just as she stepped from the moving stairs on to the third floor of the department store, she caught sight of a man who looked like Tim walking away from her through haberdashery towards the sign for the lifts. A tall blonde woman walked beside him. He had his hand on her arm, held just above the elbow, self-consciously.

Pippa stopped, started, then stopped again. In a few seconds they would be gone. In a few seconds she would never know. She began to run, dodging women with large handbags, children in push-chairs and signs about price-cuts and fashions. She got there as the lift was closing, only just managing to put her hand to the door in time. As it pulled back to allow her access she saw, not Tim, but Julia, standing with a man whose face looked nothing like Tim's, although his hair and build were similar.

'Pippa—' Julia, who was with a man spawned by the computer dating-service, blushed helplessly. 'How nice to see you – this is Alan—'

'Lambert.' He held out his hand with a formal smile, revealing a gap of at least two millimetres between his front teeth. 'Which floor?' His finger hovered over the panel of buttons. He wore several heavy rings.

'Ground, please.' It seemed an age before the doors slid shut so the lift could begin its lumbering descent.

'Lovely dinner for Michael, Pippa – thanks so much. It seems ages ago now.'

'Yes, it was fun.' Pippa patted her hair and clung to her handbag. 'Tim's taking me to Africa. I'm shopping for the trip. Can't find a thing.'

'How exciting.'

'Julia and I have only just become acquainted,' said Alan Lambert, in a voice just high enough to make you notice. 'We're going to lunch at La Brasserie, Sloane Street – just round the corner.'

'How super,' said Pippa, puzzled.

The doors finally opened and the three of them stepped out in a jumble of 'after-yous'.

'We've been having coffee on the third floor,' added Julia, as if this might throw some light on her companion. 'They've just opened it. Lovely place – full of hanging plants and the smell of coffee beans. But I expect you'll get plenty of that in Africa – Kenya beans and all that.' With a look of embarrassed apology she turned to follow her escort out of the shop.

'Have a nice lunch,' called Pippa, suddenly flooded with a shaking relief that the man had not been Tim, that – for that day at least – she had been saved from the horror of confrontation and its consequences.

Michael returned to the table with a packet of crisps between his teeth and a pint of beer in each hand. 'They'll bring our food out to us. We're number fifty-two.'

They were sitting at a wooden bench in a courtyard at the back of the pub. People were sprawled everywhere, trouser-legs and shirt-sleeves rolled up, slotted into patches of sunlight like jigsaw pieces. Around them wasps hovered over sticky glasses, while flies settled for abandoned wedges of sweating cheese and half-eaten clumps of chilli con carni.

'Christ, it's hot.' Michael wiped his forehead with a paper napkin and studied the result. 'Look at that.' He held the napkin under Tim's nose. 'Lovely London grime. We'll all be wearing face-masks soon. Cheers, anyway.' He raised his tankard to his lips and let the first swig of beer trickle slowly and smoothly down the back of his throat. It was against his principles to drink at lunch-time, but the Antonia business had left him feeling in need of a pick-me-up.

'So, how are things?'

Tim stabbed a pickled onion with a cocktail stick and held it up for scrutiny.

'Not good, Michael, not good.'

'Join the club, as they say. I'm beginning to think about

making a move – switching to another bank – what do you think?'

Tim shrugged, which was unusual for him, since such questions usually prompted a volley of hearty advice. Having escaped the confinements of answering to an employer, he liked to comment sympathetically on the career-paths of his less adventurous friends.

'So, what's up with you?' Michael was offended by this lack of response. He did not see how troubled Tim was, judging the saggy greyness of his face to be from over-heating rather than unhappiness.

'Oh, nothing much,' Tim sucked in his breath, 'nothing more than bankruptcy.'

He spoke so steadily that Michael still failed to register that anything was amiss. 'Bad month for business then?' He balanced a large square of cheese on the end of his bread and got his mouth round it just as it started to topple.

Tim laughed then, a little wildly. 'A bad month, you could say that.' He wiped his eyes with the back of his hand and snorted. 'Such a bad month, in fact, that I am shortly to join the esteemed ranks of the totally bankrupt.' He carefully replaced his drink, putting it directly on the wet-mark it had left on the table.

'My God, you're serious.'

Tim looked away, down towards Wandsworth Bridge and the sludgy swirls of the shrinking river. He pulled a packet of small cigars from his breast pocket and lit one, inhaling deeply.

'Don't tell Pip, there's a good man – about the smoking, I mean.' He slapped his thigh. 'That's good isn't it – don't tell the little lady about the really important thing—'

'Does she know?'

Tim shook his head, preoccupied with swallowing a cough.

'But are you sure, Tim? I thought things were going so well—'

'Oh, they were, they were. Back in the blooming bloody eighties. But it's the fucking awful nineties now, Mike. I guess I over-reached myself. At one stage it looked like I couldn't put a foot wrong, I was so sure—' He tailed off and Michael didn't know what to say.

'Pippa doesn't have any idea. I just can't bring myself to tell her yet.' He pushed his untouched food away and leant on his elbows, head in his hands. 'She loves that sodding house. And the garden—' He thought of their garden, a kaleidescope of colour – hundreds of little petalled flowers, none of whose names he knew, bobbing in trim lines round the rich green of the lawn, like patterned lace. And thinking of this brought to mind the small hands of his wife, working neatly with trays of bulbs and buds, pressing the earth around them, settling them gently but firmly, for hour upon hour, kneeling there, sprinkling them, cosseting them, nourishing them. 'You see, not having any children and everything—'

'I know, Tim, I know.' Where a woman would almost certainly have encouraged the spilling of such unmentioned agonies, wanting to draw them out, knowing the relief of release, Michael did the manly thing and begged his friend to stop. 'I'll get us some more drinks, shall I?'

For the rest of the time they took shelter in the business aspect of Tim's predicament. Small travel companies were folding all the time; people simply no longer had the money for adventure holidays. Travelmania was so deeply in debt that there was no hope of attracting a buy-out.

'I should have seen the writing on the wall. If I had got out at the beginning of last year I'd be laughing now.'

'Don't, Tim – there's no point in looking back.'

'Absolutely not.' He clapped his hands with a bright energy that fooled neither of them. 'I'm going on a trip – Zambia, Zimbabwe, Madagascar – call it a last holiday. It was organised and paid for months ago. I'm taking Pippa. A treat for her.' His voice trembled for the first time. 'I'll probably break the news while we're out there.'

'Well that will be good – the trip I mean.' Michael had the grace to feel inadequate; calamity on such a scale was not something their friendship was used to; it was hard to know how to tackle the thing without making Tim feel even worse. 'Look here,' he went on quickly, aiming for a tone that was casual rather than concerned, 'why don't I have words in a few ears – see what leads I can rustle up in the city—'

Tim cut him off with a dismissive wave. 'It's far too late to go back. Thanks all the same – thanks very much indeed, Mike.'

He stood up and pressed the palms of both hands to the sides of his head, as if trying to smooth away the curls. 'I expect things will sort themselves out somehow.' He reached under the table for his briefcase. 'The first thing is to tell Pippa.'

'Yes, of course,' mumbled Michael, downing the last mouthful of his pint. As he got up to follow Tim from the pub he wished for the briefest of moments that he had misfortunes of equal gravity to offer as a reassuring counterpoint to such woes; at least then he could have felt something other than pity. After they had shaken hands he stood watching Tim's stooping, deflated figure traipse up the road, thinking how ill-suited men were to bad luck, how unattractive it made them.

At first glance, Earnest Lytton's house looked like something out of the suburbia of eastern America rather than the Kentish coast of southern England. This illusion was created by the porch, which Earnest had tacked on himself, during the months immediately following his wife, Edith's, death. He was a good carpenter and could have completed the job within a week or two; but since it was fulfilling a greater, unspoken need within his lonely self, he dragged it out, seeking perfection within perfection, so that several months passed before he pronounced the project finished to his satisfaction.

The porch, or verandah, as its creator preferred to call it, ran round all four of the grey stone walls of the old farmhouse and was generally regarded as something of an oddity, like the old man himself. Neighbours (albeit quite distant ones, since the house possessed two acres of rough land and was several miles from the nearest village), scoffed at this grandiose, incongruous attachment, murmuring that, with sweet old Edie gone, the old man really had gone soft in the head. But Earnest Lytton had got safely past the age where he gave a damn what other people thought. With the English summers turning so much hotter, it made sense to have a sheltered place outside from where he could appreciate the bright sun and blue sky without being harmed by them. He spent many an hour sitting with only his pipe for company in an old wooden rocking chair, staring dreamily into the middle distance, across the tangled copses of his own land to the plump hills that skirted the coastal town of Crestling beyond. The first two summers following the completion of his wooden masterpiece were among the wettest on record. But he sat outside none the less, watching the raindrops form along the bottom of the painted slats of timber, dabbing his eyes, which these days watered of their own accord, as if making up for a lifetime of being set in a face too proud to cry.

He still thought of himself as being married to Edie, even though it was over six years since she had died. After three decades in the north of England, they had moved south on account of Edie's lungs, but by then it was too late for any amount of sea air or warmth to stop the process of slow suffocation that her illness involved. She bore it all with a wrenching stoicism. Even when the very worst of the coughing would start, when her bird-like frame could barely stay upright under the strain of each thick, rasping hack, she would keep one hand raised in the air, fending him off, shaking her head till he backed away. Over the years Earnest had suffered far more in his relationship with God than he ever had with his wife. His calling had come as a result of the war, or, more specifically, as the result of a deep friendship with the regiment chaplain, one Harry Hughes, who died of hepatitis on the way home, three days after armistice. Earnest's acceptance of God had been relatively easy in the beginning, with the fervent memories of the war still pulsing through his system and the bright banner of Hughes' faith to light the way. The questioning started later, after the girls were born, so shrunken and pink, when Edie nearly died of a broken heart and he could think of nothing to say – not one thing – to ease her pain, or his.

'Dad, hello there.' Michael, never natural with his father, held out his hand, ruffling Tom's hair with the other, glad that his son was there, between them, deflecting the focus of the reunion.

'Jane with you, is she?'

'She certainly is.' They both turned to watch Jane making her way up the gravel path; she was bent almost double, to accommodate a precarious Harriet who was riding piggy-back; one hand was twisted behind to keep a hold on her daughter, while the other clutched a bulging canvas bag. She started to smile at her father-in-law long before she was close enough to greet him, her affection radiant as always. None of the old man's vile habits, like grinding his teeth when he ate, or farting when he thought no one was within earshot, had ever bothered her in the slightest, while they left Michael cringing with suppressed irritation.

'Let me take her,' said Earnest at once, after he had kissed Jane.

Oh God, thought Michael, Harriet will cry and cling to her mother. But Harriet sat proud and high in her grandfather's arms, allowing him to carry her round the garden, pointing out flowers and birds, between tickly-pokes to the tummy.

The joy that Earnest derived from his two grandchildren had come as a pleasure – and something of a surprise – to them all. Neither Christopher nor Michael had been particularly close to him as small boys; there were no warm, fuzzy memories of a dad who pushed swings, kicked balls and built meccano sets. He was always too busy, either holed up in his study or bouncing off round the parish in his dirty green Morris Minor, cracking grown-up jokes about the lost souls of rural England.

After they had unpacked the car Earnest solemnly requested Tom's assistance on a trouble-shooting tour of the woods.

'We'll take good care, won't we now?' he said placing one hand lightly on Tom's bobbing shoulder. 'Should be back before Christopher gets here, at any rate.' He handed Tom a knobbly walking-stick. 'That's for fighting the wood monsters,' he whispered. Tom raced off with a war-cry and Earnest threw his head back and laughed with pleasure, a throaty laugh, full of pipe-smoke and the confidence of old age.

'I didn't realise Chris was coming,' said Michael, tensing his jaw and trying to sound casual. A small pulse beat in the side of his face, Jane noticed, near the entrance to his ear.

'Didn't I mention it?' Earnest set off after Tom. 'He should be here by tea-time,' he called, waving his own stick in farewell, without turning round.

'Silly bugger's getting so forgetful.'

'Oh, I wouldn't be too sure about that.' Jane busied herself with unloading bottles of milk and cereal packets.

'What's that supposed to mean?'

'Perhaps he thought that if you knew Christopher was coming this weekend, you would find a reason not to come yourself.'

'I've never heard anything so ridiculous.'

Jane, not wanting to trigger Michael's irritation into anything more serious, spent several moments reading the small print on a cereal packet.

'Christ, Jane, you come up with some absurd ideas some-times—'

'I'm a great fan of absurd ideas.'

'Christopher.' Both Jane and Michael spoke at once, their faces flushing at this unexpected entrance. He was standing in the back doorway of the kitchen, a dark figure framed by the light of the sun behind. It was impossible to see his face, impossible to judge how much of their conversation he had heard.

'How are you both?' He gently placed his holdall on the kitchen table and pulled out a bottle of red wine, its label smeared and torn. 'College wine cellars – the best off-licences in the world.'

'Still got your contacts then,' joked Michael, a shade too heartily.

'Where are the children?' Christopher directed the question at Jane who had run out of things to unpack and was now tussling self-consciously with empty plastic bags, stuffing one inside the other with vigorous punches.

'Tom is in the copse – with your father, of course. Harriet is—' Harriet chose that moment to reappear from the garden. She had brought a small stone with her which she placed carefully on the table, next to Christopher's wine, before clambering on to her uncle's lap and making clip-clop noises with her tongue.

'Hatty, not now—' began Michael.

But Christopher immediately launched into a tuneful and gratifyingly energetic rendition of 'Ride a cock horse,' which so far exceeded his niece's wildest expectations that she fell quite silent with joy.

'Come here, you,' said Jane when Christopher finally stopped. She held her arms out to lift her daughter from his lap. His shorts were brown and crumpled. A large crescent of a scar curved round one side of his left knee, an island of silver amongst all the black hairs.

'She looks so like you, it's incredible.'

'Really? Most people say the opposite.' Harriet felt floppy and hot. 'I think I'll take her up for a sleep – excuse me.'

When Jane returned to the kitchen Michael and Christopher were drinking beer and talking about football. Not wanting to disturb such a rare display of filial accord, she took an empty basket down to the overgrown patch where Grandma Edie had once nurtured fruit bushes. Earnest was good with his hands, but only when they wielded a hammer and nails. Gardening held no allure for him at all, though – thanks to a small tractor of a lawn-mower, which Edie had given him the year she died – he liked cutting the grass. In the summer he could be seen twice a week at least, steering his old machine round and round the garden, taking the corners at full pelt, like a child with a small racing car. Though the vegetable garden had long since been reclaimed by briars and weeds, raspberries still grew, and could be reached, for the price of a few scratches and stings.

Small thorns tagged at Jane's skin, criss-crossing her hands and forearms with minute trickles of blood. The sun on her back felt hot, soon producing the tickling cool of a sweat on her legs and tummy. After a while she pulled a cotton scarf from her pocket and tied it round her head, to keep her hair out of her eyes. In spite of the discomfort – or maybe, in some strange way, because of it – she was enjoying herself. The pin-pricks of pain were somehow reassuring – little tugs on reality, sensations she could relate to, while all else quietly fell apart.

'I will tell him tonight,' she thought suddenly, the inside of her stomach heaving. 'It has gone on long enough.'

Jane looked up to see a figure approaching from out of the glare of the sun. Only when she squinted could she make out the tall frame of Christopher, his dark brows screwed up against the light. He wore a wide-brimmed straw hat of his mother's, perched Huckleberry Finn style on the back of his head; in his left hand he carried a cereal bowl.

Christopher had been watching his sister-in-law for some minutes before making his approach, intrigued by her look of absorption, hesitant of intruding. The scarf, tied so casually round her head, suited her well, he decided, setting off the high colour of her cheeks and the rich gloss of her hair.

'I've come to offer my services.' He waved the cereal bowl at her.

'What's Michael doing?'

'We fell out over Arsenal,' he said with a grin, edging closer to her, cursing the persistent clinging of the brambles. 'I left him rummaging impressively in his briefcase, in search of worthier pursuits, no doubt.'

'He's never far from his work,' she said, hoping she sounded impassive.

'Dad and Tom have returned,' he went on, 'plus one rabbit without a hop.'

'Poor rabbit.'

'Conserve your compassion. They are, as we speak, designing the most elegant of cardboard homes – complete with window shutters, a sprung mattress—'

'Wall-to-wall carpeting and a fitted kitchen – I know.'

They laughed together.

'He is the most perfect grandfather,' she sighed, smiling only lightly, but still causing a half-dimple to dent each cheek.

'First rate. Making up for his ineptitude with the last generation. Move over – you're hogging all the best bits.' The two of them were now tightly ensconced in the prickly thicket. The picking and the talking proceeded hand in hand, with an ease that seemed to arise quite naturally from the simple business of being involved in a common task.

'Earnest wasn't really inept as a father, was he?'

Wanting to answer truthfully, Christopher hesitated and frowned. He put a plump raspberry in his mouth and looked at her as he chewed it slowly. He saw then that the colour in her face was deceptive, wrought by exertion and heat. The rims of her eyes were red, undershadowed by grey smears.

She doesn't look happy, he thought, wishing he could ask her why.

'I wouldn't say inept, no. Just a bit cold – a rather formal father, was Earnest. Though he's more than made up for it since.' He ate another raspberry. 'I think we came too soon after the death of the girls, my sisters. People say that if babies die you should have another one quickly, but I'm not sure. There has to be mourning, doesn't there? I think, perhaps,' he spoke very slowly and quietly, so that she found herself holding her breath to catch all the words, 'at first he was too scared of loving us, in case he lost us too. I think he held back to protect himself in some way. Does that make sense?'

She nodded, amazed and touched by his frankness.

'Love is such a troublesome business, don't you find?' he said, turning to her with a smile.

'It certainly is.' She spoke quietly, concentrating hard on the fruit, easing each raspberry off with a gentle squeeze. 'So Earnest has discovered fatherhood in grandfatherhood.'

'That's a neat way of putting it.' Christopher considered her words. 'Yes, I like that.'

'Perhaps Michael will do the same,' she blurted, not having intended to say anything so confiding – so indiscreet – about one brother, her husband, to the other brother.

'Not exactly a hands-on sort of dad, is he?' he responded easily, lifting the awkwardness from her in an instant.

Just then Michael's head appeared at an open window.

'Jane – Harriet's bawling her eyes out – can you come?'

They burst out laughing.

'Coming,' she called. With her free hand shielding her eyes from the sun, she began stepping gingerly backwards, trying to work her way out along the path she had come.

'Jane, are you coming or what—' shouted Michael.

'Yes, yes, oh hell – I'm caught – ow.'

'Don't pull – I think I can reach. Keep quite still.' Several inches of thickly barbed briar had hooked itself into her hair. 'Here – hold my bowl and stop fidgeting.' As he reached across to her, his fingers working firmly but gently to tease the bramble free, she caught a faint smell of him, a sweet, sweaty, manly smell, and shivered involuntarily.

'There. A free woman.'

'How kind – thank you.' She walked on self-consciously, only looking back to wave when she felt at a safe distance.

11

Jane and Michael were in the master bedroom. Soon after Edie died Earnest moved himself into the smallest of the spare rooms, as if he were a lodger from the old days up north, when a steady stream of scrawny schoolteachers and students had wolfed down quantities of Edie's crispy fried bread and contributed measly but vital sums towards the rent. Now Earnest felt comforted by the lack of space, by the way his narrow bed hugged the wall, cornered into it by the chest of drawers that had belonged to his father and the side-table which Edie had chosen on a rainy day at an antiques fair in Durham. The smell of Edie wasn't so strong in that room. He could bear everything else – all her embroidered seats and cushions, her collection of miniature cottages, the painful sharpness of the photographs, but the faint odours of her clean, sugary scent came at him like salt to an open wound.

Jane moved steadily, blindly, through the rituals of preparing for bed. The bedroom was large, with a soft, grey carpet and curtains of faded pink. Being on the corner of the house, it had windows on two of its walls. She had opened both these to their full extent, hoping to shift some of the stuffy heat that had settled on the top floor during the day. The children lay peacefully in the room next door, their faces flushed, arms and legs spread-eagled against the hot night.

Michael was in the small bathroom that adjoined their bedroom, cleaning his teeth rigorously. His cheeks were rough and dark with stubble. Having spat into the basin he looked up at her reflection in the mirror when she appeared beside him. 'You've caught the sun.'

She nodded, saying nothing, studying the two of them in the glass as if they were unknown characters in a play, a woman with a red, shiny nose, the man tousled and unshaven. She felt nothing as she looked, nothing except the chill of the cold linoleum on her bare feet.

'Michael,' she turned round to face him, her hands feeling for the familiar chip along the edge of the old china basin.

'Christ, I'm tired.' He padded through to the bedroom, leaving her there, on the edge of the precipice. She had to go to the toilet before following him out; fear had liquidised her stomach, drained her face of blood.

Michael lay on the bed in just his pyjama bottoms, hands behind his head, eyes on the ceiling.

'There are cobwebs all over the place – this room is filthy.' He lowered one hand to the white flat of his stomach and belched quietly. 'I think we should make our excuses and head off early tomorrow. That way we'll miss the worst of the traffic – have time to sort ourselves out the other end—'

Jane leant against the bathroom door, curling her toes into the carpet as if to secure herself more firmly. It was tempting to respond to the small issues – the dirt and leaving early – but she knew that if she did she would lose herself, drown in detail and perhaps never claw her way back to the rocky resolve that had been settling within her all afternoon.

'There is no easy way to say this, Michael,' she began, her voice hoarse.

'Let me guess.' In one abrupt movement he swung his legs over the side of the bed and sat up. The left leg of his pyjamas stayed hitched up over his knee. 'You don't want to go back early. You never do. You want to pick raspberries and dawdle down here until the point where it will take us four hours instead of two to get home again.'

'No, I want – I mean, I think we should separate.'

'Separate?' He was so unprepared. And even for her, after all the months of silent arguing with demons inside her head, the moment, now that it had come, was horrifying.

'We've been separated, mentally, for years. I can't – I won't – live like this any more.'

'What do you mean "like this"?' He stood up. The hitched

pyjama dropped to the appropriate ankle. She looked at his feet, at the sprouting dark hairs on his toes, and backed into the wall. 'I don't understand – what is this?' While his mind grappled with the shock, he took refuge in anger. 'Separate?' He gave an abrupt smack of a laugh and shook his head in disbelief. 'I work my balls off twelve hours a day – ship the whole family to bloody Cobham just to please you – and this is the thanks I get. Separate? You've got to be bloody joking.'

So many different reactions were pushing inside his head that it was hard to follow each one through; outrage, suspicion and then a great sense of injustice overwhelmed him. What about all of her inadequacies and infuriating ways, for God's sake? It hadn't been an altogether easy ride for him either—He was about to embark on this tack, when a smouldering spark of suspicion caught light, bursting through his confusion.

'What's really behind this?' He threw himself back against the pillows and studied her through narrowed eyes, silently congratulating himself on displaying such composure. 'Come on, out with it. What's really going on – or should I say Who?'

Jane licked her lips, which felt dry and crusty. An urge to laugh almost overtook her. Given that her life was spent largely in the company of domestic appliances and shopping trolleys, the thought of having the opportunity – let alone the time – for a serious affair suddenly struck her as hysterically funny.

'There is no "who", as you put it.' She hugged herself, feeling very vulnerable suddenly in her flimsy cotton nightie. 'There is nobody else.'

'Oh yes, I see.' He folded his arms. The anger was almost palpable now; his arms trembled from it. How dare she, how dare she.

'It's just no good – we are no good – we don't talk or care or give – we don't love—' she tailed off, her voice trembling, and moved across to the largest of the windows, away from him, seeking courage and air. But outside all was thick and still, a moonless, starless night, stuffed with cloud, offering no cosmic perspectives of beauty or mystery to ease troubled souls.

Down below, a small square of light fell across the lawn from where Christopher still lounged on the sofa with a final glass of wine and a book on the stately homes of England. He stared not at the book, but out of the window, at the same suffocating blackness beheld by Jane. A large moth was trying to get into the room, throwing itself at the wrong side of the glass, with all the drunken determination of a flagging boxer. As Christopher watched, the creature's efforts grew weaker and weaker, until it finally dropped out of sight.

Upstairs Michael was fighting with a dry, gagging lump that had lodged at the back of his throat, like the stopper on a rising swell of panic. Until this moment he had always been absolutely sure of his power within his family – a subtle, heady power to do with being a successful husband and father, as well as a promising businessman. Thanks in part to years of acquiescence and protection from his wife, Michael's fine, solid image of himself had never before been called into question, remaining fundamental to his own lazy self-regard.

'Please Jane,' he begged, swallowing the lump, which hurt and which only sprang back again, exploding into sobs that shocked him quite as much as her.

She went to sit next to him on the bed, taking his head in her arms and pressing it to her chest. The urge to comfort was reflexive, arising out of pure pity. She stroked his hair and rocked him, as if he were Tom, woken by a nightmare and needing her comfort in the dark.

And Michael let the tears flow, crying for himself, rather than their marriage. Even as he buried his head in the familiar musky smell of her, feeling her warmth, a cold secret part of him mushroomed with loathing at this desperate show of weakness and at all her emotional claptrap about not giving and not loving. But he let the strange dry sobs go on, surrendering himself to them, sensing that for the moment at least they were his keenest weapon.

The weather broke that night; an ugly, wet explosion against the heat.

Christopher, who had fallen asleep on the sofa, awoke with a throbbing head and a furry tongue, shortly before six. He swivelled his head slowly, massaging the stiffness from his neck. He had got out of the habit of drinking so much. A few years back, before France and after, twice that amount of wine would have left him with a clearer mind.

Something had disturbed his sleep, of that he was sure. He crept into the hall and peered up the staircase. All was dim and quiet. Then the kitchen door banged. He ran through just in time to see Jane standing on the verandah, struggling with the zip of a large black anorak.

'Do you know something the rest of us don't?' He had to shout to make himself heard against the wind, which was flinging the rain at them, slinging it sideways through the open arches of Earnest's porch.

Jane jumped round, her face pink and wet. 'Oh, Christopher, I'm going on a walk.'

'So I see.' He couldn't help smiling. 'And in my coat.'

'Your – oh, I didn't realise – only I didn't bring one and—'

'I'm not complaining, indeed I am flattered.' He cocked his head at her, wiggling his toes in his socks, which were already soaked through from the puddles of rain on the verandah floor. 'I don't suppose I could ask where you are going at six o' clock on this delectable morning?'

'Not really, no.'

'I thought so. Will you be long?'

'Not long, no, I shouldn't think.'

'Not doing a Captain Oates on us or anything then?'

'A what? Oh, I see.' She smiled then and some of the startled look dissolved from her eyes, so that the green of them looked softer and less dazed. 'No, not this morning anyway.'

'Fine.' He rubbed his hands together briskly. 'I'll put the kettle on then. Does madam take tea or coffee with her breakfast?'

She hesitated, distracted for a moment by the thought of Michael's tea-making gift; having been deprived of sleep, her mind kept darting off in wilful directions of its own.

'If you don't want to discuss that either, then that's fine by me – some things are just too private.' He was trying to tease her, wanting to make her smile again. She looked so forlorn under the giant hood, her pale, pixie face half-drowned in its blackness.

'Coffee would be lovely,' she said briskly, turning to make her way down the steps.

'Careful not to slip,' he called, because he wanted to say something and could think of nothing better.

Jane slithered through the mud towards the phone box half a mile down the lane. She needed to talk to Julia and was fearful that Earnest's big black heap of a telephone, which made a violent tringing sound for every number dialled, would wake the whole household.

Julia wasn't very good in the mornings. Coherent thought or speech was unthinkable before at least three cups of strong, black coffee and several bouts of news, blasted first from the radio next to her bed and then from the mini TV, which lived in the kitchen, squashed between the toaster and a small potted plant that never flowered but steadfastly refused to die.

When Jane called, she was asleep, not deeply but pleasantly so, lost in a fantasy of speculative pleasure about a man she did not know. The dream was full of the promise of erotic sensation, of things felt rather than things seen, a writhing, crimson indulgence from which she withdrew with some reluctance. Her telephone was set into the tiled wall of her kitchen, below a calendar of medieval brass rubbings.

'Jane? Has someone died?' Her voice was croaky with sleep.

'I've woken you up – I'm sorry.'

'No, no, I always leap out of bed at six fifteen on Sunday mornings – hoping to receive calls from my dearest friends.' She groped in her fridge for some orange juice, drinking straight from the carton.

'I'm sorry—'

'For God's sake stop apologising, will you? Christ, have you seen the weather – it looks like the end of the world from up here.' With one eye on the sheeting rain, unburdening itself on to the rooftops of Marylebone and Paddington, Julia reached over to press down the switch on her kettle and then settled herself on a kitchen chair, pulling her knees up under her nightshirt for warmth.

'I told Michael last night. I told him I thought we should separate. He cried – it was so unspeakably awful – far worse than I could have imagined.'

'Oh no – Jane, I'm so sorry.'

'He said he wouldn't agree, then he got cross and then just terribly sad. I didn't know what to do.'

'I don't mean to sound brutal, but you didn't really expect him to leap at the idea, did you? Have things really been so bad?'

Jane leant her head against the grimy panes of the phone box, trying to ignore the foul stench of tobacco and urine. She felt as if she was running out of love, that one day she would look inside her heart for affection and find that there was nothing there, just the dried kernel of a person who had once had something to give.

'I don't love him,' she said simply. 'And I know he feels very little for me. He won't admit it – he wants us all to conform to some grand image of a "normal" family that functions in all the expected ways. He just doesn't seem to believe that the emotional side of things is necessary or important. He never has.' She paused, but Julia said nothing.

'The awful thing is, that's what probably attracted me in the first place – when I needed someone cool and hard-headed to keep me on the level.'

The switch on the kettle popped amidst great billows of steam.

'But love changes,' said Julia at last, 'even I know that. After years of marriage, it must do . . .'

'Oh, I know, I know.' Jane traced her index finger round the scratched image of a heart with the letters 'C loves J' scrawled inside it. 'But this is far, far more than that. It's not just that I've gone soft in the middle – though I probably have.' She paused again. 'We should never have married.'

'Jane – don't say such things, it isn't remotely helpful.' Julia wanted to mention the children, but felt it would be too mean, too obvious. Instead she suggested a compromise, in the form of a two-week family holiday.

'I know it sounds corny, but it might help. You haven't been away properly for years. Go somewhere hot and exotic. It might work wonders.'

Jane took some persuading. The thought of the pair of them under the spotlight of each other's scrutiny, away from all the safety valves of home routines, the props that helped them communicate or ignore each other without it being so obvious, was positively frightening. It would be so false, so raw. But in the end she agreed. Because of the children. Because, after so many years, it was the least she could do.

She traipsed back up the muddy lane to the house, where Christopher's pot of coffee sat waiting.

'I'm planning a holiday,' she said brightly, towelling her wet hair with a tea-cloth.

'A surprise for Michael, is it?' He eyed her quizzically.

'Sort of.' She stirred her coffee hard. 'Can you recommend anywhere good?'

12

Thanks to the timely cancellation of a divorcing couple, the Lyttons were soon able to take up residence in a gleaming white villa in southern Portugal, on the concrete outskirts of what had once been the fishing village of Milfontes. The luxurious facilities included a swimming pool and a maid called Maria-Marta, whose beady black eyes immediately alighted upon the children as legitimate pretexts for neglecting every other domestic duty itemised on the list provided by the travel agent.

Michael, who minded about this more than Jane, devoted considerable time to communicating these short-comings through an elaborate sign-language that had little effect beyond prompting a series of nodding smiles. The beds remained unmade and the bare floors quickly became covered with a film of invisible grit that worked its way between the toes and into the bottom of the bath. Dirt of a more obvious nature, together with quantities of a mysterious fluff, rapidly accumulated in impressive piles under the beds and round the edges of each room.

Jane found it hard to care. She even came to enjoy Michael's gesticulative confrontations with their employee, all the while nurturing a secret admiration for Maria-Marta's carefree obstinacy. What mattered most to her was that the children – for whom the trivial question of language presented no insurmountable barriers – thought Maria-Marta was heavenly. Clearly sensing that here at last was a true grown-up ally, Tom and Harriet entrusted themselves to their Portugese friend from the moment she beckoned to them with a shy smile and two lollipops in her hand. After a couple of days, assorted black-eyed nephews and nieces would appear from behind gates and bushes, eager to join in with orgies of ice-cream eating and endless games in the shallow end of the pool. While Michael huffed and waved his hands, Jane could only smile, enjoying this unexpected relief from parental responsibility.

Politeness raged between them. Never had Jane believed that kindness could feel so cold. Michael enquired how she was more times in a day than he usually managed in a year. He asked if her book was good, whether she was thirsty or hungry, hot or cold, tired or refreshed. Any attempt of Jane's to break this mould, to force him into a discussion of the bigger issues that towered, invisible and hard, between them, were either quickly rebuffed or simply ignored. On the odd occasion that Maria-Marta was not there, Michael would embark on self-consciously jolly rituals to entertain the children, horsing round like a child himself, supposedly having fun, but with one eye nailed to his wife.

Jane would take refuge in the shade of the patio, with a novel or a pad of paper, trying not to watch her husband as he was watching her. Each display of civility and merriment seemed to her to be tinged with contempt and a sickening self-righteousness. Look at me, he was saying, look at me being perfect; you have no grounds for complaint, Jane Lytton; the failure is all yours.

The patio was besieged by flowers: scarlet bells, white clusters, purple horns with long furry stamens, that dangled – faintly obscene – like earrings from the velvet cases of their homes. Jane's fingers slid down the pen and her palms stuck to the paper. By the morning of the seventh day she had succumbed to the temptation to write to Julia. Having written the date, she stopped and looked down. Beads of moisture clung to the tiny fair hairs between her breasts, like tiny glass insects. Her turquoise bathing costume, accustomed only to the neon lights of the Guildford swimming pool, had faded quickly in the sun to an unbecoming mottled green.

Michael and the children are asleep [she wrote], *wrung out by the heat. They say it's unusually hot for the time of year. No matter how much we drink, it all pours out in buckets. The children are on salt tablets, which they loathe. I bribe them with slabs of melting chocolate, while Michael scowls disapprovingly in the background.*

But then, he's never understood the moral value of bribery where small children are concerned.

I suppose it's rather lovely here – flowers and birds in Technicolor etc. – but give me a windy seaside in England any day. The air-conditioning works, after a fashion; it groans every five seconds or so, like a beast in pain. I've grown to know it rather well; I even feel sorry for it, sometimes, in the mad small hours.

But I suppose you are wondering about other things. Michael is, I have to say, trying very hard. So hard, indeed, that he has given new meaning to the notion of politeness. And I am nice too, violently so. We pass the salt and discuss whether to apply lotion before or after a swim; we read our children bed-time stories and drink wine together until the clock has edged its way round to a respectable hour for going to bed.

Having taken the precaution of hiding the letter in her bag and hurling the stub of her cigarette well into the bushes, Jane walked to the edge of the kidney-shaped pool. She could feel the heat of the stone rising through the thin soles of her espadrilles. Not the faintest ripple defaced the surface of the water: a perfect pearly-green, so shimmeringly bright, it made her eyes ache. She plunged straight in, a messy dive, which none the less felt glamorous and daring, as the balmy cool engulfed her, sucking her down to the bottom of its mosaic-tiled walls. Oh for a life of sensations rather than thoughts, sang her mind, while she blew irreverent bubbles and hummed a tuneless tune, luxuriating in the extended caress of the water.

She opened her eyes to find Michael watching her, from behind the flimsy façade of his sunglasses and an open book. It disturbed her, like the thought of an eye through a bathroom keyhole.

'This isn't so bad, is it?' he grinned. An air of self-satisfaction hovered about him; his confidence, badly knocked by recent events, was slowly reassembling itself. Still smiling, he patted his stomach which had developed a small – almost dainty – pot since their arrival and offered her a swig of beer.

The smallest gestures and questions now vibrated with the hum of bigger issues. Jane took the bottle, but quickly handed it back again.

'No thank you. I'll get my lemonade.'

Michael watched her walk over to the table to fetch her glass; she moved very deliberately, very tightly, with only the faintest swing of her slim hips. She was so small, a woman in the guise of a girl. Her hair, which she had kept short for so many years, had grown quite long again and reached almost to her shoulder-blades. The dense curls were thicker than ever, making her head look very wide from behind. He could feel the distinct stirring of arousal as he studied her. She looked so separate and determined. It was infuriating and provoking. An urge to grab her took hold; an urge to be rough – to shake her, to pull her, to press on to her, into her, to make her submit physically, if nothing else.

'Shall we go for a walk?' she said, having drained the last warm dregs of her drink.

As they strolled down the cobbled street that led into Milfontes, he took her hand. They could have been two lovers, on a second honeymoon, out for a Sunday amble.

They headed towards the old part of town that lolled around the crumbling ramparts of a medieval castle, on the edge of a sandy estuary, a couple of miles from the open sea. A stray cat scurried past them, angular and wary. The rest was silence, the closed-shutter quietness of siestas, interrupted only by the brief bark of a dog, the cry of a child, the slamming of a door.

After crossing the main square, past the rusted bronze statue of a conquering hero, Jane released his hand and followed him up the long stairwell of chipped and loose steps that led to the most preserved of the castle walls. Once at the top Michael made a big show of looking through the telescope while she sat with her legs dangling carelessly over the warm, smooth stones, her toes pointing to the water a hundred feet or so below. A whisper of a breeze, as soft as muslin, blew over her face; she closed her eyes, enjoying the feel of it in her hair.

Michael wrestled with the telescope which, in spite of having consumed several coins, still offered no vision beyond a cloudy blur. He shook it and then hit it hard with his fist. Two coins tumbled back out of the slot and landed at his feet. Having pocketed the money he strode along a portion of the rampart, and squinted at the glinting sea. Whatever poise he had recaptured earlier on in the day was gone. He felt unbalanced and cross. Jane's dreamy silence only riled him more. How dare she, he thought, not for the first time, and without quite pinpointing exactly what it was she had dared to do, beyond shatter his sense of equilibrium.

'Come and sit down, Michael,' she said, her eyes still closed, her small chin lifted slightly, pointing towards the lemon sun.

Misled by her outward tranquillity, he imagined that she was going to embark on the long-awaited reconciliation. It still had not crossed his mind that they would ever really separate, such conviction arising from stubborn pride rather than any serious analysis of his own feelings.

'It's not going to work,' she said quietly.

'Jesus Christ,' he threw up his hands and hit his legs hard, before swivelling round to face her.

They were side by side on the wall, very close but not touching. 'What do you want? What the fuck do you want, woman?'

'I don't know.'

'Well, that's great – so the rest of the world sits around waiting for you to decide.'

'I only know what I don't want,' she began, but he cut in.

'Oh, that's charming, I must say.' His tone was richly sarcastic. 'Perhaps you could endeavour to throw a little more light on this intriguing state of mind. Please, spare no thought for my feelings.'

Taking a deep breath, Jane stood up to face him. 'I feel as if I've been living in a daze, as if I've been steadily losing touch with myself.' She spoke terribly fast, as if pausing for breath might cause her to lose courage. 'I just wanted things to be all right day by day. I never faced up to what was really going on. I have allowed myself to become so buried by domestic things that I have forgotten how to make myself happy. I have literally forgotten what I like, what makes me laugh, what makes me get out of bed in the mornings, beyond the fact that you've got a train to catch and the children are howling for food.'

Michael was not really listening. When she got like this, he always hated the things she said. Still sitting on the wall, he opened his legs and reached for her hands. They felt moist and hot.

'Why are you being so melodramatic about life suddenly? Everybody has things to put up with that they don't like. My job drives me crazy half the time—'

'You love your job. And if you don't, then you should leave.'

He shook her hands away so roughly that she stumbled on the loose stones and almost fell. A young couple, with identical white-blonde hair and chunky, tanned bodies, had arrived at the telescope and were having a friendly tussle about who should look through first.

'For God's sake,' Michael lowered his voice to a harsh whisper, 'how can you say such stupid things and pretend to mean them?' He glared at her. 'Life is not perfect, Jane, and it never will be – the sooner you realise that the better for everybody.'

A tiny thought entered her head then, to do with reaching forward and pushing hard, so that he somersaulted backwards into the air. She had seen someone fall like that once, a long time ago, with her parents on a beach; a woman had lost her footing on a sea-wall and fallen backwards, her legs flying over her head. But the drop had only been six feet or so; and the woman had landed, laughing, on her bottom, pooh-poohing the buzz of concern.

'But haven't we got to try and make life perfect – as perfect as possible . . .'

'I give up.' Any semblance of patience or a desire for peace had dissolved. Self-pity prowled nearby. 'I have tried everything. I've done my best to work things out. But I see now, that there is no point.' With these words, he strode away, swinging his long arms fiercely, the back of his dark head set firmly against her for good.

The young couple, engrossed now in a serious embrace, felt neither threatened nor interested by this public separation of the Lyttons. Love was for them alone that day.

Jane finished her letter to Julia later that night, while Michael pummelled pillows and sighed loudly in the next room:

I'm afraid that things remain as bad as ever. The problems lie too deep for salvaging. Michael will not face up to the blank feeling where once there was a kind of love. He believes we should soldier on regardless. But if I do that I shall simply become po-faced and embittered – like all those grim-faced women you see in supermarkets who steer their trolleys like battle-tanks and yell at their children because they themselves are unhappy.

It is selfishness, I suppose, to want to leave Michael. But it feels like bravery too.

Before their return to England Michael also wrote a letter – or rather a postcard which he concealed in an envelope.

Tim, [he wrote], *I have to say I feel pretty bad being over here while you're going through such dreadful trouble over there. (I haven't breathed a word to anyone, by the way.) But I may as well tell you that I too am experiencing something of a crisis – though of a rather different nature. The plain truth is, I don't think that Jane and I will be together for much longer. This whole business was started by her. I've pulled out all the stops, but nothing I say or do seems to make any difference. Taking her on this holiday was my last effort, and it doesn't seem to have worked. The thing is, I was wondering if you and Pippa could see your way to putting me up for a couple of nights, just while I sort myself out. We get back on Friday. Yours as ever, Michael.*

So Michael and two suitcases went to Dulwich, leaving Jane in a confused state of relief and guilt that focused, alarmingly, on a fresh longing for her parents. Childish conversations with them would start up in her head, little-girl voices that wheedled for their forgiveness and some home-spun wisdom to see her through.

In practical terms little had changed, but while Jane eagerly slithered back into the safe trench of daily life, with all its comforting rituals of feeding and clothing two small children, the full weight of what had happened blocked her mind, making it hard for her to focus on anything else at all. She told Tom and Harriet as much as she dared, explaining that Daddy would see them often, knowing that they had no hope of yet grasping what had happened, but wanting above all else to be honest. In spite of trying not to, she fretted terribly over the two of them, irritating them with unwanted hugs and tiptoeing into their room long after they had abandoned themselves to sleep, so that she could watch the innocence of their moon-shaped faces and suffer, a little self-consciously, on their behalf. It was only in the evenings, when there was no meal to worry about, no conversation to be negotiated, that her heart would sometimes surge with a kind of happiness – a rare confidence that she had acted for the best. And she would sit quite still then, watching and listening in the lovely late hush of the night, as if waiting to see what might emerge, what she might do next.

'Of course you'll have to find yourself a lover,' remarked Mattie, stabbing a long chip into a blob of tomato sauce and sucking the end.

'Dearest Mattie, not all of us are so completely tied to hormonal impulses as you. A lover is – to put it bluntly – the last thing I require at the moment.'

'What's a lover?' asked Tom, his mouth bulging with hamburger and soggy bun.

They were in a McDonald's on a rainy Saturday, after a record-breaking tour round an exhibition of modern art. Having spent some time pretending that the bored caterwauling of her niece and the simulated machine-gun fire of her nephew were not disturbing other patrons, Mattie had finally given in and confessed a longing for large quantities of junk food. The declaration proved popular and was acted upon at once.

'A lover is someone you love,' said Mattie promptly, 'and don't talk with your mouth quite so full. Try half-full like mine – see?' She opened her mouth wide, revealing the congealed remains of her chip and then made a roaring noise, which was greeted with loud applause from the children.

The family excursion had been Mattie's way of trying to help her big sister celebrate her newfound freedom. Given that Jane had initiated the separation herself, Mattie found it hard to understand the look of dazed glumness that overtook her features whenever she was off her guard. Personally she had never liked Michael very much. And now that Jane was apart from him, she felt at liberty to express herself freely on the subject.

'Michael was so pompous and correct,' she said, talking as if he were dead, rather than merely absent. 'Crippled by propriety – I read that somewhere – but I do think it is apt. It was this guy in a book – brilliant read, though not quite your thing – anyway, this guy was so knotted up about the right way of doing things, that he never truly let go, that is, not until he meets this girl—'

'Mattie, sorry to interrupt, but we'd better go. These two look terribly droopy.' Jane hid her disappointment in her sister as best she could, fixing her smile in place and stacking the tray with empty cartons and cups. It had been reckless to imagine that Mattie could begin to appreciate the weird cocktail of emotions that besieged her each day, the bewilderment of being alone and yet so tied up in the lives of other people.

'I do feel quite sad too, you know,' she ventured a bit later, when Mattie had taken her up on her offer of a lift home.

'Poor Jane – of course you get lonely. Believe me, I know all about that. Which reminds me.' She tipped the contents of her bag on to her lap and began rifling through them. 'You don't keep any make-up in the car, do you? I can't find – ah, here we are.' Holding up a fragment of a mirror she began, with a remarkably steady hand, to blacken the rims of her eyes. 'I may have a visitor tonight.'

Jane was on the point of enquiring further, when her eye was caught by a polythene bag filled with small green and white capsules.

'Are you ill?'

'No, why?' Mattie was examining her teeth, running her tongue along the edges and clacking them together.

'The pills. They look like antibiotics.'

'They are nothing.' Mattie began stuffing things back into her bag.

'If they're nothing, why are you behaving as if I'd said something obscene?' Jane gripped the steering wheel and turned into Mattie's road.

'I'm not. You're just so bloody nosy sometimes – it drives me crazy.'

Jane set her lips together, determined not to say anything predictable, an exercise of control which was rewarded by Mattie taking pity on her at the last minute and bending down to the car window.

'They're called Prozac. An American friend gave them to me. They're clinically-everythinged and they make me feel very good. Okay?'

Mattie's face, now powdered and highlighted, looked sinister to Jane, like make-up on a little girl.

'Fine. Great. Thanks for telling me.' She drove away very fast, hating the unavoidable burden of feeling like a worried parent – as if her own two weren't enough. She glanced at them in the rearview mirror with a tummy-lurch of love. They had fallen asleep against each other, two floppy puppets, with ketchup-stained cheeks and open cherry mouths.

Where Mattie's attempts at consolation tended to get side-tracked by preoccupations about herself, Julia shied away from them altogether, no doubt having decided – with her usual brand of pragmatism – that moping would do no good at all. Whenever they spoke, Jane found herself bombarded with a volley of practical suggestions that left no room for the admission of sadness. Her marriage needed mourning, she felt; it hurt that not even her closest friend would acknowledge this properly.

'You'll need to get a job. Brush up your cv – put in phrases like "articulate self-starter" and "motivated high-achiever" – that's the kind of stuff that goes down well these days. Pretend you haven't got children and put your wedding ring on the other hand. Perhaps you've done that already?'

'No, I haven't.'

'Don't sound so icy. I'm only attempting to inject a soupçon of realism into that dreamy head of yours. It's all very well jettisoning husbands, but the consequences have to be confronted. I know I sound fierce, but you'll be grateful in the end.'

Jane did not feel grateful. She wanted to say that, cowardly though it may seem, she was not yet ready to think too deeply about bank-balances, that she hoped to entrust such niceties to lawyers. She wanted to say that the children's trust in her left her weak with guilt; that, while she did not miss Michael himself, she missed the notion of having a husband very deeply. She wanted to say that being a single mother, though she had often felt like one during her marriage, was faintly terrifying and that the fat lady at the DSS had shown her as much consideration as she would a colony of lepers who had taken up residence on the doorstep.

Shortly after Michael moved to Dulwich Jane had answered the telephone to be greeted by an unidentifiable whisper, which proved to belong to Pippa.

'How are you?' she rasped.

'On top of the world,' said Jane extra loudly. 'Why are you whispering?'

'Michael and Tim are next door.'

'Pippa,' said Jane somewhat wearily, 'I'm sure there's no need to whisper. You're allowed to ring me, you know. I'm a friend who has separated from her husband, not an escaped convict.'

'Oh Jane,' Pippa sounded close to tears, 'it's so awful.'

'Look,' went on Jane more gently, marvelling at the recurring sense that she was the one being called upon for reassurance, 'call me another time, when you're alone and feeling strong. I'm quite all right, you know, and so is Michael, from what I can gather. Thank you both very much for taking him in. It means an awful lot.'

But Pippa was too nervy and distraught for another phone call; instead she wrote to Jane, posting the letter on the morning that she and Tim set off for the airport. Only used to receiving Christmas cards from her, Jane found Pippa's tiny, spider-writing hard to decipher; it was quite faint too, as if the biro was on the point of running out.

Dearest Jane

I cannot not tell you how sad I am that you and Michael have run into some trouble. But something has happened to me recently, which I feel bound to share with you, because I just know it will help. Tim, I am now certain, has been seeing someone else. There we are – it looks so simple and easily managed when it is written down like that, as a fact. At first I was resolved to leave – all the expected feelings of betrayal and rejection overwhelmed me for a time. But then – partly because of the importance to me (to us, I hope!) of having a child – I worked through all that to a realisation of how important our relationship is. I have come to appreciate just what a volatile thing marriage is, that it lives and breathes and cannot therefore be boxed or pinned down to conform to a set of rules. And I realised too, that in spite of everything, I love Tim very deeply. Oh dear, I'm being long-winded and sentimental, which I didn't intend at all.

Although I know no details of your situation, I suspect that Michael, like Tim, has perhaps given you similar cause for grief. They are attractive, our men. We should not be so surprised if temptation beckons and they fall prey to it. Forgive him, Jane. Have him back. He does look so lost without you. If my experiences with Tim are anything to go by, guilt and remorse will make him kind – kinder perhaps than he has ever been before. There is always good to be had from bad.

I feel so much better for writing to you. I could never have said half of this to your face. We set off on our travels tomorrow morning, leaving your dear husband to hold our fort for us. I hope so much that we return to an empty house.
With fondest love, Pippa.

Jane read the letter while standing amongst an assortment of parents and push-chairs at the gates to Tom's school. Its contents so amazed her that she emitted a small shriek and clapped her hand to her mouth.

'Good news, is it?' volunteered a mum whose son played with Tom sometimes, and who had heard rumours of the separation and wanted to say something kind. Brief exchanges on doorsteps before and after children's parties somehow didn't feel enough to warrant a more intimate enquiry.

'What?' Jane looked up, having skimmed through the letter again, scanning it for some redeeming feature. 'No – it's nothing. Just a letter from a friend.' She quickly stuffed the envelope in her pocket and followed other herding parents into the playground.

For Michael too, the effects of the separation were confusing in ways that he least expected. He told his secretary at once, in the hope of minimising the rumour-mill round the office, and proceeded to throw himself into his work with a frenzied determination. The disquieting sense of being the focus of sympathetic curiosity – the feeling that one's name had been on everybody's lips just moments before entering a room – lasted only for a week or so. Far more humiliating was the bungle he made with Antonia during the course of a Friday lunch, when a bottle of wine induced him to mistake the gleam in her eye for something other than raw ambition. Although Michael's ego had, by and large, fought admirably on his behalf, slaying demons of self-doubt on all sides, there still lurked a prickly sense of failure which no amount of extra paper-work and office-hours could erase. With the unhappy encouragement provided by alcohol, this tingling insecurity surfaced that day in the form of a severely ill-timed proposition.

'I suppose you know you're sexy as well as brilliant.'

The razor-look of her eyes should have warned him. 'Oh yes, I know that all right.'

'I don't see so much of you these days. I'd like to see more.' He flicked his eyes down over what the restaurant table allowed him to see of her body, lingering on the large gold button which he imagined marked the point between her breasts. She sat back and folded her arms across her chest, causing the slightest crease in the skin visible above the line of her round-necked dress. This movement and its consequences gave Michael – for some unfathomable and misguided reason – enough hope to continue.

'I'm not suggesting a hotel or anything crude. The house I'm in has the biggest bed you've ever seen.'

Antonia simply stood up and reached for her jacket and bag.

'I've screwed in big beds, thank you, Michael.' She slung her bag over one shoulder and bent nearer him. 'If you talk to me in such a way again I shall submit a formal claim of sexual harassment.' The gold button was now very near his nose. 'And I shall be asking Mr Glassbrook if I may now commit all my time to the South American markets.' As an afterthought she pulled two ten pound notes out of her bag and threw them on to her side plate, where they stuck firmly to a small pat of butter. 'Don't worry – I won't tell him why. Not this time.'

It may have been this incident that lay behind the slovenliness that now overcame Michael when he was on his own, like the onset of some insidious disease. For he was not, by nature, a slob. Indeed it was one of the more obvious discordant themes of the past, that while he liked to return to a house free of clutter, Jane could step – happy and unseeing – between heaps of laundry and discarded trains.

Now, every morning, Michael pulled a new bowl out of the cupboard in order to eat his cornflakes. When the everyday set had all been dirtied he spent several minutes looking for the Noritake rather than place his hands amongst the greasy jam of crockery in the sink. He applied the same principle to his use of spoons, progressing from dessert spoons to teaspoons, from stainless steel to silver – the latter requiring him to break open Pippa's lovingly wrapped felt and cellophane bundles in the top two drawers of the old cedarwood dresser in the dining-room. His supper invariably came out of cartons and boxes, the remains of which were then jammed into one of the bulging, smelly bags that slowly multiplied in the far corner of the kitchen.

He rented videos nearly every night, usually from the 'adults only' section at the back of the shop. But the gratification they provided was so short-lived and filled him with such self-disgust, that he rarely watched any of them all the way through. He became a channel-flicker par excellence, juggling images in his head, sandbags against loneliness, which only succeeded in keeping him awake, since his mind, unlike the television, could not be switched off at will.

Whenever Jane rang, he found it hard to concentrate on anything beyond the desire to make her feel bad. She would enquire – using an infuriatingly soft voice, hitherto reserved for when the children were sad or sick – when he wanted to see Tom and Harriet, whether he had contacted a lawyer, whether he wanted to collect more things from the house. And he would fire short, stalling answers, hoping to make her guilty and wretched – not because he wanted to go back, but because his feelings were crystallising into a kind of hatred and he wanted her to suffer.

'This is hopeless,' said Jane one night, after a particularly aimless exchange. 'We're getting nowhere.'

'I couldn't agree more, my dear. But it's what you wanted.'

'No it isn't,' she cut in. 'This is just a mess.'

Michael looked about him. There were three socks on the rug in front of the television. Six empty beer cans huddled on top of the video recorder, a sign that the wicker waste-basket in the corner had long since toppled over from too great a demand on its capacity for accommodating such things. Ancient rice grains were strewn across the coffee table, amongst several vintages of pizza-crumbs, melted blobs of ice-cream and coffee mugs, layered to varying degrees with a custardy scum.

'Well, it's not my fault,' he retorted, slamming down the phone.

But he rang her back, much later that night, when his head was spinning and his stomach ached from too much cheese and wine.

'Just tell me,' he croaked, trying to sound more pained than he really was. 'Is there some other man? Someone I know?'

Jane was lying flat on her back in bed, her hair a dark fan against the white of the pillows. Through a chink in the curtains she watched the moon, the merest thumbnail of a silvery slit.

'There is nobody else,' she said, slowly and quietly.

'I'll ask for nothing in the divorce if you swear never to marry again.'

She sat up in bed, wide awake, gripping the phone with both hands. What new kind of game was this? 'Don't be absurd.'

'So you don't rule it out then?' he said, in a small, mean voice.

'I don't think about it. But no, I suppose not. I don't rule anything out.'

He was silent for several seconds.

Jane looked at her watch. It was nearly two o clock. 'Michael, this is pointless,' she began, but he interrupted.

'You'd better start looking for a job,' he said, wanting to make her afraid again.

'Yes, I—' she faltered, experiencing with fresh intensity the curse of being so completely dependent, so tied by money and material needs. The whole system was meaningless without love.

'It's a bad time to sell the house though—' he sounded sleepy now, as though his mind was wandering, less tuned to its task. 'I miss Tom,' he said, after a long pause.

'Yes,' she replied softly, wanting to cry suddenly, knowing this to be the most sincere thing he had said to her in months.

14

Although it was several miles from Hendon to Paddington Christopher decided to walk. He wanted to clear his head. The party the night before had been a classic of its kind, burgeoning from something quite mellow into rowdy scenes of unbecoming abandonment that had lasted well into the small hours. For the first time in a very long while, he had lost control. Ruthless images of things he had said and done kept cutting into his mind, adding the pulse of self-reproach to the painful throbs of alcoholic dehydration.

Having taken the opportunity of school half-term to come up to London for an informal meeting with his publishers, Christopher had invited himself to stay overnight with Greg Chambers, a wild friend from his college days, whose endeavours to prove that wildness grew more frantic with each passing year.

It had felt good to get away from school, the clatter of the boys, the oppressive beauty of Oxford and all its associations with his own muddled past, all those messy decisions and blurred opportunities. For many years Christopher had clung to the assumption that, as life unfurled, the picture would become clearer, that confidence in himself would blossom from the bitter bud of youthful uncertainty – which had so sharply flavoured his adolescence – into something more concrete, more reassuring. Instead, though objective perceptions of the world and of literature developed steadily enough, his own self-regard, together with any true sense of direction about the life he led, remained murky and full of doubt.

Teaching was his refuge. He felt safe amidst the bantering

hierarchy of the staff-room, where he was known for a dry wit and an amusingly irreverent view of the world. In the classroom he was securer still, sure of his ability to inspire fear and laughter amongst the bobbing, cropped heads of the prep-schoolers, all the while plugging and planting them with facts – just enough to see them through exams but not so much that they grew listless. He handled them well, remembering only too vividly what it felt like to be twelve: to be bored, yet afraid, desperate to be manly, yet longing for home and the soft, bosomy embrace of a mother. All that vile confusion of growing.

He walked fast, hands tucked into the baggy pockets of his faded-green corduroy jacket, shoulders hunched against the world. For November it was mild, but still chilly enough to feel threatening. The red-brick faces of Hendon suburbia crouched behind the sparse protection offered by their front gardens. Dark leaves hung, poised for the cold axe of winter, swaying slightly in the cool breeze. Overhead the sky was patched with grey clouds that teased the sun with gaps, before closing ranks in panels of steel. As Christopher turned on to the upper stretch of the Finchley Road, already jammed with a medley of impatient vehicles, uncomfortable snap-shots of Jane's sister pushed themselves at him, thrusting through the fog inside his head.

Mattie had been at the party. She appeared in the doorway of the kitchen just as Christopher was banging an ice-box on the rim of the sink; several cubes flew into the air and skidded across Greg's terracotta flagstones, stopping inches from Mattie's painted toes. She wore a purple and lilac kaftan, with a wide black belt pulled tightly round her small waist; black leather sandals with intricate cross-straps encased her bare feet. Although out-dated in every way, the outfit suited her well. A blue scarf was entwined prettily amongst the bushy ringlets of her hair, drawing attention to the heavy blue of her eyes and the darkened lines of her brows. She was clearly Jane's sister – dark-haired, with that small, neat figure – yet in every detail of line and colour so completely different. Jane's eyes were full of green, her nose was longer, her lips fuller, her chin more pointed. Whereas Mattie's petiteness was focused on the tidy features of her face, the close-set, penetrating eyes, the sharp triangle of her nose and the fine lines of her lips, tonight carefully defined with a pinky-rose gloss.

Mattie had had a bad week. The pills had all gone, as had the friend who had supplied them. Without any chemicals to ward it off, self-doubt was seeping through the cracks in her system, dampening her confidence and drowning her hopes. Where once the monotony of typing had fired her determination to continue as an artist, it now did little more than dull her senses with its tedium, utterly defusing whatever nerve it was that had once empowered her creative drive. Too much time had passed without change. These days the only artistic encouragement she got came from men, who gasped dutifully at the bright, angry splashes of her work before pushing her through to the bedroom and gasping rather more loudly amongst the bedclothes.

'I'd prefer a drink with my ice,' she said, using the tip of her sandal to kick the nearest ice-cube back across the floor.

'What are you doing here?'

'I believe there's a party. Or do all these people pay rent?' She had to step back to make way for a girl with spiky white hair and a cigarette glued between ruby lips. As the girl bent down to get something from the fridge, the red-frilled edge of her panties peeked out from beneath her skirt, which was shiny-black and tight, and made Christopher think of dustbin liners.

When Mattie saw Christopher staring so intently, with a wry half-smile on his face, a shiver of irrational envy passed through her. The girl was very young and tall, with pencil ankles that balanced precariously on the tower-block heels of her gold flecked shoes.

'And what – come to that – are you doing here? I thought you lived the cerebral life of an Oxford schoolmaster.'

'It's never cerebral,' he laughed. The skinny girl, now in possession of a large wedge of processed cheese, darted back out into the hallway, nibbling her find like a wary animal.

'Greg's an old friend,' continued Christopher, 'we meet about once a year. Our lives have taken rather different roads, as lives tend to do.'

Christopher's state of mind was not so very far removed from Mattie's, though he had already imbibed enough to float, temporarily, above it. After six gin and tonics, the world was looking as pleasingly assailable as the soft gloss on Mattie's lips.

'So why are you in London?' She sipped her drink and leant up against the fridge.

Christopher swung one of his long legs astride a chair, resting his head on his arms across the back of it and focusing his dark eyes upon her in a way that she found unnerving. Strains of seventies rock music drifted in from the sitting-room, where chairs and tables had been pushed aside to make room for dancing.

'To see my agent – publishers – that sort of thing.'

'Another definitive biographical critique on the way? We'll have to queue for your autograph soon.'

'I highly doubt it.' Christopher put his hands to his temples, which were pounding. If his bed had not been piled almost to the ceiling with coats, he would have retreated to it. The meeting, which had been about his idea for a novel, had not gone well. Both his agent and editor wanted another critical book first, for marketing reasons. Christopher had lost his temper and ranted unattractively about the urgency of personal creativity.

Mattie asked him if he had a joint. She was jigging from one foot to the other, twitchy and wide-eyed.

He shook his head and shrugged, watching the walls of the room heave with a kind of detached interest.

'You don't want to dance, I suppose?' She put her glass down on top of the fridge, next to a large packet of breakfast cereal, and turned to him with a pouting smile.

Christopher, for whom the prospect of rising to his feet suddenly seemed daunting, felt little inclination to accept Mattie's request. But she stepped daintily forward and helped him up from the chair.

People of all ages and sizes lined the walls of the house, slouched in doorways, sprawled on the stairs and along skirting-boards. Christopher and Mattie tunnelled their way through to the sitting-room. The leggy blonde girl was dancing opposite Greg, swaying slowly with her eyes closed. Greg, his tie fastened round his head and his shirt unbuttoned to expose a line of dark, silky hairs, was gyrating furiously, mouthing the words and striking at imaginary guitars.

The two of them joined in with a more conventional disco-jig. Christopher, who found it hard not to lean at dangerous angles when he moved his upper body, clapped loudly at the closing chords of the song and jerked his head towards the kitchen.

But by now Mattie had other plans. A new challenge had presented itself and she wanted to see it through. The next song was soulful and slow, impossible to dance to alone with any conviction – though Christopher did his best. But Mattie moved forward and put her arms around his waist. It was good to be held; he felt much less giddy in the frame of her embrace. As he stared over her head, his nose tickled by a frizz of hair, his eye was caught by a picture of a young version of Greg, with boyish hips and skinny arms, his head thrown back in laughter. It was a far cry from the businessman now slumped on the sofa beside them, one arm round the blonde, the other flopped across the swell of his belly. His chin had fallen on to his chest, revealing the sparsity of the thatch on top; the glimpse of circular flesh underneath looked white and afraid. Christopher closed his eyes, wishing he could close his mind as well. Mattie pressed her fingers gently into the small of his back, drawing him closer, feeling the familiar stirrings of arousal at the prospect of a new man.

Christopher had by now reached the outskirts of Hampstead. The shops began to take on a glossier look; window displays had lost their washed-out air of neglect; coffee shops released aromas of freshly ground beans and baked croissants, instead of the greasy whiff of fried eggs and sausage. He marched onwards, head down, trying not to tread on the lines of the pavement squares, fixing his mind on any detail that might block out the night before. It was a long time since he had made such an ass of himself.

A few yards short of Swiss Cottage he succumbed to the sweet, creamy froth of a cappuccino, relishing its warmth in the empty pit of his stomach. It was well past ten o'clock. On seeing a payphone next to the door to the toilets, he debated whether he should call Julia first. He had decided to see her because of something Mattie had said – one of the sharp splinters of memory embedded in his head from the night before.

Jane and Michael had split up, Mattie said, after they had

screwed each other, hastily exploring the blind alley of lust that led to nothing but itself.

Jane and Michael had split up – for good maybe, she wasn't sure – but Julia would know, because Jane always told Julia everything and Mattie nothing. She licked his shoulder with her dry cat's tongue and began to trail her fingers through the mass of wiry curls across his chest. But Christopher pushed her away. He needed water and aspirin. He needed to think.

Sitting on the hard stool of the coffee bar, the full force of Mattie's tipsy tears of rejection came back at him, stoking up the guilt and the regret. If only she had told him before. Before they had shimmied their way down the corridor, towards the half-open door of Greg's study and the alluring blackness within. Before he had unbuckled the thick black belt and moved his hand up under the swirling purple of the kaftan to feel the moist warmth of her skin.

While blaming himself, Christopher was also struck by the gross unfairness of what had happened. It was months since he had kissed a woman, years since he had got so drunk at a party that he had encouraged the attentions of a female whom, in the sober light of day, attracted him not at all.

It seemed the cruellest irony that Mattie should have materialised before him like that, all sad and silky-mouthed, when all along she held within her the breathtaking fact that Jane and Michael had separated.

Julia's shop was artfully arranged – full without appearing cluttered. Table-sized cabinets of trinkets dominated the centre of the room, while the larger pieces of furniture, together with displays of china and glass, were set back against the walls. Christopher came in, setting off the jangle of her doorbell, just as she was wrapping a seed-pearl brooch for an old lady who had asked for three duplicate copies of the receipt. The lady smelt strongly of lavender eau de cologne and possessed a face so heavily powdered that the bracket smile-lines beside her mouth were visibly clogged with the stuff, deep gullies of fine beige sand.

'There we are.' Julia handed over the receipts and flicked her eyes up to locate Christopher. He was standing before a small rosewood desk in the furthest corner of the room. She walked up behind him, noiseless on the royal blue pile of her imitation Windsor carpet, and lightly tapped his shoulder. He jumped round, his pale face pumped for an instant with the blush of surprise.

'I am honoured indeed. Are you being charitable, sociable or genuinely interested? It's so hard to tell with one's friends.' She smiled, wishing he did not look quite so alarmed.

'Certainly not. I mean, I'm not being charitable,' he flustered, touching the crown of his head, where the hair was sticking up at odd angles, as if blasted by the wind. 'I am genuinely interested – you've some lovely things – especially this.' He turned to the desk. 'Is it Victorian?'

'Queen Anne. And I'm afraid it's got a rather lovely price on it too.'

He examined the small white tag dangling off the top right drawer and whistled. 'Out of my league, I'm afraid.'

'What a shame,' she teased. 'When I've made my second million, I'll start doing discounts for chums – and their relatives. Though I should be quite sad to lose this. Look.' She proceeded to pull out some of the small pencil drawers, unable to resist showing off the clever jigsaw of tinier drawers and spaces behind. Her long hair fell forward over the desk, satin on shining wood. She handled the parts of the desk very gently, as if wary of causing pain. 'You see, it looks so simple – so straightforward – on the outside, when really it's a maze of complexity on the inside.'

'Like a person.'

'I beg your pardon? Oh, I see.' She eyed him curiously. 'Yes, I suppose so. But some people are pretty complicated on the outside too.'

'Yes, yes, indeed – of course they are.' He cleared his throat and jangled the change in his pockets.

She clasped her hands, trying not to appear baffled. 'Did you want anything in particular?'

Behind her, the doorbell chimed as someone else entered the shop.

'There's always lunch,' he said suddenly, looking at his watch.

'Oh, I'm sorry Christopher – I don't close for lunch on a Saturday, it's just too busy. I scoff Mars bars behind the counter when no one's looking. Was there something— ?'

But he was already backing towards the door, worn out by embarrassment and the dawning sense of the impossibility of discussing the subject that drummed in his head. 'I was just passing. I do that sometimes – act on impulse – that sort of thing.'

'How marvellous. I'm a dreadful one for planning things years in advance – can't do a thing unless it's inscribed in the diary—' She pursued him to the door. 'Thanks for coming.'

'Not at all.'

He sped off, turning up the collar of his jacket against the cold.

15

'You look funny,' remarked Tom, eyeing his mother's made-up face with suspicion.

'Mummy's trying to look extra nice so that someone will give her a job.' Jane placed two squares of buttered toast in front of Harriet and licked her fingertips daintily, mindful of disturbing her lipstick.

'Like Daddy?' continued Tom.

Jane hesitated, unsure where the interrogation might be leading and wanting to have some control over its outcome.

'Yes, like Daddy. So that we have more money.'

'Don't you have enough then?' For Tom, whose piggy bank was impressively weighted with coins, the concept was puzzling.

'I have heaps at the moment, but we might need some more later on.'

'I wish Daddy was here.'

She reached down to touch his head, but her hand was shaken off with an angry toss. The rebuff hurt, pulling at the ever-present noose of guilt and injecting her eyes with tears. Quickly turning away so the children wouldn't see, she tore off a square of kitchen paper and dabbed carefully at her mascara. Having none the less succeeded in removing most of her make-up, she screwed the paper into a ball and hurled it despairingly in the direction of the kitchen bin. It did not matter to the children that Michael had, in many ways, been negligent as a father, that he had always been more readily responsive to the demands of his work than the needs of his family. Though Harriet, at the robust age of two, showed little obvious signs of stress at Michael's absence, Tom's increasing awkwardness made Jane long for the bad old days sometimes, with an intensity that scared her.

Tom was now staring at the cartoon figures on his empty plate, swinging his small legs back and forth underneath the chair, very fast.

'Daddy's taking you to Chessington Zoo next Sunday, remember? Just the two of you men together.'

'I'm not a man, silly, I'm a boy,' he shouted, jumping down from the chair, seizing Harriet's remaining piece of toast, and running into the hall.

As Harriet screamed, Tom began a jeering war-dance in the doorway.

Jane was on the point of brokering a peace when the phone rang. It was Mrs Browne from down the road, trumpeting coughs and apologies to say that she couldn't manage Harriet that morning after all and did Jane mind.

'Of course not,' she chirruped, the sound of Mrs Browne's catarrh-laced cough making an appeal impossible. 'I'll be fine,' she promised, saying what she had to say, while her heart sank low at the prospect of a bad day getting worse.

The traffic in Guildford was not sympathetic to the predicament of a panic-stricken woman map-reading her way to her first interview in ten years, with a whiny toddler for company in the car-seat behind. Made reckless by desperation, Jane hurled biscuits and juice-boxes at Harriet and tried to keep her eyes off the flickering green figures of the digital clock. The minutes advanced with disturbing rapidity, while the car got sucked round the mysterious ducts of a one-way system that seemed to bear little relation either to the map or to her intended destination.

By the time Jane and Harriet stepped into the lift of the high-rise rotunda that catered for the multifarious requirements of Grove Employment Agency they were thirty minutes late. Harriet, on seeing the lift buttons, resolved to press each one. Frustration at being forbidden this small indulgence induced a magnificent howling, followed by an unhappily conspicuous entrance into the hushed concentration of the open-plan offices of the fifth floor.

Cabinets and desks crouched amongst rubber plants and

rippling blue walls like props in a surreal holiday commercial. Jane steered her weeping charge between them, ignoring the turning heads and trying – with less success – to block out the sense of the great divide she now faced: the Workers and the Home-Stayers. Those to be admired and those to be pitied. This is not life, she told herself, this is a bad day. She hummed a song about a rabbit into Harriet's ear and imagined recounting the details to Julia later on; how she would make her laugh.

Mr Jenkins, who sat at a desk with expansive views of a multi-storey car park, did little to alleviate Jane's sense that she had entered a war-zone. Though Harriet's sobbing had quietened to barely audible sniffles, he peered at the two of them over the top of his hexagonal-framed spectacles in a schoolmasterly manner that suggested the requirement of absolute silence.

Harriet found solace in a crumbling breadstick (extracted with a triumphant flourish from the side-pocket of Jane's handbag), while Mr Jenkins started asking questions and filling in boxes on forms with ticks and squiggles. But peace, like the breadstick, was predictably short-lived; once Harriet had grown tired of sprinkling crumbs on to the carpet, she turned her attention to the tasty array of items on Mr Jenkins' desk. Between fielding questions about her career prospects and experience, Jane had to dissuade her daughter from eating two biros, a saucer of paper-clips, a stapler and the deliciously curly flex of her interrogator's push-button telephone.

'You have arrangements for child-care, I take it, Mrs Lytton?' he asked, without looking up from a particularly intricate squiggle.

'Yes – absolutely,' she shot back; though in truth she still hadn't quite asked Mrs Browne – only hinted, to prepare the way, terrified that she might refuse. Harriet was very fussy about her friends.

'Recent experience?'

'Moretons Publishing . . .'

'Yes – I think we've covered that. Anything a little more recent?'

'No. Just the children. They're quite an experience.'

His smile was deeply polite. 'Yes, I'm sure.'

I'm quite clever, she wanted to say; I got a prize for my paper on parliamentary reform; I could have been quite the career girl; but things took me in other directions, as things do.

'There's not much, I'm afraid. The recession is hitting hard.'

'I thought there was a great demand for women in the workplace. Isn't that what the statistics say?' Her courage dissolved at the realisation that he was bored with her.

'I don't know about statistics, Mrs Lytton. What I do know is that a lot of people are looking for work – unqualified, or at least untrained, like yourself – and it's very hard to fit you all in.'

He removed his glasses and began polishing the lenses with a tissue from a box on his desk. The skin round his eyes looked white and puffy; an angry red crevice was carved deep into the bridge of his nose. He looked so raw and unprotected that Jane, experiencing a surge of something resembling compassion, felt obliged to look away until he had finished.

'I'm afraid there's nothing in any of the areas in which you have expressed an interest – though in London you might be luckier, of course.' The spectacles were safely back in place. 'The only local possibility,' he thumbed expertly through a file, 'is something clerical. Ah, here we are.' He blew on his hands and rubbed them together.

She watched him intently, full of dread.

'Guildford General Hospital requires a couple of part-time clerical assistants, receptionists, that sort of thing. Not bad money either.'

She swallowed. 'Is that it? Is there nothing else?'

'Not unless you are prepared to consider full-time employment.'

'No. Not full-time. Not yet.' She hugged Harriet, who had curled into a sleepy ball on her lap.

'They're interviewing from tomorrow. Here are the details.' He pushed a sheaf of papers at her.

'Tomorrow?' Her tone was incredulous. Half-term began tomorrow.

He let out his breath very slowly before speaking. 'The interviews will be conducted over several days. I could perhaps arrange for you to be seen early next week.'

'That would be better. Thanks so much.'

He extended one hand across his desk. 'We'll be in touch then.'

Jane reached round the sleeping Harriet with difficulty, to a handshake that was limp and moist.

She rang Julia the moment she got home, only to be greeted with the unsympathetic beep of her answering machine. 'I'm aiming for a career in filing,' she said into the silence that followed. 'History degrees were definitely a no-no, but when I said I could tackle tea-bags things really took off. Fingers crossed for the interview. Call me when you can.'

The only consolation came in the form of a card from Michael's father.

'*Come down with the children any time,*' Earnest had written in a loopy scrawl across a sketch of some daffodils, '*open house here as always.*'

16

It was unfortunate for all concerned that Pippa and Tim chose to return to England several days early without forewarning their house-guest. When Tim, carried away on a swell of bravery induced by three pina coladas, at last broke the news of their impending bankruptcy, Pippa begged to go home. Instead of breaking down as he expected, a steeliness he had never known before seemed to take hold of her, a cold control that shut him out and was worse than anything. Though she insisted, many times, that she did not blame him, that soft frailty of hers, which had always beckoned for his affection, vanished overnight, as if that too had been a luxury allowed by money.

'At least we don't have any children to worry about,' she said, shortly before they touched down at Heathrow, her face flat and grim, her hair pulled back into a tight, thin pony-tail that imprisoned the wisps he loved.

Michael was in the shower when they arrived, which spared him the sight of their faces when first confronted with the grimy chaos that he had created and fed, like some cadaverous monster, during the weeks they had been away. While he lathered his belly and armpits, humming and rubbing to a spirited rendition of 'My Way', Pippa was spinning through the downstairs rooms, emitting high-pitched gasps of disbelief. Tim followed slowly behind, equally appalled, but his mind working along the more pragmatic lines of assessing damage and the possible effect on the sale price of the house.

Slightly moved by the heartfelt gusto of his own singing, Michael had embarked on a throaty repetition of the chorus. As he stepped out on to the peach pile of the floor-mat in the Crofts' en suite bathroom, Pippa appeared in the doorway. True to the reflexes bred in all civilised beings, Michael dived for a towel, but Pippa, who stood closest to the heated rail and whose instincts were following a somewhat baser trail, immediately pulled all the towels to her, forcing him to stand cowering with his hands cupped over his groin.

'Please, Pippa,' Michael begged, now shivering visibly.

If Tim had not arrived on the scene, Pippa would have withheld the towels indefinitely. She loved her house more simply and more completely than she loved her own husband; years of tender work had gone into its decoration and maintenance. She had been longing to get back, to enjoy a few last, precious weeks of living there before they had to sell and move somewhere poky and cheap to start their lives again. What Michael had done was, in her eyes, nothing short of desecration. If there had been a knife to hand she might have stabbed him.

'For God's sake give the man a towel.' Tim wrenched one from her and threw it at Michael, who wrapped it hastily round his waist, feeling miserable and foolish.

'I'm so sorry – I wasn't expecting you . . .'

Pippa turned on her heel and left without a word.

'Tim – I know it's a bit of a tip – I'll clear it all up.' Michael felt better now that it was just the two of them.

'It's a fucking mess,' said Tim softly, 'and we've got to sell this place for every penny we can get. You've seen how Pippa is – she's so – Christ, Michael, what's got into you?'

Michael was struggling with his underpants; in his eagerness to get dressed he hadn't dried properly and the result was making everything hard to pull on.

'I'm truly sorry – I'll clear it up – get cleaners in, hoards of them . . .'

'Talk about abusing a favour.' And with that Tim followed his wife out of the room.

When Michael came downstairs carrying his suitcases and a bundle of laundry, he found Pippa sitting motionless on a chair in the hall. She stared straight ahead, her lips pursed shut and her hands laced tightly together in her lap.

Tim was in the sitting-room, stuffing debris into a large black sack. Michael hastened to help him.

'How many slobs were living here anyway?'

'Just the one.'

Tim stopped and looked hard at his friend.

'So it's still no-go between you and Jane.'

Michael nodded, keeping his head bent so that Tim could not see the tears of self-pity that were blurring the patterns of the carpet.

'It's only mess, after all,' said Tim gently. 'I'll finish up here. Why don't you make a start on the kitchen? Then we'll call some cleaners or whatever.'

After the worst had been cleared away and Michael had reiterated his promise to foot the cost of professional cleaning, he left to stay in an over-priced London hotel near the office. Of all the nights he had spent since separating from Jane, this was by far the worst. Throughout the black, indulgent misery of it all, the mindless channel-flicking and munching through minipackets of over-salted peanuts, Michael knew – even as he endured it – that he had reached the lowest point, that he would never permit himself to feel so bad again. His feelings for his wife took a fresh turn that night, reaching a fever-pitch of frustrated rage. Jane alone was responsible. She had done this to him, reduced him to a hard bed and a sleepless night in a stuffy hotel when he should, by rights, be tucked up in their soft kingsize, the dark outline of her body curved reassuringly beside him, there to touch if he wanted.

Anger did wonders for his resolve. After a hearty breakfast of solidified egg and cold toast he phoned his secretary to say he would be taking the day off. Drawing up the high-backed bedroom chair to the dressing-table, as if it were a desk in an office, Michael proceeded to make a list. On a blank page at the back of his pocket diary he wrote:

Lawyers
Blank cheque and letter to Tim
Estate agents
Hair
Julia

The list helped enormously, like a signpost for the way forward.

Several times during the course of that day he patted his breast pocket, where he could feel the comfortable shape of the diary, slotted next to his wallet and fountain pen. There were things to be achieved after all.

Towards the end of the afternoon, as he sat enjoying the sensation of having his hair blow-dried into a quite unmaintainable position, Michael took out his pen and diary and placed generous ticks beside all but the last item on his list. Having tipped the hairdresser very generously, he walked briskly back towards the estate agents, whistling softly through the small gap in his teeth.

17

'Michael's told me about the two of you,' said Earnest, after he had kissed her cheek, before she had time to feel awkward. 'Things will work themselves out. They always do, in the end.'

Tom, doing a dance of delight around them, pulled at his grandfather's hands and trousers.

'How's my bunny? How's my bunny?' he sang.

'Fat as a cat and big as a house,' chuckled Earnest, sucking on his empty pipe and feeling in his pocket for a grey hanky to dab at the drip on his nose.

'Come on, Grandad, let's see.'

Harriet, certain that she was being left out of something, but not entirely sure that whatever it was warranted the stressful business of abandoning her mother, buried her head in Jane's kneecaps, whimpering with indecision. Prehensile clinging was a new, distressing hobby of her daughter's, for which Jane – interpreting it as a symptom of the separation – blamed herself. If one parent could leave, what was to stop the other following suit – unless she was held very tightly, all the time?

The hallway was freezer-cold, but the old black aga pulsed heat round the stone tiles of the kitchen and a spitting fire blazed in the wide hearth of the sitting-room, its flames gleaming in the sheen of brass and fire-irons surrounding it. Jane set about boiling water for hot-water bottles, to air the damp coolness from the beds. She hummed quietly as she moved around, enjoying the familiar creaks of the floorboards and all the grunts and whispers of the old house. It felt safe to be in the country with the old man – unthreatened and simple. There was no burden of communication, no sense of a mess that needed sorting out. He would potter along as he always did, absorbed in his routines, happy for her and the children to fit round him, happy to help if he thought he could, but never to interfere.

Looking out of the window on to the back garden, she saw Tom and Earnest staggering under the weight of a hefty plank of wood, skirting round the brown, earthy humps of the mole-hills, which Earnest lamented but couldn't quite bring himself to destroy. It was typical of him to let Tom carry his full share, to know that stretching his grandson would make him far happier than fobbing him off like a toddler.

Jane sighed and smiled, hugging the hot-water bottles to her chest and rocking slightly, like a child with a favourite doll. The hair which had flopped into her eyes all summer now tucked smoothly behind her ears, showing off the full, strong triangle of her face and the pearly smoothness of her skin. Without the fringe to hide behind, her eyes looked bigger and somehow deeper, as if their flecked green surfaced from a bottomless well of colour inside.

At the entrance to the big bedroom she paused before stepping gingerly inside, half expecting to hear dim echoes of all the failed conversations of her marriage coming at her in waves from the dark corners of a room that had seen it all. But the creaky hush felt kind. A bunch of rough greens and late flowers had been squashed unceremoniously into a tall glass vase on the dressing-table, where they bathed in the lemon light of the autumn sun. So welcoming was the sight of them, the warmth of their fading colours, that Jane found herself rushing to heave open the sash windows, even though the air outside was hard and cold. He was right, she thought, looking down fondly at Earnest pushing her two children in the swings that he had made for them, things just might work themselves out in the end.

In her own house she always felt rushed, cajoling the children through each day, like an ill-prepared commander going into battle with a small, reluctant army. She sometimes wondered if she offered Harriet and Tom anything beyond a tedious string of mysterious deadlines, based on clocks they couldn't read and schedules they didn't need. But at the old white house now, a heady idleness was seeping into her, relaxing her mind, edging out the tension. When the children were hungry they ate their tea. When they were tired she bathed them and put them to bed. The simplicity of it all filled her with joy.

As the smell of Earnest's beef stew wafted up the stairs and into her bedroom, she slipped out of her clothes and into the soothing luxury of a deep, hot bath. Liberal amounts of red wine, garlic and onions had gone into the preparation of supper. Jane had watched in admiration, as Earnest carefully peeled, chopped and tasted with the expertise of one used to living alone. Thinking of her own customary evening snacks of cheese and tinned soup, she had felt quite humbled by such application. Cooking was the perfect way to spoil yourself, he had remarked, if you had no one else to do it for you.

Sinking low in her bath, her chin resting on a frothy plateau of bubbles, Jane felt rather spoiled herself. She raised one leg, dripping and crested with foam, and eyed it critically, like an object apart. If she held it straight, the small silver stretch marks on her inner thigh barely showed. Raising her other leg out of the water, she pointed both toes at the ceiling and did a few small scissor movements, crossing her ankles back and forth, until her stomach muscles burned with the strain. Letting both legs down with a splash, she held her nose and thrust her head back until her face was completely submerged, her head resting on the hard bottom of the bath. She stayed like that for as long as she could, enjoying the tickling in her ears as the water filled them, feeling every quick thud of her heart, starving her lungs until they were ready to explode. She surfaced panting and happy, intensely alive.

Once the steam had cleared from the mirror, she attended to herself with much greater care than usual, combing out her wet hair gently and massaging moisturiser into her face with none of her usual dabbing aggression. I want to look after myself, she thought, feeling pleased at the idea, knowing that it meant progress of some kind, deep within her.

'Well, well,' said Earnest when she appeared in the kitchen, her cheeks glowing, her hair just dried and full of shine.

They drank beer together – a sweet, thick home-brew that slid, velvety-smooth, down her throat, making her dizzy and warm. While he stirred and sniffed at the casserole dish, Jane drained carrots and peeled the tin-foil off their baked potatoes. A comfortable silence settled between them, punctuated only by the rhythmic ticking of the kitchen clock and an occasional comment about the meal or the children. And Jane marvelled at the strangeness of life – at how uncomfortable she had grown to feel in the company of a man she had known, intimately, for a third of her life, while his father, this old man whom she knew half as well, could fill her heart with a sense of calm acceptance.

They had barely raised their first mouthfuls to their lips when there was a sharp knock at the front door.

'He's early,' was all Earnest remarked, pushing back his chair and going into the hall.

'Who?' she asked, but getting no reply.

Muffled greetings could be heard through the wall, followed by the front door slamming. Then Christopher came into the kitchen, blowing on his hands and stamping his feet. His face looked pinched with cold. He wore a baggy grey jumper over jeans and a pair of ancient trainers; blue sock bulged through a slit down one side and the heels were caked in a dry, white mud that was soon lying in flakes on the floor.

'Sorry to intrude – I had no idea that you – it's my half-term, you see.'

'Ours too. There's loads of food.' A shining, determined smile had affixed itself to the lower part of her face.

'Trust you to arrive just as the meal's being served,' humphed Earnest happily, as he handed his son a knife and fork and returned to his seat. He turned to Jane with a rare grin, showing off a graveyard of yellow teeth. 'I wasn't expecting him until tomorrow. Here, get some of that down you, Chris – that'll warm you up.' He pushed the jug of beer across the table.

'No thanks, Dad, not tonight.'

'Don't be daft,' was Earnest's response, as he poured beer into a fresh tumbler and refilled Jane's.

Mercifully, the smile was easing off, though all the discomfort remained. Had he heard about her and Michael, she wondered, as she carved chunks of beef into unnecessarily small portions and sipped daintily at her beer. For whatever reason,

Christopher too seemed ill-at-ease, shuffling in his chair and concentrating with equal intensity on his plate of food. With his arrival came the need for conversation; the silence which had felt so settled, was – for Jane at least – now flecked with awkwardness. Only Earnest appeared undaunted.

'Not on the bloody wagon again are you?'

'No, Dad, nothing like that.' He took a long swig of beer to prove the point and smiled properly for the first time. Unlike his father's, his teeth were pressed close together and unusually white. His lips were thin but wide, attractive when spread into a smile, but alarmingly severe when closed.

'He had a bad patch, didn't you, Chris – a while back now.'

'Really?' Jane, remembering how Christopher had brought shame upon the proceedings at his mother's funeral by lavishly anointing the vicar with wine and then subjecting his mousy wife to a loud – and rather convincing – diatribe on the idiosyncracies of the female orgasm, endeavoured to appear incurious.

'I drank a lot, rather too often.' If he was bothered by his father bringing up such a subject, he didn't show it. Instead, he seemed to relax. 'Dad sorted me out.'

The two of them exchanged a look of mutual appreciation and fell silent. Jane was almost shocked: Michael certainly had never attained anything like an intimate relationship with his father. She wondered that she had never noticed this alliance before and felt, not for the first time that evening, that her sensibilities had entered a new arena – more dangerously exposed, yet more rewarding.

'I was very mixed-up at one stage, with an awful lot of pointless things to prove to people who weren't even looking.' Christopher paused for a moment, casting a glance at Earnest, who was chewing slowly and steering his fork in circles through what remained of his meat and gravy. 'I was shamefully unpleasant to my mother. And then she died and I did a guilt-trip in classic style.'

'By drinking.'

'Among other things.'

She raised her eyebrows, but he said no more.

'He was a right pain in the arse, if you want to know, Jane.'

Earnest patted Christopher's arm and then carefully placed his knife and fork together. 'Don't hurry, you two, I'm off for a smoke.'

And they were left, the flagon of dark beer between them and their plates still half-full of food. The unanswered question of Michael, his glaring absence, ballooned in the silence that followed.

'Michael and I—'

'I know,' he put in quickly, 'I'm so sorry.'

The manic smile was hovering again; she longed to push her plate away and escape into the sitting-room. If only she had known that Christopher was coming – they could have arrived earlier or not arranged to stay for so long. She was tempted to ask when he planned to leave. Instead, she found herself saying, 'I had no idea you and your father were so close.'

He looked up, an expression of pleased surprise bringing colour to his pale face.

'We understand each other, I suppose. We've got better at it as we've got older.'

Jane gave up on the last of her stew, which was rich and filling, and poured more beer into both their glasses. Christopher made no protest. He was watching the way the kitchen light shone down on to her head, illuminating shadows of dark auburn and black amongst the rich brown. Such depth of colour.

'How did you know about Michael and me? Did Michael call you?'

He shook his head, using a mouthful of food as pretext for delay, wondering how much to tell her, wishing he could tell her everything. 'Julia,' he said at last, 'I saw Julia at the weekend.'

'Julia?'

'I was up in London, staying with an old friend not far from her shop. I dropped by on a sort of whim.'

'That was nice.' An odd prickle at the back of her neck – a frisson of some emotion that she could not identify – prevented her from saying more.

'How are you really, Jane?' he asked suddenly, with a quick intake of breath, leaning forward on his elbows.

The invitation was so straightforward, it was impossible not to respond. She felt bound to speak, drawn in by the dark intensity of his eyes and, perhaps, by the sense of trust that his own effortless confessions had generated.

'I don't know how I am. I really don't. I feel as if I'm waiting to find out.' She lowered her eyes, focusing on a brown blob of gravy to the right of her plate. It was shaped like a pear, a perfect, muddy tear-drop. 'It was the right thing – to split up – I'm sure of that – just.' She gave a little half-laugh. 'But there are so many other things – what with the children and everything. Harriet is more or less okay, but Tom is impossibly grumpy. I think I'd feel guilty anyway – just at having failed at the fairy-tale ending – at not having managed to live happily ever after.' She paused for breath. 'I did it for myself, you see – that's the hardest thing. It felt a little brave at the time, but now I wonder if I haven't just been the most unforgivable coward.' She was pressing a small piece of tin-foil into a tight ball, moulding the silver with her fingers till it was no more than a pellet. Unlike Julia, who meant well but interrupted all the time, Christopher said nothing. 'The joke is that I miss him – for all the wrong reasons of course—'

'What reasons?' When he spoke it was so softly, so smoothly, that the question merely eased her on, helped her through to the next stage.

'Because being a single mother is grim. Because I get the spooks locking up the house late at night on my own. Because of money. Because Harriet has started grabbing the legs of strange men and saying Daddy. Because Tom is unremittingly horrible. Because I feel so guilty at what I've done to them all that I don't think I can ever be happy with the result. Which makes me wonder if I have been mad as well as cowardly.'

'It's hard to be sure of anything where feelings are concerned.' He locked his fingers together and squeezed the knuckles hard. 'What we want from other people is so complicated, so tied up with what we want from ourselves, what we want for ourselves.'

'Michael and I were skiing in Austria when my parents died – but then you knew that.'

'I don't know anything,' he said.

'We flew back at once, only to find that Mattie had disappeared.'

Christopher did not flinch, though his heart lurched at the sound of Mattie's name. Face composed, eyes burning, he willed her to go on, cherishing this unexpected gift of finding her here, cherishing above all the fragile intimacy granted by being cast in the role of confessor.

'Michael was incredible. He took over. Finding Mattie, the funeral – everything. It transformed him for me – from being a student with grand ideas and too much impatience he suddenly became a wonderful man who could save me and keep me safe. And in the midst of it all I thought I had grown up too. By the time we found Mattie – squatting in some armpit of a place calling itself an artists' commune – I was awash with common sense and authority. I, the big sister, would see her through. Getting married was so obvious after that. It was the next step in coping, in showing that I had grown up and survived. Does that make any sense?'

He nodded slowly. 'Most of us couldn't begin to be half so coherent about what we have done and why.'

She placed her hands on either side of her head and shook it slowly. 'The worst thing – when I think back to those times – is realising that losing Mum and Dad was what brought Michael and me so close ... it's as if grief can somehow magnify everything, make all other emotions seem bigger, disproportionately so. Did you find that?'

'I was too busy running away to notice,' he smiled broadly, wanting now to ease the sadness from her face.

'Have you ever been in love, Christopher?' she asked suddenly.

'Oh, my word, yes,' he said at once, touching his upper lip with his tongue and starting to laugh. 'I loved an actress once, when I was going through my artist-in-a-garret phase in Paris.' He put his hands behind his head and tipped his chair back to an unnerving angle, before coming slowly forward again, soundlessly letting the front legs rest back on the ground. 'I was rather stubborn about it, as one is about these things. It took a visiting professor from Milan to bring me to my senses.'

'Oh? How did he do that?'

'By making love to her for so long that they were still at it when I returned one evening.'

She put her hand to her mouth, trying to feel horrified, but wanting to laugh.

'It was quite a shock, I can tell you,' he said with a wry smile, 'the sight of all that heaving flesh in my bed.'

'Oh dear, I'm so sorry.'

'Don't be, please.' He laughed himself, wishing he could erase the memory of the night before, the images of Mattie's flesh, that kept replaying in his head like a video gone wild.

'What is all this?' roared Earnest, his bushy eyebrows waggling in mock severity from the doorway. 'Haven't you even put the coffee on – you useless so-and-sos?'

18

It was with the best intentions that Julia accepted Michael's invitation for a drink. He wanted to talk about Jane, he said, sounding unremittingly forlorn, and conjuring up poignant images of a man in mourning, needing to recapture some essence of the person lost. Curiosity played a part in her compliance, as did a tenuous, mushy hope that she might even act as an agent of reconciliation and bring everybody to their senses. Jane had been sounding so hopelessly forlorn herself that Julia was rapidly coming to the conclusion that the separation had been ill-advised in every aspect. Being such a resolutely independent soul, she found it hard to dish out heavy doses of sympathy for anyone who had made such a drastic bid for freedom, only to show so many signs of not coping with it.

Michael's own motives were more blurred. It felt daring to contact Julia, and he liked that. But he was also troubled by pestering clouds of non-comprehension; discovering a logical reason for the breakdown of his marriage would make it more tolerable. So he clung to the pragmatic belief that it was just a question of seeking answers in the right places. His wife's closest friend was an obvious, and most attractive starting-point.

As their date approached, Julia found herself irritatingly preoccupied by it. It felt odd to be meeting Michael – odd enough for her not to mention it to Jane and for her to spend some considerable time determining what to wear. Without being sure of her exact role in the proceedings, it was hard to settle on the appropriate clothes. Everything looked either too dressy or too sombre. With half the contents of her wardrobe strewn across her bed and floor, she angrily pulled on her dressing-gown and padded through to her kitchen with the intention of fixing herself a drink and calling Jane. If she told her, she would feel better, she was sure. But though the drink was poured – a dissatisfyingly weak gin without lemon and barely a bubble to the tonic – the phone-call was never made. She lay on her bed instead, flattening a heap of rejected outfits, and mulling over the irony that her first date in weeks was to be with the almost ex-husband of her best friend. Her commitment to the dating agency had faded fast after her rendezvous with the toothy Alan Lambert and a couple more like him, who had undertaken the business of starting a relationship with all the delicacy of heat-seeking missiles. Feeling disappointed, but resigned, she had fallen back on the rigorous demands of book-keeping and french polishing, interspersed by the occasional outing to avant-garde films with her gay friend Robbie, who was terribly kind.

'It was good of you to come,' said Michael, opening wide the door of his new flat and kissing her swiftly on the cheek. He was always surprised by her height; even in pumps her head was level with his. Jane would have reached only to his chest in such flat shoes.

'Not at all,' she replied, surreptitiously studying his face for signs of strain. Though thinner, and even a little greyer, he appeared impressively composed.

The flat, which was situated in one of the dingier streets off Clapham High Road, lacked furniture and warmth. While he led her down the narrow hallway and into the mustard-walled living-room she effused about its potential, to hide her dismay. It was a far cry from the bright, cosy squash of Cobham, with all its heaving bookshelves and rampant pot-plants.

'Jane's keeping the furniture,' he said, as if reading her thoughts. 'I'm not bothered, quite honestly. It's all down to the bare essentials now – there's a sort of freedom to it all – a beginning-again feeling which isn't too bad.'

'You're being brave,' she said accusingly, because she felt sorry for him.

'Oh, I'm not saying it's been easy – far from it. Staying at the Crofts' place was pretty grim.' He stopped abruptly, detecting her pity. Though he had relished the idea of evoking Julia's sympathy, of winning such an ally, other instincts were now taking hold – the desire to appear strong being foremost among them.

'They've had their own troubles, the Crofts, as I expect you've heard.'

'No. What troubles?'

'Tim has gone out of business. They are having to sell everything. He's talking of running a camp-site in Cornwall – of all things – some place near Helston.'

'Oh dear, oh dear.' The constraints of her own life, which had looked so impossibly gloomy that afternoon, suddenly gleamed with potential. 'The poor things.'

Michael clapped his hands suddenly, making her jump. 'Now then, now then,' he said, several times, as if he were hosting a quiz show. 'Take a pew.' He gestured at two shiny-brown velour armchairs, whose single redeeming feature seemed to be that they blended well with the muddy decor. Julia, who had an almost physical need to surround herself with beautiful objects, perched on the very edge of her seat, feeling out of place and increasingly out of her depth.

'Red or white?' he asked, elaborating the question with a theatrical flourish of bottles.

'White would be nice.' She lit a cigarette, in a desperate bid to feel more poised and bold. 'I'm not entirely sure what I am here for, Michael.'

'Neither am I.' His face creased into a grin and he chinked his glass against hers. 'I thought we could go round the corner for a bite.'

Though Julia had never entertained the idea that the evening might continue long enough to involve food, the prospect of escaping the oppressive tawdriness of the flat was instantly appealing. 'That sounds great.' She took an unseemly swig of wine and looked round for a receptacle that might serve as an ash-tray. 'I gather Jane is on the point of getting a job.'

'Is she?'

On seeing his flush of anger, fused with an attempt at indifference, the last flutter of an idea about brokering a reconciliation collapsed.

'Just say whatever you want, Michael,' she blurted, gripping her wine-glass hard, 'get it off your chest, ask questions, moan. Do whatever you want.'

He studied the texture of his trousers for a few seconds, flicking at an imaginary speck of fluff.

'I want, principally, to understand.'

'Oh, is that all?' She smiled, vaguely flattered that he should believe she could help with such a thing. 'Well, I wouldn't mind a morsel or two of understanding in all this myself. It's pea-soup for me, I can assure you, uninitiated as I am into the mysteries of co-habitation.'

'But you two talked—' he began, trying to express the dim notion of apparently effortless female intimacy, a notion which had always left him feeling profoundly threatened.

'Oh yes, we're great talkers, Jane and I – usually about non-sense on the telly, or things that make us laugh. I'm afraid we've never been ones for rip-roaring discussions on the inside leg measurements or nose-picking secrets of the men in our lives.'

Not quite believing her, he said nothing.

'I think Jane has changed a lot in the last ten years,' she went on, feeling compelled by his downcast silence to offer an explanation – however hackneyed – for something she barely understood herself. 'Perhaps more than you have. Those changes added distance between you – a distance that Jane could no longer manage.' She stubbed out her cigarette in the lid of her empty packet and stood up, wanting to nudge the evening onward. 'There's no doubt that she has gone a little crazy.'

'Do you really think so?'

Julia spoke with deliberate brashness, trying to lighten the atmosphere and bustle him out of the flat. 'She had many things that a lot of women would die for – kids, man, mortgage – so she must be slightly insane.' The fondness for Jane that underlined these comments was wasted on Michael. As a man who took things literally and as one in dire need of reassurance, he received Julia's words with a degree of relief and conviction that, had she perceived it, would have alarmed her greatly.

So successfully did she defuse his sense of failure and awkwardness that later on, in the restaurant, he felt bold enough to ask her, straight out, why she wasn't married herself. Since

Michael had always assumed that such decisions were made on the basis of opportunity not personal choice, it had long puzzled him. Julia was so good-looking. Just making their way to the table everybody had turned to stare, even the women.

'Not being married – or "attached", shall we say – is sometimes a great burden to me,' she replied slowly, 'as I think it is for many women in their mid-thirties. It's grossly unfair.'

There was a studied nonchalance to her, he decided, a careful indifference to the impression she made on other people, which only succeeded in spicing up her attractions.

'An unmarried woman of a certain age is still regarded as something of a belisha beacon, signalling for attention and pity that is usually not required and almost certainly unwise. Take me for example: I'm marvellously efficient at attracting the most unsuitable characters; bus loads of people – including myself – get unspeakably soppy and hurt, and then we all end up withdrawing under a hail of self-inflicted fire. It's all very tiring.'

Michael, unused to Julia's hyperbolic style of self-mockery, was feeling somewhat under fire himself. 'My goodness,' he muttered, 'that sounds sort of – tragic.'

'Oh lord, then it's time to go home. I talk too much. I need to be told to shut up occasionally.' She was in danger of enjoying herself and felt guilty. 'I thought we were here to talk about you. I wish I could be more helpful.'

'It's just good to spend time with someone who knows all the sordid details. Work has been fairly hellish.' He tore at a crust of brown roll, pulling it into large crumbs.

'Would you go back to her?'

He thought of Tom and shrugged. 'Maybe.'

Julia, imagining that his thoughts had turned to Jane, reached out and patted his hand, her long red nails faintly scraping the surface of his skin.

In fact any remaining tenderness for his wife now constituted only the finest thread in the tangled web of Michael's mind, charged as it still was with anger and hurt pride. As the evening progressed, the desire to understand the failure of his marriage grew less urgent. Instead, a tingling sensation of power teased his thoughts. For the second half of the meal he felt brighter and wittier than he had for months – quite his old self in fact.

'I'd like very much to do this again,' he ventured, after he had won a pleasant tussle about paying the bill and only the thick dregs of their coffee remained. 'I can't tell you what a help it's been.'

While the evening had been unexpectedly pleasant, Julia felt all the inappropriateness of repeating it. They should have spent more time talking about Jane or the logistics of filing for a divorce. 'I'm not sure . . . has it really helped?'

'You can't imagine how much.' He tried to catch her eye, but Julia, now coming to her senses, knew better than to cooperate.

'Perhaps you just need to start going out a bit more,' she suggested briskly, 'you need to get used to being a single man again.'

'You could help me feel that way.' It was his turn to reach for her hand, but her long cool fingers slithered from his grasp.

'I've helped all I can,' she said tightly.

'We could help each other,' he persisted, enjoying the quickening of excitement in the pit of his stomach.

'I think you know that is impossible, Michael. I am deeply sorry if I have misled you in any way. I really thought you wanted help – over Jane – over coming to terms—'

'But I do, I do. That's just what I mean.'

She looked at him steadily, her blue eyes fearless and distrustful. 'I don't think it is.' There was sadness as well as a warning in her voice. What a fool she had been to come. What an even greater fool to speak so freely about herself, to be borne along by the misplaced confidentiality that their meeting had allowed.

As he watched her leave, Michael felt positively triumphant. She had enjoyed herself, he was sure of that, never mind the business at the end, when he pushed things a little too hard. He would leave it a week, he decided, then call her again.

19

Nosing deeper into the soft duck-down of the pillow, Jane stretched her legs luxuriously, seeking the cooler, untrammelled regions of the wide bed. Her mind drifted back towards the outposts of sleep, dimly alert for waking-up noises from the children across the landing. But all was quiet.

After a few minutes of trying, unsuccessfully, to return to a dream that had left her mysteriously content, she threw back the sheets and padded over to the window-seat. Her head throbbed slightly in protest at being brought upright, reminding her of Earnest's beer and the rather astonishing frankness she had shown in conversation with Christopher the night before. An uncomfortable shyness now stole over her at the prospect of seeing him again. He had said something about going off for the day; she half-hoped he would make an early start.

Lifting one weighted corner of the old pink curtains, she caught sight of Earnest in the garden below, putting the finishing touches to the climbing frame. He wore a check cap, which he kept tweaking at his handiwork, as if doing little salutes to the bits he liked. His lips were pursed together, whistling in a way that reminded her of Michael.

The sun was high in the sky, coyly dodging behind cotton-fluff clouds of the kind that Tom now liked to draw, wedged between squadrons of battle-planes and clusters of stars. Thinking of Tom, and realising that all was far too quiet, she dropped the curtain and hurried out on to the landing. The door to the children's room was wide open, displaying an empty cot and Tom's train pyjamas, lying in a multicoloured heap beside the potty. Harriet's rag-doll, wedged between the wooden slats of the cot, surveyed the scene with unblinking button eyes.

They were in the sitting-room, wearing a startling cocktail of clothes, but well covered and certainly happy. Christopher had a mauve tea-cosy on his head and was brandishing a wooden spoon. Tom wore a dented panama pulled well over his eyes, while Harriet was curled, tortoise-like, under a wide-brimmed straw hat of Edie's.

'We're playing a hat-game,' remarked Tom by way of an explanation.

Christopher touched the cosy with a self-conscious grin and shrugged helplessly. 'I'm just following orders.'

'I'd no idea it was so late.' She pushed her hair back from her face, still trying to focus her thoughts. 'I've left my watch somewhere.'

'We thought we'd give you the morning off. I hope you don't mind.'

She looked so sleepy and surprised, standing there in an old dressing-gown of his mother's, the stitching loose at the collar and one pocket ripped at the seam, that he quickly turned his head, to hide a smile.

'Mind? How could I mind being given my first lie-in in six years? I just hope they haven't been a bother.'

Harriet, recognising her mother's voice, wriggled out from under the hat to wave, before burrowing back again.

'Harriet wants to be a whale,' complained Tom.

'Can't whales wear hats?'

He rolled his eyes in despair.

'I brought you a cup of tea,' put in Christopher, as she was about to retreat back upstairs, 'but then didn't have the heart to wake you.' There was a shade of guilt to this admission; she might guess that he had lingered for some seconds longer than necessary, enjoying the sight of her lost in sleep, lips fractionally apart, her chest rising slightly with each intake of breath, her eyelashes long and soft, silky jets along the papery whiteness of her eyelids. One hand had rested by her cheek on the pillow, the fingers pointing to the soft fair down beside her ear, the wedding ring shiny-bright, so new-looking, so unspoiled.

'Oh.' She was momentarily nonplussed. 'Have they eaten any breakfast?'

'Bowlfuls.'

'Thank you.'

'We've had a good time, haven't we, Thomas Lytton?' He patted the flat of Tom's head.

'Uncle Chris is cool,' conceded his nephew.

'High praise indeed,' smiled Jane. But then a shiver skipped up her spine, reminding her that it was cold and that she wore nothing but a faded green robe. Pulling it more tightly about her, she sought refuge in some needless bossing that instantly made her ashamed. 'Now give your uncle some peace. He's got other things to do today besides entertain you two.'

Christopher removed the tea-cosy, feeling as let down as the children. The intimacy of the night before felt remote and impossible – maybe even imagined.

'I was going to visit a church – perhaps you would like to come too? It's for some research I'm doing—'

'That's very kind, but I don't think so – thank you.' Oh Christ, she thought, his pity knows no bounds.

'But the Normans built it – they threw the bell in the river and it's got real skeletons inside,' shouted Tom, jumping to his feet.

Christopher looked sheepish.

'Oh.' She tried to slip her hands into her pockets, but they found only air, like a foot missing a step. 'Well in that case, I suppose we'd better see it,' she said, wondering if her reluctance seemed rude or polite.

They went in Christopher's car, waved off by Earnest, who had fielded all invitations to accompany them with rambling commentaries on the state of the garden. The car was an estate of some kind, big and old, with wide leather seats and no belts in the back. The children, rolling from side to side like pillion riders, thought it heavenly. Jane, sitting in the front, sank low inside her coat, steeling herself to remain cool and strong, resolving never again to invite anyone in to trample round the mess of her life with doses of unwanted compassion.

Christopher spoke little during the drive, instead devoting a dangerous proportion of his attention to the vagaries of a cassette player that was slotted into the side pocket of his door, amidst a tangle of brightly-coloured wires. After considerable rummaging amongst a sea of tapes, strewn across the dashboard and floor, he at last unearthed one that he wanted and deftly slotted it into the machine beside him with a satisfying click.

A glorious mellow trumpeting started up from two small black speakers affixed to the top front corners of the car. Christopher sighed and visibly relaxed, the music seeming to move through him in waves. Jane watched, a little fascinated.

'It's Verdi,' he remarked, without turning his head, 'a bit like the Gloria, but written some time before – I prefer it to the real thing.'

Spurred on by the fact that the children were in an advanced state of uncle-adulation, the outing proceeded with astonishing smoothness. Jane's reluctance to be there gradually slipped away, though she remained on her guard.

Inside the small, round-stoned church the reverential chill affected them all – even Tom, who contented himself with some awestruck gasping at the sight of the promised box of human bones, and Harriet, who made small hooting noises as she skipped up the aisle, thrilled at the satisfying echoes of her own voice.

'What did you say your research was for?' Jane enquired as they left the graveyard, following the path Christopher assured them the bell had taken on its doomed journey from tower to river.

'A book.'

'Yes, my limited intelligence had staggered that far all by itself.'

'Sorry.' He smiled apologetically. 'It's just that – well, it's a different kind of book.' He stooped to pick Harriet up and place her on his shoulders. She clung tightly to clumps of his hair and to his ears, but he didn't seem to mind. 'I'm trying to write a novel – much to the disgust of my agent – and I've discovered that I can't do it without fixing real places in my mind. Even if I barely describe them, I find that I have to be able to see the background properly in my head in order for any coherent thoughts to emerge. It's a tiresome business really – I expect I shall give up long before the end.'

Jane wanted to ask more but was distracted by some alarming acrobatics performed by Tom, who seemed bent on diving into the water to retrieve the legendary bell himself. To assuage such aquatic desires, Christopher suggested a walk along the beach before returning home. They bought fish and chips for lunch and sat daringly near to the waves, the pebbles bruising their bottoms and a sharp wind cutting up under their legs and coats.

In spite of every effort to divert him from the idea, Tom remained adamant that some part of him should get wet that day. His wiry six-year-old frame was in perpetual motion, spurred on by the brisk sea air. Christopher laughed aloud when Jane finally gave in and agreed to accompany her son on a paddle in the sea. He remained sitting, with Harriet snuggling for shelter under the lee of his wide black coat, watching her balance first one leg, then the other, daintily removing her shoes and socks and rolling up the legs of her jeans.

'You're frowning,' he laughed, 'it doesn't suit you.'

'Shut up,' she retorted, throwing a shoe at him, which he caught and promptly hurled back again. 'You're in a very weak position. I suggest absolute silence as the only honourable course of action.'

'But I'm looking after Harriet – someone's got to.'

Jane set off towards the water, stepping gingerly between the sharpest looking stones, hating the icy squidge of the sand between her toes. Tom was already prancing in the froth of the breaking waves, looking tiny beside the heaving grey sea.

'This is horried, Tom,' she shouted, beginning to enjoy herself, her feet numbing to the cold.

They returned triumphant and fairly soaked, cheeks burning, hair blasted wild by the wind.

For a while Jane felt wonderfully refreshed, as if all the cobwebs of the preceding weeks had been blown away for good. A sense of profound independence – from everyone, even from Christopher – began to settle over her. But such feelings were short-lived. Within a few minutes of starting on the drive back she found herself breathing deeply from nausea rather than exhilaration. After an unseemly panic to wind down the window, Christopher pulled over in a layby so that she could finish vomiting into a bush rather than down the side of his car.

The children sat, curious and subdued, watching the ever-unfolding mystery of adult behaviour through the car windows. Christopher, after a moment's hesitation, had hurried up behind Jane to put a steadying arm across her shoulders.

She was too wretched to shake him off or to bother with embarrassment. The retching turned into a kind of sobbing, as it often did with her. He wiped her face with a large blue hanky, very gently, as if she were a child, and then pulled her to him so that she could finish crying on his shoulder.

'Was it the fish or the company?' he murmured.

'Definitely the company – or perhaps just the company's car.' She shuddered. 'Where did you get that tank anyway?'

'An auction. I'm very fond of it. I'd prefer you to blame me.' She was still in his arms, but beginning to ease free. He held on for a moment longer, grateful for her sickness, grateful for anything that let him hold her – for the first time, really to hold her, to feel the warmth and movement of her, so long imagined.

She was back in control now, separate. 'I seem doomed to make an idiot of myself when you're around.' She put his handkerchief to her mouth and took a deep breath. 'I'll wash all offended items of course – including your beloved car.'

'No need. There's no harm done. Are you sure you're all right?' Her composure felt like a door shutting him out.

'Oh yes, fine now.' They turned back towards the car. 'Thank you so much – for everything. Sisters-in-law aren't supposed to be this much trouble.'

Though Jane claimed to be fully recovered, she went to bed shortly after the children. Christopher knocked quietly a couple of hours later, expecting to find her asleep, but she opened the door herself and nodded meekly at the idea of soup.

'I hate being ill,' she admitted with a rueful smile, as he placed a tray across her knees.

'Yes, I can see that.' He watched her intently; her upper lip had the tiniest pout, that moved as she spoke, disappearing only in the broad embrace of her smile.

'Are you happy, Christopher?' she asked suddenly, as he was on the point of leaving.

'What a question – I think I prefer you languishing in humble gratitude at my accomplished services as a nurse.'

'Do you like teaching?' she persisted.

He put his hands in his pockets and leant against the wardrobe beside the bed. 'Ah, that's easier. Yes, I like being a teacher very much. Though, when I started it was a form of running away – failed academic flees in terror.' He paused to smile, shaking his head. 'I couldn't take the pressure of trying to get into print all the time, of scrabbling out an area to claim as one's own – it dried me up completely. For years I barely wrote a thing. But the moment I moved into the school the writing came easily.'

'I am afraid I've never read your book on Clough,' she admitted.

'I'm relieved to hear it. Unreadable stuff – specially designed for verbose undergraduates and lazy tutors. It would probably put you off poetry for life.'

'I don't believe you for a minute. I will read it one day. Though I should probably read some Clough first.'

'That might help,' he conceded with a laugh.

She sipped at a spoonful of soup and scowled, wrinkling up her nose.

'That bad, is it?'

'Just hot,' she rasped, fanning her mouth.

He suspected that she wanted him to go, but couldn't quite bring himself to move. 'What about you then – seeing as we're on impossible questions – what makes you happy, Jane?'

She put her spoon down abruptly. 'Once upon a time I thought I knew.' She paused, 'but now—.'

'And what did you once think it was?'

'Love,' she said simply.

'Oh dear me, is that wrong then?' He feigned panic, but she barely managed a smile.

'It's too complicated for happiness. Even loving the children is fraught with danger. Like Tom by that water today – loving brings this terrible fear of losing. It's a kind of suffering.'

'But isn't that just the point?' he said urgently, thrusting his hands deeper into the pockets of his jeans and walking round to the end of the bed. 'There has to be a price. Without the suffering there's no value.'

She sighed and returned her attention to the soup. 'I suppose so. But it's full of trickery too.'

'That's half the fun—'

'It wasn't fun realising I didn't love Michael,' she interjected quietly.

'No, no, of course not.'

After he had left the room, closing the door softly behind him, he stood for several seconds outside her door, gripped by an almost palpable urge to rush back in and tell her what had happened in London. Not saying anything felt as bad as lying. But in the end, rational argument got the better of him. Mattie would probably never mention the incident anyway. She knew, as well as he, that it had all been a mistake – two drunken adults, copulating because they were sad. The only lasting relevance of the whole sordid affair was that, had he known of Jane and Michael's separation, it would never have happened. And that was something that would be rather hard to explain – impossible in fact, without saying a lot of other things that would either set his sister-in-law laughing or sprinting for cover.

20 ∫

Christopher was lying on his belly studying the entrance to a rabbit burrow with Tom when the phone rang. The tone was only faint, but he looked up none the less, a pin-prick of foreboding in his heart. Harriet was close by, being pushed by Earnest in the swing; she had kicked off her pink wellingtons into a patch of stinging nettles by the garden fence and was flapping her small feet in celebration at the achievement.

Jane, feeling much better, was sitting at the kitchen table dissecting a cauliflower when the phone rang. One small green worm had already wriggled indignantly on to the chopping board and she was undertaking a thorough search for its mate. The cauliflower, which had clearly been resident in the house for quite some time, had been presented to her by Earnest when he caught her sneaking out of the larder with a bag of frozen florets in her hand.

'You can't do a decent cauliflower cheese with those things,' he humphed, 'try this instead. There's plenty of cheese in the butter-dish.'

With one eye still on the cauliflower, Jane reached up for the phone which, for some unidentifiable reason, lived on top of the fridge, behind a stack of Edie's cookery books.

Mattie's voice, nasal and whiny with a heavy cold, came on line. She sounded very poorly and appeared, in some measure, to hold her elder sister responsible.

'It's taken bloody days to run you to ground,' she sniffed, omitting to mention that one phonecall to Julia had easily solved the mystery. 'I thought you were supposed to be job-hunting.'

'What's up, Mattie?' Jane leant up against the side of the fridge and stared out into the garden as she talked. Christopher glanced in the direction of the house, but was quickly tugged back down to the ground by Tom. She wondered what they were doing, beyond the understandable pleasure of rolling amongst Earnest's beloved mole-hills.

'Oh, nothing's up – nothing at all.' There was a loud, snorting sound, as Mattie made a big show of blowing her nose, followed by an uninviting silence. 'How are you then?' she asked at length, so grudgingly that Jane couldn't resist saying that though she had thrown up the day before she was feeling fine – surprisingly happy in fact.

'Oh, well, I don't want to drag you down or anything—'

'Come on, come on, Mattie.' Jane turned to face the gleaming blankness of the fridge in an effort to wrest her mind from the dreamy, unfocused state induced by watching the intriguing activities going on outside. Tom and Christopher had started beating at a thatch of towering stinging nettles with long sticks, like knights charging at the lists. 'Talk to me properly. Tell me what's wrong.' She rested her forehead against the cool metal side. Her voice, so soothing and kind, worked on her younger sister as it always did, in the end.

'I'm a mess,' sobbed Mattie at last, 'I hate myself.'

'I'll be back in Cobham at the weekend – come and see me then. Stay the night and we'll have a proper talk. Michael's taking the children for the day on Sunday and Julia's coming over – but not until lunch-time.'

'No – I mean, I can't wait – I need to talk now.'

This was dramatic, even for Mattie. Jane felt the palms of her hands go clammy. Maybe something had happened. And a terrible fear, based on the ineradicable insecurity of having once before had bad news down a phone-line, seized her somewhere about the neck and throat.

'Whatever is it Mattie? What has happened?'

'Don't sound so panicky, for God's sake. I just need to talk to you about something – I can't tell you on the phone – I just can't . . . could I come down there?'

'I'd have to ask Earnest,' Jane faltered, her alarm being replaced by a flicker of resistance at the thought of Mattie arriving in Kent.

'Ask away,' boomed Earnest, coming in from the hall with Harriet in his arms, her socks caked in mud and her boots jammed on to her hands like fluorescent boxing-gloves.

'Hang on a minute,' Jane covered the receiver with her palm. 'It's my sister – Mattie – something has upset her – she wondered if she might come down—'

'Arrange anything you want, love,' said Earnest easily, more intent on rubbing some warmth into Harriet's toes. He pulled off her socks and blew noisy raspberries into the soles of her feet, before rubbing them briskly between his bear-like hands.

'Earnest says that's fine – if it really can't wait till I get back.'

But Mattie, instantly transformed at the notion of escaping the office, was already enthusing, uncharacteristically, about fresh country air and the delights of rural life. 'It'll take me a couple of hours to sort things out up here,' she went on. 'Has Earnest got a washing machine – I'm right out of everything but laddered tights – I'll have to bring a load or two – thanks so much Jane – I'll call from the station.'

When Jane told Christopher of the imminent arrival of her sister, he nodded quickly, as if he had been expecting it, and then went noticeably quiet. With the strong sense that she was somehow responsible for ruining something, yet unsure exactly what, Jane found herself apologising.

'I'm sorry – but she did sound a little desperate – I really felt I couldn't say no.'

Christopher's face tightened into a smile. 'Of course you couldn't. You're close, you two, as siblings are supposed to be.' He spread an old newspaper on one end of the table and began easing clods of mud off his boots with a long, pointed knife.

So he doesn't like Mattie, thought Jane, with a reflex of protective anger.

'Did she say what the matter was?'

'No, but I think I know.'

'Really?' He stopped, knife in hand.

Jane, unaware that Christopher's heart was racing with a futile hope that this sisterly crisis would have no bearing on him, was happy to continue, happy above all that his curious bout of awkwardness had come to an end. After the unexpected events of the last two days she had got rather used to talking openly with him.

'Oh, it will be man-trouble, I expect. And her painting. And her hateful job with that seedy group of architects. Every so often it all blows up in her mind – the misery of realising that she is so far from achieving what she wants – and I have to remind her that we're all miles off such things, that she's no exception in making a muddle of her life.'

'Does she always tell you everything then?'

'Everything,' she echoed, brushing aside the thought of the little pills in Mattie's handbag. 'Here, I believe this belongs to you.' She handed him a dry pellet of mud which had flown from his boots on to a yellowy head of cauliflower. 'If the children are very lucky, they'll have dirt as well as invertebrates to chomp on. Earnest is determined we should eat this thing, but – just between you and me – I think it's been used as a block of flats by a group of militant worms. They're green but quite sweet-looking – no hairs or goggly eyes. I caught one, but it got away.'

'Why do women have to be so confiding in each other,' he interjected, thinking only that he had to leave.

'But we're not. Mattie has always loved to talk about herself – to splurge out all the gory details – but Julia isn't like that, and neither am I – not usually anyway. My emotional catharses tend to be much more drawn out and agonised.' She smiled timidly, thinking of all the things she had told him, without quite meaning to.

'Mine too,' he said, folding up the newspaper and squashing it deep into the bottom of the bin.

While Jane grated cheese into the white sauce, he hovered in the doorway, brooding for the last time over the best course of action to take. Having washed her hands, Jane smoothed her hair back behind her ears, from where it promptly bounced forward again.

'I think I'd better be getting back.'

She looked quite startled. 'So soon?'

'I'm afraid so.' He ran one hand back across the top of his head and looked away. 'I've loads to be getting on with, what with the book and so on.'

'Of course,' she murmured.

'I should never really have come at all.' He left the kitchen at great speed, emerging some ten minutes later with his holdall packed and the shapeless grey sweater back on. Coming up behind her as she stood at the sink, he placed his hands on her shoulders and quickly kissed the top of her head. There was a faint, soapy smell to her, deep in the dry softness of her hair. 'I really do have to go, I'm sorry.'

'Well I hope we can do this again,' she said, struggling out of her rubber gloves, her voice sounding false and jolly. 'I might call you,' she offered, as a bold afterthought.

'I hope so.' After a bout of playful farewells with the children, he strode out of the house and down the front path, his bag slung carelessly over one shoulder, tossing his car keys from one hand to the other. Earnest was waiting by the gate. Jane watched as they exchanged a few words and Earnest raised a hand to Christopher's back, touching him only briefly, before opening the car door and waving him off.

It didn't take Mattie long – just two cigarettes and a cup of tea – to get to the point. They were sitting toe to toe on the window seat in Jane's bedroom, a box of tissues between them, like huddling teenagers. Bruised as she was by self-blame and insecurity, total honesty was not Mattie's highest priority in telling her tale of seduction. Truth was there, but shrouded amongst wishful thoughts, to do with unspoken understandings and whispered promises that had taken place only in the ferment of her mind. Without these trimmings, her story would have sounded too sordid and pointless to evoke the sympathy she craved.

'Christopher? Christopher Lytton? Are you sure?'

Mattie, hunched over her mug of tea, a cigarette wedged between two bitten nails, was too preoccupied with her own train of thoughts to register the scale of reluctant disbelief in Jane's response.

'Your dear brother-in-law. I couldn't believe it – seeing him there, at Greg's. It was like – I don't know – fate or something. He didn't waste time, I can tell you.' She shook her dark curls, which looked dull and greasy. 'Talk about exploitation.' She gulped, assailed by a fresh wave of self-pity.

'Poor Mattie.' Jane touched her arm.

'He used me . . . Christ, I didn't even qualify for a post-coital cuddle.' She lit a new cigarette from the burning stub of an old one and then offered it across to Jane who shook her head. The desire to smoke had, curiously, departed with Michael. She watched, motionless, as Mattie succumbed to the dramatics of a chesty cough. She looked quite terrible, the worst Jane had seen her since her teens, when she ran away and tried to starve herself to death. 'I mean, that's the usual joke isn't it – I bet even you've had that one.'

'Which one?' The smoke was making Jane feel sick. She swung her legs to the floor and took refuge on the bed.

'You know – the man falls instantly asleep after bouts of meaningful, torrid sex, leaving you to confess heartfelt emotions to a wall of snores.'

'I don't think I'm best qualified to talk about torrid sex,' she remarked absently, wanting suddenly to be left alone.

'Well, Christopher,' persisted Mattie, 'didn't even have the decency to fall asleep. He left.' She threw up her hands, scattering a fine spray of ash over the faded-velvet seat cover. 'No lover of mine,' she spoke gravely, aware that Jane's attention was wandering and wanting to wrest it back, 'has ever treated me like that before.'

'It is truly awful, Mattie, I'm so sorry.' No wonder he ran off like that, she thought, all quiet and cowardly.

'These bloody Lyttons,' sighed Mattie, 'now they've ruined both our lives.'

When Jane had left to check up on the children Mattie pulled a small leather pouch out of her jacket pocket and examined the contents. Four pills left and one squashed joint. Having carefully repacked some of the tobacco and rolled the thin paper back into shape, she wrapped the joint in a tissue and placed it gently along the bottom of her pocket. She would save it till later – smoke it out of the window when everyone was asleep. The tablets, which were the kind she had once reserved for all-night partying, were less easy to resist. Her energy-levels were so low these days. After some consideration, she broke one in half and nibbled it slowly, loving the tingly feeling it brought and the way her head began to clear.

Back in Cobham, the house felt chilly and unwelcoming. With their break in the country coming to such an unsatisfactory conclusion and her interview at the hospital looming, Jane felt all the bleak apprehension of a child facing the prospect of school.

She was standing in her towelling dressing-gown, absently ladling sugar into a bowl of bran flakes, when Michael turned up to collect the children for what had been billed as a final half-term treat. He greeted her with a disarming smile, while Tom and Harriet screamed their welcomes and pulled on his arms. Something's happened, she thought at once, he looks different.

She was still puzzling over it when Julia arrived.

'Michael looked odd today.'

'Oh?' Julia glanced briefly up from the colour supplement on her lap. 'What sort of odd?'

'I don't know – pleased with himself.'

Julia, who could usually be relied upon to wade in with amusing, if inaccurate, suggestions at such a comment, remained curiously intent upon her magazine. 'Perhaps he's finding his feet,' was all she said, as if the subject bored her deeply.

Jane, a little offended by this reticence, but knowing better than to show it, set about preparing lunch.

'Did I tell you I saw Christopher last Saturday?' said Julia at length, throwing the magazine to one side and helping herself to a raw carrot from the pile Jane had just peeled.

'No, you didn't, but I know anyway.'

'How come?' She gnawed neatly round the sides, leaving the long sweet core till last.

'He was in the country. It was his half-term too.'

'How did he seem?'

'Fine.' Jane was at the draining board now, hacking great chunks off the bottoms of Brussels sprouts; clusters of tiny green leaves fluttered into the washing-up bowl.

'I only ask because he seemed rather out of sorts when I saw him – positively distracted – quite the mad professor. I half wondered if he was ill.'

'Really.' It was a statement not a question. 'He was probably rather tired.' She ran vicious jets of water into the bowl, making the sprouts jostle like penned animals.

Julia began banging open cupboards and drawers in a haphazard search for useful things to lay on the table. 'He certainly looked tired – all black-eyed and dishevelled – rather handsome, really, in a gaunt kind of way. Where does the pepper mill reside in this worthy establishment?'

Jane pointed in silence at the table, where the salt and pepper cellars could just be seen peeking out from under Julia's discarded magazine.

'It was rather astonishing, him popping in like that, out of nowhere and with absolutely nothing to say.'

Having given up on her half-hearted attempts at assistance, she was now perched with her bottom on the edge of the table, facing Jane's back. 'Do you think I should start getting ideas?' She giggled, 'What a thought – Christopher Lytton and me—'

'I'm not really that interested in what the hell you think he wanted,' snapped Jane, hurling the vegetables into a sieve and shaking them with unnecessary vigour.

'Whatever is the matter?'

'Look, I wasn't going to mention it but—' she took a breath, 'Christopher was in London last weekend for a party.' She crossed her arms, endeavouring to appear matter-of-fact rather than angry. 'I know because Mattie was at the party too. He led her on and the two of them ended up in bed. Shortly after which, without so much as a goodbye, he leaves her – apparently to see you and then to have a quiet two days in the country.' She uncrossed her arms and began wiping down surfaces, making messy swathes through the heaps of green and orange peelings. 'Quite what he thinks he's playing at, I have no idea. I think the whole business is shameful. Mattie, as you might imagine, is pretty shaken by it all.'

'Goodness.' Julia was intrigued. 'That does sound a bit much. What a strange way to behave.' She rubbed her hands, 'Christopher and Mattie – whoever would have thought—'

'There's no need to get all gleeful about it.'

Even given the nature of Christopher's puzzling misdemeanours, Julia was shocked by the vehemence of Jane's response. Mattie, from what she knew of her, was quite capable of handling her own lovers, without requiring her big sister to get up in arms on her behalf.

'Let's leave the subject of your brother-in-law, shall we?' she suggested with icy sweetness, 'it seems to be making you rather cross.'

After such uncharacteristically tense exchanges, the two of them found it hard to regroup into anything like their usual attitudes towards each other. Though Julia stayed for coffee she left much earlier than she had intended, bowed down with frustration at Jane's unpredictable moods. At least when she had been harnessed to Michael she had had a fixed stand-point from which to rejoice or complain. Since the separation she had grown so much harder to talk to; there was a prickly touchiness to her now that Julia found quite impossible.

After all the build-up towards leaving Michael, she felt justified in feeling a trifle impatient that Jane's altered situation seemed to be giving her even less satisfaction than an imperfect marriage.

As she pulled away from the kerb, offering a departing toot of inappropriate cheerfulness at Jane's closing front door, she resolved to leave her old friend alone for a while, to give them both time for a little readjustment.

With the dubious challenge of her interview to face (though it turned out to be nothing more than the most unflattering formality) followed by a hurried introduction to the vast filing systems of Guildford General Hospital, Jane's thoughts of Christopher began to simmer with less intensity. There remained only the irksome feeling that he had let her down in some way, that he had led her on too – though not in quite such an obvious direction as Mattie.

For Christopher, the intervening weeks were less kind in assuaging his sense of loss. From the silence that ensued, he guessed that Mattie had told Jane everything and that the two of them had turned against him for good. The old demon of self-loathing, which he thought he had slain for good, began to creep up on him again, like an enemy intent upon revenge.

The prospect of a family Christmas fuelled his hopes for a time. But he and Earnest dined alone that Christmas day, while Jane and Michael tried their hands at some stiffly executed charades for the sake of Harriet and Tom. There was little pleasure to be had in either camp: though Earnest and Christopher steadily applied themselves to the task in hand, no amount of claret or vintage port could pad out the sense of aloneness that hung around the beams of the old house like ghostly mistletoe. Earnest asked no questions, but his son's shame and sadness were plain to see, infused as they were into every angle of his bony body and the way his dark eyes were hooded with a new wariness of the world.

Back at school Christopher took on every extra-curricular activity that he could, surprising his colleagues with a hearty energy that never quite rang true. While the more sensitive among them guessed that he sought such distractions for unenviable reasons, others began to whisper about the new, distasteful thrust of Lytton's ambitions, and withdrew from him accordingly. Outings, plays, poetry groups – nothing, it seemed, was safe from the voluntary involvement of the once pleasantly inactive English master.

If ever Christopher found himself alone, without one single essay to mark, not one lesson to plan, he worked on his novel – not out of love or any heated desire to create, but with gritted teeth and a burning mind, fearful of being abandoned to the downward spiral that whirled within. It was escapism of sorts, bringing little satisfaction, but at least dulling the edges of his brain with tiredness, so that sleep without whisky was possible. He never drank alone now, for fear of where it might lead. When all else failed, he clung to the feather of a hope that Mattie had been too proud to say anything, and that Jane would call him soon.

One of the few people in the world Jane had ever trusted to drill holes in her teeth was a Mr Philip Newel, who practised near Dulwich, in a quiet residential road off Denmark Hill. Pippa had recommended him, when Jane was pregnant with Tom and all the nerve-endings in her mouth had felt as though they were trying to crawl out of her gums.

As Jane reclined, her mouth open to the glare of Mr Newel's angle-poised light, enduring an examination with a silver hook that she tried not to think about, it was Pippa who most frequently came to mind. She focused on the bobbles in the ceiling, endeavouring to avoid the sight of Mr Newel's nostrils, which were wide and lined with fine dark hairs that twitched as he talked. A piece of tooth had fallen out during breakfast the day before, dislodged by a challenging crust of toast. While Tom and Harriet peered eagerly into her mouth, thrilling to the idea of tooth fairies and money, Jane nurtured less romantic feelings, to do with decrepitude and middle age.

'We can save the tooth,' announced Mr Newel happily, 'no need for a crown at all.' He started pulling on thin rubber gloves; condoms for the fingers, thought Jane, looking once again at the ceiling, while the inevitable, unimaginable needle was prepared.

The subject of Pippa provided a welcome counterpoint to the speckled craters on the ceiling, as well as a much-needed distraction from the certainty that searing pain was merely biding its time, coiled deep within each vibration of Philip Newel's unspeakable gadgets.

Since Pippa's ill-judged letter, which still lay crumpled up in the left pocket of Jane's overcoat, the two women had not spoken at all. On subsequently receiving news of the Crofts' financial difficulties Jane had embarked on the first of several efforts to get in touch. Though she quickly grew to know the chirpy spiel of their answering machine off by heart, no message of hers was ever rewarded by a return call. Even a letter, the result of several hours of careful composition, had met with an equally blank response. Try as she might to brush the business aside, discounting it, as Julia advised, as one inevitable casualty of her separation from Michael, Jane could not help feeling uneasy about the rift. Pippa had many problems and very few friends. It seemed too awful to give up on her just like that, to abandon her without the tiniest fight.

By the time Mr Newel had reached the final stages of the treatment, when the hinges of her jaw were aching and her dry lips were crying out for a tongue-lick, it had occurred to Jane that Pippa might be acting under pressure from Tim. Perhaps he had simply forbidden her to get in touch. The thought blossomed wildly. Perhaps Pippa was no better than a prisoner, a slave to Tim's philandering and to his unfortunate mishandling of their business affairs.

'Rinse thoroughly, please.'

Pink liquid dribbled unmanageably from the numbed corner of her mouth.

A little while later, when she tried to smile into the bite-sized mirror in the surgery's toilet, her lips merely quivered, looking lop-sided and unconvincing. The point of her nose was frozen too, and there was a numbing sensation in her right eye-socket, as if cold water had been injected up under the cheek-bone. She drove down Denmark Hill with one eye closed, massaging the right side of her face with her fingertips.

A plump woman was half-way up a tall ladder in front of the Crofts' house, cleaning a bedroom window. Though the weather was cold for March, she wore only a jumper and a green tartan skirt; she was polishing the glass in sweeping circular movements, her wide skirt jigging with each motion.

It was only when Tim emerged through the open front door with a mug in each hand that Jane realised that the woman cleaning the windows was Pippa.

She had parked her car across the road, not quite opposite the house, behind a white van. Having watched quite openly until this point, Jane raised one hand to the side of her head and peered through her fingers. Now that Pippa had come down the ladder, Jane could see her face quite clearly; it remained curiously unchanged, as fine-boned and sharp as ever, though incongruously small on top of the freshly-rounded pear of her body. Her hair, which was swept tightly off her face into a straggly pony-tail, seemed to have grown considerably, its longest strand pointing well down between her shoulder-blades.

Such a physical transformation was somehow deeply shocking. Jane caught her breath and gripped the wheel of the car with her free hand, wanting, more than anything else, to accelerate away. The two Crofts were now sitting side by side on their doorstep, chatting over their tea like pensioners with time on their hands.

Ever since Michael had left, Jane had been clinging to the increasingly untenable hope that, though one major element of her life had failed, the rest of it could continue much as before. Yet it struck her now, peeking through her hands at the bloated, flushed figure of Pippa, and Tim, looking so solemn and wan beside her, that nothing was the same, that nothing ever would be the same again, in her life or anyone else's.

As she gently pulled the keys from the ignition and flexed her thawing mouth into what felt like a normal position, she had the honesty to wonder whether her resolution to make an approach stemmed from a need to reassure herself, or from a genuine desire to offer support. She only knew that to have come so far, and then to slink away without saying a word, would have felt like failure of the most unforgivable kind.

'Hi there,' she called, even before she had crossed the road, wanting to give them fair warning. Tim got to his feet at once, while Pippa simply looked up slowly, no readable expression on her face.

'I'm not sure this is a good idea, Jane,' he said, coming to meet her, putting himself between his wife and their visitor like some noble protector.

'I've come to see Pippa,' said Jane firmly, feeling shaky at the very physical sensation of being so unwanted. 'I'm so sorry about your business, Tim. I only heard a little while back. I've tried to call . . .' Through the open door behind him she glimpsed bare floorboards; pictures leant against the walls, beneath grey, square shadows of their former homes; a large cardboard box was acting as a door-stop.

'This is not a good time. I must ask you to leave.'

Jane stood her ground, deliberately not looking at the almost comic expression of hostility on Tim's chubby face. Behind him, Pippa was behaving with a nonchalance that encouraged Jane to hope. Having tipped her head back to swallow the last warm drops of her tea, she carefully placed the cup on the window-sill and started climbing back up the ladder, cloth in hand.

'Pippa,' Jane called loudly, 'can we talk?'

'Don't you think you've done enough?' Tim took a step forward, coming so close that the possibility of physical violence even crossed her mind.

'I've done nothing – not to you.'

'Like hell you haven't.'

She looked to the top of the ladder where Pippa was rubbing a window; the same one as before, Jane noted, with a little twist of alarm.

Tim was sounding more confident now, getting into his stride. 'It's not just Michael – though what you've done to him is bad enough.' He poured the remains of his tea on to the gravel between them, so close to her feet that a few brown drops splashed on to her shoe. 'But the way you led Pippa on too – all the business over children, special treatments, expensive clinics, getting her hopes up.' He lowered his voice. 'I don't know how you dared. As if you were ever in any position to offer advice on being a parent.' He stopped abruptly, as if completing the expression of such base sentiments was impossible.

Jane knew that she should defend herself, to explain how it really was – not just about Pippa and babies, but also about the intolerable loneliness of being married to Michael. But Tim's expression, his whole stance, the way his stocky legs were planted so firmly against her, his hips thrust out, his arms crossed over his stomach, did not invite explanations of any kind. Instead, she made a sort of run at the ladder, charging in a way that felt at once melodramatic and necessary. Grasping a metal rung with both hands, resisting the urge to shake it hard, she called up to Pippa again.

Tim walked past her into the house, with an odd half-smile on his face. 'She won't talk to you. Loyalty means something to us.' And with that he disappeared inside. Jane was still staring after him when Pippa began to descend, taking each step very slowly, her wide skirt swaying. Jane waited, relieved that the two of them would at last have the chance to talk alone. But having reached the ground, Pippa simply collected her mug from the window-sill and followed Tim inside, like a sleep-walker. The rebuff was so surprising, that Jane did not move for at least a minute after the door had closed behind them.

To be ostracised in such a way was almost laughable; she strode out of their driveway riding high on incredulity and the exhilaration of being so unjustly treated. But by the time she had settled back into the car, any consoling puff of self-righteous triumph had been superseded by a much more wob-bly feeling. Her tooth was throbbing badly and her fingers trembled as she groped for the ignition. The white blur of Pippa's face appeared at a window as she drove away; though Jane slowed and stared hard, hoping – in spite of every-thing – for a wave, for some signal that what had taken place was not for real, there was no movement, not even a twitch.

On arriving home she resisted calling Julia. The urge to discuss the depressing and bizarre events of her day was strong, but she found herself in the unusual position of dreading how Julia might react, how she might blast the incident apart with the impatient scorn that seemed so quick to surface these days.

It struck Jane that night, as she lay blinking at the darkness, how very much alone she now was. While nothing as sinister as regret threatened to descend, she caught herself fighting the notion that she was completely adrift, that without the children and a standing order from their father there would be no direction or possibility to her life. Sleeplessness at last drove her downstairs, where she went through the ritual of preparing a hot drink before resorting to the medicine cabinet and the aspirins, which she bolted with an eagerness suggestive of a hope that the small white capsules might hold the panacea for self-doubt.

23

Returning to the neon-lit warmth of Guildford Hospital the next day was quite a relief. From her first day in the place Jane had derived an unexpected pleasure from being in an environment where nobody knew anything of her background, where there were no expectations of her beyond the limited demands of her work. She was quite happy to spend large segments of her time on her own, putting away and pulling out trolley loads of fat beige files from the cadaverous basement on the lower ground floor. It was warm and dim under the building. She liked the hush of it, the neat click of her heels on the concrete floor and the gentle gurgles of the pipes that pulsed warm air to the upper levels, like the arteries of some great metal heart.

In spite of an opening lecture from the dapper, double-breasted head of administration on the importance of keeping busy at all times, Jane often found herself dawdling dreamily between the long rows of shelves, studying X-rays of blurred lumps and fuzzy bones, or skim-reading illegible notes on symptoms and treatments. With her own life in such disarray, she found it perversely reassuring to look through these documented keyholes, to spy on the thankfully mysterious world of human sickness and diagnosis.

Her other duties ranged from answering phones to helping out with the paperwork in busy clinics. With staff shortages being a problem common to every department, Jane quickly got to know her way round the disinfected labyrinth of corridors and stairs, with their slippery, brown linoleum floors and endless stretches of peppermint walls.

Her most daunting challenge was the vast hospital canteen,

where the feeling of being new, part-time and friendless was unavoidable. After a few days of such awkwardness she took to tucking something to read under her arm before joining the queue for food; reading as she ate made her feel much less conspicuous.

In fact Jane was growing to like her own company to a degree which she suspected might be considered unhealthy by anyone in a position to scrutinise her lifestyle. She had felt so abandoned being married to Michael – living with the recurrently thwarted expectation and hope of his company and understanding – that it could only feel less stressful to exist as she did now, without any such expectations and the inevitable pattern of disappointments.

It was on a wet April evening, just two days after she had signed her divorce papers, that someone did at last emerge from the mass of her fellow employees to lure her out of this self-imposed exile. Dr Anthony Marshall, who headed up the team running the asthma research programme on the third floor, had just turned out of the hospital car park when he caught sight of Jane Lytton grappling with an inside-out umbrella, its nylon material flapping in the wind like the broken wings of a large black bird. The rain had plastered thick strands of hair across her mouth and cheeks; the wide panels of her long blue skirt billowed up round her knees, revealing the slim legs which he had long suspected of being there, but which were always hidden by trousers or irritating hem-lines.

Anthony Marshall liked women; it was one of his most pleasurable hobbies to observe them in detail, to second-guess their preoccupations and hopes, and sometimes, to play a key part in influencing such things. Jane Lytton had caught his eye not only because of her petite, dark looks, but because she seemed to exist in a bubble-world of her own, enchantingly oblivious to the people and goings-on around her. Though he had seen her often enough in the canteen, absorbed in a book or newspaper, it was only recently that they had been introduced. The asthma research programme, to which he allotted two days each week out of his busy private practice, had entered its final year and was in danger of being drowned in unsorted paperwork and unprocessed data. Jane Lytton and two of the other more intelligent part-time clerics were being drafted in for a couple of hours each day to help sort out the filing system and generally clear the way for a final analytical assault on the findings.

By the time Anthony pulled up alongside the bus stop Jane had given up on the umbrella and was holding her handbag over her head – in a desultory way that suggested defeat – while she endeavoured to make sense of the bus timetable.

He pressed one of four buttons on a panel in the dashboard, bringing the front passenger window down with a slick humming noise.

'Let me give you a lift,' he shouted. 'It's Jane, isn't it? For God's sake jump in and I'll drop you somewhere.'

Jane bent down, peering in at a safe distance from the open window, as if wary of being guillotined, when in fact her main concern was not to drip into the car. Her hair, heavy and shiny-black from the rain, was spreading huge damp patches across her shoulders and chest.

'Dr Marshall . . . I'm fine really . . .'

'Nonsense. Get in at once before I'm arrested for illegal parking. No time for politeness in weather like this.' Divine intervention, in the form of a gratifying crack of thunder overhead, prompted Jane to yank open the car door and slither into the seat beside him.

He pulled away from the kerb at once, with a tummy-turning burst of acceleration that made her suspect that the car was something impressive.

'Where to?' he asked with a grin, weaving so expertly through the rush-hour traffic that the prospect of asking him to stop was formidable.

'This is terribly kind.' She found a soggy tissue in her jacket pocket and blew her nose. 'I'm afraid I'm going to make your smart car horribly wet.'

'Bit of rain won't harm. Are you warm enough?' He pressed a switch and a jet of warm air began circulating pleasantly round her feet and calves.

'My car wouldn't start,' she explained, 'it's been sounding funny all week – sort of clunky deep inside – and then this morning it gave one throaty gurgle and died on the spot.'

'I can recommend a good garage, if you like.' He sped through an amber light, and pulled out to overtake a bus. 'But what you need, my dear, is a drink.'

'Oh no, I couldn't possibly. If you would drop me anywhere near the main station, I'll be fine – it's only two stops to Cobham . . .'

'Cobham is practically on my doorstep. I wouldn't dream of dropping you anywhere but your front door. But first we're going to have that drink.'

Jane laughed nervously at his insistence. 'You are very kind, Dr Marshall, but—'

'Anthony, please. And I'm not kind, I'm bloody thirsty. There's a good pub in just a couple of miles – on the Cobham road – we'll stop there for a quick one and you can call your baby-sitters or whatever and explain.'

Jane, a little impressed, decided to accept defeat and enjoy the ride. She leant back into the snug curve of her semi-reclined seat, from where she could observe her rescuer without it being too obvious. With her habit of scurrying, head down, through her chores at the hospital, there were few opportunities for scrutinising colleagues. It was only now, reclining gratefully in the dozy warmth of his purring car, that Jane allowed herself to take what felt like the very large step of noting that Anthony Marshall was probably rather attractive. Though his nose, when considered in isolation, was a trifle beak-shaped and small, it was more than made up for by his wide, blue eyes and the most impressive shock of silky fair hair that fell forward, a little roguishly, over one side of his face. The smile lines round his mouth and eyes suggested he was over forty, but the overall impression was of a man far younger.

Leg-room in the front of the car was limited; after trying and failing to cross her legs, Jane noticed how Anthony's long body was bent almost double, his knees barely an inch from the steering wheel. A flash of an image of Christopher popped into her head from nowhere, skating over the memory of their drive to the coast, how his feet had worked the pedals of the old green motor like an organist.

'So, you're among the noble ranks of the working mothers,' said Anthony easily, after he had placed two gin and tonics on the table and she had returned from telephoning

Mrs Browne to explain her delay. 'I know all about them, believe me.'

'Does your wife work then?' Jane enquired, happy to get the subject of spouses out in the open, as if doing so lent some justification to the dubious business of swigging gin with an attractive husband. Yet she still felt shy about revealing the exact nature of her own marital circumstances, wary that there might be something innately pitiful in confessing to being a single mother of two.

'Barbara runs a boutique in Godalming – Octavia's – perhaps you've come across it?'

Jane shook her head. The gin tasted good.

Anthony, watching the way her throat moved and her eyes closed as she swallowed, laughed. 'I told you you needed a drink. Though I must confess I'm not in the habit of picking women up at bus stops,' he added, with just a tic of a thought about a lover called Sally, whom he had rescued from a taxi-rank. 'But you looked like a woman in need, if ever I saw one. Tell your husband you're to have a hot bath and a massage when you get home – doctor's orders,' he went on, flirting imperceptibly, enjoying the thought of her neat figure being warmed and rubbed by a man's hands.

'Actually,' Jane cleared her throat, uncertain whether she was now speaking out of a healthy need to confront her new status, or for less honourable reasons to do with the penetrating blue of Dr Marshall's eyes, 'I'm no longer married. I separated from my husband six months ago.'

'I'm so sorry, Jane – I had no idea – how unforgivable of me to blunder on like that.' He touched her hand for the briefest moment and then shook his head. 'This really is bizarre. You see, I know exactly what you're going through.' He paused, running one hand through the sleek wave of his hair, his eyes illumined with the subtlest flicker of suffering. 'Barbara and I are well down that road ourselves.'

'Oh dear,' Jane considered whether to touch his hand, in a mutual show of support, but shyness got the better of her. 'So you have children?' she asked gently.

'Three girls,' he replied in a subdued tone. 'It's not much of a joy-ride for any of us – but then you know all about that.'

Jane looked at her glass which seemed to have emptied very quickly. 'I really ought to be getting back,' she said. 'Thank you so much for the drink.'

'The pleasure was all mine, I assure you.' It wasn't until they were in Cobham itself, when he was half-way through a fascinating account of some of the theories behind the rise in the presentation of asthma symptoms, that he suddenly broke off to ask her out to dinner. As she opened her mouth to protest, he chipped in quickly, expressing sentiments carefully designed to make acceptance easier. 'I spend a lot of time on my own too, these days, with things the way they are at home. It would really be such a treat to go out for the simple fun of a nice meal and pleasant company. We could do it after work one Thursday or Friday, when I'm in town. You open negotiations with your squadron of child-minders and I'll book a restaurant.'

By the time he turned into her street Jane had agreed – with an attractive flurry of reluctance – to the idea of dining with him. Quite flustered by it all, she did her best to make a smooth, dignified exit from the car, only to be thwarted by an inability to locate the door handle.

'Allow me,' he said, reaching across her, so that his head came close to hers and she could smell the unfamiliar scent of his hair and feel the faintest pressure of his arm across her chest.

'But everything's still completely under control,' she assured Julia, one Sunday several weeks later, as they strolled round the edge of the boating lake in Regent's Park. Tom and Harriet each had a bag of stale crusts, which they were trailing behind them to a posse of waddling ducks. The unexpected boon of an early heat-wave had bestowed something of a holiday atmosphere upon the park; the grass and paths were packed with picnickers and strollers in carefree mood, prepared for once to smile at each other, as strangers do when acknowledging the simple pleasure of a cloudless day.

'Oh yes? You've gone all pink just talking about him. Doctors always do that to women – there's something sexy about the idea of them. Maybe it's because looking at naked bodies is often a part of their job; so we have a secret little notion that, because they know the female body so intimately, they should also know their way blindfold round all our erogenous zones.' She gave a mock shudder and waved her fingers. 'Ooh, the thought of unleashing all those pent-up desires . . .'

'For God's sake – I've told you – nothing has happened. Why can't anyone believe in platonic friendships any more?'

'Because they are not possible,' replied Julia flatly, 'except between adults of similar sexual inclinations, like you and me, or me and my friend Robbie. Your doctor sounds right up his street actually – fair hair and blue eyes, fortyish – he eats that kind of breakfast, given half a chance.'

Jane tried to concentrate her thoughts on the burning blue of the day; tilting her face to the sun, she walked with her eyes half-closed, pretending not to be annoyed. By the time they had crossed a bridge and started up the other side of the lake Tom and Harriet, having long since used up their supply of stale bread, were flagging badly, complaining of boredom and heat. Carrying a child each, their conversation was temporarily interrupted by a piggy-back race to the ice-cream kiosk, followed by the palaver of commandeering a paddle-boat. With the children squashed behind, their heads only just peeping out from under enormous life jackets – guaranteed, joked Julia, to drown any infant under ten – the two women took charge of the twin sets of pedals, giggling together for the first time that day, as they set off in a gentle zigzag across the water.

'He's divorced, you say?' said Julia, hitching her skirt almost up to her pants, more intent on getting some sun on her long, creamy legs, than in pedalling very hard.

Jane, feeling resignedly unglamorous in her knee-length khaki shorts, slowed her own pedalling so that the little boat could advance in something more progressive than a circle.

'Not quite, but getting that way.' She pushed her sunglasses further up her nose and turned to face Julia, who remained staring fixedly ahead. 'Look, we meet for drinks and the occasional dinner, during which we talk about our children, asthma and the weather. Christ, Julia,' she waved her arms in frustration, causing the boat to wobble alarmingly, 'I was dumb enough to think you might be pleased for me.' She almost said – only just managing not to –

that only envy could account for a response of such heart-lessness.

Julia, reclining in her small seat, was unmoved. 'Dearest Jane, call me a cynic, but the man is married, you are only very recently un-married, and the whole thing sounds highly unwise.'

Jane gave up and they finished their tour of the lake in silence.

It wasn't until they got back to Julia's shop and were sitting with cups of tea in her small, walled garden, at a safe distance from their unsatisfactory exchanges in the park, that Julia dared to bring up one of the main reasons behind her invitation to have Jane and the children over for the day.

'I have something to tell you,' she ventured, drawing deeply on her cigarette and eyeing her friend through a swirling screen of bluish smoke.

'Don't go all serious on me – I couldn't bear it.'

Julia picked a crumb of tobacco off the tip of her tongue and flicked it into the air. She was sitting facing the immaculate mound of her herb patch, her bare legs stretched out in front of her so that the longest of the chives, curving with the grace of weeping willows, tickled her ankles.

'I don't know if it is serious, or not. It rather depends on how you choose to react.'

'You're getting married.'

'No, idiot.' She threw her packet of cigarettes at Jane, who caught them neatly in one hand.

'Have one if you want.'

'No thanks.' She threw the box back again, though Julia fumbled the catch and they landed on the ground.

Wanting to make a dig about smoking and doctors running asthma programmes, but checking herself just in time, Julia pressed on with the matter in hand.

'What I was going to tell you is that Michael is seeing someone else, someone from work called Lisa.'

'Really? How on earth do you know?' There was some relief in feeling nothing more intense than a jolt of curios-ity.

Julia undertook a detailed examination of the stripes on her skirt, unaccustomed and uncomfortable at being so at a loss for words.

'He's been phoning me – sometimes – over the last few months – to talk.'

'Michael has? What for? I mean, what do you talk about exactly?'

'I've been a sort of emotional crutch, I think.'

'I think you could have told me of this blossoming friendship a little sooner,' Jane retorted, getting up from her deck-chair and stuffing her hands deep into the pockets of her shorts. Then a notion far more distasteful than the unattractive image of her best friend and ex-husband discussing her, took hold. 'Didn't you just say,' she began, watching Julia intently, 'that platonic friendships with men were impossible, especially with ones that happened to be still half-married.'

Julia, in all her mental preparations for this conversation, had failed to anticipate the possibility of such a parallel being drawn. Being caught off her guard made her vicious.

'As sexually desperate as you may consider me, I am not in the habit of flirting with my friends' husbands – cast-offs or otherwise. A series of one-sided phone calls is hardly in the same league as canoodling, candle-lit dinners and getting kicks out of meaningful if-only looks over one too many gins.' Seeing the way Jane flinched, she stopped abruptly, and took a deep breath. 'All I can say is I'm sorry you've taken it so badly.' She reached down to retrieve her cigarettes, feeling a little startled at the surge of vitriol that had momentarily overtaken her. 'He doesn't call any more. He's too busy with his new girlfriend. But perhaps you're going to protest about that too.'

Jane was summoning the children and gathering up her things. 'I have no regrets, you know. In spite of your opinions on the subject, I am happy to be without Michael. Just as I am happy that he has found someone else. I simply remain curious that you don't seem to find it appropriate that I too should embark on new friendships.'

Julia, knowing that she had made a complete mess of things, tried her best to make up for it, with offers of fresh tea and apologies for being fierce. But Jane was unreachable; she had withdrawn into herself, behind a veneer of such icy politeness that Julia even experienced a stab of retrospective sympathy for Michael.

24

Christopher lay on the sofa staring up at the patch of damp staining the ceiling. He had been reading a novel, but could not keep his mind upon it. His own novel lay, complete but for the final paragraph, on the desk to the left of the fireplace. He could not write the closing sentences because he did not yet know whether there should be a stab of hope amidst its dark conclusion. He rather thought there shouldn't.

From his vantage point in the bay window of his sitting-room, he could enjoy a picture-postcard view of the school grounds, laid out to his left like patched green carpets, bordered with the feverish colours of the hydrangea bushes, reluctant homes to a medley of lost balls. As the end of term approached he found himself longing for the boys to be gone, for afternoons such as this when he could enjoy his idyllic surroundings in peace. The energy of the children made him feel stale. Yet the moment they were gone, when the thwacks and shrieks of ball-games no longer interrupted his train of thought, he found it harder to concentrate than ever. His ears strained for signs of life outside, as if he needed to feel the existence of others to be sure of his own.

But it was to the mottled shape on the ceiling that his eye kept returning: a shape of infinite possibilities, growing imperceptibly, like a slowly evolving cloud, inviting the imagination to play games. A donkey. A boat. A house. A dinosaur. It was always a dinosaur of one sort or another – long neck, small head, a clump of a tail. The school bursar, a man with beady eyes and a nose for economies, had been promising to replaster the place ever since Christopher had moved in, years before, when the damp patch had been no bigger than a hand-print. But now it did not matter.

The cottage was to be uprooted, making way for a computer centre. Work was scheduled to begin that autumn.

Christopher had, in a detached fashion, been looking into the possibility of renting near by. He had also been pursuing, with only a shade more vigour, an advertisement for a tutor of English at the University of Georgetown in Washington DC. An application form, filled out but unsigned, lay beside his typewriter, together with a photocopy of his cv and a couple of passport photographs, taken in the grimy booth at Oxford station the day before. The pictures were not flattering. Christopher, his black hair cropped short, his eyes staring and vacant, had the look of a suspect in an identity parade: motionless, but shifty, hoping to slip by unnoticed.

He got up from the sofa, wrenching himself with enormous effort, forgetting the book on his chest, which slid to the floor with a thump; it landed awkwardly, a wad of pages folded backwards, tearing the jacket. He crouched down and rearranged the pages tenderly, before placing the book in the bottom of an open packing case. As if fearful that any further delay might weaken his resolve, he then moved swiftly across to his desk, picked up his pen and signed his name at the bottom of the application form, before slipping the documents into a large brown envelope. The deed done, he put both hands behind his head and tipped his chair as far backwards as he dared, until only an inch or two held the balance. He maintained the position for several seconds, poised and tense, before letting the chair crash back into place.

Christopher's progress with the packing cases was severely hampered by the need to create order amongst his unruly belongings. Piles of unsorted letters, photographs and papers covered every available surface; a large green sack was propped open by the door, empty and gaping, as if hungry for scraps. After sifting through one such pile and extracting only one used envelope to hurl at the sack, he turned his attentions to the less demanding task of emptying bookshelves. Picking up five or six books at a time, he rubbed the dust off their covers with the sleeve of his jersey, before stacking them into boxes. Having quickly filled all available receptacles, he wandered back over to his desk, pressing his favourite recording of Mozart's Requiem into his tape-deck on the way. The haunting beauty of the music swelled inside him, as it always did, bursting the bubble of efficiency, stirring his emotions into a mood of irresistible indulgence. Only half-concentrating, he reached down and tugged out the lowest of the desk drawers, the one that was least attended, because its runners stuck so infuriatingly. Sitting with his back against the wall, he tipped the entire contents on to his lap: bank statements, an ink-stained ruler, school photographs – curling and faded – several folders, a pad of paper that looked old but unused. Flicking through the pages, checking to see how many were blank, his eye was caught by some writing at the very back – a spider-script in smudgy biro, which he recognised at once as his own, dating back to a time before the loops and dashes of haste had taken over completely. Thinking he had found the draft of an old essay, he started to read it, curious to see whether any of his youthful ideas could impress him now, as a middle-aged English master:

Another gem of a family row to add to our collection. The usual order of play – the usual trivia to start us all off, like the bell-ring in a family quiz show. Michael took Mum's side – what a surprise – while Dad stomped off and left us to it. I mean – HAIR – for fuck's sake. Who gives a fuck? How can I live with the knowledge that I have a brother who pays money to have his hair cut once every SIX WEEKS?

I sometimes imagine what it would be like to have a sibling whom I could respect. But how can I give a toss for a man who preens himself like a fucking peacock, who reads two books a year, who thinks poetry is 'gibberish' and who believes Success=Money.

But he surprised me yesterday, turning up with that girl. Jane something. I don't think it's been going on that long. He's brought her home to show her off, before they go skiing to wherever the hell it is. A designer holiday no doubt, perfect haircuts beneath bobble hats and Ray-Bans.

I thought I knew what to expect from Michael's women, but this one is different. There is a lightness to her, a quickness, that makes you look twice, to be sure she spoke, to be sure she's really there. She's very small, with loads of hair and such strange eyes – green with black and brown – that make you want to stare.

Dad looked pretty smitten too, when she kissed him at the gate, her cheeks all pink, her ski jacket zipped up to her chin, with hair tumbling everywhere. All I got was a handshake; her fingers were icy cold and small in my palm.

When Mum and Dad had gone to bed, the three of us played cards. After a couple of rounds Michael gave me one of his looks, which of course made me more determined to stay, sod that I am. But she seemed keen enough to carry on as we were. I fetched some drinks, while Michael sulked, trying to get her attention. He put his arm round her once, but she shook it off, a glimmer of beautiful impatience crossing her face.

Michael, being Michael, played to win. She and I lost outrageously. As Michael steadily amassed his fortune, we laughed at our diminishing piles of matchsticks and formed hopeless alliances against him. I suppose I flirted, but so did she, I think. We were on whisky and Coke, but Michael stuck it out with black coffee and water, a look of self-righteous superiority pinned to the flat mask of his face. Every so often he would try to stop the game, but we were determined to lose everything. He didn't dare get really cross, because of her.

It was juvenile of course, the whole thing. But thrilling too, to feel so in league with someone like her, co-conspirators against my brother. When I finally went to bed my head was spinning from whisky and a weird kind of elation. I kept thinking I could love someone like that; that this thing between her and Michael could not last – that she was too lovely, too true.

But this morning everything was different, like nothing had happened. She hardly even looked at me. Perhaps he braved the creaky landing to enter her bed. Something must have happened to make her butter his toast and pour his coffee like a waitress. After a while I couldn't take any more and left them to it. But I keep thinking of her and of those exotic flowers, that only open at night—

Christopher stopped, mildly embarrassed for himself, then and now. Without reading another word he tore the pages from the pad and threw them into the fireplace, where he tossed a lighted match at them. The paper arched and curled, a second of resistance, before submitting to the flames, sinking down into grey feathers of no substance at all.

Their engagement had come as something of a shock. Christopher, though he was aware of her family tragedy, did not see Jane again until the day of the wedding, which he approached with philosophical coolness, immaculate in his hired top hat and tails, determined to throw confetti with the rest of them. But when she first entered the church, leaning slightly on the arm of an uncle, for a moment all he could see was a tiny bird, drowning in a sea of white. Her luxuriant hair, bound on top of her head in intricate sweeps and braids, laced up with ribbons and flowers, looked to him like a strangulation of beauty. His ushering duties complete, he stood with his eyes fixed on the crazed pink plumage of a hat in the next row, unwilling to turn his eyes to the aisle as she walked by.

But, with only a little effort, the moment passed. That she was radiantly happy there could be no doubt. Michael too seemed quite transformed by the occasion, hugging Christopher goodbye as if their brotherly love had never once been darkened by shadows of mutual incomprehension.

Over the next few months he caught himself manufacturing excuses to visit them, partly out of fascination for the way Michael – his physical presence, his every utterance – seemed to absorb her. It was like watching a person bewitched. She deferred to Michael in everything, presenting her own opinions shakily, with one eye searching the room for his nod of concurrence, as if some spirit in her had lain down in the cause of love. After a time Christopher could only find such subservience deeply depressing. The spark of intimacy, or whatever it had been, on the night of the card game, showed not the slightest sign of reignition. Realising the impropriety of waiting for a glimpse of such a thing, he withdrew from the tramlines of their marriage completely, to get on with pursuing the puzzle of his own life.

In spite of his capacity for such things, Christopher took care not to pass through the next decade like some Heathcliffean figure, punished into an exile of frustration and silent torment. If anything he went to the opposite extreme. Sometimes, in the heat of other relationships, he forgot about Jane entirely. Only when he saw her again, at a family gathering, or heard her quiet voice down the end of a telephone line, were his emotional recollections set jangling with the faint sense of missed opportunity.

It wasn't until he began to detect some element of real unhappiness in her bearing, during the charade of a dinner at the Crofts, that more vehement feelings rushed upon him, like creatures released from banishment. He was shocked by the pastiness of her face, the heavy look of her brilliant eyes. There she had sat, the husband-pleasing wife, looking so left out, so anxious to be somewhere else, that he longed to abandon their cheery banter for the cold shock of real conversation. Only fear of embarrassing her prevented him. Meanwhile Michael basked in the glow of self-importance that Pippa's surprise gathering had allowed, toasting his own success, uncaring and oblivious – so absolutely neglectful of his wife that Christopher had trudged back to his car afterwards feeling quite bruised and powerless.

The dinosaur had turned into a map of North America; a few bits were missing but the essence was there. Christopher frowned at his enigmatic companion. The prospect of Washington was attractive as an escape, but not as a future. America was nothing but a bolt-hole for the monster, a way to survive. Mustering the last reserves of a detached pragmatism for which he had once been famous, Christopher strove to look forward to the prospect. After all, he had been given his chance with Jane and thrown it away with quite astonishing aplomb. Or perhaps, as he now began to wonder, there had never been a chance. Perhaps, during those few days in Kent, the bright scenario of romantic possibilities had clung to life purely by virtue of his own imagination. The tangled history of his feelings for Jane had formed a pattern inside his head alone; there was no proof that she had ever, consciously, played a part in it. And now, there was nothing but the thought of her disdain to contend with, echoing at him in her resounding silence.

After stretching his long body so high that he almost touched the damp shape overhead, Christopher returned once more to his desk, resolved, though by no means refreshed. With the three fingers he used for typing he began to compose the closing lines of his book. There could be a blink of hope, he decided, because there always was. Not that he felt it now, but he knew it was there, lying low, waiting to pop its silly head up just when his eyes had grown accustomed to the dark.

25

The moment, when it came, was so much anticipated as to be something of an anticlimax. The committedly passionate way in which his tongue flicked in and out of her mouth felt more strange than arousing. I do not know this man, she thought, as her lips struggled with an appropriate response, and her hands made no attempt to stop him from unbuttoning her shirt and starting to caress the silky channel of skin between her breasts.

They had been to the cinema, to see a titillating Hollywood remake of an old classic, in which every nuance of charm from the original had been sacrificed to the cause of pressures at the box-office. To Anthony's credit, he kept his hands to himself throughout the film, even when promising shivers of electricity seemed be charging haphazardly round their forearms and elbows. Jane was grateful for this show of self-control, even though she knew such reticence had nothing to do with what would happen later. It would have been unseemly to neck in a cinema, that was all. They would do it at his place instead, at the little flat he had mentioned, where a table of supper awaited them, where she had agreed to go, like some kamikaze fly into a glittering web.

The flat was disappointingly bare, furnished only with the essentials. Jane, knowing full well that she was entering his lair, having at last admitted – if only to herself – that Julia's unwholesome views on friendship were mostly right, had expected more of a velvet lining to the place. Romance did not exactly dance upon the brown formica table and its four matching chairs. Nor did the padded satinette of the headboard make her feel any more lost to the moment, as the pressure of Anthony's embrace steadily compelled her to fall back into a conveniently horizontal position.

The most entrancing thing was Anthony himself, who more than lived up to her expectations as to what a new lover should do and say on such occasions. He was tender, unhurried and quite impressively adept throughout the potentially clumsy business of progressing from the front door to the bedroom without improper haste. He looked the part too. Michael had always looked funny lying down – quite disappointing compared to the vertical version: his face seemed to sag and the texture of his skin, when seen close to, looked open-pored and uninviting. Anthony, on the other hand, glowed as he drew her closer; his hair flopped becomingly into his eyes, and his nose, of which she had once been so critical, seemed to disappear entirely.

While Jane's body submitted welcomingly enough, her mind obstinately refused to climb into bed alongside. A curious, almost comical detachment overtook her, focusing unhelpfully on the improbability of her circumstances and the uncharacteristic recklessness of her compliance. At some unidentified point during the preceding weeks this coupling had become inevitable, something towards which she had begun to move with a curious, almost existential sense of necessity. Even when the snake-tongue had started its disconcerting darting-ritual, making her long for the slow, sensuous kissing of which she and Michael had once been capable, way back before the hurried mouth-pressing of latter years, even then she felt unable and unwilling to call a halt. This was what she had expected, dreamed about, flirted for and come for. There was almost a duty about seeing it through to the end.

'I'm not sure you were quite with me,' said Anthony afterwards.

'Oh, but I was,' she replied quickly, knowing only too well about the paradoxical game of reassuring a man for any shortfalls in her own enjoyment of their love-making. 'It was lovely.'

Clearly heartened, Anthony then leapt out of bed, with admirable immodesty, and proposed they adjourn for food. Jane, who felt far less inclined to offer up the flawed attractions of her own body for closer scrutiny, wrapped a bath towel around her chest before following him through. She was not hungry in the least, but remained fearful of making him feel that their evening had failed in some respect.

There were smoked salmon sandwiches, pots of exotic, ready-mixed salads and a bottle of white wine. Anthony was eating with some enthusiasm, his handsome face attractively flushed and full of smiles.

'What lovely food – thank you.' She sipped some wine and bit a small corner off a sandwich. She wondered, watching him eat with such apparent abandon, whether thoughts of his wife had invaded his mind quite as much as Michael had entered hers.

'So Barbara knows about this place of yours?' she remarked, echoing her understanding of the 'open-marriage' scenario which he had constructed with some dedication during their last few meetings.

'Yes – sort of – I mean, it's one of those I-know-you-know situations.'

'Oh, I see.' So she doesn't know, she thought, but he had to make me believe she did, in order to get me this far. This realisation brought surprisingly little acrimony or regret. Suspicions about the separation, which was so imminent but never quite happened, had always hovered close by. Talk of his marital problems had simply served as a convenient crutch, a justification for her to continue with the pleasurable and almost forgotten process of being wooed and won. It had taken away the guilt, as Anthony meant it to.

By the time he had eaten his fill, she was still nibbling through her first sandwich; the salmon tasted dry and salty. She wanted to ask for lemon, but felt it might seem ungrateful.

'Can we do this again?' he asked, reaching across the table to stroke her cheek. In spite of everything he was left with the damnable impression that she remained aloof from him, that there was some deeper, inner sanctum which he had yet to discover. She looked up, her black-green eyes momentarily startled, before they quickly softened with her smile.

'My baby-sitters will mutiny if I go out much more.'

'They can start a world war for all I care.' He picked up her hand and pressed it gallantly to his lips. 'I need to see you again,' he whispered, thinking at the same time how curiously more alluring it was to pursue a woman than to ensnare her. Though he had found considerable satisfaction during the last couple of hours – Jane's petite figure had proved pleasingly supple and soft – her silence had been the source of some disappointment. Anthony liked a bit more of a show from his women, more of a sense that he had them in his thrall. 'Same time next week?' he ventured, kissing her hand again, but this time more fervently, licking his tongue round her finger-tips and sucking her nails. I'll get a moan out of you yet, he thought, his blood quickening at the thought.

But all he got was a 'maybe,' before she firmly pulled back her hand and starting to gather her clothes up from the floor.

26

Mattie's invitation could not have come at a worse time. Not only was Jane reeling from her encounter with Anthony, but Tom was on the point of spending three weeks with his father. She felt irrationally insecure about leaving him at home, even though he was already in bed, with the inestimable Mrs Browne just a flight of stairs away. Though she knew she had no right to mind about Tom staying with Michael, it was hard not to feel some resistance to the idea. It was the thought of the new woman that troubled her most; sharp images of an unsympathetic, unmotherly female playing nursemaid with her son, glowered unhelpfully at the back of her mind.

Tom himself, ignorant of his mother's muddled anxieties, was frantic with excitement. For days he had been boasting to the bewildered Harriet of how many hamburgers he would eat, how many late nights he would have, watching telly with his Dad. 'Not your Dad,' he sniped, when he thought Jane wasn't listening, 'mine, mine, mine.' There had been no question of Harriet going too. Aside from the limited space in the flat, there was the more critical, but undiscussed, problem that Michael – who was taking time off work for this episode – felt daunted by the thought of coping with the two of them at once. Harriet was still a lot trickier than Tom, requiring much more diplomacy and ritual in the challenging areas of food and sleep. Though he used to criticise Jane for mollycoddling their daughter, he could not have faced implementing the regime of 'solid discipline' that he had himself so firmly espoused but never quite put to the test.

It was a sticky July evening, the sky crushed by cloud, when

Jane reluctantly descended the steps down to her sister's basement flat. Though she had done her best to postpone the dinner, the last-minute invitation had been delivered with such a frenzy of insistence, that she had felt bound to accept in the end. As always with Mattie, there burgeoned the little mushroom of a thought that something was seriously wrong, that she needed bailing out of some imminent disaster or other.

Jane placed her sandalled feet carefully on each of the narrow black metal steps, eyeing the chipped, week-old nail varnish on her toes with some distaste. It looked so vulgar that she wondered, not for the first time, about the health of the state of mind that had induced her to apply it. Her private life having responded to motives of the most dubious and confusing kind, she was in no mood for Mattie and the counselling sisterly role that would no doubt be expected of her.

Since there was no response from the doorbell, she climbed half-way back up the iron stairway and leant over a congestion of cracked flower-pots and smeary milk-bottles to tap on the kitchen window.

'Coming,' called Mattie, in a tra-la-la kind of way that reminded Jane of their mother. Her frizz of hair was gathered into one exploding clump on the very top of her head, from where it cascaded over her eyes and ears like a silky mop-head. She was wearing skin-tight black cycling shorts and a lime-green T-shirt that stopped somewhere around her rib-cage. Her stomach looked very white and flat.

'I'm on an up,' she announced brightly, her eyes glinting with a mauve eye-liner that matched the rather alarming shade of her lips. Having offered her cheek for a kiss, she promptly disappeared into her bedroom, ordering Jane to make herself at home.

Since there was no visible inch of surface in the kitchen, Jane took her handbag and bottle of wine through into Mattie's living-room. The place looked as though it had been the scene of a small riot. Overturned drawers, cardboard boxes, shrivelled pot-plants, untidy piles of clothes and stacks of canvases competed for floor space – as if all the inner muddle of her sister's life had finally hurled itself into the open, demanding attention.

'A bit late for spring-cleaning, isn't it?' she called, perching on the arm of a chair and fanning herself with an old magazine.

Receiving no reply, she got up to negotiate her way to the bathroom. This required sidling through a cupboard of a spare room which Mattie had once called her studio, but which now more closely resembled a dumping ground for things that had outgrown their usefulness, but which had not yet been abandoned long enough for assignment to a dustbin. A dented lampshade and a badly stained blanket toppled off a heap of paintings as she pushed open the door. In bending down to pick them up her eye was caught by the words *Triangles of Love* written in italic script on the corner of a page. Easing it out, she found herself confronted by a dense mass of black and red triangles, overlapping in dizzy mirror images of themselves. Right in the centre sat the smallest triangle of all, dripping colour at its corners – globules of red paint, like fat tears.

'Oh Christ, not that,' exclaimed Mattie from the doorway, none the less pleased to have something of hers examined. 'My geometric phase,' she snorted. 'You can keep it if you want.'

Jane, who thought the painting horrid, said she couldn't possibly.

'By the way, I'm giving up – that's one of the things I wanted to tell you.' Mattie took the painting from Jane and held it at arm's length, scrutinising it as if for the first time. 'Mediocre Mattie. A little bit good at lots of things. Not very good at anything.'

'Which means you're a damned sight more able than most of the human race,' put in Jane, feeling guilty about not liking the picture.

'That's what you always say.'

'Then I'm always right, aren't I? Anyway, you can't mean it – about giving up. Some of your stuff is excellent.'

'Oh, I do mean it.' Mattie smiled. 'Period. Final. I should have done it years ago. You can't imagine the relief,' she stretched her arms and arched her back to emphasise the point. 'You simply have no idea how awful it was to live with the guilt of not painting.'

She laid the triangles gently on top of a battered brief-case which Jane recognised as belonging to their father. The gold inlay of his intials, *DSB*, had worn away to the faintest imprint.

'Let's eat. We can take our plates into the garden. Her upstairs,' she made a face and scowled at the ceiling, 'is slobbing in Corsica – the third time this year.'

It was only as Mattie was ladling dollops of livid curry on to Jane's plate, splashing their mounds of sticky white rice with ample blobs of green, that she got round to explaining the mess.

'Moving? Where on earth to?'

'I'll tell you in a minute,' she called, leading the way up the steps, past the front door of the main house, down along the dingy side-alley that housed the dust-bins and into the garden at the back. An ornate set of heavy white furniture, high-backed and curly-legged, awaited them.

'Come on – don't keep me in suspense.'

The curry, in spite of its lurid appearance, tasted good.

'Things are falling into place at last, Jane, they really are,' Mattie gushed, unable, after so many years, to shrug off the childish sense of wanting – needing – to win approval. 'Do you remember my amazing trip to Boston – that cheap flight deal when I slept in the airport to be first in line – when I met that incredible man, who'd been involved in that famous bridge project and the university rehousing scheme?'

Jane, who remembered only that there had been a man, but nothing about bridges, nodded, dreading what was coming next.

'Well, the incredible thing is, he called the other day – just like that – and it was like we had never been apart – I mean, it was like we knew exactly what the other was going to say, what we were thinking – it was unreal. And then he suggested,' she swallowed, as if to contain some of her excitement, 'that I go out there – to live with him.'

Jane hoped her face gave only the slightest indication of her feelings.

Mattie was now vigorously spooning curry into her mouth. 'Don't you think that's wild?' she said with her mouth bulging, her eyes all poppy and staring.

'It certainly is—'

Mattie put down her plate and raised both hands with a jangle of bangles and rings. 'I know what you're going to say, so don't. I am going for broke this time. I'm packing up the flat, I've handed in my notice at work – I've been buried in shit, Jane, and it's taken a chance like this to make me realise just how deep.'

Jane did her best to be gentle. 'How well do you really know this man, Mattie?'

'We had those amazing weeks together – it was, like, really intense. Phil was married then, which kind of made things complicated – but that's all over now. He's had a really hard time,' she added solemnly.

'So . . . do you mind my asking . . . if you love him?'

'Love?' She picked up a grain of rice from the edge of her plate and placed it on the tip of her tongue. 'Oh, I gave up on all the sloppy stuff years ago. Love doesn't guarantee survival – of itself or anything else. It's a pain in the arse as a matter of fact.' She put her bare feet up on the table, showing off a pretty ankle bracelet of twisted gold. 'Phil is okay, really he is. And what's more important he's unattached and quite wealthy and – for some amazing, incredible, reason – he wants me.' She nudged her plate further away, using the side of her foot. 'I tell you, I've had it with one-night stands and getting pissed at lousy parties.'

'But what if it doesn't work out?' asked Jane weakly, cringing at the image of Mattie hurling herself across the Atlantic like a dice across a board.

'Then I'll stay and make a go of it on my own,' she retorted, crossing her arms and sticking her chin out, as she always did when she was being particularly determined.

'I'm just worrying for you, Mattie. I'm the big sister, remember? Worrying is my thing.'

Suppressing a flurry of uncomfortable thoughts about the implications of her own recent behaviour, Jane pressed on with the necessary business of being sensible; a process she was rather good at when undertaking it on someone else's behalf.

'But you need green cards and things over there.'

'I've got a tourist visa that's valid for sixty days. But once you're in, you're in – everybody says so. Loads of people work over there without proper permits.'

Jane shook her head, unconvinced of the depth of her sister's knowledge on the subject; Mattie's views of the world had always been based on the most attractive ideas around her at the time, a hotch-potch of hope and half-baked truths.

'Why not just keep it as a holiday?' she suggested, aiming for a tone that was friendly rather than judgemental.

Mattie only rolled her eyes at the darkening sky.

'Going away won't change you, Mattie,' Jane persisted, more urgently now. 'I can't help thinking that a part of this madcap plan is all about trying to run away from yourself, from what you are, who you are—'

'Put a plug in it, can't you? Christ, I should have known you'd be like this. You, who have made such a perfect success of your own life.' She got up and banged the plates on top of one another, so that the cutlery stuck out awkwardly at the sides. 'Get real, can't you? It's hard work on my own.'

There wasn't much to say after that. Mattie led the way as they filed back down into the stuffy flat in silence. Coming in from the shimmering green of the garden, the misty dusk of the summer night, Jane felt more sympathetic about Mattie's compulsion to leave. It must be like living in an airing cupboard, she thought, seeing again the cramped spaces of the flat, thinking of the hated job, the discarded paintings, the history of men who never called back.

She was about to go when Mattie, a little mollified by Jane's air of repentance, suggested that she have a rifle through some of the heaps on the floor.

'It's all going. A man from the Salvation Army is coming tomorrow. You might as well see if there's anything you want.'

Since their taste in clothes had never shown the slightest hint of overlapping, it was purely in the interests of their fragilely reconstructed peace, that Jane knelt down to examine some of the rejected items from Mattie's copious wardrobe. From the sound of things, it might be quite some time before they saw each other again.

With some relief, she extracted a silky blue scarf, which Harriet would certainly enjoy even if she could find no occasion to wear it herself. 'This is very pretty,' she said, spreading it across her knees and stroking out the creases.

Mattie made a face and flapped her hands dismissively. For her, clothes were full of associations. While other people remembered smells, or music, or food, Mattie's recollective energies always focused on dress. The blue silk scarf had been part of her costume on the night of the vile party in Hendon; the purple kaftan was further down in the same pile, ready to be put to some inspirational use by the Salvation Army.

'A witness to my seduction of your poor brother-in-law, that thing. I'm not having it anywhere near me on my journey to a new life.'

Jane stood up so quickly that something clicked in her spine, not painfully, but with a little jarring feeling of a nodule moving out of place.

'Seduction?'

Mattie smiled, rather immodestly, puckering her lips. 'Naughty I know – but it hardly matters now.'

'But I thought . . .' Jane was gripping the scarf tightly, weaving it round her fingers.

'I guess I was just in one of those moods that night,' Mattie went on cheerfully, hindsight and her present optimism granting a belated blast of honesty. 'You know – looking for an ego-boost, sort of thing. I think I'd have slept with a terrorist.' She began to laugh, but stopped the moment she saw Jane's expression. 'Oh Christ, don't play the prude with me.'

'Sorry – I mean, I'm not. I'm just surprised. You see, I thought you said it was the other way round, that he took advantage of—'

'You should know better than to listen to me when I'm upset,' cut in Mattie impatiently, not liking the look in Jane's eyes and thinking suddenly how wonderful it would be to get away from big-sister judgements. 'Anyway, it was true that he was unforgivably cold afterwards. He could have made a pretence of affection at least – played the game a bit – it might have made both of us feel better about being so drunk and silly. But I got my own back,' she added slyly.

'You did?'

'He wrote a letter – a grovelling apology – which isn't exactly flattering, if you think about it. And then he tried to ring a couple of times. I switched him through to the answering machine. It may sound mean, but it made me feel better. Anyway, situations like that are always so awkward, don't you find, when neither of you knows where you stand or how best to sort it all out?'

'Yes,' murmured Jane, 'I suppose they are.'

She was half-way up the steps when Mattie suddenly rushed back inside, reemerging with the picture of triangles.

'A goodbye present,' she said, very sweetly, laying a breathy kiss near Jane's ear before scuttling back into her burrow of a home.

27

There was no need to go out that Saturday afternoon. The forecast was rain. Outside, a grey drizzle was already speckling the air, flecking the windows with a damp mist. The house felt unnaturally quiet without Tom. Jane even missed his war-games, and the way he slid head first down the banisters in order to beat Harriet to the bottom.

Harriet missed him too, placing far greater demands on her mother to provide entertainment. After whining all morning, she had finally settled down to a whispering game involving Tom's trains – hallowed, untouchable objects when her brother was around – and several chair legs. Jane sat nearby, doing her best to cobble together a shopping list. There was nothing to buy, no reason to go out at all. Tom was the only one who ever ate anything in any quantity. Both freezer and fridge were stuffed to bursting point. After a few minutes she wrote the word 'broccoli', very slowly and neatly on the back of the old Christmas card in front of her, before pausing to suck the end of her pencil. Could she really be bothered to cook herself something so advanced as a vegetable? Harriet hated broccoli; she had been known to sub-merge quantities of it in her milk rather than suffer the repulsion of placing it in her mouth. Chucking the pencil down with some impatience, Jane sat back and watched as it rolled to the edge of the table and on to the floor. Harriet grabbed it with a squeal of triumph and began beating a blue engine across the back, scolding it in squeaky whispers for some unforgivable deed.

'Come on, you, we're going on a drive,' said Jane firmly, reaching for their raincoats and ignoring Harriet's yowls of dismay.

It was only as they approached the outskirts of Godalming, when the rain started to pound the windscreen with tropical fervour, as if trying to force her to turn back, that Jane realised she had come in search of Barbara Marshall's boutique.

With the grey afternoon stretching ahead and Harriet obligingly asleep in the back, three trains clutched fiercely to the frilly yoke of her pinafore dress, there was no need to hurry. But a panicky feeling overtook her none the less, like the sensation in a bad dream when unknowable deadlines and ungraspable challenges press upon the mind, when some awful truth is about to dawn. She drove jerkily but systematically through the grid of narrow streets round the town centre, craning her neck to see through the sheeting rain. The windscreen wipers worked furiously, squeaking in spite of the profusion of water.

It had been easy not to think about the wife. Anthony was very helpful in this regard, never complaining about his marriage, but referring to it just occasionally, with becoming hints of sadness and weary resignation. While never stating it outright, he had hinted on a couple of occasions that Barbara too had had affairs. With such skilful connivance from him, it had been easy for Jane to feel unthreatening. Barbara, from the hazy impression that she had of her, as a bored, wealthy wife who dabbled in prissy shop-keeping, did not sound like a woman capable of too much angst.

The door jingled as Jane and Harriet entered. A ten- or eleven-year-old girl sat behind the counter, reading a comic and sucking the ends of her pigtails. On catching sight of them, she immediately clambered down from her stool and came round to say hello, cooing at the one train that had been allowed to accompany them this far and unwisely surrendering her spectacles to Harriet's determined, grasping fingers.

A woman appeared from a door behind the counter. 'Can I help at all?' she asked tentatively. 'Or would you prefer me to leave you alone?' Her hair was fair and very fine, cut short round her ears and up the back of her neck. She wore a matching set of earrings and necklace – large bobbles of black and gold, to which her fingers kept returning in a fidgety way, as if to a string of worry-beads.

'I'm just looking, thank you.' Jane shuffled through a couple of racks of clothes, her heart pounding, wishing she had never come.

Everything was on sale – fifty per cent off the marked price. The styles were attractive too, sensible without being dowdy. Thinking of her pathetically limited supply of skirts for work, she began to look with more genuine application.

'It seems only yesterday that mine were that age,' said the woman dreamily, refolding some sweaters near Jane and nodding at Harriet, who was going through her lengthy repertoire of animal noises for her new audience.

'How old is your daughter?'

'Trudy is twelve. I've got two more – thirteen and fourteen – all girls.'

So it was Barbara Marshall. Curiosity, the ostensible reason for her coming, suddenly felt like no reason at all. A chilling sense of something like evil tiptoed up the back of her neck; here she was, no better than a voyeur, dabbling covertly in other people's lives, playing games with their emotions. Instinct told her to flee at once from this pleasant, skinny woman, with her bony cheeks and big smile, but Harriet was chortling with Trudy and Barbara was still talking about babies.

'I certainly had my hands full when they were small. Oh, but they're worth it, aren't they?' She hugged a sweater to her chest, lovingly. 'My husband would love another – even now. He wants a boy of course, like all men. But I just don't feel I've got the energy to go through it all again. It's been so long – I don't think I could face it. Is that terribly selfish of me?'

'Oh no – I don't think so – not at all.'

Barbara disappeared behind a grey curtain beside the changing cubicle. She was much taller than Jane had imagined, and so painfully slim.

'You're very good with her,' she said to Trudy.

'I love babies,' she sighed, pushing her spectacles back up her nose.

Jane was eyeing the main door longingly when Barbara reappeared, brandishing a dress of emerald green with a cream belt and cream trim round the sleeves.

'I don't often do this,' she said, sounding a little breathless, 'but I really do think this would look rather splendid on you.

It was in the stock room. With the closing sale it's at a very reasonable price. It's wild silk. The colour is just so perfect – for your eyes.'

'Thank you, but I really don't—' she faltered. Barbara swung the dress from side to side, making it shimmer in the light. 'Well, I suppose there's no harm in just trying it on, is there?'

'No harm at all,' agreed Barbara, smiling with great confidence now, the worry-beads forgotten.

'Did you say this is a closing sale?' Anthony had never mentioned anything about that.

'Unfortunately. Trade has been poor for quite a while now,' she explained, twirling her wedding ring round her finger and casting her eyes sadly round the cosy interior of the shop, which was decorated more like a living-room than a place of business. 'It was so easy when we started out. On a Saturday you couldn't move for customers.'

'This rain can't help,' put in Jane, wanting to be kind.

'No, no of course it doesn't.' She sighed. 'It's a shame to sell. But my partner and I – she doesn't come in at the weekend – think it's best to get out now, before things get too desperate. They say lots of small businesses are being hit at the moment, what with the recession and everything. It's all supposed to be getting better soon, but we haven't seen any signs of it.'

'I'm so sorry.'

'Believe me, so am I.' She gave a short laugh. 'It's really kept me out of mischief, this place – and the girls love helping. I'm a sports widow, you see – used to be rugby, but now it's golf. Does your husband play golf?'

Jane shook her head.

'Well, don't let him,' she warned affectionately. 'Once they start you've lost them for good. Though it keeps them out of mischief too, I suppose,' she added with a faint smile.

Jane shuffled behind the curtains to change. In her hurry over the zip she got it caught in the lining and had to come out for help. Barbara sorted out the hitch with an expert yank and then stood back admiringly.

'I knew it,' she cried, clapping her hands, 'I just knew it.'

The dress felt smooth and cool. When she turned to look at

herself in the full-length mirror, its skirt swung out effortlessly with the quiet whisper of fine silk. The main bodice was snug and flattering, following the line of her bust and waist as if it had been specially tailored for her alone. It was impossible not to be thrilled.

'You shouldn't be leaving this business,' she said quietly, 'you're far too good at it.'

'Here, try these.' In an instant Barbara had slipped off her shoes and was offering them to Jane. 'To get the full effect.' They were made of soft black leather with a small pointed heel; since their feet were clearly of a similar size and there was no question of wearing her own scuffed plimsoles instead, Jane reluctantly felt compelled to accept. She slid her feet easily into the faintly repellent warmth of Barbara Marshall's shoes, her toes curling on contact with the unfamiliar grooves inside. After only one hasty twirl she stepped quickly out of them and handed them back.

'I'd love the dress, but I think I'd better let you hang on to these.'

Barbara carefully folded the dress amongst quantities of crisp tissue paper, before Sellotaping it into a large white cardboard box that had OCTAVIA printed across one corner in large blue letters.

'If your husband throws a fit you can always bring it back – though I hope you won't. You need a wedding or something. It would be perfect for that – with your hair up, perhaps a cream ribbon of some kind—' Having put her hands to her own head to demonstrate, she dropped them with a quick laugh. 'Goodness, you're lucky to have hair like that. All mine fell out after Trudy – it's never been quite the same since.' She tugged ruefully at a few short strands.

'I think it looks very nice,' replied Jane firmly, looking round for Harriet. Trudy led her over and hugged her hard before waving goodbye. Harriet waved the train in response, as she trailed after her mother out of the shop.

Though the rain had stopped the pavements were pitted with puddles. The air smelt fresh and moist. Jane walked fast, with her head down, feeling like a spy, expecting every second that

Barbara would come racing up behind her, knowing who she was, what she had done. Harriet trotted happily beside, steering a course through every crack of water, her white socks getting soggy with rain and mud.

The wife was no longer the wife. She was thin and kind and full of hope. What Jane had chosen to regard as no more than a harmless, grown-up game, now glowered in the lurid spotlight of unforgivable dishonesty. If love had played a part, she might have felt better. Where its absence had once helped her feel less guilty, now it only made things seem worse. Anthony was an attractive tonic for everyday pain, nothing nobler than that, nothing addictive or justifiable.

That evening, when two glasses of wine had begun to iron out the significant creases of the day, Jane filled her old fountain pen and settled down in the deepest of the armchairs, with a block of writing paper on her knees. The nib, thick and worn smooth, moved with gratifying ease across the chunky whiteness of the page, as if wanting to help her in her task. Contemplative, but sure, she started at once, barely pausing until she had signed her name at the bottom:

Dear Anthony
I do not have to tell you how much your friendship has meant to me over the last few months. My pleasure in your company is not easy to hide.

But recently our relationship has entered new territory – territory in which, I have to confess, I feel far less comfortable. The trouble is, as I think you must know, there is no going back with these things. Feelings cannot be stacked away in boxes and told to behave. So I'm afraid we must stop arranging to see each other. I am not even sure how this will affect you, though I suspect it might make you cross or sad.

No doubt, if my own marriage had not failed, I would not be so sensitive about the situation in which we find ourselves. Emotional deceit was the ruin of me once, and I have vowed never to fall into such a trap again, with myself or anyone else.

I do not know your marriage. I have tried hard not to think about it. But, perhaps the support you want is there waiting for you, if only you would turn and look. The thing we all love most is to feel needed – it brings out the best in us. Whereas the hardest thing – sometimes – is to show that need.

With love, Jane.

The letter helped the guilt. And there was relief too. Wanting Anthony, enjoying his calculated attentions, now seemed little better than a way of giving up; it was good to realise that she wasn't quite ready for such a surrender. It also made her think more tenderly of Mattie, with all her crazy plans about America and the divorced man who designed bridges.

After reading her letter through just once, Jane sealed it in an envelope ready to take to work on Monday. It would be hard of course, eyeing each other across photocopiers and down the length of corridors, seeking refuge behind pillars and newspapers; but it felt unquestionably right. A new peace of mind – a fresh trust in her own instincts – settled upon her as she fell asleep that night, sinking deep into dreamy swirls of shimmering green and flickering light.

28

Michael shifted the car down into second gear, ensuring that the movement caused the knuckles of his left hand to brush against the exposed inches of Lisa's stockinged thigh. As Julia had correctly reported, Lisa Reubens worked at the bank. Though she had begun as a temp for the whole department, her finger-clicking command of keyboards and fax machines had quickly made her indispensable to several of her employers. Her indispensability to Michael, which was of a rather different nature, had been set in motion during an encounter beside an office drinks machine, whose notoriously eccentric treatment of ten-pence pieces had generously allowed them the most promising of introductions.

Having gallantly bashed buttons on Lisa's behalf, persuading a creamy-brown liquid to spurt into the awaiting receptacle, Michael took the opportunity of keeping her by the machine a little longer.

'That doesn't look like a very healthy cup of coffee.'

'It isn't.' When she smiled, he noticed a fleck of red lipstick on one of her front teeth. 'It's hot chocolate.'

'That would it explain it then.'

Lisa took a dainty sip. 'I love hot chocolate. Perhaps it's the continental in me. My grandmother was Spanish.' It was one of Lisa's endearing – and yet to some, irritating – habits to talk exactly as her mind worked. Once she started, thoughts could trip off her tongue in quite random sequences, leading down avenues that sometimes surprised even her.

As a single woman in her late twenties, recovering from the shock of losing a long-standing boyfriend to a flat-mate, Lisa was alert to the possibility of a fresh affair – preferably with the prospect of some permanence. Michael Lytton, with his swarthy looks, had already been an object of some interest, even before Rosie in Personnel had mentioned his recent divorce.

She stood to one side, feigning concern about the machine, while Michael fed ten-pence pieces into the slot to secure a cup of coffee for himself.

'Horrible, really,' he remarked, taking a swig and scowling. 'Perhaps I should switch to that stuff.'

'Oh, you should, you definitely should.' And with an instinct perhaps inherited from the Spanish grandmother, who had once graced the Milan stage for a living, she chose that moment to spin on her heels and saunter back down the corridor, her impressive chest pushed outwards, the full curve of her bottom rolling with each stride. After a moment's hesitation, she turned and smiled at him before disappearing round the corner, relieved to find that he had indeed been watching. No harm in being friendly, she told herself – and Rosie when they discussed the incident over lunch the next day.

Although Michael had the wit to recognise a crude bid for attention when he saw it, he was flattered – and lonely – enough to feel inclined to pursue it. Since Antonia had thankfully been transferred to their New York office, the business with Julia, to whom he had devoted many hours of time and energy without any success at all, had left him freshly embittered. Having felt more than a wisp of encouragement during their dinner together, he still found her subsequent reaction, her steadfast refusal to do anything beyond talk to him down telephone lines, hard to understand. It was yet another body-blow to his teetering self-confidence. Without any family intimacy to fall back on, and with Tim buried in the West Country and Jes working for serious money in California, Michael had begun to feel, for the first time in his life, as if there was no one to turn to.

Having settled the car back into a comfortable cruising speed for the last section of motorway before the Westerham exit, Michael reached for the hand of his lover and gave it a squeeze. With the prospect of an evening in a pampering country hotel before them, he could afford to feel expansively happy, thoroughly soaked in feelings of warmth towards the world in general and the woman on his left in particular. Lisa squeezed his fingers back, as he had known she would, before raising them to the painted heart of her lips. She savoured the moment, enjoying the soft, salty taste of his skin on her tongue. It had been an irksome habit of her ex-boyfriend, now married to the audacious flat-mate, to shun all physical demonstrations of affection unless they were a prelude to sex. Whereas Michael's craving for hand-holding and hugs was like an unquenchable thirst. She stroked his ear with her free hand, enjoying the swell of nurturing love inside her, a swell that had begun the moment she saw him stare with such lonely gloom into the frothy depths of his styrofoam cup, searching for something to say – anything – to keep her from going.

All her life, it seemed to Lisa, she had been searching for just such a man, a man who buried his head in her big bosoms as much out of lust as a hunger for a mothering love. Up until Michael, the men she had loved had pushed the smothering aspect of her away, wary of such a blatant capacity for commitment, seeing it as more of a threat than a treat.

Michael bent his head slightly towards her, to show that his left ear appreciated the caress. He had forgotten about this feeling of being cared for in an overt, generous way, when everything was still to play for, when nothing had turned sour. When they went to bed together, nine days after their prosaic exchanges about the varying qualities of manufactured hot drinks, he had been almost shocked – not to say thrilled – by Lisa's unashamed desire, by all the writhing and moaning that went with the unhooking of her indescribably splendid underwear. Having stopped believing that women in real life could behave like that, he immediately blamed Jane for his loss of faith.

From the luxurious standpoint provided by his intensely spoiling new lover, Michael began to feel a belated sense of injustice at how little attention he had received during the years with Jane, regarding such neglect in a similar light to the criminality of not providing services which had been paid for in advance. Without the application or know-how to ask himself why the relationship had evolved in such an unsatisfactory way, he began to excel at feeling hard-done-by, fostering a new, more ugly brand of self-righteousness about his marriage. Once the divorce papers had been signed he began to do what he had secretly vowed to avoid doing: to complain about Jane's failings, without restraint, to Lisa, who in the early days accepted such confidences greedily, receiving them as reassurance for the security of her own status in his life.

As time quickly proved however, there was no reason for Lisa to feel insecure. Michael decided, barely two months into their relationship, even before his and Jane's separation had been made legal, that they should marry. Through Lisa he found himself rediscovering lost pleasures of everyday life, pleasures that he regarded as his basic right: a welcoming smile at the end of a long day, the caresses of an unquestioning love, the sense that he was interesting. When Michael spoke, Lisa listened, wide-eyed, nodding, apparently made happy just by the sound of his voice. It was rejuvenating in the most fundamental way.

But he did miss Tom, especially since having him to stay. The visit had gone very well indeed. They got on much better without Jane around; Michael could lay down his own rules, indulge or castigate his son as he thought right, without fear of provoking any parental cross-fire. Tom seemed to enjoy it too, rising well to the challenge of being treated more like an adult. Jane had always babied him so.

It was partly because he wanted to talk about Tom that Michael had booked them into such a splendid hotel for the night. The other, more ostensible reason for this indulgence, was that the hotel was not many miles away from Crestling and the old white house. Part of Michael's plan was to spring a visit on his father. Though he knew only too well how fond Earnest was of Jane, he remained convinced, in the heat of his own ardour, that Lisa would win the old man round in seconds. He even hoped that by introducing his lovely fiancée he might improve things between him and Earnest, give them all a fresh start, so to speak.

While happily oblivious of these deeper motives behind Michael's strategies for the weekend, Lisa had the sense to be apprehensive.

'What if he doesn't like me?' she asked, for the fifth time, as they pulled into the driveway of the Country Inn, the wheels of the car crunching through the deep gravel.

'My love, he will adore you,' replied Michael patiently. He found her worrying quite touching.

Unconvinced but encouraged, she smiled in response, pulling her skirt a fraction lower, so that it met the top of her knees.

After a promising start of cocktails and a three-course dinner that left them replete – but neither too tipsy nor too full for some inspired love-making – their evening came to an unsatisfactory conclusion. The prophylactic burst at the critical moment, blasting the gossamer of romance they had so devotedly woven and forcing a discussion of the very subject which Michael had planned to introduce with the utmost subtlety and control.

'Are you likely to get pregnant at the moment? I mean – are you in the fertile bit or the safe bit?'

'You make me sound like a plant or something.' She tugged a pink silk nightie over her head and started combing her hair, which was thick and black.

'Don't be like that, darling.' He sat up behind her and placed a hand on one of her bare shoulders, massaging gently in a way he knew she liked. 'It's just that . . . well it would be something of a disaster if it happened now.'

'Our child, a disaster, I like that.' The thought of such criticism being levelled at a miniature version of her or Michael was enough to cause real tears to gather along her eyelids.

Michael, amazed and horrified by his apparent cruelty, hastily put his arms round her. 'Oh darling, don't get upset, please.'

These bouts of tears alarmed him more than anything; Lisa's lachrymal ducts flowed freely and often, smearing her lovely cheeks with dark rivulets of non-waterproof mascara that somehow intensified the impression of suffering.

'Lisa, darling, the idea of you and I having a child of our own is wonderful – I've told you that – but at the right time. That's all I mean.' He bent his head next to hers and breathed a kiss into her ear. 'I would hate anyone to think we were getting married for any reason other than our love for each other.'

She liked that and snuggled closer, clinging to his encircling arms like a child.

'You will make the most perfect mother, I know that – which is one of the reasons I feel so sure about us having Tom.' She tried to interrupt, but he gently covered her mouth with a kiss. 'I've thought about it a lot recently – especially about the timing side of things and – if you agree of course, my sweet – I would like Tom to come and live with us as soon as we are married.' He was speaking in a rush now, anxious to express the thoughts that had been fermenting for several weeks. 'Then we could have a child of our own, say three, or perhaps two years after that, when Tom is settled in a prep school.'

'Oh, but that's such a long time to wait,' she whispered, torn between wanting to please him and asserting her own desires. Coming from a large Catholic family herself, Lisa had been longing for several years to start producing children of her own.

'Please, Lisa,' he wheedled, winding a tress of her hair round his index finger, 'you can't imagine what it would mean to me to have Tom. It might be a long, hard process. I need to know that I have your full support. He likes you so much – anybody could see that. We did have fun when he came to stay, the three of us, didn't we?'

She drew away and went to sit at the dressing-table. 'Yes, we did have fun. He's a lovely boy, Michael. I would always love him anyway, because he is yours.' She sat staring solemnly at him through the lacy frame of the mirror for a few seconds, her hands folded neatly in her lap, before offering terms for her surrender.

'If we had Tom, I'd have to give up work—'

'Give it up – tomorrow.' Sensing victory, he could not suppress his jubilance.

'Tomorrow is Sunday, mi amor,' she replied, smiling at his eager face, liking the way his hair looked so romantically tousled, thinking he looked not unlike Richard Gere, even though his eyes were grey not brown. 'Come here,' she murmured, turning from the dressing-table and holding out her hands to him.

He came at once, obediently, walking the short distance from the bed to the stool on his knees. 'You have promised to marry me, haven't you?' he growled, clasping his arms about her waist and laying his head in her lap.

'I'll marry you next week, if you like,' she said lightly, as if she might only be joking, relishing the power to tease.

'Next week it is,' he murmured, raising his head to her breasts, gently biting between kisses, the flimsy material of her nightdress sticking to his lips and tongue.

The prospect of visiting Michael's father the next morning generated an unease which they both found hard to hide. On the short journey from Westerham to Crestling they hardly spoke a word, except for each to enquire of the other, every two miles or so, whether everything was okay. Each answered yes and wished it were so.

The day was hot. Lisa could feel her bobbed hair sticking unpleasantly to the back of her neck, destroying all the hard work with the hair-dryer that had made her late for breakfast. She was a great believer in appearances, in the importance of a first impression. For Earnest she wore her best summer frock, which was tight-fitting and bright yellow, with white broderie anglaise skirting the neck and sleeves. Her legs, freshly waxed the week before, were smooth and bare; her small feet were tucked into yellow leather shoes with spiky heels that sank deep into the earthy mounds of Earnest's grass, so that she had to walk on the balls of her feet, balancing uncomfortably all the way up to the steps of the porch.

The front door was propped open with an iron hand-bell that Edith had once used to summon Earnest back up to the house for meals and telephone calls. Entering the cool dimness of the hallway, the faint smell of linseed and boot polish fuelled Michael's sense of stepping back in time, so that he moved closer to Lisa to catch the sweet scent of her perfume, dabbed daily behind her ears and between her breasts. The past could be such a lead weight, he found, pulling at him for recollection and reconsideration, when, now more than ever, all he wanted was to move onwards.

His father was nowhere in sight. They looked upstairs and down, calling his name and banging doors.

'He must have gone on a walk or something,' said Lisa, worried by the furrows in Michael's brow.

'Damn. We could be here all day waiting for him.' Suspense,

disappointment and a faltering confidence in the wisdom of their visit underlined his impatience. 'He's probably hard at work in that jungle of his that he calls a copse.'

'Working at what?'

Michael shrugged. 'Oh, I don't know. He clears ditches and ties bits of string round broken fences – all that sort of Heath Robinson stuff. Pointless in the extreme, but I suppose it helps him pass the time. There's not much else for him to do these days.'

'Poor old man.'

He laughed at that. 'Don't waste your lovely pity on my father. He's fine. Very selfish and very happy. Always has been.' He thrust his hands into his trouser pockets and wandered back out on to the verandah, whistling quietly. 'I suppose we could go down there and look for him,' he suggested at length.

'Down there?' Lisa squinted at the ragged horizon presented by the tangle of trees at the bottom of Earnest's broad garden. 'Into those woods?'

'It's hardly a wood, sweetheart.'

'I couldn't possibly – not in these shoes. Surely he'll be back for lunch?'

'I don't think he bothers much with lunch. He's incredibly thin.'

Lisa sucked in her stomach – a purely reflexive action prompted by the notion of a slimness to which she constantly aspired but never quite attained – before marching, with great vigour, back into the house. After a few minutes she called out to Michael, who was still hovering, very much at a loss, on the verandah steps.

'Come and look at this. What do you mean he doesn't eat? I've found loads of things – fresh bread, cheese and half a chicken. Why don't we lay the table, get everything ready, as a sort of surprise for when he comes out of the woods?' Having made up her own mind on the subject, she was already bustling round the kitchen, unearthing plates, glasses, knives, forks – even three napkins – and placing them all neatly on the table.

Michael felt his frustration dissolve at the sight of her, the way she made herself so at home, arranging things with busy precision, her cheeks flushed, her hair bouncing tidily. He went up behind her as she was stirring milk into two steaming mugs of coffee and kissed the nape of her neck, just above a small mole that gleamed with minute, silky hairs.

'Have I ever told you I love you,' he murmured.

'Not enough, not enough.' She leant back against him, offering parted red lips up to be kissed.

They drank their coffee in the kitchen, keeping guard over wilting lettuce leaves and taking it in turns to bat flies off the chicken. Every so often they kissed, only to part at the slightest rustle of a sound from outside. As the minutes chugged by, the tension of waiting began to mingle with the gradual arousal caused by their intermittent embraces. The day was getting hotter. Michael took off his tie and rolled up his shirt sleeves; Lisa kicked off her shoes and put her feet in his lap, wiggling her toes provocatively.

'I can't take much more of this,' he grunted, not making it clear whether he was referring to her teasing feet or the prolonged absence of his father.

'We could always start eating,' She tore off a shred of lettuce. 'He can't be much longer, surely – we've been here for hours.'

'Silly old fool. What can he be up to?'

They made love on the kitchen floor. The delicious coolness of the tiles helped Lisa forget the discomfort, but their hardness left a small patch of bruising at the base of her spine, a blue stamp of a memento that stayed with her for weeks afterwards. The excitement for her was bound up with a realisation of her power – that she could induce Michael to take such a risk. For him, terror at the thought of Earnest's wrinkled face appearing at the door sharpened the edge of his sexual appetite, intensifying the pleasure of gratifying it. And there was a part of him too, the young boy part, who felt the child triumph over the adult, once and for all.

The exertion and pump of adrenalin left them so thirsty and celebratory that Michael proposed they look in the cellar for a bottle of wine. As he groped his way down the dark steps, Lisa, following closely behind, put her arms round his neck and nuzzled his hair. The light switch was half-way down on the left, in the middle of the wall somewhere. The instant he made contact with it, Michael lost his balance and pitched forward. There was time, a split second, for him to anticipate pain, before something broke his fall at the bottom of the steps. He heard Lisa scream before he saw that he had landed on the body of his father.

29

The sex made it so much worse. The thought that the crumpled body, with its blood-caked head, had been lying just a few feet beneath them as they hip-thrusted into each other on the cold kitchen floor was too macabre for words. It made Michael feel barbaric and unsafe; unaccustomed to the rawness of such emotions, he threw himself into all the business that followed with a frenzied energy, as if activity alone could shield him from the confusing assault of guilt and sorrow. After Lisa had been persuaded to stop crying, there were all the phone-calls to make: to the necessary authorities, to Christopher, who was leaning against a tree in the park in Oxford when it happened, watching a cricket match.

On hearing the news Christopher was at first enraged. Those stairs had been a death-trap for as long as anyone could remember. Only a few months before, Earnest had said, not for the first time, that he really ought to have the light-switch moved up the wall, so that it could be reached with greater ease. Such a stupid minor detail, a design fault, had no right, he felt, to be responsible for the taking of a human life. Something more momentous, more significant in every way should have done the deed.

The two brothers met in the Country Inn on the Sunday morning following Michael's unhappy discovery of the body, while Lisa stayed upstairs.

Suffering, the grey gauntness of their faces, made the two men look more alike, than at any other time in their lives. They sat in the mock-Tudor dining-room sipping their coffees and struggling to talk, groping for a way of sharing the experience more fully. But a romantic unveiling of brotherly love was not to be, though each had half-hoped it might be so. Michael was too absorbed by images he would never reveal – Lisa with her yellow dress up around the white mound of her stomach, her eyes blinking and brown; the eyes of his father, staring, gooy with blood.

'It must have been rough on you two – finding him like that. I'm sorry.'

'You've no idea how rough . . .' Michael felt again the weight of Lisa upon him, her arms round his neck at the top of the stairs, bearing down on him as he fumbled for the switch. He remembered too the triumph of the secret sex, the sweet taste of it, before satisfaction had turned so sour. And he envied Christopher, as he always had, for being close to Earnest, and now for being able to mourn him simply, with none of the complicated, uneasy feelings that surged in his own heart.

'Have you told Jane?'

'Not yet, no.'

'Would you like me to?'

'You? Christ, no. Why should you? Of course I must tell her.'

'Will you say Lisa was with you?'

'I don't know – I expect so.'

'Are you quite sure you don't want me to tell her—'

'Stop going on about it, for God's sake, Chris.'

Their fellow breakfasters looked round, momentarily diverted from their buttery eggs and flaky croissants, releasing vibrations of disapproval at raised voices in such a place, so early in the morning.

Michael lowered his voice to an impatient whisper. 'I will deal with Jane. I have some sense of duty in that respect, you know. There are plenty of other things for you to be worrying about.'

Their discussion of arrangements for the funeral did not proceed any more smoothly. Earnest Lytton had, to put it in his own words, resigned his commission from God – or at least from the God whose demands were laid out in the New Testament he had once preached so evocatively. In the light of this, Christopher suggested that he might appreciate being buried on his own land, in a clearing in the copse, perhaps.

Michael was appalled. 'Bloody hell, now I've heard it all,' he whispered furiously. 'The very idea of getting the coffin and the priest and the rest of the bloody lot of us down there—' He threw up his hands in a gesture of contemptuous despair and flung himself back in his chair.

'Forget it.' That they were capable of arguing over such a matter was enough to make Christopher withdraw. 'We'll stick to the safety of the churchyard, shall we? Just in case there is a God and he has a strict sense of protocol about such things.'

Lisa chose this moment to make her entry into the hushed elegance of the dining-room. She had suffered a great deal, she felt, and walked accordingly. Christopher had met her only once before, when the two of them treated him to lunch at the Randolph. It was on this occasion that Michael, capitalising on one of his fiancée's curiously frequent visits to what she referred to as the powder room, had confided that he and Lisa were 'very serious' about each other. While being unable to regard their relationship with equal gravity, Christopher could see that they were reasonably well-suited. Lisa was much more overbearing than Jane, much more bossy and cosseting; Michael, he realised at once, relished this side of her, perhaps because of the security it offered, the sense it gave him of being looked after.

On seeing Lisa now, a black mohair cardigan draped over her shoulders, her face a becoming composition of pallor and sorrow, he could not help thinking that the part was over-played somewhat, given that she was in mourning for a man whom she had never known. As with their previous encounter, when he had chewed politely on dry pheasant that had stuck to the roof of his mouth and caught between his teeth, Christopher could think of nothing to say beyond obvious pleasantries.

'It was such a shock – for both of us,' she responded hoarsely, laying her hand on Michael's arm and shaking her head. Her dense black hair swung from side to side in a single motion, like a curtain with a curled hem. The large diamond on the fourth finger of her left hand sparkled prettily in the morning light.

'We're going to have the funeral on Wednesday, darling.'

'I'd like to be there.' She sipped Michael's coffee, leaving a pink smudge of lipstick on the rim.

'If you don't mind – I really must be going now – so much to do—' Christopher spoke stiffly, a compelling need to get away rising inside him like nausea. 'I go along with everything you've suggested. I'll be around if you need me.' He managed a ridiculous half-bob of a bow to Lisa, before plunging through the chairs and tables for the door.

Before going into the house itself, he sat in the rocking chair on the verandah, running his palms over the worn grey wood of its arms until they were warm. The chair smelt of pipe smoke. Floating on the wisp of a breeze were voices and laughter, whether from recent times with Jane and the children, or from more distant days, he did not know. Nor did it seem to matter. A scruffy sparrow, its feathers tufted and fluffed, landed a few feet from him, its eye darting to and from a crumb of something near Christopher's left foot. After cocking its head a few times, sizing up the risks, it hopped closer. But at the last minute its courage failed; it soared off into the sanctuary of the silver birch, the one that had died, but which Earnest could never bring himself to chop down. The departure of the bird, its essential timidity, depressed Christopher beyond words, heightening his sense of abandonment.

Inside, the house was stuffy and still. There had been more life outside, where some substance of the old man seemed to linger in the warm air. Christopher forced himself to open the door to the cellar, to feel his way down the top three steps and grope for the elusive switch, the trigger of death. He had a sudden thought then, poised in the dark, that perhaps it was Michael who had killed their father, squashing the life out of him when he fell. Falling in darkness, like life, he thought.

A pungent smell wafted up from the bottom of the steps; blood and disinfectant. Someone had made a bad attempt at clearing up. A botch job. Something about this, the fact that no one had been caring or strong-stomached enough to clean the blood away properly, broke the last small twig of his defence. Sitting on the bottom step, his feet where his father's head had been, Christopher wept. It was not only from a sense of loss that he cried, but also for himself, for his own derisory attempts at being happy, for all his failures and cowardices, for the fact that he was already half-way through his life – now without even the buffer of a parent between him and the thought of death – and yet still felt weak and worthless.

With a cloth and a bucket from under the sink he set about clearing the blood away properly. He had only just finished when the phone rang. Though recoiling at the noise, hating the sense of intrusion, he felt bound to answer it.

It was Jane, as yet ignorant of what had happened, calling to invite herself and the children down for a weekend. The shock of hearing Christopher's voice, sounding so hostile and low, made her sparky and false.

'Oh, so you're there this weekend are you?'

'I, yes, I—'

'How lovely. I'm hoping for an invitation myself – but not for this week or anything terribly soon – is he there?'

'He – he – he—'

'He's in the garden, don't tell me. Well, don't summon him in or anything – I can easily ring back. Just say I called, would you? Thanks so much.'

It all happened in the weird double-time which accompanies calamity – the slow-motion of the unavoidable that happens in a flash. The moment her voice had gone Christopher knew he had done wrong. He should have been able to swallow the lump in his throat far down enough to say something. No matter that Michael had staked his claim for breaking the news to her; he, Christopher, should have said something.

Without thinking, fumbling with the receiver, he began to dial her number. But when he got to the eighth digit he made the mistake of pausing – to think the last part through – and promptly forgot it entirely. The numbers simply evaporated from his mind, floated away, like figures in a dream. After redialling, incorrectly, several times, he undertook a frantic search for an address book, a note-pad, anything of Earnest's that might have contained Michael and Jane's number. He had rifled through kitchen drawers, old phone books, even the desk in the sitting-room, before the sweet recollection of the existence of directory enquiries eased its way back into his panic-stricken head.

The number, when they released it, was so obvious, so blindingly familiar, that he wondered if he was going insane. With trembling fingers, he dialled for the last time, then settled himself to wait, leaning his forehead against the cold metal side of the fridge, as Jane had done, so many months before, when Mattie phoned all weepy and full of cold. One, two, three, four, five, six, seven rings. There was no reply.

He banged his head hard against his metal support, welcoming the distraction of physical pain. Moving slowly, half-stunned, he then replaced the phone, put the cloth and bucket back under the sink and returned to his car, locking the front door behind him.

So Michael told Jane after all. She expressed so little emotion that he almost felt cheated. He hated her control over herself, the way it shut him out. Before calling he had half-imagined her breaking down on the telephone – a fantasy of need in which she sought his comfort, as she once had, a long time ago, when they had confused such emotions with love.

Perhaps because of her restraint over Earnest, which Michael's state of muddled shock caused him to receive as some kind of an affront, he was cruelly blunt when it came to his other news.

'Lisa and I are getting married – in spite of the funeral. We feel that's what he would have wanted.'

'But he didn't know her, did he?' Jane had slumped to the kitchen floor with the phone gripped between her ear and shoulder. She was finding it hard to concentrate.

'No, but if he had, he would have, if you see what I mean.' No single aspect of their conversation was proceeding as Michael had intended.

'Oh, I see,' she murmured, not seeing anything at all. 'Just so long as you're happy—'

He felt sure she was mocking him. 'Of course I'm not happy about Dad, if that's what you're implying.'

'No, no Michael, of course not.' Jane wished only for the conversation to end. By the time he finally released her, she was trembling from the effort of suppression. In trying to put on a tape of cartoons for the children her fingers jerked uselessly over the switches, so that Tom, tutting with impatience, snatched the remote control from her and did it himself. Removing the lid from the biscuit tin and leaving it invitingly on the table beside them, she bolted up the stairs, two at a time, to seek sanctuary behind the bathroom door.

As she sat on the toilet seat, leaning back uncomfortably against the cistern, the flush handle digging into her left side, a towel pressed to her face, Jane, like Christopher, found it hard to think beyond her own loss. No more of that quiet reassurance, that unvoiced affection of which she had felt so sure; no more building and fixing for Tom; no more rocking on the verandah for Harriet, wrapped in his liver-freckled arms like a baby in a blanket, the rhythmic creaks of the chair soothing her to sleep. And as she remembered him, his thick shock of white hair, the small, bony features of his face, the crinkled, stretched-leather look of the skin under his eyes and around his mouth, the image blurred and fused with an impression of her own father and how he might have looked, had he lived so long.

A bathroom had been her refuge then too, in the cramped skiing chalet full of friends who had taken it in turns to knock on the door and beg her to come out, fearful – as they later admitted – that she might cut her wrists. Looking now at the pink disposable razor reserved for her armpits, Jane didn't fancy her chances of death. Nor had it crossed her mind that evening in the Austrian mountains. She had sat on the loo then, staring, not at the assortment of shaving appliances marshalled round the basin, but counting the cracked tiles on the floor and walls, waiting for something, for some clearing of vision, some emergent sense of what to do next, before she got on the plane home. It had presented itself in the form of Michael, hurling himself through the door, breaking the flimsy lock, like some superman of the slopes. 'It will be all right,' he had said, grabbing her hands in his, soggy pieces of toilet paper falling to the floor at their feet, 'you will come through this, I promise you.' It was his strongest moment, Jane saw now, the climax of all the time they spent together, before or since.

No more weekends in the country. Lisa and Michael would no doubt take it over as a cosy rural retreat for themselves, she thought, as she ran cold water on to a flannel and pressed it to her eyes. Or perhaps, even worse, they would sell it, to buy somewhere more convenient for London, closer to shops and motorways and cinemas.

Later on that evening, when Harriet was asleep, Jane brought Tom downstairs for a last story, pulling him on to her lap and kissing his soft, ruffled hair. He hadn't fought or sulked quite so much recently, perhaps because she had taken some time off work. Whatever the reason, he seemed marginally happier and more relaxed – more like the Tom of before, when nothing more serious than an irritating little sister had threatened to cloud his day.

'Darling, I'm afraid I have something sad to tell you.'

He sat up at once and studied her with such solemn eyes that all her bravery threatened to collapse in an instant.

'Grandpa Lytton has died,' she said, biting her lip.

There was a moment's pause.

'Is that because he was very old?'

'Partly . . . yes, he was very old, so he was going to die quite soon. But he – he died because he fell down some steps and banged his head very hard.'

'Did it hurt him, when he died?'

'No, I'm sure it didn't. It happened far too quickly for it to hurt.'

'So does that mean he's gone to heaven?'

'Yes.'

Another pause, longer this time.

'Will I go to heaven when I die?'

'Yes, of course you will.' She tried to hug him but he remained upright, unyielding.

'So I'll see him then, will I?'

'Yes. Yes, you'll see him then.' She lifted him round to look at the book, so that he could not see her face. The tears crept noiselessly down her cheeks, salty-warm on her lips and tongue, while he turned the pages and she whispered the words.

30

Julia arrived on the doorstep the day before the funeral like Mary Poppins, complete with umbrella, carpet bag and hat, the latter being of black velvet, with a wide, floppy brim, pulled, twenties style, down over her eyes and ears. She looked marvellous, though Jane worried for the hat. Harriet liked hats, not just to wear, but to chew and jump on, to fling, Frisbee-like across a room. The carpet bag was full of presents, perfectly wrapped parcels with dainty tags, invisible Sellotape and mesmeric patterns of teddy bears and trains. They were to be rewards for when they were good, she said, little milestones to get them through the next two days with the minimum amount of pain.

It had been Julia's own suggestion to come and take over the running of Jane's house for two nights, so that she could approach Earnest's funeral in peace, with time off either side to prepare and recover. On hearing Jane's subdued voice on the Sunday night, telling her in dull monotones of Earnest's accident, Julia's system had flicked into crisis-management mode, when she camouflaged all her concern with the most flagrant and tender bossing.

'I shall arrive on Tuesday and leave on Thursday. Book yourself into somewhere spoiling. Drink large quantities of whisky at all times. I did it when Dad died and it helped enormously – especially after breakfast, when things have a tendency to look their worst.'

Though she approached the idea of caring for Jane's children with no small degree of apprehension, there was a certain appeal too, not to mention curiosity, in playing at parenting for such a safely limited period. Deeper still, lay the sense – unmentioned, yet very real – that an unwelcome distance had opened up between the two of them, a distance which might best be tackled by a strong show of support at such a time.

The hand-over threatened to take all afternoon; after a conducted tour of the fuse-box, the immersion switch for the hot water, the surgery leaflet on first aid, the medicine cabinet and the children's wardrobe, Julia ordered Jane to shut up and go.

'But there's the dish-washer. I haven't explained—' Julia picked up her small suitcase and handbag and held them out to her.

'Kiss your infants and go – now.'

'Humming's okay – that's normal – but if it gurgles for anything more than five minutes you must switch the knob back to the green bit and then forward to the blue bit again – very fast or it doesn't work. When the humming comes back you can breathe again.'

'I shall breathe regardless. Go away.' Julia was now standing beside the front door, keeping it open with her foot and pretending to frown.

'I gave you the number of the guest-house?'

'At least three times, though why you can't go somewhere that sounds a little more promising I cannot think—'

'And if they're monsters – Tom especially can be horrid then get as cross as you like – or call me – thank you again so much.'

'If you thank me one more time I shall run screaming from this house and never return.'

'Don't forget to hide your hat,' she yelled through the car window as she drove off, her heart lurching at the sight of Julia with Harriet and Tom either side of her, all of them waving like mad.

Though Julia would have grieved deeply at the sight of the Sea View Motel, whose bedroom windows offered little view of the coast except for those patrons inspired enough to have come equipped with a telescope, Jane did not care in the slightest. She felt utterly remote from her surroundings, disconnected; luxury of any kind would have been wasted on her. Even when the bath taps vomited pipe-fulls of air and brown water, and the fan whirred and stopped the moment she plugged it in, she could not muster the strength to mind. Having lain on her lumpy, narrow bed for twenty minutes, trying to relax and appreciate her solitude, but feeling only hot and alone, she resolved to go out for a walk.

'Do some shopping at the very least,' Julia had commanded, 'treat yourself.' Since Jane was too unfocused to do any such thing, she bought T-shirts for the children, white splashed with paint-boxes of colour, and a cheap straw hat for Julia, which she ended up wearing herself, because the sun was dazzling and she had forgotten her sunglasses.

It was strange to feel so solitary amidst the hoards of people who flip-flopped around her in their beach shoes, making their way towards the next ice-cream, the next fizzy drink or simply back to the inches of stony sand which they had claimed as their own. Having yearned so often for just this sense of being alone, Jane wondered increasingly what she was supposed to do with it. Without Tom and Harriet she felt like a balloon lost to the sky, a pin-point on a blank canvas. Loose images flitted about inside her head; the children waving, Barbara Marshall smiling, Julia's hair, tumbling out of her velvet hat like a shower of gold; Christopher, Michael, Earnest – the Lytton men, a triangle of men. She stopped then, when the triangle came to mind, like a sleep-walker coming to her senses. The symmetry of it was appealing: Christopher, Mattie and Jane; Michael, Julia and Jane; Michael, Lisa and Jane; Michael, Christopher and Jane; like Mattie's horrid picture, triangles over-lapping, leading nowhere. Remembering the red paint dripping in the middle and thinking of Earnest smashing his skull in the dark, she shuddered, hating the notion of such patterned evil, even if it was only the mental meandering of a sad woman, drifting alone on a hot day.

The stone face of the angel peered down from her safe niche on the pillar, an expression of haughty pity on her grey, pock-marked face. Apart from the two brothers, Jane knew no one. It was a small gathering, made up of locals from the village and distant relatives whose faces were hazily familiar from family albums and the Lytton turn-out for her marriage to Michael. Earnest had been an only child and Edith's family came originally from north Scotland, so contact between the various factions was rare.

Jane had taken the precaution of arriving late, so that she could slide into a back pew unnoticed. Christopher and Michael were sitting on the right at the front, in the same row, but several feet apart. On the aisle side of Michael bobbed the unmistakable figure of his fiancée, buttoned into an elegant black chiffon dress and sporting a pillar-box hat that crawled with black lace. She kept touching her face, tweaking the netting this way and that, nervously glancing at Michael between tugs.

The coffin looked far too small to house Earnest's long, wiry frame comfortably. Did the body shrink after death, Jane wondered, without the soul to pad it out? Instead of singing, she was capable only of opening and closing her mouth, while her fingers gripped the order of service so tightly that the edges of the paper were soon damp and torn. She would have liked to have sung, to have wished him farewell with her voice; but the notes in her throat wavered so – like the terrified tremolo of a bad soprano – that she did not trust herself to release them, knowing for sure that tears followed only half a beat behind.

Outside, the burning wheel of the sun mocked their long faces and sombre clothes. The handles of the coffin glinted, flashing a last valediction, as the box was lowered into the deep hole. Jane, having kept well back till then, away from the small crowd, stepped forward at the last minute, to throw a tiny bouquet of marigolds as her parting gift. Moments after the 'dust to dust' passage, she tiptoed away, taking the long route down through the graveyard to the back gate, anxious to avoid the small-talk over sausages on sticks that was scheduled to take place afterwards.

She almost got away. Her fingers were on the rusted latch when a hand touched her shoulder, causing her to spin round at such speed that she cricked her neck.

'Michael, you scared me.'

He stood very close to her, unsure how to proceed, a visible sheen of sweat covering his white face. In the background, she could see Lisa eyeing them anxiously from behind the black cage of her hat, her head half bowed, in imitation of prayer. Christopher had his back to them, his dark head unmoving, either ignorant of – or studiously oblivious to – the side-show going on behind him.

'Thank you for coming.' Michael pulled a yellow handkerchief from his breast-pocket and dabbed at his temples. 'You don't have to go running off, you know.' He wondered how she could look so cool, in her long-sleeved black dress and dark tights.

'If that's an invitation to stay, then thank you.' Her fingers sought the latch and lifted it. 'But I don't really think it would be appropriate.'

'But there's something I want to give you, something he would have liked you to keep—'

She stopped. 'What?'

'The carriage clock, the one you always liked, on the mantel-piece in the sitting-room.'

She blew her breath out, not knowing how to respond without sounding forced. He really had surprised her. 'That's an extremely kind thought. Thank you, Michael.'

'And Lisa would like to meet you,' he added, terribly quickly, flicking his eyes away and fiddling with his hanky.

A carriage clock for a handshake with the bride.

'Really, Michael.' She almost laughed. 'Whatever for?'

'She doesn't want any animosity, you see.'

'Animosity?' The impulse to laugh faded as the absurdity of the request sank in. 'Animosity?'

Her handbag swung out as she turned back from the gate to face him properly, wanting him to look her full in the face. 'There is no animosity, Michael. There is nothing. What she thinks of me, or I of her, is an irrelevance. It does not enter into the situation at all. I am very happy that the two of you have found each other, truly, I am. I wish you every success in your marriage. There. Is that enough? Can I go now?'

'Would you say that to her?' he asked, pleading now, making her realise – with some amazement – that he was acting under the strongest of directives.

'But why should I? It is the most fatuous request I have ever heard.' She could feel her patience melting in the heat.

Michael too, appeared to be sagging under the burden of

his errand, coupled with the constraints of his heavy black suit.

'Because it would mean a lot to her,' he replied miserably, eyeing the funeral party with longing. He no longer cared about the outcome of the conversation; it was Lisa who had suggested it, the idea of happy families taking root in her head quite suddenly, but with tremendous force and such noble arguments to back it up that he had felt powerless to resist.

The cortege was now heading back inside the church for a final hymn. Lisa, issuing a piercing glance in their direction, was the last to step out of view.

Jane, who had skipped breakfast and eaten only a sandwich the night before, began to feel a numbing dizziness crawl over her, starting at the back of her neck and working upwards behind her ears and through her temples.

'Look. I will think about it. I will sit in the car and think about it. That's the best I can offer.'

She was in such a hurry to get through the gate that she caught the strap of her handbag on the side post. Michael, already making his way back up to the church, did not notice.

'But if I do come, I don't want the clock,' she called back, freshly appalled at the naïve duplicity of his tactics.

It was with considerable relief that Jane stepped under the cool canopy of trees that arched over the narrow road like the vaulted ceiling of a cathedral. Only pin-pricks of light broke through the dense, leafy roof, catching the auburn blackness of her hair in the cross-fire of their small beams. A swarm of gnats suddenly flannelled her face, causing her to screw up her eyes and run, arms flapping, to be rid of them. She arrived, panting, at her car, the last in the long line of vehicles parked up on the soft verge of the road, its wheels parallel to a dry slit of a ditch that was full of dead leaves. As she was about to get in, a white envelope, pinned under the windscreen wiper, caught her eye. With an eery snap of a sensation that she was being watched, she looked quickly over her shoulder. But the glade was cool and quiet. Distant strains of the last verse of 'Lead Kindly Light' filtered through the trees. Something scuttled in the hedge.

A cuckoo cooed, a brief cry of dismay from the matted roof overhead.

> Dear Jane
> I am sorry I must resort to the drama of a letter. It comes from having lost faith in my own voice. I certainly lost it when we spoke on the phone the other day and Dad was dead and I couldn't tell you. I tried to ring back, but you had gone out.
> My silence stemmed, I think, from shock, and, I suppose, cowardice. And Michael had said he wanted to be the one to tell you. All these things made me dumb.
> Forgive my timorousness
> Yours, Christopher.

Jane was not to know that it had taken several drafts to wring out the yearning that had seeped through his first attempts like air through a cracked door. In the end, formal brevity had been the only way to block it out. He had planted his letter when the mourners first filed out into the graveyard, slipping through the side door of the church and jogging along the line of cars, waving the gnats away, as she had done. It never crossed his mind that she would attend the reception afterwards; it was so obvious that she would hate it, knowing only him and Michael, and with Lisa there too.

Having read Christopher's apology just once, Jane carefully folded it back into the envelope and put it in the side pocket of her bag. It was a good letter, honest and to the point. She was very glad that he had written it. Standing for a few seconds beside the open door of her car, she tried to imagine how he must have felt, returning to the white house on that day, how difficult it must have been, just to answer the phone.

After driving along winding country roads for fifteen minutes or so, blowing her nose and taking deep breaths, she made her way back to Earnest's house, approaching it with all the wariness of an animal who has caught the scent of danger on a drifting breeze.

But the world has to be faced, she told herself, as she switched off the engine and began walking purposefully towards the house.

31

The first person Jane saw was Pippa, carefully descending Earnest's narrow verandah steps; one hand gripped the slender balustrade to her right, while the other patted the scant bun of grey hair that sat on top of her head like a worn pin-cushion. Jane stopped at once, overcome by timidity and awkwardness. Recalling the trance-like state in which Pippa had floated past her a few months before, she braced herself for something similar.

'Jane,' exclaimed Pippa at once, her heart sinking, 'how lovely – Michael said you might change your mind. How are you?' She made a show of hurrying over for a kiss, her round face beaming in an effort to disguise the uncomfortable twist of embarrassment and guilt coiled inside her. Something like terror had descended at the sight of Jane's composed, small figure, neatly, and so tastefully attired in the simplest of black dresses; it made Pippa feel more than usually large, clumsier and uglier than ever. She found herself longing to be back in the West Country, amongst her new friends, people who had not known her before the disasters of the previous year, people who did not know she had ever wanted a child, people who accepted her size without a little intake of breath, never imagining that it was a physical condition so recently acquired. 'It's been so long – too long – and such a sad occasion too – poor Michael seems very shocked. Hardly surprising – finding the body like that – quite unimaginable. We felt we had to come – for Michael's sake – to offer support and so on.' Her fingers patted and pressed the hairpins in her skimpy bun as she talked, while her eyes gleamed with an unnatural light, warning Jane off any notions about plunging in with references to the past.

Unnerved by such an adroit display of normality, Jane rose less fluently to the challenge herself. 'Pippa – I didn't know you were here – I didn't see you in the church.' It was impossible not to be startled again by the sheer size of her; the person she had once known seemed to have been swallowed whole, submerged by an alien body; all the original fine features were only just discernible, like the parts of an unfinished sculpture emerging from a huge rock. With her old lady's bun there was also something of the Mrs Pepperpot about her, something at once comical and sad.

'The awful thing is, we just missed it – the service, I mean – such a shame – though we set off at the crack of dawn—'

'Oh dear – was it the traffic?'

'Not the traffic, no,' Pippa replied, 'there was another reason. If you come with me, I'll show you.' She flashed a stiff smile, wondering if time might erase some of the confusing layers of anger and guilt stacked inside her. For the moment it was out of the question. There was too much hatred still, not just because of what Jane had done to Michael, but, more unforgivably, for the way she had cast aside the gift of a conventional, balanced family life, a gift for which Pippa would have sold her soul. Shutting Jane out, turning Tim against her even more than he was already, had seemed to Pippa's mind the smallest of revenges, the least and easiest thing she could do in the circumstances.

Curious, and a little concerned, Jane turned and followed Pippa towards the cluster of cars parked in the field on the opposite side of the road.

'What are we going to see?'

But Pippa was walking briskly ahead, her black tent of a dress hitching up round the back of her knees with every stride. When she got to the back of a dusty old estate, she opened the boot and pulled out two hairy terriers which she held expertly under each arm, while they licked her cheeks and nibbled her ear-lobes.

'Meet Lottie and Lionel,' she announced, trying to keep her lips and chin from their busy pink tongues. 'They're dying for a walk, poor loves – it's been such a boring day for you, hasn't it, my darlings.' They yelped their agreement, while Jane watched, at a loss for words. Having returned them to the car with the aid of several handfuls of multi-coloured, bone-shaped biscuits, Pippa slammed the boot shut and leant back against it with a satisfied sigh.

'Don't tell me – child-substitutes – I know.' She stared boldly into Jane's silent face, wanting more than anything to blast away the shadow of pity that lay across it. 'That's exactly what they are, and I don't care a bit. I'm going to breed them.'

'They look very sweet,' said Jane quickly, relieved that Pippa had voiced the obvious conclusions about babies and puppies which had so speedily formed in her own mind.

'Tim isn't quite so keen, but he'll come round, I know he will. We might even make some money out of it one day.'

'I think it's a wonderful idea.'

'I can't tell you how much we love Cornwall,' she gushed, overcome by the need to make Jane believe she was happy. 'We wouldn't go back to London for anything. Funny how things work out – with Michael and Lisa and so on.' She reached into the front of the car and pulled out two leads, one red and one blue, causing the little dogs to leap at the windows in a frenzy of enthusiasm. 'Lovely girl, Lisa – the best thing that could have happened. And of course you're all right too,' she added briskly, peering in at her dogs. 'As you might have guessed, these two darlings are the reason we were so terribly late. They tried their very best – I know they did – but we still had to stop rather a lot. Lionel's good, but Lottie hasn't quite come through the potty training stage yet.'

Jane waited for an indication that irony as well as humour lay behind this last comment, but Pippa was already leaning into the car, tussling with clips and collars. When she straightened herself, her entire face was bright pink and her breath was coming in wheezy gasps.

'Maybe I'll see you when we get back from our walkies,' said Pippa, without conviction. 'Tim's in there somewhere,' she waved at the house, 'if you felt like saying hello.'

Jane nodded bleakly, knowing that few things would make her more uncomfortable. As she watched Pippa's wide frame trot off in its unfamiliar rolling, ponderous way, both round white arms stretched out in front of her by the eager pulling of the little dogs, it suddenly struck her that her altered appearance was perhaps no more than a layer of protection. Maybe Pippa felt safer buried in her own body, knowing that pity and politeness would keep other people from probing too deeply.

Caterers in black dresses and frilly white aprons had taken over the kitchen. As Jane entered the house she was struck by the volume of noise coming from the open door of the sitting-room, where the french windows had been thrown open to the back garden. As she stood hovering in the hall she heard two female voices coming from the top of the stairs, one of them particularly loud and shrill. This is Lisa, she thought with a flash of something that felt like intuition. She walked forward stiffly, composing a smile, thinking through the brief well-wishing that she was prepared to offer, because Michael had begged her to, and because it could do no harm.

Then the shrill voice said, just as two fish-netted calves came into view: 'Michael wants the son, Tom, to come and live with us. He feels—' The voice faded fast at the sight of Jane standing at the bottom of the stairs. As her female companion disappeared across the landing, Lisa hurried on down, a smile fluttering at the corners of her lips.

'We haven't met,' she said, extending a hand, 'I'm Lisa Reubens.'

Jane did not move.

Lisa looked round for support. A waiter, a tray of full glasses balanced on the flat of one hand, walked quickly between them with a murmur of apology.

'I think I'd better find Michael,' she said, distressed by the expression on Jane's face.

By happy coincidence Michael chose that moment to emerge from the sitting-room. 'Ah, glad to see—' he began, before realising that the situation was not as amicable as he would have wished.

'She—' Jane pointed a finger at Lisa, 'she says – Tom.' Sentences would not form. She started to move towards him, causing Lisa to shuffle protectively into the crook of his arm.

'Tom?' he said, still unsure as to the exact nature of the crisis.

'She says you want Tom.' This time the words came out rather loudly, almost like a scream, which had the effect of alerting some of the other guests to the unfolding drama.

'I've only been thinking – I was going to tell you,' he muttered, hugging Lisa more tightly and using his free hand to loosen the knot of his tie.

I might hit him, thought Jane, moving closer still. But someone stepped between them.

'Come now,' said Christopher, 'come with me. Michael upstairs. Jane come with me.' She allowed him to propel her away, out through the front door and round the side of the house, down to the bottom of the garden where the swing and climbing frame sat, looking so dejected in their fresh coats of red and yellow.

'They want Tom,' she said. 'Did you know?'

'No. I would have told you if I had.'

She sat on the swing while he leant up against one of the supporting legs. The guests, knowing only snippets of the story, huddled up by the french windows, wondering at the soap-opera going on about them, and trying, every now and then, not to stare. Michael watched grimly from an upstairs window, hands pushed deep inside his pockets, his jaw grinding furiously. He would never have expected Jane to cause such an embarrassing scene, even given the circumstances. But after a couple of minutes his thoughts turned to the more soothing notion of his future wife and he smiled; how composed and beautiful Lisa had seemed next to the shrieking, dishevelled thing that had confronted them; his smile deepened; such neurotic outbursts could only strengthen their position with regard to Tom.

Christopher did not know how to offer comfort. His brother could be a determined, ruthless man; with the back-up of a new wife and a deft lawyer he might well win custody of Tom. He could think of no reassurances for such a prospect.

Jane was swaying in the swing, her head leaning against one of the ropes, her stockinged toes tracing lines in the thick clover at her feet. Her shoes were in her lap.

'Perhaps I should give him up.' She sounded dazed. 'Perhaps I should spare Tom the battle. What do you think?'

'That would be hard.' He crossed his arms, to stop them dangling, wanting so obviously to reach out to her.

'I'm so sorry about Earnest.' She spoke to the grass at her feet. 'I loved him very much. Losing a parent is always such a shock, however – whenever – it happens.'

'You would know,' he said gravely, watching her intently, wanting her to look up, but knowing that if she did he would feel scared and look away.

'There's this sudden realisation that the fun and games are over, that now it's for real, that the business of being grown-up, for which one had longed as a child, is actually very unrewarding. It's all a big con.' She pulled roughly at her tights, hoicking them up from the ankle, drawing his attention to the slimness of her legs, the bony, schoolgirl knees. 'Thank you for your letter,' she said suddenly, having only just remembered it.

'I felt so dreadful – you ringing and—'

'I know. It doesn't matter now.' She got off the swing and smoothed her hair, tucking the long front pieces behind her ears, before slipping her shoes back on. 'I'd better go before I assault somebody – a menace to society, that's me. Would you walk with me? I couldn't face meeting anyone on my own. I know they all think I'm mad.'

'Don't be so hard on yourself. Mad people have a lot to offer. Personally I prefer them to the sane ones.'

They strolled round the side of the garden, steering a safe course away from the cluster of guests, following the dusty path that snaked past the old silver birch. Though the uncut grass beside them looked lush enough, the ground under their feet was cracked and dry; the wind that greeted them from round the side of the house was warm and unrefreshing, more like a blanket than a fan. 'When does life stop being such a bloody mess, that's what I want to know.' Jane kicked at a hard clod of mud, covering the tip of her shoe with a fine layer of reddish dust.

'I'm hardly in a position to comment on that.' He even smiled. 'I've made the most terrible mess of things.'

'No you haven't – not really – not compared to me. The sum total of my achievements is really quite hard to match.' She held up her fingers to enumerate them: 'My marriage has failed. I may lose my son. I have a career as a part-time filing clerk. And I may have caused someone to fall in love with me when I had no business doing any such thing.'

He thought for one crazed moment that she meant him, but her attitude was too cool to sustain the illusion.

'I bet you can't do better than that,' she went on, now rummaging in her bag for her car keys, 'mess-wise, I mean.'

'I am alone, discontented and emotionally dishonest.' He wanted badly to ask her about the person who might love her, but couldn't think how.

'Oh, but I'm all those things too,' she replied airily, the glitter of self-deprecation in her eye. 'What a fine pair of no-hopers.' She brushed his cheek with a kiss. 'Thank you for rescuing me from making a total idiot of myself,' she said, getting into her car.

'About Mattie,' he blurted, bending down to her open window, just as the engine roared.

'It's all done with, Christopher,' she replied, having to raise her voice above the sound of the revs. 'Mattie told me everything. It doesn't matter. None of it matters.'

Christopher stood watching long after her car had disappeared round the bend, staring at the settling trail of dust thrown up by her wheels with a blank heart and blinking eyes.

The insides of Jane's cheeks were raw from where she had chewed them in a successful bid not to start crying. Now that she could weep without fear of embarrassment, the urge receded. Though her head throbbed badly, she felt some small stab of satisfaction at having – albeit with Christopher's help – regained some measure of control. To have let go of herself in front of all those people, on such an occasion, would have been humiliating beyond words.

Their talk by the swings had calmed her wonderfully. There was something about the stillness of him, the sense that he could listen without judging, that lured her out of herself, made her want to say things that were really far too confiding, given that he was a man she really didn't know very well, but who, now she thought about it, always seemed to be there, a backstage player, waiting to step in from the wings.

32

It wasn't much fun at all. In fact it was really rather awful. Tom's wilfulness, of which Julia had only ever had glimpses, was quite frightening. He seemed to relish the challenge of trying to make her cross – an emotion at which she had never excelled, anger, like confrontation, having always been an unwilling component of Julia's emotional vocabulary. Though she was good at appearing tough, there lay at the heart of her a solid belief in safely traditional things like fairness and goodwill, qualities which meant little to a raging seven-year-old.

'I'm going to eat this rubber,' Tom announced on the first morning, after three bowlfuls of Coco Pops and half the contents of the sugar bowl.

'You'll get tummy-ache.'

'Won't.' Tom raised the rubber to his lips.

'Don't be silly, Tom. Give the rubber to me.'

'Won't.'

'Silly, silly Tom-Tom,' chanted Harriet; an attempt to show solidarity with Julia which only succeeded in encouraging the opposition.

Tom bit the rubber, his impish green eyes fixed on Julia's face.

'I'm not going to watch. I've never seen anything so stupid. Come on, Harriet, let's go and read a story.' Julia swept out of the kitchen, sneakily grabbing the first aid leaflet on her way. Weed-killer, plastic bags and boiling water featured in several sections; but rubbers didn't get a mention. She even tried to ring the surgery, but the number was constantly engaged. When Tom reappeared, patting his rib-cage and making disgusting burp-like emissions from the back of his throat, she abandoned her search for medical assistance, deciding that death might be the best option after all.

As the day wore on Julia found herself clock-watching in a way that she hadn't done since her days as a sales assistant at Nelson's Antiques, where lolling of any kind had been forbidden and the small of her back had ached for the pleasure of being allowed to sit down. Ten minutes before what Jane had declared to be the witching hour, she clapped her hands and chased her charges upstairs to the bathroom. What she had envisaged as a short, routine procedure, took nearly an hour. Half-soaked and worn-out, she finally abandoned them to bedfuls of books and toys and staggered downstairs in search of a drink and a smoke. Having managed to hold back all day, she felt badly in need of a reward.

Jane's drinks cupboard was a disgrace; its contents offered nothing more fortifying than an empty gin bottle, a quarter of an inch of whisky and a sticky bottle of sweet Martini that had been there so long it was glued to the bottom of the cupboard. Settling for whisky – with a splash of water to make supplies last – she flopped in front of the television. A hospital drama was well under way: three plain nurses were confronting a rather attractive doctor with accusations of sexual harassment at a departmental party. Julia found herself siding with the dishy doctor, who was just about to give his angle on events when Tom appeared beside her, declaring firstly that he was starving and secondly, that Harriet had peed into his policeman's helmet in preference to the potty.

This proved to be merely the first in a series of interruptive episodes that lasted well beyond the ten o'clock news and a documentary on breast cancer that she had been most keen to watch. When Tom finally surrendered, a small heap of crumpled peace on top of his duvet on the floor beside his bed, Julia agonised for several minutes before admitting that she had neither the courage – nor probably the strength – to move him. Fear that one or other of them would wake granted her only the flimsiest of sleeps herself, panic whirling in her stomach at the slightest sound.

They had been doing guard-watch at the window for at least

an hour when Jane's grey Rover finally pulled up outside the house. Harriet ran shrieking to the door, while Tom promptly hid behind a book on prehistoric animals.

Jane looked pinched and tense, though her face broke into a grand smile at the sight of Julia and the children. 'Oh, I missed you all,' she cried, trying to hug everyone at once.

'Was it ghastly?' asked Julia, noting Jane's pallor and the grey smudges under her eyes. 'Have you been miserable? There's gallons of coffee.'

Though Tom had allowed himself to be kissed he returned at once to his book, leaving Harriet to continue the welcome in the kitchen.

'This place looks suspiciously tidied-up and spotless,' remarked Jane accusingly. 'I expected jam smeared on the walls at the very least. Have they been more or less okay?'

'We've had our moments.' Julia made a funny face at Harriet, unwilling to reveal the full extent of the battles that had been waged and her own desperation in dealing with them. 'Persuading them of the joys of sleep proved something of a challenge.'

'Oh dear, they've been awful, I can tell.'

'Not exactly awful, no—' She smiled. 'I think they just knew they had an amateur in charge – and took full advantage. We'd opened all my presents within about two minutes of your leaving – it was my fault, I caved in completely. Then it rained for the rest of the day. Yesterday was better – we spent so long at the park that we got locked in, but a kind man on a horse undid the padlock. Food hasn't been a problem. Tom ate a rubber in the morning – but seems to have digested it okay – and Harriet wanted sausages for every meal.' She poured out two coffees and dolloped milk into the mugs. 'Tell me about the funeral.'

Jane shrugged. 'Grim, but bearable. Until the reception. Michael talked me into going.' She took a sip of her coffee. 'I saw Pippa there. Honestly, Julia, you wouldn't recognise her. She introduced me to two yapping dogs and said she was happy, but I wasn't convinced. Perhaps I've got it all wrong, but I can't believe that being huge is part of being happy.' She shuddered at the thought of Pippa's pink, puffy face. 'She's sort of inflated sideways. I know it's not remotely politically correct to say such things, but I think she looks awful – like one of those Americans whose idea of a high-fibre diet is onions with a hamburger and two black mushrooms on a pizza.'

Julia burst out laughing. 'I must say, you don't exactly conjure up the most sympathetic of images.' She wiped her eyes on the cuff of her sleeve. 'Poor Pippa.'

Jane pulled Harriet on to her lap and pushed her coffee to the other end of the table, out of her daughter's reach. 'But it was after that when things nearly got out of hand.'

'Oh yes?' Julia eyed her quizzically. 'Were you drunk and disgraceful?'

'Not quite – though I nearly hit Michael.'

'That does sound exciting. Did he run away?' Her flippancy faded quickly as Jane, speaking very quietly, went on to explain about Tom.

'Christ – Jane – how awful. But they haven't a hope, surely?'

'I don't know,' she replied slowly, 'but I think they're going to try all the same. They'll be married any minute – having a shiny-new wife who doesn't try and hit people might strengthen Michael's case considerably.' She rested her chin on top of Harriet's head, loving the sweet smell of her hair. 'I just don't know. Tom is so wretched sometimes – the thought of Michael and me fighting for custody is unthinkable – it would confuse him beyond words.'

'Yes, Tom is sort of – full of rage – I'm not sure I was terribly good at handling it—'

'You've been completely wonderful.'

Julia drained the last of her coffee and began gathering up her things.

'Oh, I've just remembered, your friend Anthony called. I said you'd be back today.'

Jane made a face.

'Did I do wrong?'

'No, no – it's just that – well, the truth is, things did get somewhat complicated – don't say I told you so or I'll scream – and I've been trying to persuade him to concentrate a little more on his wife.'

'I hope he listens.' Julia pulled her hat on, right down over her ears, so that her eyes were only just visible under the brim. 'My hat survived several ordeals, but that weird picture of triangles lying on your bed wasn't quite so lucky. It got ripped, I'm afraid – by the fairies according to Tom – but I think it's salvageable. I've got it here' – she patted her bag – 'I'm going to put a frame on it for you. Strange piece – wherever did you get it?'

'It was a parting gift from Mattie. It gives me the creeps, actually, but I couldn't refuse. Don't worry if you can't fix it.'

'Any word from the migrant sibling?'

'Just a postcard of a New England forest, all multi-coloured and pretty. She didn't really say anything though. I give it six months at most.'

As Julia was on the point of going Jane called to the children to come and say goodbye. Harriet obligingly embarked on a volley of sloppy kisses, but Tom, having slouched as far as the bottom of the stairs, refused to speak.

'It doesn't matter, Jane, really,' whispered Julia, feeling miserable at the sight of the egg-shaped head, so sullen and bowed.

'But it does matter. It matters very much. Julia has been kind enough to look after you for two days, Tom. She has given you presents and taken you to the park. Now, say thank you, please.'

Tom remained silent, looking hard at his trailing laces, his hands clenched into fists inside the pockets of his baggy trousers.

'Tom. I am still waiting.'

'I hate you,' he shouted, turning to run up the stairs. 'I hate all of you. I want Daddy, I want Daddy.'

'Don't worry,' Julia touched Jane's arm, 'he will be all right. He's just in such a muddle right now.'

Jane shook her head, 'I thought it was getting better. Oh God, I shouldn't have gone away – that must be what's brought this on. I should have taken them both – I should have known—'

'Blaming yourself is by far the easiest option and won't get you anywhere,' put in Julia, being stern, as she always was when Jane's emotions threatened to drown her capacity for rational thought. 'Women, especially mothers, are famous for being far too prone to indulge in guilt-trips on everyone else's behalf. It may be,' she hesitated for an instant before gathering her courage to continue in such a forthright vein, 'it may be that Tom might benefit from some counselling.'

'You mean—'

'It's only a thought. Our bodies get to see doctors often enough – why not our minds? My friend Robbie swears by it – he gets the shakes if he doesn't have a chat with his therapist at least once a week.' She swung her carpet bag over her shoulder. 'All I'm saying is, don't rule it out.'

During the course of this conversation the phone rang twice and then stopped. Jane thought nothing of it until Julia had gone and Tom came downstairs looking unaccountably happy.

'That was Daddy on the phone. He wants me to go to Cornwall with him and Auntie Lisa and I said yes. We're going to camp at Uncle Tim's and make a real bonfire.'

The moment her car was out of sight, Julia lit a cigarette, wound down the window and put a Whitney Houston tape on at full volume. Any nagging sense of failure or disappointment at herself was vastly superseded by relief. She had baby-sat for Jane in the past, for short spells, when the children were younger and easier; but never before had she experienced the all-embracing nature of the task, the relentlessness of all those demands and needs. The thought of her shop, her tidy, clean flat, the single mug, bowl and spoon that sat in the drainer after breakfast, her solo routines for taking care of herself and her business, filled her with a deep gratitude. Having stubbed out her cigarette, she picked up her car phone and dialled the number of the shop.

'Good morning, Lisson Antiques, how can I help you?' came a male voice with a hint of an accent, which Julia had originally had trouble in identifying, but which she now knew to come from Sweden.

'Olaf, hello, it's me. Just checking in to see if the place has burnt down or been robbed.'

'No. We are in excellent condition. How was your god-daughter?'

'A lot more demanding than my business, I can tell you. I

should be with you in an hour or so. Can you hang on that long? The traffic is unspeakable.' She was sitting in a jam that appeared to stretch right up through and beyond the Kingston bypass.

'Of course. I am getting paid, remember?'

She laughed. Olaf dealt in antiques himself, but only by way of a serious hobby. Having run a successful computer company for most of his life, he had recently sold out and was adjusting to the pleasures of retirement. They had met when he came browsing round the shop a few weeks previously and argued over all her prices. His payment for two days of shop-sitting was, by his own suggestion, a Victorian porcelain figurine of a deer and hunter. He had one very like it already, he said, and relished the idea of an almost-matching pair.

33

Though Jane had read about fathers who developed irrational desires to keep their hitherto uncherished children with them en route to a new relationship, she was still amazed that such a course of action should appeal to Michael. Apart from perhaps the event of birth itself, he had always been such a reluctant parent, so short-tempered and unwilling to be involved, that she could only assume his motives were of the basest kind, to do with getting back at her more than wanting to bring up their son. And she suspected the awesome Lisa too, of being a driving force behind it all.

But how could a mother refuse a child a camping holiday with his father? It would be impossible to explain her reservations to Tom without alarming him and adding to the turmoil of his new one-parent world, a world in which grandfathers died and mothers and fathers took off from the family home, apparently at random.

As it was several days since she had eaten anything hot or nutritious, Jane decided to cook herself a proper meal that night. Tom and Harriet, no doubt exhausted by the antics to which they had subjected poor Julia, complied with uncharacteristic docility to the process of being washed and shoe-horned into bed. When all was silent upstairs she opened a bottle of wine from under the sink, switched on the radio, and began preparing rice and vegetables to go with a frozen chicken breast which had been wedged into the ice-packed rear section of her freezer. It was almost certainly ill-advised to eat such a thing, given that its position suggested an occupancy of several months, but it appealed more than the sausages, chicken nuggets or fish fingers, which comprised her meagre list of alternatives. She felt a belated twinge of guilt about Julia, who had clearly survived her two days on a diet of ancient cheese and squidgy fruit.

The radio programme was about black holes in outer-space, invisible vortexes of nothingness. Though Jane tried to concentrate on the scientific explanations, she found her mind wandering down far less sensible – but irresistible – avenues lined with notions about after-life and God. She longed for faith in something; it would be so much more reassuring to believe that someone, at least, was in control; she was sure she'd worry less about black holes and Tom's sulks if she could be sure there was a grand plan behind it all, even if the master of that plan was crazed or evil. Preparing a meal to such a background inevitably made her think of Earnest, bringing echoes of his comments on the importance of spoiling oneself to mind. It seemed justification enough for refilling her glass, which she did – liberally – before having a little weep over the thawing chicken. It looked rubbery and grey; Earnest would certainly have hurled it into the bin.

On going upstairs to find a jumper, she couldn't resist pausing in front of her wardrobe mirror, to see whether she looked as bad as she felt, after all her crying for Earnest and now with the worry of Tom screwed up inside her too. In recent weeks the weight had been falling off, to the point where the scales registered several pounds less than when she was a student. While a part of her relished this process, from a deep-seated female impulse to see virtue in weight-loss, it didn't suit her to be so thin, as Jane could easily see for herself. Her breasts were in danger of disappearing altogether; her bottom when viewed side-on looked agedly flat instead of round; and her chin jutted sharply out of her face, drawing attention to the hard triangle created by the ridges of her cheek-bones. Her eyes sat deep in their sockets, all hollow and staring, as if shrinking back from the outside world. Even the tightest of her trousers hung so loosely on her hips that she had taken to keeping them up with an old leather belt of Michael's, which she had found under a wardrobe on an afternoon of adventurous Hoovering.

The jumper improved things, hiding the baggy effect created by the belt and the purple stain left by Harriet's sloppy drinking habits at tea-time. Resolving, with a spurt of self-conviction, that being alone was no justification for going to seed, she slipped out of her flattened espadrilles into some leather shoes and gave her hair a vigorous brushing. A grey hair gleamed amidst the mass of dark brown. Her eyes watered as she yanked it out; but when she looked down she found two precious brown ones in her hands instead. The offending hair having mysteriously disappeared, she completed her attentions by settling a fine, black velvet hairband amongst the dark curls, before hurrying downstairs to check up on her food.

An internal debate as to whether it would be in some way slovenly to round off her feast with a few spoonfuls of the children's easy-scoop, bright-yellow vanilla ice-cream, was interrupted by an impatient knocking at the front door.

'Who is it?' she called, making a tentative approach, images of men with hatchets and sawn-off shot-guns leaping unhelpfully to mind.

When the letter-flap popped open, she hopped back in fright.

'It's me,' said a familiar voice. 'I've been ringing the doorbell for hours. May I come in?'

'The doorbell doesn't work. Is that Anthony?' She reached for the bolts and unhooked the latch.

'The very same.' On stepping inside, he whipped out a small box of mints and a bouquet of red roses from behind his back, presenting them both with a bow and a knightly kiss to the knuckles of each hand. Such flourishes, though a little hackneyed, had never failed him in the past. Jane looked gratifyingly surprised, if a little tired. There was a disappointing redness to her otherwise magnificent eyes and not the faintest hint of colour to her face. While this image did not quite match the one Anthony had been carrying round in his head, it did make him feel pleasantly protective; it held a novel appeal, to find her looking so domestic and alone.

'Christ, I've missed you,' he growled, moving forward for an embrace. Jane found herself encircled amongst rose-buds, arms pinned to her chest, while his lips pressed not very pleasantly on to hers, his tongue wiggling along the sealed line of her mouth. His breath smelt strongly of garlic and wine. It took several minutes for her to work herself free. Time enough for Tom, sitting on the top stair, to have an unrestricted view of the proceedings.

'Mum.'

'Oh my God, Tom.' Dumping her gifts on the hall table, Jane rushed – two stairs at a time – to where he was sitting, his pale face resting on cupped hands, his eyelids heavy with sleep. 'Darling, I had no idea you were awake.' She pulled him on to her lap, her heart thudding, breathless with guilt.

'Who's this then?' asked Anthony, in a jaunty, unnatural way that broke the silence like the scrape of a nail on a black-board. She held Tom closer and raised a finger to her lips, motioning him to be quiet.

She staggered and nearly fell as she carried the dead-weight of him back to bed.

'You're a lucky chap to have such a lovely Mummy,' Anthony called after them, pleased that the child was being removed from the scene.

'Who's that man?' asked Tom, as she was pulling the bed clothes round him.

'A friend of Mummy's. Now go to sleep.'

'What was he doing to you?'

'Darling, he's just a friend. Friends kiss each other sometimes.'

'Not like that. That was in-love kissing.' He screwed up his face and made a sound that quite effectively expressed his disgust.

'Well, it wasn't meant to be,' replied Jane a little desperately. 'I don't love him at all. He's going in a minute. I'd like you to try and forget all about it. Go to sleep now, there's a good boy.'

Back downstairs she found Anthony in the kitchen, drinking wine from the glass she had left on the table. His hair, which she had once perceived as flopping with roguish attraction over one eye, now looked sloppy and unkempt.

'Anthony, this really is not a good idea. I'll call a taxi.'

His elbow slipped off the table as he tried to lean on it. 'Don't do that, old girl. We've got some unfinished business, you and I. Don't tell me you don't remember?' He smiled in a way designed to be alluring, but which drew not a flicker of response from Jane's face.

'I explained in my letter—'

'Oh yes, your fucking letter.'

Jane tensed, sensing a nastiness to him, the flip-side of his never-ending charade of gallantry. I don't know him, she thought, I never have.

'Could you pour me some wine, please,' she asked, willing herself to remain cool. 'Here, help yourself to some more too.' She handed him a clean glass.

'Where've you been, anyway?' he asked, now sounding like a grumpy child. 'Couldn't find you in any bloody place.'

'I took some holiday.'

'Go anywhere nice?' He swirled the wine round his glass, sniffing it.

'I've been at home.'

'Barbara's in France. I'm supposed to be going out there tomorrow. Three weeks in some decrepit farmhouse with green scum on the swimming pool and mould round the taps.'

'It might be lovely.'

'I'd be a lot happier staying here with you.' He patted his knee. 'Come here a minute, there's a good girl.'

'I don't think so.' Taking her wine, trying not to hurry, she walked over to the telephone and dialled the number of the local cab company, which was pinned to her cork board between Mattie's postcard and Harriet's first picture of a human with limbs as well as eyes. When he realised what she was doing he hit the table hard, making her supper things rattle.

'I don't believe this. Put the bloody phone down and come here.'

Determined she would ignore him no longer, he impatiently pushed his chair back and went to put his arms around her, burying his face in her neck, licking her ears and forcing his hands up under her jumper. Jane gripped the receiver hard, giving out details of her address in clipped, subdued tones, telling them to hurry.

'Hurry? There's no hurry, is there?' He tried to turn her round to face him, but she broke free and ran into the hall.

He followed slowly, hands raised in a show of despair. Anthony wasn't used to women running away from him. It felt insulting. He hadn't done anything to warrant such unpleasant behaviour. There was no justification for it, not after so many weeks of such unbridled encouragement.

'I think you've been playing games with me, Mrs Lytton,' he

said quietly, his smile suggesting a friendliness that was not there. 'Come on, own up.' He raised a scolding finger at her. 'You've been having a little fun at my expense, haven't you?'

He was now in the hall; Jane stood just a few feet away from him, with her back to the front door.

'We've both been playing games. I'm sorry, but it couldn't go on. It wasn't leading anywhere.'

'But it was fun, wasn't it?' he said, stepping closer, his tone softening. 'Don't tell me you think there's something wrong with some harmless fun . . .'

'It's not harmless. There's Barbara.' She was speaking quickly now, her hand closing tightly round the handle behind her, ready to fling the door open and run, screaming if necessary, into the middle of the dark street. 'You know, I'm probably just like her. I mean, the whole business of having an affair with someone like me would be utterly pointless. It would be like having a second wife. I'm very neurotic and insecure and fussy when it comes to relationships. I'd make all sorts of wifely demands – I know I would – so you'd feel more burdened than ever.'

'I like the thought of you making demands—'

He was only a couple of feet from her now. She pulled open the door. 'Please leave,' she said, her voice wavering hopelessly.

'Leave? I've no intention—'

He was cut short by the brilliant headlights of a car and a loud hoot.

'Coming,' Jane shrieked, waving her hands on the doorstep like a demented thing.

Anthony folded suddenly. The skin of his face seemed to sag and his shoulders caved in. His head was pounding terribly. 'Perhaps we could—' he began.

'No,' she said, giving him a small shove. 'It's all over. Go to France. Swim in your scummy pool. Be nice to your wife.' And with that she closed the door, leaning up against the back of it with the deepest sigh of relief, unable to shake off the conviction that danger had been close at hand, that it had not just been her imagination playing tricks.

'So, what is she like, this friend of yours with all the troubles and the terrible children?' Olaf kissed one of Julia's breasts and then sat back, as if to study it more intently.

'Oh, very normal. And the children weren't terrible – I was.' She yawned, reaching back above her head to grasp the bedstead, so that the compact mounds of her breasts rose too, causing her lover to smile in appreciation.

He started to kiss her again, this time with rather more vehemence. She nuzzled the top of his head and then pushed him away.

'I thought you were supposed to be tired.'

'I was. But who are you to complain? You should make the most of such times as this – I am an old man, remember?'

'I hate your old man jokes. I won't listen to them.' She threw back the sheets and swung her legs over the edge of the bed. 'It's late. My shop opens in half an hour. Get some sleep, old man.'

He sat up and placed his arms firmly around her waist, before planting a small kiss on the mole by her left shoulder blade. 'Let us just talk some more. To lie in bed with you is my greatest pleasure. Don't leave for your workshop yet.'

She loved the way he talked. The grammatical, textbook English, learnt to perfection but still pitted with phrases that sounded somehow incorrect – subtly inappropriate or too formal.

'We shall discuss your friend, Jane Linton.'

'Lytton.' Julia flopped back amongst the pillows. 'Five minutes. Then I'm in the shower. You can brew us some of that wonderful coffee of yours. Why are you so interested in Jane anyhow?'

'Because she is your great friend. And because I am interested in you. Would you like me to meet her?'

Julia had to think about this for an instant or two.

'Do you have an embarrassment about me? Because of my age?'

'Oh no, silly Olaf. It's not that, not that at all. It's just that I haven't told her about you yet – she has so many complications in her own life at the moment – I'd feel almost guilty admitting to being happy myself.' She paused. 'And we don't talk like we used to – not nearly as often anyway. We're both so hopelessly busy.'

'That is not an excuse between friends.'

She stroked the thin smattering of grey hairs on his chest. His skin was smooth, but slightly loose-fitting, as though designed for a man one size larger. He had spent most of the summer at his house in the Swedish archipelago and was still tanned a light olive-brown. The hair on his head was steely blond and very thick; his eyes, though beset by lines – crow's-feet gone wild – were so richly blue that she had originally suspected him of wearing tinted contact lenses. But the reluctant unveiling of some gold-rimmed, half-moon spectacles in the semi-darkness of a cinema had soon put paid to that theory.

'You're right, I know.' She paused, torn for the first time in a while between loyalty to Jane and the desire to unburden herself to someone whose intimacy and opinions she already cherished very deeply. 'There was a time – a while back – when I unwisely allowed myself to become embroiled in the break-up of her marriage.'

'You made love with the husband?' The blue eyes were fearless, softened only by concern for her.

'Oh no, nothing like that, thank goodness. But we met once – a big mistake – and then he used to call me a lot. Looking back, I'm sure he saw me as the way to avenge Jane. I don't think he's a very nice man. Anyway, when I finally mentioned it to Jane – though I didn't tell her everything, only that he had called – it made things very difficult between us. In fact the whole business of her marriage going wrong has sort of upset things – I can't really explain it.'

'Call her now. Tell her we shall take her out for a dinner. Tell her it shall be the gift of your good friend Olaf Lindquist.'

Julia kissed him very tenderly, running her tongue along the dry pink of his lips. 'You are a lovely man. Thank goodness you stepped my way. We shall take Jane out to dinner soon – but I won't let you pay. Can I have a shower now?'

'No, you cannot.' He pulled her down beside him, rolling her body over to face his. 'Before drinking my coffee you have first to earn such a reward,' he whispered, brushing the hair from her eyes and kissing her nose.

34

The week that Tom was in Cornwall slouched to its conclusion like a beaten dog. On the days she was at home Jane undertook major cleaning missions to the basement and attic, filling the empty hours with a manic desire for order, as if rows of tidy boxes might impose discernible patterns upon the dishevelment of her own life. Harriet did little dances amongst the dusty heaps, flicking her feather duster at dead spiders and spraying aerosols with carefree abandon. She liked housework. She had recently acquired a Hoover of her own, which rattled and whirred very satisfactorily, and which she drove with great vigour over anything that crossed her path, a look of serious intent on her pixie face.

September, the husk of summer, imprinted its own stamp of melancholy on those days. The nights were noticeably darker, the sun whiter. The unmistakable heartbeat of winter pulsed quietly in the background, filling Jane with a kind of suspense, a dull, unpleasant sense of waiting, that cast its shadow over even the brightest moments.

Some part of this tension was lifted when she found herself called to the head of administration's kingdom of an office to be informed that, due to budget constraints beyond his control, all of the part-time clerical staff were to be 'released'.

'You mean we're being made redundant,' said Jane, which caused some embarrassed squirming before the discussion was shunted quickly on to the less painful question of financial settlements. An absurd sense of rejection accompanied her home – an inescapable feeling of not being wanted, of not having been good enough for even the lowest rung of a ladder.

'I've tried thinking of the Crofts and blaming the economy, but it doesn't help a jot,' she confessed to Julia over the phone later that day. 'How would you feel if you'd failed in the dizzy career heights of clerical assistant?'

Julia could not help laughing. 'Try not to take it so personally. The country is going down the tubes and we're all going with it. If it wasn't for that little trust-fund of my father's, I'd have landed on a park bench years ago. Anyway, look on the bright side – won't it ease the pressure on your love-life? Or am I jumping to conclusions?'

'No you're not and yes it will.' Jane sighed. 'You sound rather jolly. Have you won the pools or something?'

Julia hesitated. She hadn't been entirely honest with Olaf. There were a few qualms associated with admitting to Jane that she had fallen in love with a man thirty years older than herself, a man who wore half-moon spectacles.

'Come and have dinner', she commanded. 'We'll go out. My treat. We haven't seen each other properly for months.'

'Oh Julia, I'd love to, but not this week. Can we leave it till Tom gets home – till he's settled back at school and so on? I don't mean to seem ungrateful – it's just that I'm not at all jolly myself at the moment – I'd be lousy company, truly I would. I'm good for nothing but chasing dustballs and filling sacks for the dump. It's very cathartic. The house will be quite empty soon and I'll have to stop. I really wouldn't recommend me to anyone. I'll ring you when I'm more myself, when things are back to normal.'

On the morning that Tom was due back Jane received a starchy white envelope, addressed to her in the embossed italics she might have expected on an invitation to take tea with the Queen. It turned out to be a request for her to attend the reading of the last will and testament of Earnest John Lytton, at the offices of Masterton and Daniels on Wednesday, 18 September at 10 a.m. She was just marking the date in her diary when the telephone rang. Her hand reached for it absently, her mind still on the letter.

'Jane, it's Michael.'

'Is Tom okay?' She felt a surge of adrenalin, followed quickly by relief at Michael's easy response.

'Yes, he's absolutely fine.'

'How was Cornwall?'

'Good, though it rained a bit. Pippa and Tim seem well. They've got these dogs now—'

'Yes, I was introduced – at the funeral.'

They both paused, allowing Jane a second stirring of real foreboding. 'Why are you phoning, Michael?'

'There's no easy way to say this – the plain fact is, Tom has asked – begged – to stay with us.'

'I don't believe you,' she retorted, certain it was impossible.

'Well, that's what he says.'

The complacency of his tone alarmed her more than anything. She put a hand over the mouthpiece and drew in as much air as she could. For the first time in months she found herself longing for a cigarette, something to hold, something to breathe on, to steady herself.

'Tom is confused, as you might expect. He doesn't mean everything he says.'

'He's been saying a lot of things, as it happens.' Again, there was a self-satisfied edge to his voice that put her on her guard.

'Like what?'

'Like you're always cross with him. That you favour Harriet. That he hates his school. That he doesn't like some man who comes to stay – I must say, Jane, I would have expected a little more tact from you. Tom keeps going on about seeing you kiss. It's clearly upset him deeply.'

This was too much all at once – so many missiles against an unsuspecting target – causing her to bluster and stutter her defence, like the guiltiest of parties.

'The man is nothing. He has never stayed. Tom hardly saw anything – I mean, there was nothing to see.'

'That's not what he says.'

'For God's sake Michael—' The notion that she was having to justify her behaviour to him enraged her. 'What about you and Lisa – don't you think all that might be confusing him a bit too?'

'We're very discreet. And anyway, we're married now. Tom understands that. He's clearly very fond of Lisa.' His tone was placid and slow, exuding the confidence of the player with the unbeatable hand. 'If he was happy with you he wouldn't be coming up with all this, would he now? And as for that school you picked, it clearly doesn't suit him, I've never seen Tom more reluctant about anything—'

It was hard not to shout. Panic was rising fast, as the realisation of what was at stake sank in.

'He always says he doesn't like school before term starts. After the first day he's fine. But then, you wouldn't know such things, because you were never interested. Perhaps,' she spoke very slowly, a knife-edge to her tone, 'perhaps you could take the trouble to enlighten me as to why your son is suddenly of such mighty interest to you, when you spent the first six years of his life doing your utmost to avoid him?'

'That is a bloody lie.'

'Could I talk to Tom now please?'

There were a few muffled rustles before Tom's shrill voice came on the line.

'Hello, Mummy.'

'Hello, darling. Have you had a lovely time?'

'Super.'

'Tell me some of the things you did.'

'We built a castle with ten towers on the beach, but it was too cold to swim. We stayed in a caravan with a big telly in it at Uncle Tim's and I helped build the fire. And Daddy says I can stay with him much longer if I want to.'

A desperate ache was swelling in the pit of her stomach, pushing up through her chest so that she had to fight to breathe.

'And what do you want, my love?'

'I want to stay.' There wasn't even a hesitation. An adult might have paused, to be polite.

'Do you like Lisa?'

'She's nice. She's good at drawing aeroplanes.' He did stop then, but only for an instant. 'Daddy says I could see you and Harriet whenever I wanted. He says I can go to a much nicer school than my old one.'

'I see. Could I talk to Daddy again now, darling? Remember Mummy loves you very much. I'll see you soon—' But he had already gone.

'See what I mean?' drawled Michael.

'He's barely seven. He believes what you tell him. He doesn't realise the implications of it – how the hell can he?'

'Oh, I think he realises well enough—'

A kind of hatred, a new, raw feeling had taken hold, making her voice deep and hard. 'You can't just keep him, you know. Life's not that simple, Michael.'

'You did it to me,' he said, very softly, loving the satisfaction of being able to say such a thing.

'You agreed—'

'You didn't give me much choice.'

'So this is revenge, after all. Christ, that's low – even for you.'

'It is nothing of the sort. Tom is my son too.' He cleared his throat. 'Look, I realise this is upsetting for you. Would you like me to call back when you're a bit more under control?' Lisa had come to stand beside him, laying her hand supportively on one shoulder. Behind her Tom was watching a video of Batman, using the console to re-run scenes he found particularly exciting.

Jane's voice was brittle from the effort of control. It gave Michael the most perverse pleasure to be able to make her struggle so.

'I will not get more "under control" about this, ever. I trusted you, Michael. If I had thought for one moment that—'

'Then trust me to look after him. It's what he wants – you heard for yourself. Neither Lisa nor I are forcing him into anything.' He squeezed Lisa's fingers with his free hand. 'Though I will admit to being pleased – how could I not be? Any father in my position—'

She had stopped listening. Having said to Julia that she could not stomach the thought of distressing Tom with an open fight against Michael, she now knew this to be untrue. She would fight for ever, when the time was right. For now, the only sensible course open to her was acquiescence. She stroked Harriet's curly head; as if sensing that calamity of some sort had seeped into their lives, she had crawled on to Jane's lap and was snuggling against her, as if trying to burrow back inside.

'So, when can I see him then? You're not going to change your mind about that, are you?'

'Of course not – so long as you promise to return him, that is.' That Tom himself had elected to stay had given Michael the most wonderful blast of confidence. He felt he could afford to be magnanimous. 'Let me see, we're away the next couple of weekends, and then there's the business of starting a new school . . . I tell you what, I'll call you back—'

'No. Don't call me back. Tell me now.'

'Steady on there.' He winked at Lisa. 'Let's look in the diary, shall we?' She could hear him turning pages. 'The last weekend in September looks good for us.' The casual tone of his voice cut deep; he could have been talking to a holiday tour operator.

In the end she agreed to his suggestion, because she had to. Brain-washed or not, Tom had asked to live with his father. He had not been kidnapped or drugged. He had asked to live with his father and the new wife who drew aeroplanes. Until she could get some advice on her legal position, there was nothing to do but submit; fighting too hard too soon might ruin everything. For the moment, the single overriding priority was to be allowed to see Tom again.

That night she brought a confused, sleepy Harriet into bed with her, needing the comfort, needing the clinging of the small arms around her neck in the dark.

35

Several strands of hair, thin, silver threads, stretched across the dome of the shiny-pink scalp of the man in the corner, from the tip of one protuberant ear to the other. Jane couldn't remember the man's name, but she knew he was going to tell them about Earnest's last wishes. There were many things she now had trouble remembering, her mind having taken to swimming off in directions of its own, dragging the immediate present with it and leaving her stranded in a limbo of dazed nothingness. Her eyes roamed round the room, noting the plush furnishings, the heavy burgundy velvet, the dark wood.

After sitting quietly gnawing on a bunch of keys for ten minutes, Harriet had embarked on a more detailed investigation of her surroundings, plucking at trouser-legs and lunging for teaspoons. Jane, who was the only one already sitting down, watched vacantly. The room was hot. If she stood up she felt she might collapse and drown in the deep wine-red of the carpet.

There were about ten people gathered in all, standing in a small-talking semi-circle, sipping from thin china cups, waiting for some signal to move into the three rows of high-backed chairs beside them. Michael, having come over with a stiff greeting and a hug for Harriet, had positioned himself at Lisa's side, with his back to Jane. She thought she recognised a few of the other faces from the funeral; but soon they all merged into a single blur of dark suits and ties. Except for Lisa, whose electric-blue dress and matching shoes lit up the room like a beacon. When Harriet tugged at the crisp crease of her hem, she pretended not to notice. Michael turned with a grimace for Jane.

She leaned forward heavily, still loath to abandon her chair.

'Harriet, sweetheart,' she called, in a voice so devoid of conviction or authority that her daughter did not even deign to acknowledge it.

Now huffing with audible disapproval, Michael pulled Harriet away from a precarious tower-like construction of cups and brought her, whining and wriggling like an eel, over to the other side of the room.

'Really, Jane, this is hardly the place to bring a child.'

'Mrs Browne had a migraine.'

'How unfortunate.'

'How is Tom?' She had already asked once, but needed to know again.

'I told you – he's fine.'

'And school?'

'No problems to speak of.'

'You mean, there are problems?'

'I mean nothing of the sort. Tom is perfectly well. Now if you'll excuse me—'

'Michael – it's so hot in here.' She fanned her face with her hand. 'You couldn't open the window or something, could you?'

'It is a little stuffy. I'll see what I can do. I wish to God Christopher would hurry up and get here.'

'Oh, so that's why we're all waiting.'

'What did you think we were doing? These people have got better things to do with their time – as indeed I have – but then my dear brother has never been exactly renowned for his punctuality.'

At that moment Christopher walked in, wind-swept and out of breath, looking daringly casual in his beige cords and crumpled green shirt. His hair, which had grown considerably over the summer, was wavy and tousled, contrasting sharply with the careful grooming evident on his brother's head. Lisa had spent several minutes that morning attending to Michael with her blow-dryer; after an initial resistance, he had succumbed completely, seduced by the rubbing circular movements of her fingers over his scalp and most pleased at the taming effect her ministrations had on his hair.

The moment Christopher appeared someone clapped their hands and everybody began to sit down, there being no time, apparently, for the luxury of familial greetings. Jane did her best to settle Harriet in her lap, but quiet co-operation was not high on her daughter's list of priorities that morning. After resisting fiercely for a few moments she tried to stand up, her feet digging uncomfortably into Jane's knees, while her chubby fingers clutched mercilessly at her hair and earrings.

'May I take her for a bit?'

Christopher had crept over from his place in the back row and was crouching beside them. Too relieved to protest, Jane let the eager Harriet flop into her uncle's outstretched arms and turned her attention back to the front of the room. The man with the sparse roof of hair was addressing them from behind a wide desk with a leather inlay, an angle-poise lamp bent towards his face like a microphone. He had a nasal drone of a voice that made Jane want to close her eyes.

'Thank you all for coming – dear friend Earnest Lytton – time it's taken – letter of wishes – a few surprises – honour his decisions—'

The words came at her in a broken, meaningless volley of phrases. She turned to check on Harriet, who was pulling on Christopher's nose and having her own tweaked in return.

'– come to the main point. According to Mr Lytton's wishes, his eldest son, Michael Lytton, is to receive liquid assets and stock holdings, amounting to a total value of fifteen thousand pounds. While his house,' here the lawyer cleared his throat and stroked the point of his thin nose, 'according to the said Mr Lytton's last will and testament, he bequeaths the house and its contents to his second son, Christopher Lytton and,' he paused again, 'and Mrs Jane Lytton, to be possessed jointly by these two persons.'

Without turning her head, Jane became aware of several things at once: of Lisa grasping Michael's arm, of heads swivelling, of Christopher gently releasing Harriet who toddled back up to the front. Jane, meanwhile, stared resolutely ahead, into the deep, glossy wood of the empty seat before her. This cannot be, she thought, feeling dreamy and detached, this cannot be.

The rest of the proceedings comprised formalities and details that floated over the heads of the listeners like dust after an explosion. The real blow had already been struck: the younger brother and the ex-wife of the elder brother had been favoured, together. While the elder brother had been slighted, given a mere sop in comparison. An unmistakable whiff of scandal hung in the air, lingering in the silence of unexpressed outrage, surprise and plain curiosity.

When they were dismissed, like a class of new schoolchildren, no one knew quite where to go, how to leave the room. Michael looked as if he wanted to come across to Jane, but Lisa, who had a tight grip on his elbow, led him away, the arrow of her nose aimed firmly at the ceiling. The rest followed, murmuring amongst themselves as they shuffled across the carpeted corridor towards the wrought-iron railings of the stairwell.

Only the guilty parties remained, the inheritors. There were a few moments of silence before Christopher burst out laughing.

'The old devil. What a trick to play. Poor old Michael.'

Jane found herself laughing too, jelly-like from shock and release of tension. 'I can't believe it. Why on earth would he do such a thing?'

'I suppose – I can only think – it was because he saw who needed – who would enjoy – the old place the most. You've got to admire his cheek – though I'm not sure Michael will see it in such terms.' He edged his way through the chairs towards her, his heart racing with something like euphoria, an exultation that was full of fear and pleasure. 'Congratulations, anyway, if that's the appropriate thing to say.'

'Of course it's impossible,' she began, suddenly struck by the impracticability of Earnest's scheming. 'You must buy me out or whatever one does in such situations.'

'Buy you out? I wouldn't dream of it.' The solicitor put his head round the door and quickly disappeared again, indicating with a wave that there was no immediate hurry for them to leave. 'In fact,' Christopher moved over to the window from where the roofs of cars and the striped tops of shop canopies were visible in the street several stories below, 'in fact, you can consider the place your own for the next year at least.'

'Whatever do you mean?'

'I'm going abroad.'

'You can't—'

'I beg your pardon.' He spoke quite sharply, spinning round from the open window to face her.

'I just meant—' but she couldn't think what she had meant at all.

'What were you going to say?'

The stuffiness of the office came at her again like the blast of a fan-heater. 'Nothing – I was just going to ask where you were going.' The straps of her handbag were twisted round her fingers, leather sliding on sweat.

'Washington DC. I've been accepted as visiting professor in English at Georgetown University. I applied months ago. I felt I needed a change.' He peered down at the traffic again. 'I felt I was starting to merge in with the damp on my walls.'

'Yes, I see,' she replied, in a way that made him suspect she hadn't really been listening. Harriet was lying on the carpet at her feet, sucking her thumb and winding a silky coil of hair round the index finger of her other hand. 'I ought to take her home. She's tired. So am I.' Jane stood up and stretched; her joints felt bruised and stiff. 'Thank you so much for taking Harriet. I'm feeling sort of weak today. I think I might be going down with something.'

'You ought to live there,' he said suddenly.

'Where?'

'At the white house – while I'm gone. Rent your place and move to the country. There's a good school in Crestling. Some village biddy could do your cleaning while you grew vegetables and kept chickens and things.'

She had to laugh. 'You can't be serious.'

'But I am – deadly serious. You should do it, I'll put it in writing that it's all right by me, the co-owner' – he couldn't help grinning – 'then at least you've got the option.'

'My goodness, I don't know what to say.' The idea was instantly appealing. 'But . . . I should pay you some sort of rent or something—'

'If you live in the house you'll be doing both of us a favour. Rot and wood-worm will take one look at you lot and run like hell.' He rubbed his hands together, as if absolving himself from further debate. 'Now then, how about a farewell drink?

A coffee – anything. We ought to toast our new-found wealth, you know,' he added, seeing her face assume an expression that could only be a prelude to refusal.

'I really – I think – I had better not.' She looked at her watch, without registering what it said.

'Are you thirsty, little one?' he asked, dropping to his knees to talk to Harriet, the smile crinkling the corners of his eyes. It was unforgivably devious to bring his niece into the matter, but at that moment he felt desperate enough to try anything. It might be years before he saw either of them again.

'I give in – you win. A quick coffee then, before I get clamped or towed away.'

They found a sandwich bar nearby, where Christopher bought coffee and a sausage roll for himself and an apple juice and doughnut for Harriet. Jane, suddenly overcome by something like nausea, asked only for water.

'How's your book – the novel you were planning?'

'Finished.'

'So you're free then – to go to America.'

'I suppose so.' He frowned. 'It will be less painful to receive rejection letters from across the Atlantic.'

'Oh, I think rejection hurts at any distance.'

'Yes, of course it does.' He felt foolish, but also pleased that she had not pandered to a bid for reassurance that she was in no position to give. It reminded him of her honesty, a quality which he believed, increasingly, to be of the rarest kind. He bit into his sausage roll, but then panicked at the silence between them and spoke with his mouth full, flaky bits of greasy pastry sticking to the corners of his lips.

'Were you all right after the funeral?'

She nodded and took a sip of water. It tasted warm and metallic. 'Tom is living with Michael at the moment. Had you heard that?' The monotone with which she delivered the news did not deceive him as to the effort of control behind it.

He put the sausage roll down and pushed his plate away.

'No,' he said quietly, 'I had not heard that.' He pressed his hands together, as if in prayer, matching each long slim finger to its counterpart, pushing the heels of his palms as close as they would go. 'Do you see him?'

'Not yet.' She closed her eyes and raised the misty, over-washed glass to her lips; putting her head back, she downed it all in one go, in a vain attempt to quench the raging thirst that was now burning at the back of her throat. Her neck moved rhythmically as she swallowed. He noticed, not for the first time, how thin she was, all hair and eyes.

'I wish there was something I could do to help you.'

'There is – giving me the house – I shall certainly go there for a while. It might do me good – help me too – to have a change—' her voice tailed away, leaving him feeling helpless and bereft.

Harriet had by now fallen asleep in her push-chair, half a doughnut still gripped in one hand, specks of sugar on her cheeks and chin.

Jane was talking again, absently, as if the words coming from her lips meant little to her. 'So much seems to have gone wrong – I can't help believing it must be some failure in me that has caused so many terrible—' she couldn't think of the right word 'mistakes.'

'Now, I'm sorry to interrupt, but I simply cannot sit here and grant you the monopoly on mistake-making,' he shook his head, pretending to be severe; 'I can't allow that at all. Others of us are just as adept in that area, if not more so.'

'Perhaps.' She had torn her paper napkin into thin strips and was lining them up across the table. 'I bottle things up, that's my trouble. I live so much of my life inside my head.' She looked up to find him staring at her with such intensity that she felt compelled to look away.

'When are you off?'

'Tomorrow.'

'So soon?'

'I hung on for the will – they wanted me days ago.'

'Mattie's over there, you know.'

'Yes, I know, she's in Boston, teaching art to old ladies,' he chuckled, before registering that he had surprised her. 'She wrote to me,' he went on quickly. 'Just a postcard – you know. I suppose we might meet up at some stage. Boston's only a hiccough away from Washington – by American standards, that is.'

'Yes, of course.'

They had left the cafe and were standing on the pavement outside, people streaming past them on either side. Saying hello to her is never this difficult, he thought, bracing himself.

She was frowning at him. 'Please give her my love if you see her. You're clearly very honoured. My postcard only had trees on it – not a squeak about old ladies.' The push-chair was between them. She wanted to say something more, something kind perhaps, or memorable, she couldn't quite put her finger on it. It was hard to think with her throat so sore and the drilling sensations going on behind her eyes.

'I might write,' he said, 'if you don't mind, that is.'

'I would like that.'

They kissed quickly across the rain-hood of Harriet's push-chair, before setting off in opposite directions. Jane had been walking for several yards before it dawned on her that she was going the wrong way. She wheeled round quickly, hoping to catch Christopher up, but his tall, striding figure was already lost amongst the lunch-time crowds.

36

Pneumonia wasn't diagnosed until several days after their arrival in Kent. When an elderly doctor from Crestling gruffly informed Jane that her raw throat and hot flushes were the symptoms of something infinitely more serious than a bout of flu, she found herself accepting the news as if it was no less than the inevitable, a natural culmination of all that had gone before. There was relief too, in being able to acknowledge that she felt like hell, in realising that it was not simply, as she had feared, that her capacity for resisting everyday bugs had lost some of its edge.

The obvious and most sensible course of action would have been a speedy return to Cobham, where vital amenities like Mrs Browne and supermarkets were incomparably more accessible, where mothers languishing in bed would cause the least inconvenience. But such a move held little appeal, not least because Jane felt far too weak to organise it. On top of that, she found herself wanting – very badly – to stay where she was. Having half-dreaded the thought of sharing the house with Earnest's ghostly presence, she found the place haunted only by a sense of peace and warmth. Outside, winter was emerging from behind the brilliant canvases of autumn. Earnest's copse was a shimmering fire of red and burnished gold, colours touched into life by the maddening kiss of frost. There was a bite and tingle in the air, an alertness, which affected her deeply, in spite of her imminent state of collapse, filling her with irrational surges of hope and self-belief.

Feeling like a beggar with a bowl, she rang Julia a few hours after receiving her diagnosis.

'Let me understand correctly. Though you have one of the

most serious diseases known to civilised man, you wish to take to your sick bed in a draughty old house in the wilds of Kent where neither you nor your daughter have any friends or support. You wish to do this because some sixth sense has instructed you that this is the best place to be.'

'That's about it, I suppose.' She waited resignedly for some gentle explosion on the wide-ranging, unintelligible subject of her personality.

'Well then, at least we all know where we stand.' There was a pause before Julia's voice came back on the line. 'Since I can boast of no private nurses in my small circle of acquaintances, I would consider it an honour to undertake this small challenge myself. I shall drive down at once.'

After Julia's arrival, Jane's immune system, as if realising that it no longer had to cope alone, surrendered completely. For a few days things went very fuzzy. She lay in the wide bed in the blue room, aware of nothing but heat and aching, interspersed with the sickly-sweet, chemical smell of medicine. Her only movements were trips to the bathroom: exhausting, painstaking journeys, leaning on Julia like an old lady with a walking frame.

It was several days before she felt able to sit upright to a tray of tea and toast. Julia sat on the end of the bed, while Harriet was allowed to climb in next to her mother and nibble on the crusts.

'I'll have to Hoover the sheets, I can see,' scolded Julia, thrilled to see a hint of colour in her patient's cheeks.

'This bed's quite big enough to be shared with a few crumbs.' The first mouthful of tea had snaked its way down into the empty bowl of her stomach, a warm coil of comfort deep within. 'Thank you, Julia.'

'No need. It's given me quite a kick – to feel really useful for once.' She tugged at a crease in the counterpane.

'What do you mean, "for once"?'

Julia moved closer and patted her hand. 'Letting people into your life, I mean really letting them in, so they can make a difference, is not something that comes very naturally to you. Hadn't you noticed?'

Jane scowled, but only briefly, and began licking the butter from her fingers. 'It's only ineptitude – nothing deliberate. It's just because I blunder along, letting things happen to me instead of taking control.' She let her head flop back against the pillows; it felt unbearably heavy suddenly. 'By the way,' she murmured, her eyes closing, 'could you move Mattie's triangles? Hang them in the downstairs loo or somewhere. It was a kind thought – to put them in here – but it's giving me eye-ache. All those sharp points – ordered chaos – the worst kind of all.'

'Come on Hatty, we're going to have to make some toast for ourselves now, seeing as Mummy's gobbled the lot.' She pulled a resisting, sleepy Harriet from the warm bed and held her close. 'Let's put jam on ours – potfuls of it,' she whispered, her breath tickling Harriet's ear and making her giggle. 'Strawberry or blackcurrant – or honey, perhaps – or all three – what do you think?' Harriet scrambled free and made an eager charge for the door, shouting her enthusiasm at the prospect of food.

Julia, who several months back would have been trying to persuade her god-daughter of the benefits of wholemeal bread and Marmite, allowed herself a smile of satisfaction. She and Harriet were well on the way to developing a rather fine understanding of each others needs. Having removed Mattie's picture from the wall, she leant across to retrieve the tray from the bed.

'You really ought to be getting back into your own life,' said Jane dreamily, tucking her arms under the pillow and stretching out her fingers in the dark cool beneath, 'though it's been fun having you in mine.'

'Don't be absurd. You're a sack of bones. A small gust of wind would send you flying into the nearest tree.'

'But your shop—'

'I've warned you before not to fret about my shop. I've got help. A friend – a minor patron of the arts – a brilliant haggler over prices. He's taking care of things for me.'

'He?' Her voice was lazy with sleep, but her eyes popped open.

'Don't be nosy. Return to your slumbers. He's Swedish and terribly organised.' And with that she swept out of the room.

The following week, when Jane was well enough to camp on the sofa downstairs during the day, Julia produced – like a smug conjuror with a deep hat – a young girl called Karen who was sixteen and lived a couple of miles down the road.

'Karen has a bicycle and loves children,' she announced, pushing her guest into the sitting-room while she rushed off to the kitchen to make tea and open a fresh packet of biscuits.

Karen smiled shyly at Jane, before bobbing down on all fours. Putting her face very close, she gravely invited Harriet to press the curled tip of her freckled nose, which made the most satisfying of squeaks the moment it was touched. 'We've got lots at home,' she remarked casually, getting to her feet and lifting Harriet on to her skinny hip in one effortless movement, 'Mum fosters.'

Though the purple shadows under her new employee's eyes suggested a social life somewhat at odds with the homely demands of her working day, Karen's energy and cheerfulness were limitless. Apart from a few cigarettes, chain-smoked at great speed down by the swings whenever her charge was asleep, she devoted herself wholeheartedly to their needs, cycling off for groceries, hanging out washing and wrestling with Earnest's dinosaur of a Hoover with only the mildest cursing.

After Jane had invested in a second-hand child's bike seat, Karen would pedal off down the lane with Harriet kicking in delight behind; if they weren't having picnics or running errands, they would ride over to spend the afternoon with Karen's family, where a spoiling choice of playmates was always available. The last vestiges of her daughter's clingy shyness disappeared within days; she no longer picked at her food or whined to be held. Her elfin face filled out with health and colour; sleep, once fitful and problematic, now came in eleven-hour stretches, allowing her mother to catch up on what felt like a lifetime of broken nights.

Julia took to driving down at the most unexpected times, her car invariably loaded with toys and clothes from the house in Cobham. Though she did not want to worry Jane, 23 Meadowbrook Road already seemed to her to be tainted with the neglected air peculiar to unoccupied houses – an emptiness that no amount of window-opening or duvet-shaking could erase. Thanks largely to a series of unexplained prevarications from Michael, nothing had yet been done about organising tenants.

Jane did not need any prompting from Julia to feel concern at the general state of affairs. She had tried pressing Michael into positive action a number of times, but since the reading of the will all traces of bonhomie towards her had evaporated. Falling ill had not helped matters; though he managed a get-well card, she suspected the all-powerful hand of Lisa behind it. But by far the worst thing about her illness was having to postpone her weekend with Tom; with Michael so intensely glum and hostile, she found herself wheedling and bargaining – like the worst brand of supplicant wife – for a chance to see her son.

She didn't succeed until one Friday morning late in October, when – without much explanation as to why – he allowed himself to be persuaded to release Tom for a day on Sunday. Jane, standing with a basket of laundry on her hip, debating whether the shaggy scraps of black cloud were likely to assemble themselves into something thick enough to produce rain, was elated by this small victory. It had been a long time. A whole day with Tom would be a treat indeed. Though she had promised faithfully to return him at the end of the day, hopes about winning him back burned in her mind, together with flash-light warnings about the dangers of using children as weapons in grown-up wars. Being ill had also deferred the business of seeking legal advice, a move that filled her with dread, and one which she still regarded as the very last resort.

She pegged a grey bra into the last space on the line and used Earnest's old forked stick to push the line of clothes higher, so that tights and trouser legs swung at the darkening sky like crazy flags. It was almost certainly going to rain. She sat on a tree stump to wait, pulling her long cardigan more tightly about her against the cold. Had she been wrong after all, she wondered, watching her bras and socks fight the scooting wind; was it misguided to end a marriage that had lost its heart? Was the old cliché of sticking together for the sake of the children the best wisdom in the end? Would Tom have suffered as much if they had stayed together? Would any of them?

The light crunch of car wheels on the gravel at the front of the house invaded her thoughts, but not thoroughly enough to make her move.

'Where the hell is everyone?' shouted Julia, emerging from

round the side of the house. 'What kind of welcome do you call this for a friend who has cancelled every engagement in a hectic social calendar in order to nurture a convalescent friend?'

'Hello, Julia.' Jane turned and smiled from her perch.

'Christ, it's freezing out here – are you hoping for a double dose next time around – perhaps with hypothermia thrown in for good measure? You never were one to do things by halves.' She had buttoned up her jacket and was hopping from one leg to the other.

'I was just thinking.'

'A highly dangerous occupation at the best of times.' Julia kicked the laundry basket over with the tip of her suede boot and sat down on it. 'If we're going to contemplate our navels out here I shall have to smoke. Warm lungs appeal more than the thought of no warmth at all.' The wind snuffed out the flames of several matches before she succeeded in lighting up. 'Ah, that's better. Don't worry, I'll chug into the Siberian winds on my side not yours. Even I can appreciate that a spot or two of tar might not be the best tonic for your condition.'

'I was just thinking that losing Tom would have the ring of poetic justice to it – that maybe it's supposed to be my punishment for ending the marriage. I seriously wonder whether I was wrong, that perhaps I should have let things continue after all, learnt to live with the status quo, not grumbled so much—'

'I warned you – thinking is invariably unwise – especially for someone whose brain is still addled from drugs and disease.' She stubbed her half-smoked cigarette out in the damp grass but held on to the stump. 'First of all, you are not going to "lose" Tom, as you put it. Which reminds me, I've got the number of a lawyer for you in my bag – don't let me forget. Secondly, talking in terms of punishment doesn't get anybody anywhere. To do what genuinely seems right at the time is about the most we poor mortals can hope for. Take me for example. Are you suggesting that just because I have made such a wealth of cock-ups in the past I don't deserve to take up with the right man when I find him?'

'So you have found him then,' said Jane gleefully, clapping her hands.

'That's not what I said at all.' Julia rolled the stub of her defunct cigarette between her finger and thumb. 'Though I think I might have.' She gave a nervous laugh. 'He's not exactly a conventional Romeo – not remotely what I thought I was looking for. But then most of life's problems seem to me to arise from not knowing what the hell one is looking for. We waste so much time chasing after the wrong thing, not seizing the right thing until it whacks us over the head. Do you agree and can we go inside now?' She stood up and brushed some flecks of ash from her lap. 'My nose is in danger of producing icicles.'

'Yes, I do agree,' said Jane quietly, only mildly surprised by the image of Christopher that floated inside her head. Abandoning her washing to the elements she turned to follow Julia inside. 'Though sometimes, it's too late,' she added, but only as a mutter, so that in spite of Julia's backward glance of suspicion, they said nothing more about it.

37

On Sunday Julia took Harriet to the Doll's House Museum in Crestling, leaving Jane to put off preparing lunch in favour of drifting from room to room, picking things up and putting them down, willing the minutes on towards the arrival of Tom. They were to eat shepherd's pie, his favourite, with peas and baked beans. Having gained sufficient grip on herself to peel some potatoes, she began a haphazard search for toys that might appeal to her son. Some imaginative prospecting unearthed a nest of trains under Harriet's pillow and a chain of railway track that had been used as fencing round three pigs and a chicken. Still concerned about the limited nature of her findings, she rummaged through a couple more boxes upstairs before remembering that Julia's latest hoard from Cobham still sat in the hall. This last search was the most fruitful of all, producing two tennis balls, a book on dinosaurs and a Lego kit of a space module, complete with little men in moon boots, and oxygen masks fixed to their backs.

While the potatoes boiled and then disintegrated in the bottom of the pan, she set to work with the Lego, using the top of Julia's box as a table, with the instructions propped up against the wall behind. There were eighteen separate diagrams of instructions and several missing bits, calling for some ingenious improvisation. Her calves tingled uncomfortably from being knelt on, while her neck locked into the awkward position required for fiddling with the pieces and comparing her progress to the small pictures on the flimsy instruction sheet. Though a small portion of her mind worried about potatoes, it became a matter of unrivalled significance that she should complete the kit before Tom and Michael arrived. Her toils were transformed into a labour of love, something she had to show for all the hours and days of missing him.

As the time for their arrival approached she worked faster. By eleven o'clock only the most detailed trimmings remained – some lime-green propellor blades, visors to click on to the little black helmets, a tiny flag. Ten minutes later she sat back on her heels to admire her work, rubbing the stiffness from her neck, feeling flushed and triumphant. After a few minor readjustments, she carefully set the model on the hall table, positioning its various components round a rough terrain of telephone books, pens and pads.

The potates were burnt underneath and soggy on top, but responded well to some vigorous whisking and generous blobs of butter. She hurried over frying the mince, expecting a knock on the door at any moment. At twelve she put her completed pie beside the oven and wondered seriously, for the first time, whether Michael was going to keep his word. She flicked the radio on briefly, but turned it off when she realised it might drown out the sound of an approaching car. There was nothing for it but to continue with preparations for lunch: baked beans in one pan, peas in another, kettle on to boil, ready for the peas; knives and forks on the table, glasses, water, pepper and salt, ketchup; so much hurry and then, suddenly, nothing left to do. Julia and Harriet were late too. She wandered into the sitting-room and studied the newspaper headlines with a vacant eye. A tourist bus had crashed on a motorway. She sat up. Perhaps there had been a crash in Kent too. Perhaps Michael and Tom had driven into Julia and Harriet, on the windiest bit of the road, where you always had to brake more than you thought, where there was barely room for one car, let alone two abreast.

Entwined with the worry was anger. To think that Michael could be so unthinking or spiteful as to change his mind – without so much as a phone call. She pushed open the front door and tramped outside, pulling the sleeves of her jumper down over her knuckles to glove them against the cold. But the lane was empty. Not the slightest murmur of an engine-hum filtered through the rustly stirring of old, wet leaves. Somewhere far away a tractor engine started up; an aeroplane roared overhead, sunk deep within a grey wall of cloud.

Jane traipsed back inside, helplessness now winding round her heart. The little spacemen watched her walk by, inscrutable behind their shiny-black visors, their space-guns at the ready. She was flushing the loo when the knock came – one short, sharp rap that made her heart leap with relief and fear. Julia wouldn't knock like that. Julia wouldn't knock at all.

Flinging the door open, ready with reprimands and welcomes for father and son respectively, she found not Michael, but Lisa standing before her, composed but unsmiling, Tom's hand in hers, an unnaturally clean football pinioned under his free arm.

'Darling – how lovely to see you.' She crouched down, wanting to grab him – to swamp him with her own relief – but managing not to. He stepped forward, letting go of Lisa's hand, carefully setting down the ball, hesitating for just a moment before putting both arms limply round her neck and burying his head in her shoulder. She held him then, very tightly, tighter still when she realised that he was crying. A lump came into her own throat. 'Thank you, Lisa – I wasn't expecting you – I—' At which point Julia and Harriet arrived, lightening the moment considerably, as greetings of a less intense nature were called for.

'Could we have a word?' asked Lisa, just as Jane was wringing her hands for her to be gone. Julia, rising with characteristic aplomb to the occasion, enticed the children out into the garden, though she could not resist dramatically flinging the longest of Earnest's many scarves round her head and neck, just to make the point that there was no sacrifice without pain.

Jane led the way into the kitchen, but Lisa remained hovering in the doorway. Apart from the funeral, when everything was safely bustling and different, she hadn't been back to the house since Michael's abortive attempt to introduce her to his father. Her eyes flicked down to the flagstones and up again; it was impossible not to think of the sex, the bruise which had stayed so long, the weird guilt of that day.

'Is there somewhere else? The sitting-room perhaps?'

Jane, assuming a derisory sense of decorum to lie behind the request, was tempted to say something rude. 'Of course,' she replied. But I'm damned if I'm going to offer her a drink, she thought.

'I'd love a coffee – if that's not too much trouble. The traffic out of London was frightful.' Lisa peeled off her gloves, pulling at each finger like a twenties film star, before laying them carefully across her handbag. 'Could I use the bathroom, please?'

A few minutes later they were settled in armchairs like old friends. Lisa looked around the room with a stern eye. A lingering smell of tobacco smoke still hung in the air. All of Earnest's ornaments and furniture remained exactly as he had left them; only odd details hinted at the new inhabitants: Harriet's sock over the back of the chair, a video of Postman Pat on the carpet by the television, a pile of ironing on the stool behind the door.

'A nice house, I suppose, though not my cup of tea.' Lisa stirred sugar into her coffee, eyeing Jane through a thin veil of steam. 'Michael was deeply shocked, you know, by the will and everything. He thinks you must have been having an affair with his brother. Have you?'

The audacity of it was like a slap in the face. Someone more composed might have been cool enough to refuse even to respond to such a question. But Jane had seldom felt less composed in her life. She felt idiotically polite. She looked towards the door, longing for Julia. Julia would know what to say, how to put herself in charge – because Julia was brave and said what she thought; not inept, tongue-tied by propriety and fear. But Julia was pushing Harriet on the swing while keeping an eye on Tom, who hung from the uppermost bar of the climbing-frame, his jumper riding up to reveal a chalky stomach and bony keyboard of ribs.

'No I have not. I was deeply shocked by the will too, as it happens.' She stood up in a fresh effort to wrest control of the situation, despising herself for feeling so intimidated by the perfect poise of her adversary, a poise resonant in every aspect of her being; from the way she let the drops of coffee fall from her teaspoon before placing it on the table beside her, to the leisurely crossing of her stockinged legs, the black seam a faultless line that fed unwaveringly into the back of her patent leather shoes. 'If you are only here to make accusations—'

Lisa raised her hand and shook her silky dark head, smiling for the first time. 'Forgive me, no. Please, sit down. You might be rather interested by what I have to say.' She placed her mug carefully on top of a newspaper and leaned forward. 'I am returning Tom to you.' The statement was so simple, so unexpected, that Jane did not at first take it in. Lisa stood up and went to watch the children through the french windows. 'He's a lovely boy. I know how you must miss him.' She crossed her arms and sighed. 'Michael will miss him too, of course.'

'Why – I don't understand?' A blush of joy was spreading through her.

'It won't work. I want a new life with Michael, you see. Tom is so much a part of what he had before. It's different between us when Tom's around – not how I want it to be.' She went to study the photograph of Earnest and Edie that sat on the mantelpiece. 'Michael looks so much more like his mother, don't you think?'

'Lisa, please – I don't understand what you mean.' She was beginning to think she had misinterpreted – it was too simple – too impossible that Michael should ever concur with such a decision. 'Does Michael agree to all this?'

She turned and nodded slowly. 'Oh yes, Michael agrees. You see,' she smiled very quickly, the first hint of shyness in her bearing, 'I am expecting a child myself now.' Her hand moved to her stomach, which looked flat and unmotherly. 'It's very early days yet – but I've been quite sick in the mornings – it's been hard – coping with Tom as well. Michael didn't realise at first – the strain on me – but I've made him understand.' She walked over to her coffee and took a sip while perched on the arm of her chair. 'You're supposed to go off things like this, aren't you?' She wrinkled her nose. 'But I love a good cup of instant now and then.'

'You mean,' Jane swallowed, 'Michael is prepared to let Tom live with me – for ever?' Her tone was incredulous.

'I've got it in writing – all about alimony and so on too. Here.' She unzipped a side pocket of her handbag and passed a slim white envelope across. 'It has been hard for him of course – in fact he's not been well at all recently – a bad cold. He needs a break – we both do. We're going to Spain for Christmas – to my sister's.' She was putting her gloves back on, flexing her fingers in the soft leather.

'How lovely,' Jane murmured, raising her eyes to Lisa with new respect. She had underestimated her. It had been naïve to assume that such awesome skills would be used to fight battles on Michael's behalf, when all along she had a hidden agenda of her own. Jane found herself wondering whether Michael loved or feared such manipulation. 'The – your baby – do you mind my asking – was it planned?'

'You could put it like that, yes,' Lisa's neat lips twitched into a small smile of self-congratulation. 'By the way, we've explained everything as best we can to Tom – that he can still come for weekends and things. I think he understands – though he hasn't said much, to be honest. He's a bit of a one for moods, I must say.'

Jane clasped her fingers tightly behind her back, feeling the barb of criticism within the smooth delivery of words. 'It's hardly surprising, is it? Given all that's happened—'

'Quite.' She clipped her bag shut and turned towards the door, eager to be gone and without any qualms at appearing so. 'I've got his things in the car. He did get very excited when I explained that you had moved down here.' After they had descended the verandah steps she glanced back at the house with a sniff for the peeling paint and smeary windows that made Jane feel so much at home.

They unloaded a suitcase and a couple of bags from out of the boot – such a measly amount of baggage that Jane felt a pang on Tom's behalf.

'Convenient that Christopher was starting that job in America, wasn't it?' said Lisa, casting a sidelong look at Jane. 'Nice of him to let you live here.'

'Yes, very nice.' Jane released the words tightly and quickly, detecting the renewed probe of an unhealthily curious and determined antenna.

'Your sister's there too, of course.' Lisa was looking in her bag for her keys.

Jane ploughed a furrow in the gravel with the toe of her shoe. 'Yes, she's in Boston.'

'That's right – we heard about that in one of Christopher's letters. He's written several times, much to Michael's surprise. He says he likes Boston a lot. Ah, here we are.' She dangled the keys at Jane. 'Don't bother Tom. We said our goodbyes this morning. I don't believe in making an unnecessary drama of these things. Goodbye then.' She held out her hand.

'Goodbye Lisa. I feel I have a lot to thank you for.'

'Yes, I suppose you do.' They shook hands quickly, their fingers dry and cold. 'Though I'm doing this for me too, you know – and Michael of course – a clean slate for everyone.'

As she drove away Jane found herself thinking about Boston. Christopher's letters – there had been two so far – had been full of dry observations about his Washington colleagues and the difficulties of communication in a world where irony was no more than a word in a dictionary. Some of the things he wrote made her laugh out loud. But he hadn't yet said anything about Boston.

A shrill voice from the verandah made her jump.

'All my stuff – great,' yelled Tom, racing down the steps.

'Come and give me a hand,' she called, waving him over, the thrill of having him back rushing through her again with such force that her legs trembled as she bent down to gather up the heaviest of the bags.

In spite of starting two new schools in as many months, Tom seemed happy enough for Jane to postpone all previous thoughts of therapy and counselling. His teachers said he was quiet, but co-operative; the bad old days of raging seemed mercifully to have slipped away, to be replaced by the more healthy stomping that went with being seven years old and full of plans that were either forbidden or impossible. It helped enormously to have Earnest's vast garden to charge around in, not to mention the treat of Karen, whose private habits never affected her supply of energy when it came to high-speed chases across the lawn and elaborate role-playing in the children's never-ending games of let's-pretend.

Jane, while recognising herself to be much more settled in every respect, still lived with the echo of a fear that such feelings might prove short-lived. Though the house in Cobham was safely let, though Lisa's pregnancy proceeded apace and Michael showed no signs of stirring against the wishes of his new wife, she still found it impossible to stop worrying entirely; anxiety was such an old companion, it was hard to let it go all at once.

It was only as her strength returned that Jane realised quite how ill she had been. In spite of her doctor's prescription for rest, she found herself taking long walks, exploring the pathways and thickets of the land that was now partly hers, driving herself on until her pulse raced and her lungs heaved for air. Hard though she tried, she could not block Christopher from her thoughts at such times. It was nothing but gratitude, she assured herself, while her heart skipped for reasons that felt worryingly unconnected to her lack of physical stamina; without his generosity all the peace and space that her imperfect family now so enjoyed would not have been possible. Best of all, his kindness ensured that money was no longer a worry, allowing Jane to appreciate the unsung luxury of unemployment: it felt nothing but lucky not to have a job, to have time for her children, time for herself. Such unhurried living, coupled with the return of good health, brought a new perspective on her life, charging it with a degree of self-tolerance that was almost worrying.

'I'm in danger of feeling content,' she confessed to Julia when she rang up a couple of weeks before Christmas. 'I keep forgetting to check over my shoulder for demons sneaking up behind.'

'You always were a raging pessimist at heart; you thoroughly deserve to get run over by the proverbial bus.' Julia liked not having to worry about Jane any more; it suited her far better to feel the old balance back between them, a balance that allowed her to speak her mind without fear of the consequences. 'But before such an untimely demise, could we discuss that most joyous of festive seasons, the one that tears into our bank accounts with as much fervour as it does our digestive systems?'

'I take it you mean Christmas.' Jane pulled up a kitchen chair to the side of the fridge and allowed Harriet to climb on to her lap, where she sat quietly sucking on the most reachable section of the telephone flex. 'Are you going to moan or be useful? I could do with a volunteer for the Santa Claus bit.' She lowered her voice: 'I can't say more because my youngest is eating a small portion of the telephone wire; but believe me when I say that lavish refreshments will be your reward. Michael used to like beer and cake, but the catering department might see its way to something a shade more upmarket. Actually, Michael always rather enjoyed that side of things,' she added fondly, without feeling at all rocky at doing so.

'Tempting though it sounds, wearing a sticky beard and a baggy red trouser suit was not exactly high on my list of priorities, no.' Julia paused just for a moment, showing uncharacteristic hesitancy, before going on, her voice all of a rush: 'Look here, I was wondering if you could add Olaf to the guest-list – do say if you'd rather not, and I'll try hard never to mention it again.'

'Of course Olaf can come – I feel quite awful for not having suggested it myself.'

'Thank goodness for that. We'll come down on the day itself, if that's okay with you.'

'But Tom's singing a solo – didn't I tell you? On Christmas Eve, in front of the most eye-catching of nativity scenes: Joseph is made of straw and slouches like a drunken Guy Fawkes over one end of the crib, while Mary, who was painted on to cardboard by the vicar's wife, has a highly suspect leer on her face, as if she's hoping to be ravaged by a shepherd. One of Harriet's more respectable dolls has just been chosen to play baby Jesus, which makes us all feel frightfully grand. Do say you can come – it starts around three o'clock, if the marauding hoards of angels and wise men can be assembled in time.'

'I'm sorry Jane, I'd love to, but I can't. I'm planning on keeping the shop open till lunch-time and I know I won't have bought a thing for anyone before then because I never do. Anyway I'd cry buckets and embarrass you deeply. I'm rather worried about myself in fact – weeping at fluffy animals and cherubic infants never used to be my thing, but now I do it all the time. I need Kleenex to get through the nine o'clock news these days. Do you think it's terminal or merely hormonal?'

Jane let out a hoot of a laugh. 'I can't think why you're

asking me – the biggest emotional mess to hit southern England. Postively horse-whipped by my emotions, that's me. The chemicals in my body have always played merry hell with my lachrymal ducts.'

And so she rambled on, joking easily about herself, because, as she realised with the gentlest of nudges inside her head, none of it was true. Without being able to say exactly when or how, she knew that she was no longer in a mess, that though she was still quite weak on the outside, she was getting better deep down, that she had rediscovered a belief in happiness, if not quite happiness itself.

So with Julia's abstention Jane had to cope alone with the potentially hazardous business of watching Tom's O-shaped mouth at the head of an energetically bobbing choir, whose tinsel-bound costumes rustled proudly and loudly in accompaniment to his rendition of the first verse of 'Away in a Manger'. Harriet, in spite of several of the fiercest warnings on the matter, vigorously mouthed the words, emitting the odd unscheduled squeak and waving her star-wand at her brother like a baton. Tom, though he had resorted to furious practising behind locked doors at home in order to escape the well-intentioned encouragements of his little sister, seemed suddenly to realise that he was old and wise and superior enough to rise to the awesome demands of such an occasion. He straightened his shoulders and widened his mouth, scorning Harriet by his very stance, releasing his piping treble boldly into the packed pews of the small church, without so much as a glance of disdain in her direction.

Jane, pink-cheeked with anguish and elation, sat straight-backed and still until the last note, watching her children through a blur of tears, knowing with a sudden swoop of conviction that they were definitely through the worst, that whatever lay ahead could never be as bad as what had gone before.

38

On the morning of Christmas Day Jane put on the green dress that Barbara Marshall had picked out for her; it fell out of its box of tissue with slippery ease, as if eager to be released. Though it was uncreased and as alluring as ever, she regarded her reflection with unease; not only because it felt unnatural to look quite so elegant, but also because it linked her to past muddles that she wanted to forget. She was undoing the zip to take it off when Tom ran into the room firing the rubber-tipped arrows that he had found sticking out of his stocking that morning, along with a feathered red bow which had almost snapped in two from Jane's efforts to fit it in.

'You look different,' he said, stopping at once and cocking his head to one side. 'You look like a pretty lady. Is it because it's a special day?' Harriet joined in with a chorus of appreciative oohing and aahing of her own, clinging to Jane's leg and nuzzling her face against the inviting sheen of the material with such fervour that she left a large dribble mark on the hem.

After finding a faded apron of Edie's to protect her outfit from further onslaughts, Jane pulled slouch socks over her stockinged feet and made her way downstairs for a final assault on the kitchen. The children were hearteningly keen to be involved; Tom took charge of the vegetables, refusing to be dissuaded from taking bites out of each carrot, and pulling so many leaves off the sprouts that they tumbled into the waiting colander looking like green marbles and outsize peas. Harriet, meanwhile, attended to the decorations on the cake, supervising a fight between Santa and some rebelling reindeer, using fir trees and angels as weapons, the tips of their wings gouging great holes in the icing-snow.

The house heaved with decorations, most of them manufactured on innumerable wet afternoons by Karen and the children; quantities of kitchen foil, Jane's cotton-wool balls and potfuls of glitter had gone into this minor cottage industry, resulting in galaxies of stars, angels and obese snowmen, who glowered and grinned from walls and windows in every room. Intricately unbalanced, low-slung mobiles dangled from lamp-shades and doorways, the most dramatic being a system of robins and snowballs that swung in the face of anyone reckless enough to step inside the front door. Jane had got used to it over the weeks and now did a quick dodge as she crossed the threshhold.

Julia and Olaf arrived when she was still in her baggy socks and frilly apron.

'There's brandy butter on your cheek, or something equally delicious,' said Julia, licking her lips after planting her kiss of welcome. 'Try the other side Olaf, you might find something even tastier there. I love the dress, by the way – what I can see of it. Wherever did it come from?'

'It's a long story,' said Jane, as Olaf proceeded to confuse her by first taking her hand, and then leaning forward for a kiss as well. It was still a little hard between them, each being so close to the same person, yet so many worlds apart themselves. 'And one that I'm not prepared to tell when feeling as sober and silly as this.' She cast an apologetic look at her feet.

'Well, we'd better do something about that then,' laughed Julia, pulling two bottles of red wine from down the sides of a large bag that bulged with parcels, while Jane quickly untied the apron and ran upstairs to find some shoes.

It wasn't until a few minutes after Harriet had caused general consternation by choking on and almost swallowing a silver horseshoe from the pudding, that Mattie burst into the room.

'Surprise!' she shrieked, tipping presents amongst the dirty dishes and prancing round the table bestowing kisses on the bemused faces of the children, on Julia, and even on Olaf, just as he was about to light a cigar.

She got to Jane last, hesitating before putting her arms round her, so that her elder sister had time to register the translucent glow that radiated from her – the soft, but unmistakable light of happiness. 'I've so much to tell,' she whispered, as they hugged. 'You do look well – all this country-living I suppose. Have you left us any food? We just couldn't resist the idea of a surprise – we would have got here hours earlier only the flight was delayed – typical. They gave us turkey on the plane though, which was rather sweet – and free drinks, which was sweeter still.'

It was only then that Jane realised Mattie had not come alone, that Christopher was framed in the doorway, clutching bags and waving stiffly at them all. Mattie and Christopher. They had made something of each other after all. It should have made her happy. She unearthed a second box of crackers and dished out mince pies and port, feeling ashamed at minding so much, at her meanness of heart.

After lunch and more presents Christopher lay invitingly on the rug behind the sofa, while the children, dressed in the Indian costumes he had given them, took turns to jump on him with plastic tomahawks, showing as much respect for his body as they would a trampoline. Near by Olaf and Julia sat side by side, not holding hands but clearly wanting to, as self-conscious as teenagers. Jane meanwhile, incapacitated but doing her best not to appear so, asked Mattie vibrant questions about Boston and teaching art, without listening properly to any of the answers. It was a struggle not to seek out the dark eyes of her brother-in-law; the keen urge to study his face was superseded only by the fear of being caught doing so.

After a respectable while she sought refuge in the kitchen.

'Thank you for your letter.' Christopher picked up a drying-up cloth and began helping to clear the draining board.

'Thank you for yours.'

'How have you been?'

'Fine.'

'Of course – how silly of me.' He threw down the cloth. 'You're always fine. Everything's always fine.' He thrust his hands into his pockets and strode from the room, almost bumping into Olaf on the way.

Jane stared at the yellow gloves immersed in the bowl of frothy water in front of her, as if powerless to extract them. Her mood had made him angry; he knew her too well. She could fool her best friend, her sister even, but not him. Beside her, stacks of plates, caked with congealed mixtures of bread sauce, gravy and cranberries, awaited attention. Olaf patted her lightly on the shoulder.

'I would consider it an honour, if you would let me do this washing. I have eaten so well. You are a fine cook, Jane.' He gripped an imaginary tyre of spare flesh and grinned, his eyes disappearing in clusters of wrinkles. 'I shall have to go on my diet now, or your Julia will turn me away.'

'I'm sure she won't do any such thing.'

She reached for a dirty plate, but he took a firm hold of her wrists and shook his head gravely.

'Go and sit. Talk to your sister and her friend. Julia and I will do this.'

'You heard the man, get out,' commanded Julia, appearing with a full glass of port in one hand and an unlit cigarette in the other. 'I shall direct proceedings. It will give me enormous pleasure. Find out why the hell Mattie's looking so well – I can't get her to tell me a thing.'

Jane slipped away obediently, amazed at the obtuse cheerfulness of people in love.

There was a flurry later on about beds. With the children already asleep in their separate rooms and the remaining spare room made up for Olaf and Julia, it rapidly became clear that space was going to be something of a problem. Jane had just announced that she would be happy on the sofa, when Julia interrupted to say that she and Olaf had had half a mind to go back to London anyway. Before anyone could argue they disappeared upstairs to pack their things, while Christopher went outside to fetch a suitcase from his car.

Jane, grabbing a pair of boots and the nearest coat to hand, tip-toed past Mattie, who was snoring gently in the deepest of Earnest's chairs, and let herself out into the garden through the french windows. The cold air felt good; she breathed deeply several times, dispelling the throb in her head wrought by the roaring heat of the open fire and too much wine. Her wellingtons squeaked quietly on the wet grass; her dress swished round the top of the boots, its bright green now only the merest shimmer under the shadowy moon.

She walked fast, down past the climbing frame towards the fence at the bottom that separated the garden from the copse. Leaning on the gate, her chin on her arms, she shivered against the cold. The sky was too cloudy for stars. Even the moon was struggling to get through, its light no more than a silvery haze of grey on black.

The rustle of a footstep made her jerk round.

'Christopher – I thought you were a ghost.' She was panting slightly from shock.

'Do you believe in ghosts?'

'Sort of – not really.' Though her breathing was back to normal, her voice still sounded high-pitched and strange. 'I believe in the power of the past, though I suppose that's not quite the same thing. Sometimes it's a nice feeling – like with Earnest and the house – but other times it seems no more than a horrid way of getting bogged down, of not being able to go forward—'

'Jane—' he took a step nearer.

'Hello – anybody there?' It was Julia, calling from the house. 'We're going – I'll be in touch.'

'Hang on,' Jane shouted back, 'I'm coming.' She began to run across the garden, her stockinged feet sliding round inside the wellingtons. Christopher, having jogged behind her for a couple of yards, suddenly began to run properly himself, grabbing her hand as he did so, pulling her on to match his pace. They flew across the dark, wet lawn, slowing only to negotiate the path at the side of the house. Olaf's grey Mercedes glistened in the dim glow cast their way by the porch light.

Julia took control of the farewells. 'Lovely day – I'll be in touch. If Harriet hates her jumper don't be afraid to tell me – I can take it – I'll get something else – I don't want it sitting in the bottom of a drawer – and do explain to Mattie – didn't want to wake her—' She was still talking as the car moved away.

Jane, after the exhilaration of her run, suddenly felt deflated. 'Do you need a hand with your things – I mean taking them upstairs?'

'To Mattie's and my quarters you mean?'

She nodded, starting to walk away.

'You know, for an intelligent woman, you can be astonishingly dim.'

'How kind of you to say so.' She continued walking towards the front door, quickening her stride as she saw it starting to swing shut.

'You are the only person still labouring under the illusion that Mattie and I wish to share a bed.'

She stopped and turned. Behind her the front door slammed.

'Don't you?'

'I'm sorry to disappoint you, but your sister and I haven't struggled past the rudimentaries of friendship – not since our famous but unmentionable encounter when the earth moved only by virtue of the alcohol levels in our blood streams.'

Jane remained standing several feet from him, staring at her boots. Wanting to blow her nose, she put her hands into the deep pockets of the coat she wore hoping to find a tissue; on one side the lining was ripped so badly that she could poke her entire hand through the hole; on the other side her fingers found only grittiness and something that felt like a stone, but could have been a conker. She sniffed. 'Oh, I see . . .'

'By the way, you're wearing my coat again—'

'Have you got a hanky?'

'At your peril.' He pulled a crumpled grey handkerchief from his trouser pocket and handed it to her. 'Now what was it you really wanted to say?'

'Should we go inside?'

He shook his head. 'No, I don't think that was it. Try again. I suspect it was something about Mattie.'

'Oh, it's nothing – only that,' the words came in a rush, 'you never mentioned her in your letters to me and Lisa said you'd written to Michael and that you'd spent loads of time in Boston and that you loved it up there, which is what made me think—'

'—all sorts of foolish things.' He offered her his hand. 'Come here, I've something to say.' She shuffled forward, her hands feeling clammy in spite of the cold.

'Mattie has had some problems – with drugs – but it's all sorted out—' he pressed her fingers between his. 'That's why

I got so involved. I've had some experience of such things. I didn't want to worry you . . .'

'I should have guessed – I suspected as much, before she went away – she had these funny green and white capsules – I should have done something—'

'Spare yourself the sisterly brow-beating, please Jane. Mattie is no longer your responsibility – she never really was. She's going back to the States in a few days, into the incomparably safe hands of a vegetarian baseball player who does press-ups during breakfast. He's an exhausting companion, but very well-intentioned. Mattie's in love with his triceps and he thinks he's landed an eccentric English princess. I'm not sure marriage is on the cards, but they talk frequently about producing offspring.'

Jane gave a little gasp at the impossible idea of Mattie as a mother, before her brain whirred on to an even more worrying thought. 'When do you go back?'

'Never,' he said simply, shrugging his shoulders and smiling at her look of pleased surprise. 'By mutual agreement, the English faculty of Georgetown and I have severed our contract for good, citing irreconcilable differences as the cause. They found me rather odd – far odder than the generally accepted level of lunacy expected from an Englishman.'

She giggled. 'Heavens, what did you do?'

'I forced my students to write poetry. I banned the reading of literary critics. I tore up essays that were too long – as fat as books some of them. Dreadful crimes, I know, but I'm unrepentant.' He picked up her other hand and pulled her closer. 'So you see, there's nothing to stop us now.'

'Nothing to stop us what? Had you noticed it's raining?'

'Nothing to stop us kissing.'

'But I've never had so much chit-chat before a kiss – it's rather off-putting. Frankly,' she took a step forward, 'I'm not sure I'm up to it. And we're getting terribly wet.' But she responded easily enough to the gentle pressure of his hands on her back, sliding into his arms with a strange sense of returning. Then there was nothing but his face, unexpectedly soft, his lips unhurried and deliberate, the kiss of a man with all the time in the world.

'At last,' he murmured, pulling back to cup her face in his hands, and kissing each eye in turn. 'I thought I might feel guilty, when the moment came, but I don't remote-ly.'

She brushed a curl of wet hair back off his forehead. 'But is it all right? Will we be all right?'

'I doubt it. I'll get drunk on Friday nights and beat you with a saucepan. When you get fed up with that you'll start a torrid affair with a librarian. We're almost certainly doomed,' he laughed, kissing her wet cheeks. After a final drenching shower, the rain stopped suddenly, leaving the darkness dripping quietly around them. 'I suppose we'll have to spend the night out here – what with the door shutting and your sister being in such a stupor.'

She tilted her head back to look into his face, happy to feel so small. 'You're even taller close-to – or perhaps it's just these wellies.' She stood on her tiptoes, bringing her nose level with his chin. 'Keen though I am to prolong this romantic interlude,' she said, trying not to smile, 'I feel bound to mention two things: firstly, my doctor would have a fit if I joined the queue for yet more antibiotics, and secondly, the french windows are open. Follow me.'

He pretended to go reluctantly, forcing her to tug on his arm. 'You mean we could have had this entire conversation under a dry roof? You deliberately kept me talking out here, when all along you knew of an open door to a warm hearth. As a prospective lover I consider myself worthy of better treatment. What do you say to that, may I ask?' He fell into step beside her and put his hand to the back of her neck, up under the wet tumble of inky dark curls.

'I say prospective lovers should watch their step.'

Mattie was standing at the windows looking out, one side of her face pink and lined from where it had been pressed against the side of the chair.

'Where the hell have you been? I thought I'd been abandoned to a spooky house with two orphaned children. Christ, you're both soaking? What's the joke anyway? Where are Julia and Olaf? I succumb to a spot of jet-lag and wake up to find that the whole world has changed. I wish you'd stop laughing and tell me what's been going on.'

'We'll do our best – but it's a bit complicated,' said Jane, before escaping in search of warm towels from the airing cupboard, while Christopher made coffee for them all, carrying the mugs through on a tray into the sitting-room. It wasn't until he set about rubbing Jane's hair dry, that Mattie's mouth dropped open – a spontaneous reaction which she deftly converted into the deepest of yawns, before slipping upstairs to bed, leaving her coffee to sit untouched beside the photograph of Earnest above the fireplace. The beady grey eyes of the old man seemed to glint in the firelight, fixing their stare on the corner of the sofa when Jane and Christopher were encamped, damp and happy, in a bed of towels and cushions.

'Here's to Dad,' announced Christopher with a grin, raising his coffee to salute the image of his father, 'the scheming old sod.' They chinked mugs and drew closer to each other, while the flames curled greedily around a fresh log, releasing celebratory gun-shot crackles up the blackened chimney. Outside the rain started again, hurling itself against the windows and doors, raging like an uninvited guest.